MORE PRAISE FOR JESSICA CLUESS

"Is it clear that Cluess adores the Harry Potter series and *Jane Eyre*?
Yes. So do you. So does everyone.
What matters is that her voice is her own."
—*The New York Times*

★ "[A] smashing dark fantasy."
—*Publishers Weekly,* Starred

"Jessica Cluess is an awesome storyteller!"
—TAMORA PIERCE

"A fun, inventive fantasy. I totally have a book crush on Rook."
—SARAH REES BRENNAN

"With the emotional intensity of my favorite fantasy books,
this is the kind of story that makes you forget yourself."
—ROSHANI CHOKSHI

"A glorious, fast-paced romp of an adventure."
—KELLY LINK

"The magic! The intrigue! The guys! . . . This team of sorcerers
training for battle had a pinch of Potter blended with a drop of
[Cassandra Clare's] Infernal Devices."
—*Justine*

"Your next YA fantasy obsession."
—*Bustle*

"An elegantly addictive read."
—*Kirkus Reviews*

"Henrietta Howel is a fantastic heroine."
—*Culturess*

"Fantasy fans will rejoice."
—*SLJ*

BY JESSICA CLUESS

THE KINGDOM ON FIRE SERIES

A Shadow Bright and Burning

A Poison Dark and Drowning

A Sorrow Fierce and Falling

A

SORROW
FIERCE
AND
FALLING

KINGDOM ON FIRE · BOOK THREE

JESSICA CLUESS

Random House 🏠 New York

This is a work of fiction. All incidents and dialogue, and all characters with
the exception of some well-known historical and public figures, are products of the
author's imagination and are not to be construed as real. Where real-life historical
or public figures appear, the situations, incidents, and dialogues concerning those
persons are fictional and are not intended to depict actual events or to change the fictional
nature of the work. In all other respects, any resemblance to persons living
or dead is entirely coincidental.

Text copyright © 2018 by Jessica Cluess
Jacket photograph copyright © 2018 by Christine Blackburne/MergeLeft Reps

All rights reserved. Published in the United States by Random House Children's Books,
a division of Penguin Random House LLC, New York.

Random House and the colophon are registered trademarks
of Penguin Random House LLC.

Visit us on the Web! GetUnderlined.com

Educators and librarians, for a variety of teaching tools,
visit us at RHTeachersLibrarians.com

Library of Congress Cataloging-in-Publication Data is available upon request.
ISBN 978-0-553-53598-3 (hc) — ISBN 978-0-525-70813-1 (intl.) —
ISBN 978-0-553-53600-3 (ebook)

Printed in the United States of America
10 9 8 7 6 5 4 3 2 1
First Edition

Random House Children's Books supports the First Amendment
and celebrates the right to read.

TO THE READERS WHO HAVE MADE THE JOURNEY,
AND THE FRIENDS WHO HAVE MADE IT WORTHWHILE

A girl-child of sorcerer stock rises from the ashes of a life.

You shall glimpse her when Shadow burns
in the Fog above a bright city.

You shall know her when Poison drowns
beneath the dark Waters of the cliffs.

You shall obey her when Sorrow falls
unto the fierce army of the Blooded Man.

She will burn in the heart of a black forest;
her fire will light the path.

She is two, the girl and the woman,
and one must destroy the other.

For only then may three become one,
and triumph reign in England.

—Taken from the Speakers' Prophecy

1

THE MONSTER WAS EXPECTING ME.

At least, that was how it seemed as I approached the edge of the barrier to Sorrow-Fell, breaking through the mist to find the demon Molochoron. The thought that this creature anticipated me was nonsense, of course. He was only a ten-foot-tall blob of jelly with dark, sharp hairs protruding from his so-called flesh. He'd no capacity to think or to plot. Only to destroy.

Yet as I stood before the Ancient, I couldn't shake the idea that he knew me.

The barrier was invisible, but its protection was absolute. These lands had been gifted to Blackwood's family by a faerie lord, and as such could not be accessed without a Blackwood's permission. I stood my ground and stared at Molochoron, the Pale Destroyer, studying the writhing shapes within the mass of pale jelly. Were they the monster's latest victims, now being digested?

The pain in my shoulder flared to think of it.

"There are more today, Henrietta." Maria had worn her peacock-blue cloak, providing a dab of color against the winter landscape. She pointed toward figures shambling out of the fog to stand beside Molochoron, their master. These creatures appeared human, but only vaguely. Their faces had melted, the flesh on their hands and arms bubbling with sores.

Familiars. Servants of the Seven Ancients.

Molochoron roared, sounding like nothing so much as a lion trapped in a vat of jam. The sound shook snow from the trees, but we were safe behind the barrier.

Maria was right; more creatures arrived every day. Ten this morning, I counted, scribbling the number in my journal. Blackwood had thought it odd that I'd volunteer to check the borders in the early morning. It wasn't a particularly glamorous—or warm—job. But it was the only way that Maria and I could work in secret on her, well, her particular destiny.

Being the chosen one, she'd a great responsibility.

"What've you got for me today?" Maria toed the very line of the barrier. She and Molochoron were a mere half foot from one another. I believed the ball of putrescence purred at having such a challenger near.

I slid my pencil and notebook into my little reticule and tied the strings. "Can you manage an ice tunnel from back here?"

Maria summoned a stinging cloud of needle-sharp snow, then flung it past the barrier to engulf Molochoron, who disappeared from view. The world before us turned a violent white for several minutes before Maria lowered her hands, settling the snow and ice. If we had anticipated a great, bellowing charge from the Ancient, we were disappointed. Molochoron had rolled a half foot to the left at most. Snow had settled on him like a dusting of sugar upon a cake.

"Er, perhaps not. Try something with the trees."

Maria took my advice readily, placing her hands on the earth. With a grunt, she dug her fingers into the snow.

Molochoron was surrounded on either side by tall, ancient pines. At Maria's order, they bent like graceful dancers in the midst of a plié. The branches sought to entrap the demon, who simply rolled a few yards back, completely out of harm's way.

"So far, I've a knack for moving Ancients slightly to the left," Maria muttered.

"Yes, but you do it so well." As far as encouraging words went, mine left a lot to be desired. Honestly, it felt like the bloody monster was humoring us.

Maria put the trees back in their proper place. Huffing, she stood. Her face was flushed, and not merely with the cold. Disappointment painted her features.

"Suppose that's enough for now," she grumbled, slipping her hands inside her cloak for warmth.

"I think we're making real progress."

Molochoron pulsed steadily, the noise coming from him a steady buzz; he appeared to have fallen asleep.

Bother it all. Maria led our way down the snowy path. I cast one look back at the barrier, at the rotting Familiars and Molochoron. Perhaps I was a dreadful teacher for the true chosen one. Why hadn't the prophecy come with a nice instruction manual woven into its back?

Soon we entered the forest's embrace. The trees were so dense that the bright morning darkened to twilight. The bracing air was almost enough to make me forget the pain in my shoulder. Almost. It had been months since Rook, in his transformed state as an Ancient, had bit me. Still, the bite had made me Unclean, and the pain that went with such a status varied between aching and excruciating.

Maria took her hands out of her cloak. Her left hand flexed, the fist opening and closing, a sure sign that her temper was nearing its limit.

"Remember how you bested Nemneris," I said to cheer her. In October, when the Water Spider had destroyed our boat and been about to feast on the lot of us, Maria alone had risen up and dragged the beast back into the sea.

"I was angry then. Besides, there wasn't an entire country relying upon me." We walked ten minutes through the trees before we came to the edge of the forest, looking toward the great estate beyond. She put her hand to a tree, running her fingers along the bark. "Once you know you're chosen, it freezes the mind."

Well, that feeling I understood only too well.

"All right. Maybe focusing only on your sorcerer abilities is a mistake. What about your witchery? After all, I saw you heal yourself once by taking the life of a plant. That power could be useful."

Maria's left hand tightened into a fist once more. She spoke in a lower, more womanly tone now: "Power, aye. And danger.

Killing a living thing for magic puts one on the path to losing one's soul." The "friend" Maria called Willie was making an appearance. As a child, Maria had spent a great deal of time living off the land, all alone. She'd invented "Willie" as a companion. Sometimes, dear Willie seemed to have a mind of her own. "Death can only ever master, not be mastered."

Right, we needed a cheerier topic.

"You learned that in your grandmother's coven, yes? What's a coven like?"

"Can barely recall. Elspeth—my gran—drove Mam away. She never forgave Mam for dallying with a sorcerer." Maria turned her gaze to the ground. "Called me a bastard and wouldn't take me back, even after my mother's death."

"I'm so sorry," I murmured. Apparently there were no cheery topics to be had today.

We left the forest and walked down the sloping hill to Sorrow-Fell. In the months since we'd come here, I sometimes thought of the house and its gardens as a constant flame that kept the encroaching dark of the Faerie wood at bay. The trees were heavy with Fae magic, their branches black and gnarled by it. But breaking through the dark forest and looking at the house below always felt like waking to a brilliant day after a nightmare. The green lawns now lay buried beneath snow, and the pond had frozen, but the white marble colonnade of the house, the great mansion's mullioned windows with stained glass in the image of the Blackwood family crest, shone brightly. This was my home now.

My permanent home after my wedding to Blackwood.

Which, incidentally, was today.

I tugged off my left glove for a glimpse of my engagement ring. Blackwood had gifted me with it on the day we'd arrived at Sorrow-Fell. A plain silver band set with a tiny pearl, it was less ostentatious and grand than one might have imagined receiving from a wealthy earl. But that was Blackwood: a surprise all the way through. He was elegant where others were loud, careful where others were bold.

And in a few hours, he would be mine.

Perhaps that was one reason I'd insisted on patrolling the barriers today. I'd needed time to gather myself and focus upon something else. Now, as the great house grew closer with every step, the enormous weight of becoming Lady Blackwood bore down upon me, while growing excitement quickened my pulse.

As we passed a squadron of sorcerers running drills by the frozen pond, I glimpsed Dee at his customary place in the lead. He bent his knees—even the bad one that had been smashed in our battle with Nemneris was doing well—and thrust out his stave. The other men followed his example.

"Now!" He twirled his stave with expert grace, his skill all the more impressive when you noted the three-pronged claw he'd fastened to the stump of his right arm. When Dee had lost the limb, Blackwood had been certain he would never handle a stave again. He'd underestimated Dee's ability and determination.

As one, the squadron performed their maneuver, and the surface of the frozen pond split in two with a momentous crack. The slabs of dripping ice rose into the air, then melded into a sharp-edged pyramid. With ease, the men returned the slab of ice to its original shape and laid it back over the water, so that it appeared the pond's surface had never been disturbed. My spirits lifted to see them at work. When we drilled and I felt magic surging in my blood, I believed in my heart that R'hlem couldn't possibly win.

Dee looked up and noticed Maria and me.

"Oi! Howel! Shouldn't you be dressing?" The other sorcerers chuckled. I heard one or two faint whistles as well.

"I don't see any of you fancying up," I called, grinning.

"Need an extra bridesmaid?" One of the fellows ushered a playful gust of snow to swirl around me. "I'm told pink's my color."

Laughing, I sent a burst of fire in his direction. My flame rocketed from my hand, a bright blue . . . with threads of shadow.

The laughter died. Cheeks burning, I killed the flame. No one said anything, but my new, shadowy powers—and my status as an Unclean—gave people pause. My shoulder, which bore Rook's bite marks, ached when I thought of it.

"Well. I have to give my report." I tugged at Maria's sleeve. Our shoes crunched over the ground, and the men behind us returned to their training.

Maria nudged me in the ribs. "They understand."

I puffed out my cheeks. "I know. I'll just feel more accepted after the marriage."

"Aye." Maria hooked her arm through mine. "The chapel's a sight in itself. His Lordship's made it a pretty place."

Pretty was an understatement. I'd seen the chapel yesterday evening. The walls had been festooned with holly and wintergreen branches, faerie lights twinkling among them. Blue snow-sorrows filled the space with a delicate fragrance. They were a magical flower unique to Fae lands, a riot of pale blue petals with a scent both fresh and forgotten, like a shuttered room in which a lady's perfume still lingers. Snow-sorrows grew out of the snow in winter and remained dewy and fresh for weeks after being plucked. When spring arrived, they were said to melt like the frost.

With the light filtering through the stained-glass windows, the chapel looked heavenly. The idea of marrying Blackwood there filled me with a potent mix of emotions: excitement, fear, hopefulness, and something dark and intimate that I didn't dare name.

While celebrating my seventeenth birthday two weeks ago, we'd agreed that the time had come. The war was going to end, one way or another, and we wanted to face it together. But before I could meet Blackwood at that beautiful altar, there was one more job to do.

Prior to marrying the lord of Sorrow-Fell, it was customary that the bride meet the lady of Sorrow-Fell—his mother—and receive . . . something. No one had told me exactly what.

Blackwood's mother always kept to her rooms. Only her maid—a silent, older woman who moved like a shadow—was regularly allowed inside. I had seen Eliza enter her mother's quarters several times, but only once had Blackwood gone in. He'd returned a scant three minutes later, shutting the door with more force than was strictly necessary. The one time I glimpsed Lady Blackwood had been the day she and her daughter had fled London. She'd been shrouded in black from head to foot as she climbed into the carriage. Her face could not be seen behind a thick, dark veil. Speaking with my future mother-in-law would be nerve-racking under the best of circumstances, but I had never even seen this lady's face. It was doubly frightening.

Whatever she planned to give me was part of an unbreakable tradition going back generations.

Maria and I entered the house through a front door fifteen feet tall. Sorrow-Fell had been designed for grandeur, not comfort. The ceiling of the front hall was thirty feet high, turning the faintest whisper into a sharp echo. Gothic-arched windows displayed scenes of Blackwood and Faerie history. One window showcased a tall woman wearing a crown of stars as she stamped a fanged, wriggling serpent into the earth. Flowers of ruby and obsidian flourished around the creature.

The floor beneath our feet was tiled, creamy marble with veins of pure gold. On the right side of the hall, a staircase with an elaborately carved wooden banister led up to the second floor. Every alcove was filled with portraits and busts of hook-nosed ancestors. Shields and banners displaying the Blackwood seal—a pair of clasped hands entwined with ivy—hung upon every wall. At the back of the great, echoing hall, someone had installed a fireplace large enough to house a small family. Maria and I went to warm ourselves before the fire.

"I wish we could just bloody tell them *you're* the chosen one," I murmured to Maria. She turned her back to the hearth and tossed her red curls over one shoulder.

"Not yet." She'd always watched the sorcerers with trepidation. Then again, she had no reason to trust our kind. Maria was a witch. Well, a half witch. Her half-sorcerer blood would not save her if she was discovered.

When you're the lady of Sorrow-Fell, you can change so many things.

"There you are, Henrietta! Mamma's waiting." Eliza clattered down the stairs to snatch my hands and drag me after her. I glanced back at Maria and she shrugged, content to remain where she was.

Eliza's usually sleek black hair tumbled about her shoulders, and she wore a simple muslin gown. When we'd first met, everything she'd worn had been velvet or silk. Now, with the war at our doorstep, she'd forgone glamour entirely.

"You look nice today." I smiled, but she shook her head.

"Don't worry, I'm straight off to change while you're with Mamma. You need a bridesmaid in pink taffeta, after all. One of the worst parts of the war was losing Madame Voltiana as my seamstress. I've had to make do with gowns from two years ago. Can you imagine the sacrifice?" She gave a playful wink.

"The horror!" I laughed. "Where's George?" I had to resist the urge to call him Blackwood. As an engaged couple, we could use our Christian names with each other. I'd have kept calling him Blackwood, but he'd insisted.

"On the other end of the house, naturally. He won't see you until the ceremony. Bad luck, don't you know?" Eliza plucked my notebook from my hand and scoffed as she flipped through it. "Really, did you need to make another study of those *things* on your wedding day?"

We came to the second level of the house. The coffered ceilings were lower here, the walls papered with dark green silk. Sorrow-Fell was comprised of two sections: the more modern west wing, where everyone lived, and the ancient Fae grounds in the east. People claimed those rooms were haunted.

I disagreed. Hauntings were reserved for the dead. Whatever was on the Faerie grounds felt watchful and alive.

"Once you're the countess, you'll have others to do these nasty jobs for you," Eliza said, snapping me back to reality.

"What about the countess's sister?" I squeezed her hand.

"She'll have to be your most trusted advisor."

We arrived outside Lady Blackwood's stately door. Eliza kissed my cheek and swept down the hall to ready herself for the ceremony. Evidently, she wasn't worried about this meeting. And why should she be? After all, a future mother-in-law was not nearly as terrible as an Ancient.

Then again, for all I knew, she could be worse.

Shrugging off that alarming sentiment, I forced my shoulders back and opened the door.

Candles burned on tabletops, providing dim illumination to this gloomy space. Lady Blackwood's bed lurked in the center of the room like a monolith, its curtains drawn. Deep shadows capered about the walls. A thin sliver of daylight broke through the damask curtains to cut across the floor.

"Miss Howel? Come here," a woman said from the bed.

I approached and tentatively pulled back the curtain.

The lady lay beneath the blankets, her face hidden in shadow. Something about the way she worried her thin, gloved hands made me nervous. Why was she wearing gloves in bed?

"My lady." I curtsied to her.

"As the current countess, it is my duty to instruct you." Every word she spoke sounded odd—juicy—as though her mouth was filled with saliva she could not spit.

"Thank you," I said.

"And to warn you." There was a rustle of silk. She drew closer—it was all I could do not to leap away. "You still have a choice, child. You can still run."

The wound at my shoulder exploded in sharp pain. I gritted my teeth. Just once in my life, could I meet someone who didn't have a warning to impart? Just once, I'd like for someone to give me a warm hug and a pat on the cheek.

"Why should I run?"

Silence. I summoned a ball of whispering flame into the palm of my hand and examined the woman more closely. Even in bed, her face was veiled. Low panic cramped my gut; something was wrong with this lady. Her nightdress, designed to be fashionable, had yellowed, and stained lace decorated the sleeves. The scent of camphor and sweat met me. Her gloved hands felt for mine, and I resisted the urge to pull away.

"You are not one of us." She said it flatly. Ah, so she was a snob, then? Was I not high-blooded enough for her family?

"No, my lady." I bristled. "I'm a solicitor's daughter. My parents died when I was quite young. I was born a magician, as well."

"All this I know." She tsked, and her tongue sounded clumsy. "Do you think I care a jot, girl? I was the daughter of a minor sorcerer house myself. My father sold me in marriage for the prestige of the Blackwood name. What a fool he was. Only stupid people fuss about blood. What they should care about is *power,* and you possess a great deal of that.

"Marriage is a contract." She changed the topic with a strange ease. "When you become a Blackwood, you take on a debt." My blood chilled. Did she know, then, what her late husband had done? How he had been partly responsible for the fate of this country? More than that, how he had placed the blame upon magicians and witches and spared his family from the punishment?

"A debt?" I repeated.

"Have you ever wondered why my son is Lord Blackwood, but his estate is Sorrow-Fell?" I had wondered. In a traditional house, the earl would title himself after his estate. Blackwood should really be Lord Sorrow-Fell. "Sorrow-Fell is more than a name; it is a living part of Faerie," the lady continued. "To call oneself lord of this place would be akin to calling oneself God."

"That's . . . interesting," I said. Her grip tightened; her hands were sharp and bony.

"The Blackwoods are not like other sorcerer families. Our bloodline does not stretch back a thousand years. We are a new house, a mere three hundred years old. The first earl stole this estate from a Fae lord."

"He won it, I thought."

"Stole." The s sound in her mouth was particularly wet. "The first Blackwood was a nameless blacksmith, a common man with a sorcerer's ability—likely the bastard of a well-placed sorcerer father. This nameless commoner took his family name from the dark forests that surround the estate. The whole history is smoke and mirrors. The family is cursed, my dear."

"Excuse me?" Next she was going to tell me Blackwood had buried the corpses of his previous wives beneath the floorboards.

"Cursed by the faerie queen Titania." The woman's voice rose to a frenzied pitch. "She claimed she'd free the family once they paid a blood debt, a sacrifice on the part of a young Blackwood bride. Then, only then, would she lift her curse."

"I don't understand. You're a wealthy, powerful family." It all sounded like something out of a novel, frankly. But I knew better than to dismiss something because it sounded radical.

"There was never a Blackwood heir whose end was not untimely, and never a Blackwood consort who did not waste and wither. As you see."

She released me and made a vague gesture toward herself. I suppressed a shudder. "My Eliza may be spared all this pain." The woman's voice gentled a bit. "If she married, she would no longer be a Blackwood. She would be safe."

Unfortunately, Blackwood's previous hopes for Eliza's marriage had been dashed.

"Girl, take my warning in the kind spirit in which it's meant. You can still be free of the Blackwood bane."

The Blackwood bane? My temples throbbed. I was an hour from the altar, and she shared this *now*? I studied her and my heart softened; clearly, the woman had been a recluse for years. She was not in her right mind.

"Thank you for the advice, my lady." I curtsied once more.

"You're determined to stay." She sounded resigned. "Very well. I offered you this chance. Should you choose to be the countess, you must follow tradition. I said that the future lady of Sorrow-Fell must pay a debt of blood. You must do what generations of Blackwood brides have done. Take this." She offered a cruel-looking dagger with a sweeping silver blade, slipping the thing out from the bedclothes beside her. Did she sleep with this dagger? An ivory design had been laid into the handle: a curl of ivy, Blackwood's symbol. "Do you know the old druid lands?"

I did. They ran to the northernmost reach of the estate, through the blackest heart of the forest. I didn't relish the idea of a trip there.

"With that knife, make a sacrifice of blood on the border."
She wiped at her mouth with a handkerchief, stealing up under
her veil.

"I cut myself?"

"Heavens, no. Something else."

Blast. Would I need to truly kill something? "What happens then?"

"Nothing. It is merely the custom. Once you've offered the
blood, turn around and come home to your prince."

I did not like the mocking way she said that.

"Thank you." I curtsied one last time to the lady, then hurried away. The cloying, rotten perfume of the air dispersed as
soon as I'd left. My back to the closed door, I tried to think.

Curses. Family rituals. Mad old ladies. Honestly, it was as
though I'd stepped into a Gothic tale by Mrs. Radcliffe.

At that moment, I wanted to see Blackwood desperately. I
wanted to feel his hands upon me, his arms around me, his lips
tracing mine. A hot, heavy feeling settled low in my body at
the thought of him. With him, I would find peace and security.
This was it. One more mere hurdle to overcome, and then the
chapel.

First, I needed a sacrifice.

THE WORLD WAS SMOOTH WITH FRESH snow, the air so cold that
tears at the corner of one's eye froze, needle-sharp. I'd worn
my warmest cloak, a dense gray with white fur trimming, and
even that wasn't enough. As I trod ahead, I winced to think

of the fine blue satin of my wedding gown being demolished: it was custom for the bride to make this journey wearing her gown.

I'd set off in a sled, buried under blankets, but when we'd approached the border of the wood the driver was required to let me out. The final leg of the journey must be made on foot, alone. The trees towered over me, their black branches entwining to create an arched ceiling.

In one hand, I held the knife. In the other, a red pomegranate. That had been Maria's suggestion when I'd consulted her on the offering and suggested a dove.

"Don't you dare! What did I tell you about the danger of dark magic?" She'd dragged me down to the kitchen to find what we could. "If the juice is thick and red enough, and from the seed, that'll do." She'd passed me the pomegranate, its flesh rough and deep red like heart's blood. Since I didn't actually want to kill anything, it suited me just fine.

I wandered farther into the wood, until the world around me grew silent as snowfall. I listened carefully for the sound of hoofbeats. That could signal the approach of a wild man. They said he'd the body of a stag in the front, a bear in the back, and a cruelly beautiful face with three mouths.

And to think, this was one of the light Fae's creatures. But as Blackwood had told me, the light Fae were as dangerous as the dark. More so, in fact.

There was nothing gentle in magic.

On either side of me, small white toadstools sprouted out

of the snow. They were faintly luminescent as they guided my feet along the path. The air tasted thick here; magic sat on the tongue like a sweet. Shuddering, I burrowed deeper into my cloak. Lady Blackwood's words haunted me as I walked these eerie woods. Every Blackwood earl came to a bad end; every lady withered. But Blackwood was not his father, and I would not be reduced to his mother's fate. We wouldn't be chained to the past.

I became light-headed as I pushed on into the darkest part of the forest . . . and then broke through the wood and into a clearing—a patch of stark white. The druid lands waited beyond, a blank expanse of nothing. I blinked, trying to adjust my eyes. The wind became sharper, and my shoulder pained me, a bright scream in my mind. Gritting my teeth, I held the pomegranate out before me.

"No one told me what to say," I whispered into the void. "I suppose I don't need words."

I sank the knife into the fruit and let the juice bleed over my hand. It dripped, a startling red onto the snowy ground. Three drops, then four.

There. I'd done it. I was prepared to turn and go, until the mist lifted.

The mist lifted, and I saw the stones.

2

TWELVE STONES STOOD IN A RING. I STEPPED INTO
the circle to find blue sky stretching above a lush, grassy field.
It was high summer.

Sweat dripped down the back of my neck, and I untied my
cloak and dropped it into the grass. There was a persistent buzz
all around me. It sounded like a chorus of bees, but I knew that
was not true.

The droning came from the stones.

Around me, the stones were about ten feet high, stationed
roughly ten yards apart from one another.

My stomach dropped. The markings covering them were
runes. I hurried to examine each stone. Some of these runes
looked familiar. Blackwood's father had numerous tomes on
runes, and Blackwood and I had spent time reading through
the volumes and making notes. Runes were how Lord Blackwood, Mary Willoughby, and Mickelmas had opened the world
to R'hlem and his Ancients. Runes were how we had lost my
father to that hellscape, damning us all in the process.

Some of these appeared to be porter runes for transporta-
tion, some runes for summoning. But the largest runes of all,

one carved into each stone, were unlike anything I had yet seen. They looked rough and jagged at the edges, like rudimentary weapons. There was something primitive about them. Touching one lightly, I saw

a cracked and barren plain, the earth clay red, the sky a sunset orange, the sun a boiled lump of

When I took my hand away, the image vanished. That had not been our world. I was sure of it. In my bones, I knew it had been the Ancients' home. For that moment I had stood in another world, and I had felt . . . minuscule, an ant surrounded by giants. Dimly, I recalled a dream I'd had back in Agrippa's house soon after I'd arrived in London. Nearly a year ago, but it seemed a lifetime now.

In my dream, I had found myself in this exact circle of stones. The Seven Ancients had gathered around, all of them watching. Waiting.

In my dream, the Ancients came to this place.

The idea of it filled me with a bone-deep horror.

I pressed my hand to the rune again, daring everything for another look. I winced as a riot of shapeless color and blinding light played through my head, and then

A tear in the blue sky above. The fair summer day darkens as the rift opens between this world and the next . . . the beast, bristling with hair and teeth, gnashes at the circle of stones all around. It is trapped by the circle, unable to break free and wreak havoc upon the world outside. On one side, in the space between stones, stands a woman with her hands outstretched.

On another side waits a man wielding a stave.

And then, another man, one with a golden beard and a doublet of forest green, his hand raised to the swirling maelstrom in the summer sky.

With a scream, the beast is pulled up into the vacuum above, sent to the roiling world beyond the stars. With a cry, the woman and the two men raise up their hands, and the circle vanishes.

I fell back, gasping. I stared up at the sky, my hand trembling on my stomach. That scene had played out in our world, in this very circle. I had seen an Ancient, some kind of monstrous dog creature as it was sent back to the world above. I had seen a witch—the woman, obviously—and a sorcerer, and Ralph Strangewayes, the father of England's magicians. They had all stood there, calm as you like, and worked together to send the monster back to its hell world.

Sweeping on my cloak, I grabbed the knife and tore off into the woods. I barely felt the returning sting of winter or noticed the encroaching darkness. My shoes were soaked, my toes numb, but I didn't care. I kept a ball of fire over my head to guide me until I emerged from the wood. The waiting driver put me on the sled, and we made for the house. My heart hammered as I arranged the blankets on my lap.

Bother the wedding and all the rest. I needed to tell Blackwood what I had just seen. He needed to know that the gate to the Ancients' home world rested on his own estate.

BLACKWOOD HAD TAKEN THE OLD PARLOR, as the servants called it, to change and prepare for the wedding. I knew where that was, at least.

The Faerie side of the manor was not built for humans, and sometimes the hallways did not lead straight on to anything. Rather, they spiraled like dreams, making a sharp turn here or a looping reversal there. The ceilings were so low they nearly scraped the top of my head, and the stones beneath my feet were unevenly placed. Torches flickered and smoked in the walls, granting the place the air of a dungeon. No one knew when the Fae had built the eastern wing, but it felt ancient. I had sometimes imagined the rooms carved out of time itself.

My body was still weak these several months after Rook—the Ancient that had been Rook—bit me and poisoned my system. But today, especially after what I'd seen, I felt little tiredness.

Arriving, I knocked on the door. Without even waiting on a reply, I barged in to find Blackwood before a mirror. Granted, in this room it would be difficult to avoid a mirror; they were everywhere. The only furniture in the old parlor was a high-backed wooden chair with clawed lion feet, placed in the direct center of the room. The walls and ceiling sported mirrors of every size and shape. Some were oval looking glasses encased in gilt frames. Others were square, or diamond-shaped. I looked to the ceiling and found a ten-foot mirror staring back at me. But I did not see our reflections in it, Blackwood's and mine. Rather, the mirror displayed an empty room long over-grown with moss and ivy, weeds growing wild out of cracks in the floor.

A disturbing image.

Actually, the most disquieting thing of all was parked right beside the high-backed chair: it was the *optiaethis*, the grotesque lantern-like thing we had rescued from Ralph Strangewayes's house in Cornwall several months earlier. It was small, a ball of glass caged in metal, pulsating white light trapped inside. The sight of that light made me cringe. I hated that Blackwood had taken to keeping it always with him.

But at the moment Blackwood's attention was focused en-tirely upon me. His expression lightened when I entered, and then darkened with confusion.

"Henrietta." He sounded both surprised and awed.

We stared at one another. Lord, he was . . . well. He was everything a young bride on her wedding day should want. His morning coat was dark green, which set off the brilliant color of his eyes. Tan breeches tucked into gleaming boots defined his strong, slender legs. The cut of his suit hugged his broad shoulders and tapered waist. His night-black hair had been combed back, and a lock fell before his eyes.

I felt myself flush. A part of me wanted nothing more than to drag him to the chapel, marry him, and only then tell him what I had discovered.

Sometimes, I hated being rational.

"It's bad luck to see you before the ceremony." Blackwood

strode over, taking me into his arms. I hadn't realized how cold I was until he enveloped me in his warmth.

"I gather you're not that upset about it." I skimmed my fingers through his hair.

"Not all traditions are important," he whispered, and kissed me. The dark, nameless desire that slept inside me awoke, eager for more and more of his touch. When we broke apart, I laid my head on his chest.

"You're distracting me." I smiled.

"Not from anything too important, I hope," he whispered in my ear. God, why did my resolve weaken with his touch? He kissed my cheek, then captured my mouth with his again. I wanted to forget everything else; indeed, I could barely recall why I'd come. A small voice inside me reminded me that there'd be plenty of time for this later.

"I need to tell you something." I broke away to compose myself. "About the old druid lands."

His black brow lifted. "So. You completed the ritual." Blackwood sounded pleased, even as he took in the somewhat bedraggled sight of me. My gown, which had begun as a confection of blue satin with a low, square bodice and intricate lace at the wrists, was damp and spotted with mud. I could only wonder at the state of my hair. But in Blackwood's gaze, I found desire. "You're beautiful, Henrietta." He made as if to kiss me again. The hungry part of me wanted to fold myself against him and forget everything else. But I held out my hand, stopping him before I forgot why I had searched him out.

"Yes, the ritual's done," I said. "But I wanted to talk about the druid lands themselves. When a Blackwood bride goes to make a sacrifice, what is she supposed to find?"

"Well. You're not supposed to *find* anything. Slice a dove or a raven's breast, and then—" His gaze sharpened. "Henrietta, do you mean to say that you saw something?"

"It was more than that. I've had visions before, but the circle provided more than that. It was as if I'd been absorbed into a moment in time. I'm not sure why I saw them. It could have been on account of the pomegranate."

Blackwood blinked. "Is that . . . code for something?"

"Maria thought I should sacrifice fruit, not a bird." I shrugged. "Perhaps the druid lands enjoy fruit."

Blackwood frowned. "I still don't understand."

"There is a stone circle," I said. "Twelve stones, all about ten feet high."

"Truly?"

"Yes. And they were covered in runes."

Now I had his full, hungry attention. "What type of runes?"

"All types. And when I touched the stones—"

My words were lost in a blare of horns. Even here, deep inside the great Faerie part of the estate, they echoed. Blackwood and I went to the door as the horns blared twice, then three times. That was the call of the barrier patrol. Three blasts meant that something was approaching from the west.

My stomach flipped. Blackwood and I raced out of the old parlor and back into the main house. Pain flared in my shoulder as I ran, but I forced it down. In the distance, I could hear the thunder of hooves. The ground trembled with it. Bloody hell, were the Ancients attacking en masse? Was even our ultimate stronghold unsafe from R'hlem?

From my father?

Last time I'd seen him, I'd plunged a dagger into his heart when he showed one moment of weakness and love. I doubted he would ever make that mistake again.

"My lord." One of the guards, Virgil, ran to greet us. He was a rosy-cheeked sorcerer, scarcely two years older than I.

"Is it an attack?" Blackwood glanced ahead, trying to gauge the danger. The sorcerer shook his head.

"The barrier's clear of enemies, my lord. But there's an entire army of people charging straight for us."

"Soldiers?" Hope flared through me. Perhaps some regiments in the queen's army had made their way north to us.

"They're ordinary citizens, but there are sorcerers with them."

Sorcerers, traveling with common people? I was pleasantly surprised.

"Should I call for your coach, sir?" the boy asked. Blackwood and I looked at each other. Words were unnecessary; we grabbed our staves out of their sheaths at the same time.

Yes, I wore my stave, Porridge, with my wedding gown. I was a bride, but I was also a sorcerer.

Blackwood and I summoned the wind together and flew for the barrier. The winter chill easily sliced through my cloak and silk gown. Traveling this way, the ten-minute walk to the barrier shortened to two. We arrived to find an entire battalion of sorcerers waiting shoulder to shoulder with staves in hand. Dee was getting his men into line. So was Wolff, easy to pick out because of his height. I searched for Maria but didn't see her bright red hair.

Through the clearing mist I caught flashes of movement. There was a roar from somewhere in the forest, the sound of voices shouting.

Men erupted into view, some on horseback and some on foot next to wagons and carts. Most of them didn't look magical at all. They were ordinary Englishmen, and a few women as well. Their faces were streaked with mud and ash, reddened by the icy wind. They tore for the barrier, for safety.

At the head of this makeshift army, charging toward us on a horse, was Magnus.

3

MAGNUS LEANED FORWARD IN THE SADDLE AND swung his stave, spraying snow out of the way to clear a path to the barrier. Beside me, Blackwood stiffened. Despite the war, he could never shake his hatred toward Magnus. If it weren't for Magnus, Eliza would now be safely married and in Ireland.

And miserable, but it was difficult to make him understand that.

Blackwood did not open the barrier. Instead he stood there, the only movement his cloak in the winter wind.

"We have to let them in!" I cried.

"R'hlem's men could be waiting for an opportunity like this." He kept his stave lowered at his side.

Wolff arrived beside us, slapping snow from his dark hair. His cheeks and nose were red as apples. He must have been in the middle of a patrol when the horns sounded.

"Why are we waiting?" He looked from me to Blackwood. "It's Magnus. Don't you see?"

Honestly, Magnus might be the prime reason Blackwood was delaying.

"We must let them in." I exchanged looks with Wolff, who

held up his stave in a ready pose for attack. Blackwood sighed and strode forward, leaving crisp footprints in the snow.

"Everyone prepare for the fall. Remember, stay inside the barrier line!" he shouted as the men rushed into action.

Horns blared five short, sharp times, moving every sorcerer into position. We'd never taken the barrier down before, but at least we had a plan for doing so. Six squadrons each were stationed in four different locations—north, south, east, west. When the barrier came down all around the estate, we'd be ready for anything. "Watch so that nothing inhuman comes through!" Blackwood yelled. The edge of our protective shield was marked all the way around the estate with stone pilings. When Blackwood touched the air between the pilings, the barrier would respond to his blood and sever itself.

It would remain down until he touched it again, placing the barrier back up. I followed Blackwood, my stave reassuring in my hand. I brought Porridge to the ground and whispered its name, summoning energy into its carvings. It glowed in seeming appreciation. Porridge had been out of action for so long.

So had I.

We waited until a horn sounded from each of the four corners, signifying that the squadrons were in place. Blackwood took a deep breath and touched the edge of the barrier. The air charged, crackling with energy. In an instant, the invisible shield around us died.

Blackwood and I stood ready as swarms of people ran full tilt onto the safety of Sorrow-Fell ground. Horses thundered past us, their breath steaming in the frigid air. The sorcerers came last, some wearing red army livery, others in plain clothes. I caught a glimpse of Valens as he drove a wagon, guiding the horse with a steady hand. Then I turned, searching again for a glimpse of Magnus.

There he was, still on horseback, though he'd stopped and was looking back into the forest. A cry of joy caught in my throat. All these months, I'd been certain he must be dead. And here, here he was.

I tracked his gaze and saw what had stopped him. Behind him, an older woman had fallen from one of the wagons and lay on the ground. I started forward to help, but Magnus had already taken action. He galloped the horse back up the hill to retrieve the woman.

Blackwood called my name as I hurried out of the barrier's safe zone, to give cover in case of an attack. How could I do otherwise? It was Magnus, for God's sake.

Magnus picked up the woman, and I guarded their backs as we all made our way into the barrier's protection.

Once I'd got back behind the barrier line, Blackwood put the defensive shield up again with a touch. I felt the protection form around us, a momentary pressure on the skin. Blackwood took me by the shoulders.

"That was dangerous, Henrietta!" he cried. I touched his hand for reassurance, but also to release myself.

"No harm done," I replied.

With a harsh exhale, he turned from me and went to Hawthorne, one of his most trusted men. Hawthorne was an older sorcerer who always looked suitably grim and gray-faced. Perhaps Blackwood liked him for that specific quality. Blackwood and Hawthorne spoke together, probably agreeing with each other on how reckless this had been.

Thankfully, a single, short horn called from the other four points in the barrier. Nothing had got through. I signaled our trumpeter to blast the same message and went to stand beside Blackwood. Together, we headed back through the tangle of forest to the long, sloping yard that led to the house.

Magnus, Valens, and all their people had congregated there. Men and women were climbing down from wagons or holding the reins of jumpy horses.

As the future lady of Sorrow-Fell, I ought to see to them. Whatever I had found in the druid lands could wait. I didn't think the stone circle was going anywhere.

Passing the new arrivals, Blackwood and I received bows and curtsies and cries of praise. The men and women looked tattered and relieved.

The sight of their happiness warmed me. Blackwood, however, appeared more on edge than before.

"What the devil are you doing here?" he snapped at Magnus and Valens. The two of them were taking down sacks of provisions. As we drew near, I stopped in shock. I had never seen such weary looks from two sorcerers in my life, not even after London fell.

Magnus in particular looked wild. His hair had grown

longer in the months since I'd seen him, even more outrageous and windswept. Stubble dusted his cheeks and chin, and his jacket was torn and patched in several places. His body had grown leaner, his flinty gaze more determined.

Well. He wasn't the only one whose appearance had drastically changed, after all. My Unclean marks had left me thinner, with dark circles beneath my eyes. But he didn't appear repulsed. In fact, he didn't exhibit any feeling at all upon seeing me.

I tried not to let that hurt.

"What happened?" Blackwood's tone softened.

Valens opened his mouth, but Magnus answered. "We needed to resupply." His gaze raked me up and down, and his eyebrows lifted. He appeared shocked by my silk gown. "Do you always dress so formally here? I'm afraid I left my evening garb at the last battlefield."

"This is our wedding day," Blackwood said. I noted how he made certain to hit the word *our*.

Magnus stiffened. "Ah. Apologies, Howel. Or Lady Blackwood?" He sketched a bow.

"We haven't performed the ceremony yet," I replied.

"Well, I know what an anxious bride you must be. What red-blooded woman would fail to swoon at the promise of a lifetime with old Blacky here?" He gave a wan smile. "You've someone to give you away, I suppose? For a pound, I'll take you up the aisle *and* serve as entertainment at the wedding breakfast."

"Maria's asked to give me away. She's very excited by the

idea." We couldn't have my father here, for obvious reasons, and I'd rather be given away by a friend than by an older sorcerer I barely knew.

"Yes, that sounds like her, all right." Magnus's voice warmed with real fondness.

Blackwood's arm circled me.

"You're welcome to stay as long as you need. Both George and I agree. Don't we, dear?" I said. Blackwood narrowed his eyes, but I would not let him say anything other than yes.

"Of course," he answered.

"Well, then." Magnus provided a steadying arm to the old woman he had rescued. Blood smeared the side of her head. God, she needed medical attention at once. "Where may we take the wounded?"

I pointed him past the carts and wagons. "Maria and Eliza are on hand to help with the injured."

"You can find them in the stables," Blackwood said.

Magnus snorted. "Stables? You're the soul of kindness, Blacky." He marched past, carrying the woman as though she weighed no more than a sack of flour. "Let me guess, we put the horses in the parlor? Sorrow-Fell's wonderfully topsy-turvy."

Color rose in Blackwood's cheeks.

These two were not going to get on well. At least some things never changed.

That left us with Valens, who, while not as ragged as Magnus, was still clearly the worse for wear. A short young man with shaggy blond hair and hooded blue eyes, he'd always looked perfectly groomed and presentable in London. Now his cheeks were thin from hunger, and stubble bristled on his face.

"We need more horses, supplies, water. Whatever you can spare," he said to Blackwood. "Also, these people—"

"We cannot take in those without the means to help," Blackwood said, though he didn't sound especially firm about it. The sight of the families rejoicing and crying together in huddled groups was softening him.

"We'd the choice to either take them with us or leave them to slaughter. Or worse," Valens said.

"After all, R'hlem tends to transform into Familiars any humans that he doesn't outright kill," I added. Valens nodded to me, grateful for the support.

Blackwood relented. "Very well. Medical treatment, supplies—"

"Whatever you need," I added. Valens smiled at me. Hard to believe I'd once considered him an enemy. "You'll want to warm up before we discuss any further. I'll arrange for hot soup and bread in the great hall." I smiled. "You've come at a very good time, you know. Your daughter was born last week."

Valens's face lit up, and he raced for the house. His wife had come to Sorrow-Fell with us and had given birth to a little girl, Georgiana—named in Blackwood's honor. Blackwood watched Valens go with some sympathy in his eyes.

"That would be good," he said, as if to himself. "One day, someone will say those words to me."

I blushed. He cleared his throat and took my hand.

"I don't think we can proceed with the ceremony today." He touched my cheek, sliding a lock of hair from my eyes. "So close," he murmured. My whole body buzzed to hear the yearning in his voice. I pressed my lips to his.

"We'll try again soon," I said. "After I tell you more about the stones."

"Yes, we'll talk more. Tonight?" he asked.

"Tonight."

He kissed me again, and a small, unhappy voice deep within me argued we should have the ceremony anyway.

Every day that we had been at Sorrow-Fell together, I'd wanted him more and more. As days passed into weeks, I had begun to see Blackwood anew. I had always thought him handsome, but now I found my eye inexorably drawn to him whenever he entered a room. Love had enveloped me, entwining my heart with his as snugly as the ivy on the garden wall. It was as if Sorrow-Fell itself had laid some strange enchantment upon me. I liked it.

But at the moment, I needed to do my job.

"Are you in too much pain for work?" Blackwood stroked my cheek.

"I'm fine." I tried not to be cross. He meant well, but I'd told him several times that doing nothing worsened the pain. When we'd first come to Sorrow-Fell, he'd wanted to see me resting round the clock. What he didn't understand was that rest exacerbated the whisperings in my head. Only work quieted the voices.

I sorted the wounded and brought the worst of them in a wagon down the hill to the infirmary. Then I pointed the rest of the arrivals to the front entrance of the great house. As we all walked together, someone came up beside me and tugged at my elbow.

"H'lo. Didn't think to see you again." The girl sounded cheerful, and a bit amazed. She was unfamiliar, with nondescript brown hair and a round face. No, I'd never seen this girl before in my life.

"I'm so sorry, I don't believe we've met?" I smiled, masking my confusion. She appeared offended. Then her expression cleared.

"My fault. Forgot I was wearin' this." She pointed to her nose. Odd. Then her face changed. Yes, her nose shrank, her blue eyes changed color on the spot. What the devil?

When she'd finished her transformation, my mouth dropped open. Because she was correct: I did know her. Shock and delight warmed me in equal measure.

It was the magician girl from London, Alice Chen.

ALICE AND I SAT IN A CORNER OF THE GREAT DINING hall, usually reserved for visiting dignitaries and aristocrats. The Gothic arch of the stone ceiling and the elegant mullioned windows indicated a grand cathedral, while the long table of ebony gleamed from fresh polish. Normally, this was where bone china would be laid, so thin one could see the light through it, and where hushed conversation would happen over crystal glasses of the finest wine in the cellar. It was strange now to see this room brimming with so many ragged people, grateful for a mere helping of soup and bread. Strange, but I liked it.

We huddled by one of the windows, watching as snow flurried in the yard. The sky above was slate gray, and I shivered as I pulled my cloak closed at the throat. Alice seemed to feel the cold less, or perhaps she simply felt hunger more. She drained her soup bowl and wiped her mouth.

"Me and my brother, Gordo, was always the most gifted in the family. Mum said it were special, face changin'. Gordo can turn to near any animal, but me? I can do folks as well. Humans, I mean. Saved our lives a few times." She looked out into the yard, a thoughtful expression on her face. She wore fingerless gloves, and her nails had been bitten down to the nub.

"Where's Gordo now?"

"Still alive, I hope. After London fell, we all sort of broke apart. Tried fighting together at first, but when you're twelve or twenty against a giant blob monster, all them big ideas 'bout brotherhood and standin' together sort of fall away. Plus, we learned that Hargrove were actually Mickelmas. That made him quite unpopular for a bit."

I winced. "When did you find out his real name?"

"Right after London fell. He gathered those of us he could find together and told us. Told us to spread the word, too. Said he'd had enough of lyin' to everyone and wanted a fresh go."

Very noble of him. "What happened after that?"

"Half of us got bloody furious and left. A few tried to beat him with clubs. The rest of us made peace with it, but the army were so small at that point." She pulled a brilliantly colored handkerchief from her coat pocket and fidgeted with it. "Despite what he done, Mickelmas is the only person can bring us all together. And, well, he won't be doin' that anytime soon."

My skin prickled at her words. "What do you mean?"

Alice turned her eyes to the floor, regret dancing in her expression. "I mean R'hlem's army captured him, last I heard."

My hands went up in flame. I extinguished myself fast, but people around the hall stared at us with shock.

"Are you sure?" I croaked. She nodded.

"Peg Bottleshanks was with 'im and managed to get away."

"When?" My throat went dry.

"'Bout a month after the city collapsed. He's likely dead now." She looked at me with sympathy. "I'm sorry." Alice tried patting my shoulder, which sent pain spiking through my body.

Mickelmas, captured by R'hlem and killed? I knew that R'hlem wouldn't respond kindly to his former friend. Mickelmas was partly responsible for my father being pushed into the Ancients' world to begin with. And in that final battle in London, R'hlem had begun flaying Mickelmas alive right before my eyes. Now he'd had plenty of time since capturing the magician to finish the job.

I put my gloved hand to my mouth. What if R'hlem *hadn't* killed Mickelmas?

Perhaps he wouldn't waste the opportunity to torture his old "friend" the way he himself had been tortured in the Ancients' world. He might casually peel Mickelmas like an orange. God, he might feed the magician to Molochoron, or crisp him alive with Zem's fiery breath.

What if he decided he could *use* Mickelmas?

No, surely that was a foolish idea. R'hlem was a master of magic, after all. He wouldn't need Mickelmas to teach him any tricks.

But my father, say what you would about him, was a practical man. And keeping his enemy alive, even if he despised him, would be worth it if he could receive a great deal of information from a man who knew too much. Hadn't I spent hours reading through the contents of Mickelmas's magic trunk? The man was a library of magical knowledge. With such power under his control, R'hlem could discover new ways of tormenting us.

New ways of winning.

"You all right?" Alice sucked a bit of soup from her thumb.

Murmuring apologies, I went upstairs to change into warmer clothes. My head pounded as I stripped myself of the ruined wedding gown, as I buttoned my warm wool dress and tied on my cloak again.

I wished the magician had come with us to Sorrow-Fell. I wished it more than anything.

As I headed downstairs, a wave of dizziness nearly toppled me. The pain at my shoulder burned with brighter intensity. My sight warped, the stairwell before me lengthening and contracting at once. I slid down, falling away into utter blackness. And then . . . light.

"Come on, then!" a little boy calls over his shoulder, running full tilt down a hillside. He cannot be more than eight years old and takes great, whooping leaps toward a river that sparkles in the distance.

Without pausing, the child races into the river. He is barefoot and rolls his trousers up to the knee as he wades into the crystal stream, squealing at how frigid it is. He examines his own image in the water, bright blue eyes and flaxen hair like dandelion fluff. His smile is unafraid. Turning, he sticks out his tongue as two other boys arrive. They look like older copies of the child in the river, both of them flushed with exertion.

"Oi! Stephen!" the taller one says, edging into the water. "Mum wants you home. They say the monsters are prowlin'."

Stephen only laughs and dances out farther into the stream. Cursing softly, the older boy tromps in after him.

"Stephen Poole! You stupid . . . c'mere!" The older boy grabs his younger brother and lifts him up while a wriggling Stephen laughs.

And then, with the swift transition of a nightmare, a roaring black cloud rises up behind them. The brothers are snatched away into the darkness, dead in one heartbeat. Stephen screams as massive tentacles wrap around him, burning his skin.

The vision melted away, returning me to the hall. I pressed my feverish cheek against the cold stone of the wall.

This was not the first time such images had overtaken me with a sheer power that I could not resist. Sometimes they would display nonsense images of another world. Sometimes I would see this same young boy, this Stephen.

I would have recognized that child's face anywhere. I was seeing Rook, before his scars and the loss of his family. Back when he still had a name, and brothers, and an unblemished soul.

I got up from the floor, straightened my skirts, and walked on with heaviness in my heart. Every time I saw another of these visions, I would promise over and over again to find Rook. To save him from the shadows. To bring him back.

I would do this, or die trying.

"WHAT'S THE DIFFERENCE BETWEEN AN ABRASION and a cut?" Eliza asked cheerily when I arrived at the stables. She was winding up bandages. "I thought they were the same thing, but Maria seems convinced otherwise."

"I'm not the most expert healer," I said, barely paying attention. I'd looked for Blackwood in the great hall and been told he'd come here. Now that I was here, someone had said he was in the great hall. Blast, I needed to speak with him about what Alice had said.

Eliza kept pace with me, wearing only a simple gray gown with an apron beneath her cloak. When I'd first met her in London, all those months ago, she'd seemed a regular fashion plate. I'd been unable to imagine her doing anything but attending parties and laughing at clever jokes that other people made.

She'd proved how ungenerous I'd been in my opinion of her, and indeed, of women in her circle. When Maria had asked for help tending the wounded, Eliza had paled but offered her assistance. Since then she'd become an astute learner.

The stables at Sorrow-Fell were grand enough to count as housing in their own right. The gabled roofs sported wooden beams that had been carved to depict tableaux of round-bellied satyrs bothering water nymphs. The images of the white stag, most elegant of all the light Fae's creatures, were embroidered upon tapestries and other wall hangings.

The injured had been stationed in the groom's lodge, a small but rather luxurious cabin directly adjacent to the stalls. Straw pallets and cots created something of a labyrinth, which the nurses navigated with care.

Maria was examining an older man's leg. A massive bruise purpled the side of his face, and Eliza got straight to assisting her.

"Can you help?" Maria asked upon seeing me. She pointed toward a cluster of people near the door. "They're needing more fires in the stalls outside. I want to sort out who needs a bed here and who can go in the main house."

Well, if Blackwood wasn't here, I might as well do something useful. People made appreciative noises as I summoned flame and lit the kindling. Lilly appeared at my elbow, ferrying hot drinks on a tray. Her strawberry-blond hair hung in a messy chignon, with flyaway wisps landing in her eyes.

"How are you, miss?" she asked as we walked back to the cabin. Blackwood had wanted to retain Lilly's services as my maid once we arrived at Sorrow-Fell, but I'd refused. I didn't want a personal servant when every scrap of help was needed for the war. So I didn't dress so grandly any longer, or wear my hair in elaborate styles. After all, I'd had years of practice looking after myself.

Lilly seemed perfectly fine as well. Her cheeks were rosy and her normally spotless hands and apron smudged. In London, she'd been all sweetness. She'd seemed so fragile, really. But now, as we entered the lodge, she whipped off her scarf and turned an attentive eye to each cot before snapping her fingers.

"Oi, bring that bucket here. Asked for it two minutes ago," Lilly called, briskly waving a boy over. He hurried, looking rather sheepish. She took the bucket before sending him flying off with another order. Placing the bucket beside a rather green-faced man, she skirted around one bed to the next, checking eyes and pulses and organizing who was ready to make the march to the main house.

Lilly had taken to these tasks as a duck to water. And as she stood with her small hands on her hips, it occurred to me that healing had brought out something of the general in her as well. I invited her back to the stalls, to see to the next round. She happily agreed.

As we turned into the yard, I stopped. Magnus stood before me with his hands thrust into the pockets of his coat. Snow dusted his hair. His cheeks had been whipped raw by the cold. This time, when his eyes met mine, he smiled.

"How the devil did you manage it?" He nodded at the stables. "It looks a proper hospital."

"We're a capable group," Lilly said. Magnus laughed, though it wasn't the same as before. He used to throw back his head and bellow, a rich and easy sound that came from the core of him. His laughter was not so easy now.

Not since the night his mother had died.

Lilly excused herself and hurried for the stables. I noticed she snuck a glance at us over her shoulder as she went.

"Sorry I didn't get a chance to say a proper hello, Howel." Magnus took my hand and kissed it. Once, it would have been a charming or boyish gesture, but not now. He was all business now. "Thank you for getting Blacky to let the barrier down."

"He'd have done it anyway," I said.

Magnus raised an eyebrow. "But would he have shut it before I managed to get inside? I wonder."

I frowned at that. "You still act as though he's some sort of devious maniac," I said.

Magnus shrugged, acknowledging the possibility. "I confess I was surprised to find out this was your wedding day. All these months later, and you're only getting round to marriage now?" He searched my face, as if looking for some specific reaction. "'Gather ye rosebuds while ye may.' John Donne said that."

"Robert Herrick, actually." The look of shock on Magnus's face was delicious. "'To the Virgins, to Make Much of Time' was a particular favorite of Mr. Colegrind's."

"I stand corrected. Truly, it sounds like a poem any unseemly old man would love." Magnus cleared his throat. "Do you want to wait on a spring wedding? Perhaps have Callax serve as a bridesmaid? I'm sure he'd look heavenly in pink."

"No, I think we're done waiting," I said.

"That's good." Magnus kicked at the snow. His boots were worn now—in fact, his toe was close to coming out the tip of his left boot. There was a gash down his arm that I hadn't noticed before.

"You should see Maria." I drew closer to look at it. He let me, though I felt him watching me.

"It doesn't matter. The people here have all sustained much worse," he said. We watched another group move toward the main house. Magnus squared his jaw. "At first I didn't have a thought beyond annihilation. After Mother's death, I couldn't see anything ahead for me." His voice was distant. "Now I've seen how the people lived in all the years we were under the ward." His gray eyes blazed with murderous intensity. "We should be ashamed."

This was the most un-Magnus-like thing I'd yet heard him say.

"What else have you seen out there?" I asked. He passed a hand over his eyes. All of his jovial energy evaporated.

"Liverpool's gone. It was a city of smoke when we got there." He looked to the sky, as if finding solace in the blanket of dull gray. "The Shadow and Fog was at the head of the enemy's army."

Rook. I started at that. Magnus looked at me with something like sympathy.

"I'm sorry." He examined the cuts and scrapes along his knuckles. "Howel, just so there's no misunderstanding between us." He stared into my eyes once more. "The next time Rook and I meet, one of us will die."

It was a punch to my gut, even though Magnus had more reason for vengeance than anyone. After all, Rook had sunk his fangs into Fanny Magnus's throat and ripped her apart like a wild animal.

"What if I could save him?" I blurted it out. "If I could separate him from the monster?"

Magnus sighed. "Well. I believe you can do anything, Howel." He winked, a glimmer of his former self. But I knew he was humoring me. Only I believed Rook could be rescued.

"With that vote of confidence, I'll be well armed," I drawled.

Magnus snorted with laughter. Momentarily, it felt like being transported back to Master Agrippa's house. But then my shoulder ached, and the haunted look returned to his eyes. No, we were no longer that boy and girl.

"I should check on the men. Remind them what a picture of health and vigor I am. Give them something to aspire to." Magnus turned back for the main house. Eliza materialized next to me, her eyes tracking Magnus as he strode away.

"I've got to fetch some more hot water and linen." She raced off to catch up with him.

Magnus had surprised the entirety of sorcerer society at Eliza's debut ball, declaring her his fiancée to spare her from marrying a man she did not love. It had been kind of him and bold and it had made Blackwood dislike him more ferociously than ever before. I doubted Magnus enjoyed staying on Blackwood's estate and being in his power.

I turned to go back to the stables, but another wave of dizziness washed over me.

An endless expanse of darkness, teeth and eyes on every side of me, shadows covering my body like another skin, the starless stretch of night

The vision appeared and vanished between one heartbeat and the next. Coughing, I tried to keep my feet as I lurched out of Rook's visions. The world spotted about me. Perhaps I really should go and lie down quietly for a few minutes.

I made excuses to Lilly and Maria, then turned back toward the house.

As I tromped up to the entrance, I caught movement out the corner of my eye. Curious, I walked around to the side of the house and stopped.

Eliza stood on tiptoe with her arms flung around Magnus's neck, kissing him passionately.

I was about to turn away with embarrassment when Magnus broke off the kiss. He held Eliza at arm's length. And I found, degenerate that I was, that I could not move.

"Eliza, no," he said quietly.

"But there's no reason not to." She leaned in closer. "Don't you like me at all?" She sounded hurt.

"No man could help liking you. You're everything a man desires."

Eliza blushed prettily. "Why not—"

"Because I'm the wrong man for you."

Her eyes flashed at those words. "Oh, of course. Tell me what's good for me, just like George."

"That's not it." He clasped her hands. "If you'd offered this a year ago, I'd have had us in a church in thirty-five minutes flat. Perhaps twenty-nine, if I could get Dee to serve as a witness. But now . . ."

"You're in love with someone else." Eliza did not make it a question. My entire body froze, but Magnus sighed.

"I don't see a future for me, Eliza. I throw myself into every battle as if it were my last. There's a part of me that prays it will be. You deserve someone who looks forward to life with you. Such a man would be painfully easy to find."

She cast her eyes down, and it was clear she hovered on the verge of tears. Magnus touched her shoulder.

"Think about it," he said. "Do *you* even love me?"

The tears vanished; she seemed to be thinking it through. "I mean, you're terribly handsome." He laughed at that, which made her smile. "Lord, I don't know. I'm not sure what love is, I suppose."

"And think of this: Did Blackwood ever believe for one second that you could look on blood and broken bones and never flinch?"

"No." She smiled. "He thought I'd give up after the first day."

"He loves you, but he doesn't understand you. You deserve to be understood."

Eliza was silent. Finally, she gave a smile.

"Very well." She took his arm. "But will you play the doting fiancé in front of George? It'll be sure to drive him mad."

"How could I resist such an invitation? Shall I recite poetry on bended knee?"

"If you could write a song in praise of my beauty and sing it at dinner, that would be best." She giggled. "Can you play the lute?"

Magnus scoffed. "What self-respecting bear of a man can't

play a lute?" They made to enter the house. I hurried away and tucked myself into a shadowy alcove, praying they didn't see me as they passed.

Once they'd gone I stared at the darkening sky above. What the devil was I doing?

When the dizziness of Rook's memories swept over me again, I nearly welcomed it with relief. They usually traveled in threes, these "flutters." This time, there was a flashing image of Rook mucking out a stall at Brimthorn, the charity school where we'd spent our childhood. Nothing more to be gained, merely a bubble of memory. When I came to again, there was no headache. Sighing, I trudged toward the house . . . and I stopped.

The visions before my eyes, from Rook; the visions I'd had in the circle, from touching those runes. I realized that I'd been so bloody stupid not to think of it. A witch, a sorcerer, and a magician . . . I was a sorcerer, Maria a witch, and with Alice here, I had the third.

Surely we could examine the circle together. Before I showed it to Blackwood, it might help to have a better idea of what, precisely, the thing even was. But we would also need someone whose experience with visions and psychic abilities was greater than mine.

We needed a Speaker, and I'd the perfect candidate in mind.

"HOLD UP. MY LEG'S A BIT sore from all the runnin'," Alice hissed early that evening as she followed Maria and me across the snow-packed ground toward the Speakers' chapel. With this much excitement thrumming through me, I didn't even feel my injured shoulder.

Sorrow-Fell housed two "chapels" on its property. The wedding chapel—the "proper" chapel as Blackwood called it—was on the western side of the estate, designed by Christopher Wren himself. It was an elegant building that housed stained-glass windows designed to let colored light fall upon pews filled with sedate, ordinary worshippers. The Speakers' chapel on the eastern end, however, was an old Fae construction.

An ancient stone mound, the crumbling walls were held together primarily by moss and sheer cussedness. The windows were stained glass, much like the other chapel, but these windows did not show religious figures. Rather, they displayed startling images of a man with a green face and a curling beard of ivy, of trees whose branches were ripe with many eyes, of horned men holding nubile young women in their arms. A stone altar resided at the center of the building; the ancient stains that decorated it suggested that more than wine had been spilled here in the past.

Blackwood did not think anyone in their right mind would choose to stay in such a place. He'd insisted the Speakers enter the main house, but they'd replied that being around so many ordinary minds, cluttered with so many ordinary thoughts, would cloud their own.

A bit insulting, but perhaps accurate.

Maria and I pulled open the great creaking doors and

entered, Alice close at our heels. So many bodies lay upon cots, or even on the floor, that we needed to step over them. A burnt-sugar perfume hung heavy in the air. My eyes watered, and I sneezed. Maria had drawn her cloak up to her face.

"It's the Etheria flower," she whispered. "Makes you light-headed."

That was a mild explanation. Shadows warped in the corner of the room, and I jumped a bit in horror. Maria pulled me along.

Someone was sitting on the stone steps of the altar, a blanket flung over his shoulders. Lambe looked up at me, his pale eyes a hazy glow. The rising moonlight streamed through the window at the back of the chapel. Shimmering squares of red and blue and yellow light dotted Lambe's face.

"I've been waiting for you," he whispered.

5

LAMBE SIPPED HIS ETHERIA TEA AS I EXPLAINED what I'd seen in the vision. The steam of his drink smelled foul, like boiled laundry. His eyelids drooped, and I half feared he'd fall asleep. His fingertips were stained purple, presumably from grinding the Etheria flowers. Looms dwelt in the corners of the chapel, one of them half finished with another prophecy tapestry. It appeared to display the image of a large man swallowing a smaller one while a goat watched them. Maria stared at the thing, looking rather wary. Indeed, her chosen one's "fate" had been woven upon one of these looms.

Cots creaked as Speakers moved in their restless slumber. They were abed all hours; some of them could go days at a time without rising, due to the effects of the Etheria flower. Alice stood over one of the sleepers, looking quite disgusted. One man got out of his bed and shuffled up the chapel's walk toward us, which made me jump. But he stared over all our heads, into a dream world.

Lambe seemed the most aware of any of the people here. *That* was rather terrifying.

"So you need to understand the full purpose of these stones," Lambe said into his teacup.

"Yes, I want to tell Blackwood exactly what they can do, and what *we* should do."

"Then we must go." Lambe swallowed the dregs of his tea, set the cup down, and let the blanket slide from his shoulders. "I must see this circle."

"Have we any more pomegranates?" I asked Maria as I helped Lambe into his coat and we four slipped out into the winter night. God, the cold bit me down to my bones. Why couldn't I have found this circle in the summer?

"The estate recognizes you now as its lady." Lambe chased the short length of his shadow across the moonlit ground. "The land claims you."

Well. I wished that felt comforting.

"The lady in the wood, though, lies in wait. Keep her out of the fire," he said as he staggered into the forest.

My gut twisted at his words. Months ago, he had mentioned this half-baked prophecy of a lady in a wood. If this meant some ghastly apparition was waiting behind the nearest tree to crack open our bones and eat the marrow, I was going to haunt him in the afterlife for not warning us properly.

"Cor, you aristocratic folk really go in for atmosphere, don't you?" Alice muttered as we followed Lambe. She shivered. "Haunted woods, prophets, stone circles. The rich are different."

"It's true." Maria nodded. "They also keep great hearths to

lean upon dramatically. Sure every time I come into a room, Lord Blackwood is slouched against some carved marble mantel, gazing into the flames with a dead serious look on his face."

Alice slapped Maria on the shoulder with glee.

"He's not *always* doing that," I said. Maria squeezed my hand with a humoring sweetness.

"Love blinds us all in different ways." She giggled as I sent a shower of embers upon her.

We made our way deeper into the forest's black center. The air shimmered in the moonlight. Ahead, I could swear I heard the lilting of pipes and flutes. Flashes of blue light swirled in the corner of my eye, then disappeared behind a gnarled trunk. I unsheathed Porridge and noticed Maria had her ax in hand, surveying the forest's paths with caution.

"Used to see the light court on their parades through the highlands," she told us. "They've a ghostly look about them, as if you could see through their bodies. Bit like an onion skin."

"Most faeries wouldn't like being compared to an onion," I replied. Then again, Fenswick had regarded the gift of an onion as the highest compliment, so perhaps I was mistaken. I winced to think of Fenswick. The little hobgoblin had betrayed us, it was true, but he'd also rescued us from Queen Mab. During our rescue, he'd fought a bog creature to aid our escape. I'd no idea what had happened to him on those Faerie roads, though I had my sad suspicions.

"Still think Mab was worse, though," Maria murmured. "The taste she had for memories? That was a terror."

The recollection made me shiver. Mab had forced a cherished memory from Magnus as a "toll" for using her Faerie roads. To this day, Magnus couldn't remember what she'd stolen. In times like these, one more happy remembrance could keep a person fighting. In war, good memories were few and far between.

Ahead of us, the moonlight began to grow brighter and stronger. My head throbbed, but we all pressed onward. Maria grabbed my elbow, and Alice held on to a corner of my cloak. Our destination should lie just ahead. . . .

We emerged out of the night and into the druid lands. Lambe, Alice, and Maria gaped at the sudden change. It was night here as well, but the stars above were bright. The wind was ripe with the scents of summer grass and fruit. Maria moaned and collapsed to the earth.

"Who would ever choose to leave?" She rolled onto her back. Alice plopped alongside her, head lolling back to gaze at the sky.

"I'll be stayin' on. Don't care if it's haunted."

"You two enjoy a rest." I rolled my eyes. Ahead, the stones waited. Lambe went round the circle once, twice, puzzling over it. He and I examined each stone in turn. I felt power bubbling in my blood; the pull to the runes felt stronger with Lambe and the others here. Lambe closed his eyes.

"You can hear them," he whispered.

"Hear who?" Maria called.

He put out his hand and touched a stone.

It seemed that a voice barked at us from the sky in an unknown language. Maria and Alice leaped to their feet, backs together and faces raised to the heavens. From the stars in the sky to the tips of the grass, from the smooth, ancient stones to the earth beneath our feet, there came a white-hot surge of images.

It is a blindingly bright day. An old man wrapped in roughspun cloth and animal pelts jabbers as he goes from stone to stone, tracing the runes with the tip of a finger. The stones each sport one large, jagged rune. The man, with wild white hair that streams behind him, a grizzled chin, and gleaming beetle-colored eyes, dances about the center of the circle. Above him, the sun hits its zenith, and the stone shadows disappear utterly. Then, biting into his wrist, the man flings droplets of blood onto the stones.

One by one, the blood sizzles as it strikes its targets. Above the man, the bright blue air warps. The sky rips open, and as the man falls, giant purple tentacles, resembling those of some undersea monstrosity, wriggle out of the rip.

And then, like a pricked bubble, the images vanished. Lambe had fallen to his knees, his hand no longer on the stone. I wandered to the one nearest me but did not touch it. I could feel it even now, the distant tremor of power.

"That was Wild Mordecai, the last English mystic." Lambe wavered and fell backward. Maria caught him and laid his head in her lap. "He was the first to open this circle."

"He invented the runes?" I asked. Because now I knew, all of us knew, that this circle was the beginning of magic in England.

"No. The runes must have already been here. Perhaps the Fae." Lambe swallowed. Maria laid him in the grass, came to the stone beside me, and placed her hand upon it. She hissed but did not pull away. A hum buzzed around us as Alice went to another stone and touched it. Finally, steeling myself, I laid my hand upon a stone as well. A sorcerer, magician, and witch were all in contact.

The circle vibrated, and a pulse of energy exploded skyward in a great, glowing ring. My whole body felt white-hot for one second, and then the feeling disappeared. We all took our hands away; I was mildly surprised to find my handprint had not been burned into the rock.

"You see now?" Lambe propped himself up on his elbows.

We had awoken the circle. I felt it.

"It's like bein' struck by lightnin'." Alice studied her hands. "Only without the dyin' bit."

The power in this circle was unfathomable. These were the first summoning runes. The first to send a creature back, as well as to bring it forward.

"There was something special about the time of day." Maria spoke as if in a trance. "The man waited until the sun was at its height."

"The solstice." I recalled the memory Mickelmas had shown me of himself, Lord Blackwood, and my father. They had waited until noon on a summer solstice to open that portal. "The timing has to be perfect."

Lambe's silence told me I was correct. In order to end this

war, the circle would have to open on one of the solstices or equinoxes, a moment of transition from winter to spring or spring to summer. To finish this once and for all, we would have to come out of hiding. In fact, we would have to welcome our guests with open arms and borders.

R'hlem and his armies had to come to Sorrow-Fell.

WE FOUND OUR WAY BACK TO the house as dawn lightened the sky. God, we'd spent a whole night out at the stone circle. As we deposited Lambe before the chapel, the door flung open. Wolff strode out, his sleeves rolled and his hair mussed. The poor fellow hadn't slept.

"Clarence. Where the devil were you?" He caught Lambe up in a tight embrace.

"Having an interesting walk. You should tell Blackwood," Lambe said as Wolff helped him into the chapel. He needed rest badly, and so did I. Telling Blackwood might have to wait a few hours.

When I stole back to my room, I drew the curtains and barely had the strength to remove my gown and corset before tumbling headlong into bed.

Several hours later, I awoke to a ringing in my head and a knock at the door. I sat up as Lilly entered with a tray. She kicked the door shut behind her, and it felt so like Agrippa's house that for a minute I believed these past few months had all been a mad dream. That I'd woken to another day of practice sessions with the boys.

"Lord Blackwood sent this." She deposited the tray in my lap. Smoked ham and tea, along with some brown bread and raspberry jam. My stomach rippled at the sight; I was starving.

"You don't have to bring me breakfast," I said, sheepish.

Lilly sat beside me. "It's no bother. After you eat, His Lordship asks you to come down to the library." She frowned. "Where were you last night?"

Ah, so my absence had been noted. I took a bite of the bread.

"I'll tell you. I promise," I said as I washed it down with a sip of tea. I'd have to eat fast and dress faster. Blackwood wanted an explanation? He would certainly have it.

I NEVER MINDED HAVING A REASON to go to the Blackwood library. I had always loved the happy sight of books lining a shelf. Even the smell of books was the most wonderful perfume, that musty-sweet blend of ink and paper. Any library was a good library, but Sorrow-Fell's was truly exceptional.

Say what you would about Charles Blackwood—he was a cruel scoundrel and a liar, it was true. But he had also been a scholar, and he had built a library to match his curiosity. The library was more of a palace than a room, with bookcases that stretched fifteen feet high. Every subject under the sun was collected here, from alchemy to zoology, from the wisdom of ancient Greece to the bold questions of the Enlightenment.

Long tables were stationed throughout the cavernous room, illuminated by a chandelier shaped like a sun, a candle held in each of its golden rays. The size of the place demanded a crowd. Indeed, Charles Blackwood had envisioned magical scholars from all over the world coming to his estate to study and debate with one another.

Perhaps the only decent thing he'd ever imagined. Granted, it was likely he'd had one goal in mind: the accumulation of more magical power for himself. Tucked inside these shelves, between volumes by Aristotle or Herodotus or Voltaire, one might stumble across a book of dark and unspeakable magic.

Charles Blackwood had kept books that detailed how to sacrifice an infant to attain greater knowledge, or how to read the secrets of the universe in a virgin's entrails. Sometimes, I would find Blackwood in this library, tucked into a corner and reading over one of those unholy scripts. The sight of them— often bound in a diseased-looking leather—made me shudder. He would remind me that he was searching for theories, not anything practical. And I believed him, because he was not his father.

Still, those profane manuscripts were the dark spot in this otherwise pristine library. I found Blackwood seated in a green velvet chair by the window, the sun warm on his back as he pored over a book. The light haloed his brilliant dark hair. He turned a page with slender fingers. He was beautiful and strong.

When he turned his gaze to me, his face lit up in relief. He closed the book and kissed my hand. He greeted me every morning in this way, both proper and romantic. Sometimes, if we were alone—as we were now—he might kiss me. A needful part of me wanted that.

"Let me look at you." He stood, stroking his chin as if examining a fine piece of art.

"Have I changed so drastically since last night?"

"No, you never change." A smile of pure satisfaction lit his face. "That's what's wonderful. Seeing you in that slant of sunlight from the window, it's as if you were placed there by design. Whatever room you occupy becomes your room." He kissed my hand once more, his eyes never leaving mine. "You belong in this place, as you belong to me."

"Belong to you, or with you?" Hypnotic as his eyes and lips were, I must maintain a level head.

"With me, of course." Then, "Where were you last night?"

"You were worried?" I meant to tease, but the flash of panic in his green eyes told me I'd been right. "You said yourself Sorrow-Fell was the safest place in the kingdom."

"Yes, but I can't risk you. Not ever." His hand pressed against my back, drawing me nearer. "You know what you mean to me."

"You needn't have worried. I wasn't alone on my mission. I went to the stones with Lambe and Maria. We saw so many things." I didn't bring up Alice. She'd asked me to keep her presence here a secret, until she could feel more secure.

"Saw?" His eyes grew wary. "Like what?"

"Come and see." Taking his hand, I led him from the library.

BLACKWOOD STOOD IN THE SUMMER AIR. His cloak lay on the edge of the perimeter, forgotten as soon as he felt the heat. A wondering light played in his eyes as I showed him the stones.

"Here." I pressed my palm to one of the runes, and a flurry of lightning shot through me. He put his hand alongside mine and cried out. He felt it, too, as though we were connected to it—and from it, to each other.

"The power." Blackwood tipped his chin back, the full light of the summer's day striking his face. "I've never known anything like it."

Images rioted in my mind. I saw flashes of more monsters, more Ancients. Lizard Zem, his throat swelling with fire; On-Tez, spreading her dark wings to their full expanse. In response, my own shadow abilities flourished, drawing me back into the darkness of Rook's memories.

I am lost in the darkness, until there is a flickering point of light. She walks down the cellar stairs, dressed in white and barefoot. In this dark pit, she brings me a candle and a name. Her eyes, her dark eyes, behold me utterly, and she is not afraid.

I am found.

I drew my hand away. Blackwood brought me to stand in the center of the circle. The twelve stones around us felt like witnesses. His hand rested on my back.

"Was that one of Rook's memories?" he whispered.

"You saw it, too?"

"I saw you as a little girl." He kissed my forehead. "Even then, you were perfect." Blackwood's lips found mine. The feeling of fire quickened in my blood. "You've given me such a gift." He kissed the hollow of my throat. "My love."

The pain at my shoulder had utterly vanished. It seemed that the shadows sang to be this close to him.

"Then we should plan the trap." I went to kiss him again, but he pulled away.

"Trap?"

"For R'hlem. On the equinox, we bring down the barrier. We have to get him here somehow, after all."

But Blackwood merely took my face in his hands and kissed my forehead.

"No," he said.

6

THAT WAS ALL BLACKWOOD SAID. HE LOOKED greedily from one stone to the next; apparently, our discussion had ended.

Well, it hadn't for me.

"What do you mean, no?"

He returned to the stones. Closing his eyes as he placed his hand on another rune, he was the picture of a man taking a sip of strong drink. Or a drug. "Yes. This is what we've searched for." He wasn't even paying attention to me.

"Are you listening?" I said, tugging him away. His body stiffened with annoyance.

"Yes, I can hear you. But I can't agree to what you're asking. Tear down the barrier and try to simply herd the Ancients to this spot? Henrietta, it's madness."

"Yes, but it might be the only way."

Blackwood regarded me with bewilderment, as if I'd sprouted a second head. "By bringing down the foundation of magical security? Even you've never been that reckless."

"Let's at least research the circle. Suppose this is the only way to send the Ancients home," I said, trying not to snap with impatience. Father or not, I wanted R'hlem gone. He had told me that the Kindly Emperor would come and that we would all witness his smile. That was a sight I could do without. "If we don't learn to control this opening, R'hlem might. The only way to keep this from becoming a weapon against England is to use it against him first."

"Precisely. That's why R'hlem should never have a chance to get this circle," Blackwood snapped. The wind ruffled his hair as he went from stone to stone, protectively touching them. God, I didn't want to start screaming at him, but I felt myself losing that battle. This absorption was something I'd witnessed in him before. Hunger when he read his father's darker volumes, hunger when he watched the monsters fail to enter Sorrow-Fell. Hunger when he looked at me, as he did now.

Blackwood came to me, put his hands to my face, and kissed me. I pulled away in frustration. I didn't want to be kissed and fussed over like a favored pet.

"Darling, I can't bring him here." Blackwood was attempting a low, reasonable voice, like he thought I was on the edge of hysteria. I bloody well was not.

"Lambe showed me the visions. He told me that this circle could summon monsters as well as send them back. A circle this large and powerful could bring anything to our world!" Witness his smile. "R'hlem always gets what he wants!"

"He won't get through to Sorrow-Fell." Blackwood frowned. "I've told you before, Sorrow-Fell is safe."

Safe while the rest of the world suffered. Safe for now.

"Besides, we don't know all that these stones can do," Blackwood said.

Suddenly, I understood. He didn't want to tear the barriers down, not so much because he was unsure of his power, but because he *had* power. And for a boy—a young man—who had spent his life with all the responsibility of power and none of its pleasures, he craved this euphoria.

"George. Please."

But he wouldn't be swayed.

"Thank you for bringing me the stones." He held me. "You're still my best soldier, and my truest companion."

But not his equal. I pushed him away again, startling him.

"I'm telling you, we need to act!" I cried.

Blackwood stilled, danger growing in his silence.

"Remember to whom you're speaking," he said carefully. There was no anger there, only a gentle reminder bordering on a threat.

"I can't save you from yourself," I said, and made to leave.

"Wait." Blackwood held out his hand. "I'll have the runes copied. They might be useful outside of Sorrow-Fell." He narrowed his bright green eyes. "Under my control."

Because everything must be under his control. I stormed out of the circle without permission. That, at least, I could still do.

QUEEN VICTORIA HAD BEEN GIVEN QUARTERS in the tower, on the old Faerie grounds. When she'd asked Blackwood why she shouldn't be housed in the west wing, he'd replied that the magic here would add an extra layer of protection. Her bedchamber was in a rounded turret, with two small, arched windows overlooking the grounds. There was a large four-poster bed in the center of the room with a canopy designed to look like the tree-branched ceiling of a dense forest. Tiny, menacing gargoyle faces had been carved along the corners of the walls.

When I entered, the queen turned about in surprise, and I made a clumsy curtsy. She sat by the writing desk in her room, a blank sheet of paper in front of her. Perhaps she'd been writing her prime minister. Lord Melbourne had survived the Battle of London—barely, but he'd live.

"Howel. What's happened?"

Her Majesty calmly listened to my description of the stone circle. For a woman of barely twenty-one with a kingdom under siege, she was remarkably stalwart. Still, I noted how her hands trembled lightly as she stroked her spaniel, Dash. The little dog woofed pitifully and licked his mistress's chin.

"You believe we must bring the Skinless Man down upon our own heads?" She spoke softly, as if to keep her voice steady.

"Majesty, this might be the only way to finish the war once and for all." My heart pounded as the queen considered.

"Lord Blackwood knows this?" She tilted her head, dark ringlets of hair framing her face.

"He is being difficult," I said carefully. "With Your Majesty's bidding, perhaps we might convince him to begin a plan of attack—"

"There will be no such plan." Blackwood's voice boomed as he swept up the stone steps and into the chamber. Snow gleamed in his black hair, indicating how quickly he must have come here from outside. Bloody hell, how had he known what I'd do? Sometimes I loved how attuned we were to one another's thoughts, but now was not one of those times. His eyes held mine with an accusing glare. "I can't believe you went behind my back."

"You wouldn't listen."

"Imperator." The queen rose, sliding Dash off her lap. "Perhaps you might have thought to discuss Howel's discovery with me."

"I did not think that Howel's discovery merited a discussion until I'd decided what to do." Blackwood did not tear his gaze from mine. Sparks singed on the lines of my palms.

"You're the one who decides?" I kept my fire under control, but just barely. "I found the blasted thing."

"As part of a ceremony to become the Countess of Sorrow-Fell. A discovery made on my land, by my future wife." Blackwood's gaze raked over me, ordering me to be silent. All of it on *his* land, and *his* wife.

"As your monarch, I demand a consultation," the queen said, her voice rising.

Blackwood bowed slightly, in deference. But then he said, "No, Majesty. *I* shall inform you of *my* decisions."

I stopped breathing. The sheer, bloody audacity of informing the *Queen of England* as to what she would do or say or know.

Blackwood continued, "You will, of course, remain informed of my decisions, after I consult the Order—"

"The Order no longer exists!" I cried. For heaven's sake, R'hlem had smashed our obsidian meeting places and killed most of the powerful men in our society. "The queen commands—"

"No. As Imperator, *I* will command." I was doing my best not to explode in flame. "I shall accept criticism, of course, but I must have control."

Apparently, he did not need to listen to me when he had his books, his *optiaethis,* and now his stones. All his.

"Remember who appointed you Imperator!" The queen was near to shouting now.

"This isn't you, George," I murmured. He wouldn't look at me.

"I shall inform you when plans are complete." With that last line and a glare tossed to me, he strode out. The queen collapsed back into her seat while Dash whined and pawed at her skirt.

"Are we prisoners here, then?" I didn't know if she was speaking to me or to the dog.

"Not prisoners." I narrowed my eyes as I regarded Blackwood's departing shadow. "Cherished guests. He likes to have us near." I curtsied to the queen before I took my leave. "He simply doesn't want to share any power."

Walking down the steps, I cursed myself. Bringing Blackwood into the situation had been foolish. I'd have to leave him out of my next plan.

My heart was heavy with the realization.

THAT NIGHT, I SAT ON THE edge of my bed, hissing in pain as I pulled off the bandages around my shoulder. Maria had shown me exactly how to make the ointment and wrap the wound.

I soaked a cloth in warm, soapy water and began to clean. The wounds were still small and round and the skin around them inflamed. I hissed again as I washed and patted them dry. After, I turned to the mirror that stood by my dressing table and evaluated myself.

The glistening black wounds, a few inches above my breast, seemed to mock me. They rather resembled gleaming eyes, their expression filled with wicked laughter.

Sighing, I put away the soiled rags and went to unwind a new bandage for myself.

I stopped as cries sounded in the night.

Quickly, I slipped my nightdress back onto my shoulder, threw on my wrap and boots, and hurried outside, crunching across the snow-covered lawn alongside the others. Rolling a ball of flame into my hand, I held it aloft as we all made the long trek through the woods and toward the barrier. There, outlined in the stark moonlight, I saw them.

Familiars. Hundreds of them. Ravens, Lice, Skinless all swarmed against the invisible wall like ants amassing at a picnic. I found Blackwood with his hand on his stave.

"The devil is going on?" he breathed.

Lambe had shown up as well, his coat not even buttoned, his eyes flat with fever. "The circle is awake now," he muttered.

I would bet any money that these creatures had responded to the surge of power that my friends and I unleashed in the stone circle. The Familiars' many eyes gleamed with want. They knew that the ultimate prize now lay on the other side of this dome.

A circle powerful enough to pull apart the foundation of the world.

We had told R'hlem exactly where he needed to go.

Like it or not, hiding was no longer an option.

7

I NEEDED A NEW PLAN. THE ONLY PROBLEM WAS, I didn't know what that plan ought to be.

The next day, Maria and I went to the barrier to train and check the numbers. In the early-morning light, we found Familiars beyond measure. Some of them were standing on one another's backs, clawing at the invisible barrier. Idly, I thought how if the barrier dropped for half a second, many of these beasts would fall right on their faces. It would be almost funny, except for the fact that they'd be inside Sorrow-Fell. That would be far less amusing.

"Suppose there's more to practice on now," Maria said, with forced cheer. She had practiced all the drills I set to her—with fire, with water, with a wild sweep of air—and had mastered them. The Familiars had been burned and frozen, drowned and dropped from heights. Maria had beat them, but those tests had been in a controlled environment, with her safe behind a wall. The true test against these things was to meet them in the open field.

Nothing was going to be easy, it seemed.

Though Blackwood had taken to avoiding me, and I him, at

least it seemed that others were finding some happiness. When I arrived at the Speakers' monastery with a basket of food—and some extra sugar for Lambe's tea—I found him seated with Wolff before that grisly altar, heads together. Wolff ran his fingers through Lambe's hair and looked up at me with great tired eyes.

"I should be on duty, I know. But he never remembers to feed himself," Wolff said as he took the basket from me and fished out a winter apple. Cutting it in half, he offered a piece to Lambe. The smaller boy ate with his head pressed to his lover's chest.

I envied that closeness.

And they weren't the only ones. Upon returning to the house, I found Dee and Lilly standing by the stables. She'd her back against the wall, and I didn't think the pink flush in her cheeks was solely because of the cold. Dee was twirling a flower between his fingers—a blue snow-sorrow. Lilly took the bud from him like it was a gift of gold itself. When she placed her hand on his arm, he flushed crimson.

I took those faces—Wolff and Lambe, Lilly and Dee—with me as I entered the house and made for Blackwood's obsidian room. They were the reason to fight, and to win.

Blackwood's obsidian room was the grandest I'd ever seen, with size enough to seat twenty people comfortably. The domed ceiling curved ten feet overhead, and sorcerer sigils written in firelight played over that inky expanse. There was the eye sigil that indicated psychic ability, the tongue of flame that stood for fire magic, the five-pointed star that represented sorcery itself. Standing in this midnight room was like living within an inkwell. As I entered, I pulled off my gloves and focused upon the task at hand. I needed action, and a plan. The best I had of each was using the scrying mirror to ferret out magician and witch enclaves throughout the country. It was not much, but I needed purpose.

I took water from a pitcher and poured it out onto the floor. Using Porridge, I lifted the water into the air to form a mirror. My hand trembled as I imagined Scotland, starting with the highlands. I couldn't track people in this mirror, only places.

Soon I'd a bird's-eye view of the Scottish highlands lying distant under a blanket of snow. I scrutinized the thickets and trees but found nothing. No sign of footprints, animal, Ancient, or witch. Cursing under my breath, I let the water drop back into the pitcher and rubbed my wrist. I scratched a few words in my notebook: *Feb. 20, no sign of witches near Perth.*

Perhaps I would find some glimpse of magicians in Derbyshire.

"Am I interrupting?" Blackwood's voice was a shock in the stillness. I wheeled about to find him standing in the doorway.

Blackwood kept his hands behind his back, but I read the wariness in his eyes. Since he'd argued with the queen, we had kept to ourselves. Normally, we would have supper together in the evening, or sit in the library after coffee. There would be hushed talking and stolen kisses. These past few days, though, we'd been strangers. His absence was a pain in my chest.

"I was searching for a coven in the highlands. Perhaps the witches have been moving south." I kept my voice uninterested. After all, I didn't give a damn what he thought of me. I made to walk past him, but he touched my waist. His eyes shimmered with masked hurt.

"I'm sorry I chastised you before the queen." He pressed a soft kiss to my forehead. "I can't stand fighting with you."

All my coldness melted. I wanted so badly to give in to his embrace, but remained firm. "You said you were the one giving the orders. You spoke to Her Majesty like a child."

Blackwood took my hands, his thumb tracing a circle over my engagement ring.

"I cannot bring R'hlem to the last bastion of safety in this country. If Sorrow-Fell falls, who else will be able to stand up to him?"

"I've been looking for the witches and magicians," I said, but I knew he had a point. The sorcerers had the best training, the strongest weapons. Though if my vision in the circle was true, all three races were needed to end this war.

"I would expect you to start in on a new plan." He smiled, only a touch. "I've thought we could compromise."

"The great Imperator Blackwood, compromise? Heavens, how droll." I wrinkled my nose, and Blackwood gave a brief coughing laugh. Well, if I could still make him laugh, perhaps we were all right.

"I've returned to the stones and recorded the runes. If what you say about a witch, a magician, and a sorcerer all being needed is true . . ." He ghosted a kiss across my lips, which melted my resolve. "Perhaps you, Maria, and I could attempt it."

"With me as the magician?" After all, I wasn't truly a magician now. Alice was, but she still begged me to keep her cover secure. Even though Blackwood had said I could bring magicians to Sorrow-Fell, I wasn't certain how safe she'd be among the other sorcerers, not without an army of magicians at her back.

I recalled my father bleeding on the runes. Perhaps it was blood, not magical ability, that was needed to open that portal. Perhaps the three of us would be enough.

At the very least, we could try.

"But what if the circle depends on the equinox? What if it's too early?"

"We may not even attempt an opening. Let's see how the act of carving the runes feels. Tonight, after dinner, we'll take Maria and go to the outer reaches of the barrier, away from everyone else," he said. "We'll test it. You were a schoolteacher, after all. I know that if you love anything, it's a test."

"It's wonderful, having a fiancé who knows you so well," I teased, wrapping my arms about his waist. This was compromise, and something more. He was giving me the opportunity to share in this as an equal.

I brushed my lips against his, and he deepened the kiss. How I loved his every small reaction, and how I could make him react. His soft, delighted moan when I bit down lightly on his lip, his hushed intake of breath when we broke apart.

Blackwood's free hand roamed up my back. He kissed my jaw, right where my pulse fluttered. I closed my eyes and gasped as he kissed down my neck . . . and went farther.

My neckline wasn't deep, but he pressed his lips over my heart. God, I was losing my senses. Thankfully, Blackwood brought his lips back to mine, but his fingers continued to toy with the lace at the very edge of my bodice. My skin grew wonderfully hot beneath his touch. He stopped when embers trailed from my hand.

"Sorry," I murmured, but his mouth stopped my words. My entire body was heavy with want, tense with excitement. My heart hammered as Blackwood pushed me back against the wall with his body. I was trapped and welcomed it, as much as I welcomed his hand making a slow journey up my waist. Then, barely breathing, I felt his hand skim over the swell of my breast. We'd never gone that far before, and I gasped. He pulled back as though he'd been burned.

"Sorry," he echoed me. His pupils were large and dark. He traced the tips of his fingers across my cheek.

"I wish . . ." Then I stopped, because I didn't know how to finish that sentence without sounding immodest.

"I know," he replied. His strained breathing indicated he wanted the same thing. Blackwood and I had kissed before, but never like that. Never as though we wanted to meld ourselves together. Never as though we were the only two people on earth.

"So." I smoothed my hair. "After dinner, then?"

I sounded far too bright, even to my own ears. Blackwood laughed, the corners of his eyes crinkling. It was such a carefree, easy sound.

I loved it.

"Very well. After dinner."

MARIA, BLACKWOOD, AND I ALL MADE our way to the edge of the barrier as the moon climbed into the sky. The night was cloudless and the snow so brilliant it glowed. Maria ran ahead of us, her peacock-blue cloak standing out sharply in the moonlight. She stopped in a clearing.

"This is it!"

With the moon overhead and my fire to warm us, we got to work at once. Consulting Blackwood's paper, we wrote the runes into the snow, measuring the circle to make certain it was correctly proportioned. With every new rune, I felt something coming alive inside me. The runes were power itself.

Finally, there it lay in the snow: a perfect ring. Was it my imagination, or did it vibrate?

I wanted to quash the writing out of existence. But we had no other choice, not with the swarms of Familiars amassing all around us. For better or worse, these runes were probably the way to ending the war. We needed to test them.

"My father's books all talked of blood sacrifice," Blackwood said, checking for flaws. I felt his engagement ring beneath my glove, that pearl set in that silver band. We were together in this, as we always would be. Warding a blade on Porridge, I met Maria's gaze.

"Not a lot of blood is needed," Blackwood said, as though he was worried I'd lop off an arm in my enthusiasm. "Perhaps a little from the three of us?"

Maria took out her dagger, and Blackwood warded a blade of his own. As one, we lightly cut our fingers and let the dark droplets of blood fall onto the virgin snow. The drops scattered upon the runes, and the air crackled with energy. Blackwood and Maria each appeared to feel it as well. Blackwood took a quick step backward, one hand to his chest. Maria crouched in the snow, watching the runes as they began to glow and . . . bubble. Delight and horror mixed within me, a potent hybrid.

A shock of energy, like a physical shove, erupted from the ring and knocked me to the ground. Energy shot from the ring to ricochet off the barrier. I could sense it. Maria rolled about on the ground in a daze, while Blackwood got to his feet.

"Oh no. No." He crushed one of the runes beneath his boot. The buzzing power dissipated at once.

"Nothing happened. It's all right," I gasped. But Blackwood ran past me.

"No!" Stave raised, he shot a blast of fire into the air, a warning shot. But to warn against what, exactly? The portal hadn't opened, and . . .

And then I heard the gleeful, inhuman noises rushing

toward us like a dark tide. The sound of multitudes of trampling feet came from the direction of the barrier.

The pulse hadn't opened the portal; it had knocked down the barrier.

Sorrow-Fell was open to the monsters.

8

MARIA AND I CHASED BLACKWOOD UP THE HILL. I held Porridge, and Maria kept pace with her ax. Ahead, the darkness moved like a wave. Horns sounded the alarm. As we approached the oncoming horde, I whispered, "Do you think tonight will be the night?"

"Perhaps." She didn't have to ask what I meant. Perhaps this was the moment to reveal her true nature as our chosen one. Something good might as well come out of what was about to happen, to make up for this idiotic blunder I'd led us all into. My eyes burned as I ran, the shame warming me better than any fire could. God, all I could think of was Lilly, and Eliza, and Magnus, and Valens's wife and newborn daughter. The queen, by all heaven—hopefully the queen's assigned guard was with her already.

Sorcerers flowed up the moonlit hill to follow Blackwood toward the barrier. If he could close it soon, we might stand a chance. Wolff and Dee raced ahead, the glow of a ward around them. They met two charging lice Familiars headlong—the wards brought down the spidery monstrosities, and the boys plunged blades through the creatures' hearts.

"Howel!" Dee waved me over, his hooked arm shining in the moonlight. We arrived in a flurry of snow, which Wolff was using to construct a low, solid shield of ice. We joined him, Dee and I, weaving our magic quickly. Maria held back and vanished into the trees. "How the blazes did this happen?" Dee cried, sharing my fire to weave a fast net. We launched the blue flame over three swooping ravens, pinning them to the earth. The caws and screams as they sizzled turned my stomach, as did the smoking flesh and feathers.

"The Skinless Man's trick, no doubt." Wolff spoke through his teeth, consumed in the task at hand. God, how I wished that were true.

No time for regret. More Familiars swarmed with every second. Acting on instinct, we sorcerers divided into our assigned squadrons. Horn blasts signaled squadrons to their spots on the barrier. I stood with Wolff, while Dee fell in with Valens. Together, we all met the oncoming attack.

"Fire!" Valens called as the monsters approached.

The first wave of defense ran at the creatures.

The clash of armies was immediate and gruesome. One skinless Familiar brought its sword down in a stinging arc and lopped a sorcerer's head from his shoulders. The body crumpled at my feet, blood spattering the ground and steaming in the air. With a cry, I thrust my stave forward, punching a hole through the Familiar's chest with a stream of pure fire.

Our cries seemed to rattle the very trees around us.

We pushed into battle, pummeling the demons back. God

in heaven, how many were there? Already, great quantities of blood had mixed with the snow. The ground was a soupy pink.

"Close it!" I shouted at Blackwood.

As he fought his way toward the barrier, a cadre of sorcerers kept a circle around him as protection—and some of the human men joined in as well. I hadn't noticed them until now, but they were the people we'd rescued days before, fellows with pitchforks and clubs and kitchen knives. They all ran past the barrier, doing their best to shove the Familiars out into the forest.

Valens's squadron joined them. I caught bright flashes of him and Dee as they shoved the monsters back. Dee especially was relentless; he built up a huge wall of ice and pushed it before him, crushing the creatures as they scrambled to escape. Flashes of fire, bitter swirls of ice, the rumble of the earth itself, we used them all. Still, there were so many Familiars. Always more.

Please, God, let Blackwood close the gate. Launching a fireball into a skinless man's face, I hoped against hope.

If we couldn't do this, a free England was a thing of the bloody past.

Mercifully, Blackwood made his way to the head of the barrier unharmed. I caught sight of Maria as she knelt behind a tree and unleashed a fierce blizzard that only slowed down the Familiars.

Blackwood arrived at the invisible dividing line. With a

great cry, he waved his hand across the stones. We all gasped in relief as the protection came up around us again.

Though we'd closed the gate, by my count there were sixteen Familiars still among us, and that wasn't counting what might have got in everywhere else. Organizing fast into groups of three and six, we launched into attack. Cut off from their army, the Familiars were more easily handled. They exploded or melted or froze before us, dropping like great, disgusting flies. My heart sang as we fought. It didn't matter that my corset was digging into my side, or that I had a painful hitch in my leg. We were winning.

But then, as the carnage began to subside, we all heard those fearsome cries on the other side of the barrier. Horrified, I saw that one of the squadrons had been left on the wrong side of the line. Valens's face was white with shock. The ordinary men who had come to fight with us were also there, armed with nothing but rusted pitchforks. Some pounded at the barrier, yelling to be let in.

And . . . Dee was among them. He stood beside Valens, staring across an unbridgeable gap.

"Let them in!" I shouted, and everyone around me took up the cry. But Blackwood could only look on with misery.

"Too many," he gasped, and he was right.

Out of the dense forest, over the hill, swarms of Familiars rushed forward. We'd gotten a mere taste of what was coming. Valens and Dee blasted at the attackers, but it was a losing game. The rest of us watched, helpless as children at a panto-mime.

A sharp whistle. Dee was rounding up the ordinary men to head deeper into the forest. Valens joined them and they ran. Some men fell and were set upon by monsters. Blood gushed over the snow.

By the time we'd finished slashing the beasts, our friends had disappeared into the woods. And judging by the slavering hordes pressed up against the barrier, searching for a way inside, we could not launch a rescue effort. Not tonight. Perhaps not tomorrow, either.

They'll never be seen again.

The thought slashed through my mind, a blaze of red. *No.* I hurried to Blackwood, his image blurring as tears came upon me. "Please."

"We can't." Blackwood held me tight. Not Dee. I remembered Dee treading on my feet as he taught me to dance. Dee blushing as he told me about his feelings for Lilly. Dee standing with us against Nemneris. Dee only a few days before, leading a squadron, wooing Lilly with a winter flower, doing all the things he'd never believed he could do.

"The perimeters were all down." Hawthorne came up wiping blood and ichor from his face. "We must make certain every last one of those beasts that got through is dead."

"We've a job to do," Blackwood whispered. I could feel him trembling. Dee was lost, along with Valens and so many others. Innocent men lost in those woods, left to die.

All my bloody fault.

"Come on, then." Maria touched my shoulder gently—no one had noticed her during the fight. Why hadn't she seized the opportunity? Had she, when faced with all the death and chaos around her, become frozen with fear? I could ask her later. For now, I placed an arm around her waist, and she and I walked back toward the interior of the park. We had a long night of work ahead of us.

But one of us was not ready to leave.

"Dee!" Magnus pushed sorcerers aside and propelled himself against the barrier. He beat at it, a stream of curses flying from his lips. I went to pull him away. "How did it happen, Howel?"

He thought I was ignorant of the reality. His question was a plea against simple misfortune. He assumed there was no reason for it. But I knew better.

And I had to tell him yet another lie, on top of the countless others that had already eaten a hole in my heart. "I don't know," I said.

SEVERAL HOURS LATER, AFTER A NIGHT of hunting down every last miserable Familiar that had made it onto Sorrow-Fell lands, I staggered up the stairs to my room. Lighting a candle, I poured water for a wash. The basin turned cloudy at once, pink with blood. I gingerly took off my clothes and put on my nightgown.

There'd been so many bodies. So much death.

Maria and I had gone to tell Lilly as soon as we arrived

home. She was a braver soul than I was, but she'd dissolved in tears when we told her about Dee. Maria had given her a drink and told her to sleep. Maria was the healer, not I.

The guilt ate at me. As I made for my bed, there was a knock at the door. Without awaiting my answer, Blackwood slipped inside. Closing the door, he slumped. His black hair stuck at odd angles all over his head. He still wore his muddy boots. The buttons on his jacket were undone, and a dark patch of drying blood decorated his forehead.

"What is it?" I wrapped my arms around my body. God, I was in only my nightdress.

Blackwood was crying.

I had never seen Blackwood cry before. There had been moments when he teetered on the brink of emotion. Once, when he had confessed his father's secret to me in Agrippa's library, I had seen him desperate and in pain. Now he looked as though the center had been punched out of him.

"All those people." His breathing was ragged.

I went to him. He'd lost his coat somewhere in the last few hours. We were pressed up against each other now, and the hard contours of his body warmed against mine. I felt the wild thudding of his heart in his chest. We stood there, and my own tears wet the shoulder of his shirt.

"We did everything we could," I murmured. "It's . . . it's my fault. I suggested the runes." But he shook his head.

"Howel, I'm lost."

I'd missed hearing my surname from his lips. That had

been a signal, to me, that we were two sorcerers equal in each other's company.

"You're the youngest Imperator in history, after all." I kissed his cheek. "You're bound to feel lost, but I'm with you."

"How could such a monster . . ." He paused, because we both knew he was talking about my father. He put a hand to my cheek, his fingers cold against the heat of my skin. "How could he have such a daughter?"

I recognized how close we were, and how alone. But I needed to be alone with him; him, and no one else.

"I thought of the runes." Blackwood swallowed. Shame ignited inside me, but he said, "I believe you're right, Howel. I wanted to wrest the magic from its proper place and force it to do my bidding. That is impossible, I know that now. I was rash and . . ." His words trailed away. I kissed his forehead.

"I wanted to blaze ahead without any thought to what could happen," I whispered. "For all we know, playing with the circle could have been worse." God, why had I been so headstrong? Perhaps I was so bone-weary of the pain in my shoulder that I'd wanted to hasten the end of the war, no matter the outcome.

Blackwood's lips met mine. For one blessed moment I felt safe.

"I've been the most foolish," he whispered, stroking my hair. "Every day, there are more and more of those blasted monsters. I've trapped the future of English magic inside a glass dome." He tightened his embrace. "Howel, I'm afraid." Knowing that he was still human, still mine, warmed me. My body hummed with his touch. "You are the better part of my soul," he growled. "Help me."

I slid my fingers through his hair. He gave a small, stifled gasp as I kissed his neck. "If you want me to leave, you must tell me now," he whispered. This was against everything we'd both been taught.

My fingers trembling, I undid the top buttons of my nightgown. My dress fell open to my stomach, exposing my body to him. I moved as if in a dream. I could hardly believe what I was doing . . . what I wanted to do.

With a wondering expression, Blackwood touched me. I couldn't breathe as his hands trailed up the bare skin of my stomach, skirted around to my back. His fingertips skimmed the black marks at my shoulder, but he did not appear repulsed. Impulsively, he brushed his lips over the wounds, and I gave a soft cry.

"Is it all right?" he asked. God, it had felt heavenly.

"Yes." Slowly, I tugged at his shirt, and he discarded it in one movement. His body was white in the moonlight, his form muscled and lean. I put a hand to his bare chest, to feel the pounding of his heart in time with mine.

I traced my hands over his body, shivering at how silken his skin was over such a hard physique. His kisses grew more urgent. We tore at one another, and the worry of what tomorrow might bring dispersed like smoke in the air. This might be all the time we would ever have together.

Blackwood slid my nightgown from my shoulders and let

it pool to the floor in a soft whisper. The night air should have been freezing on my skin, but I barely felt it. Lifting me into his arms, he carried me to the bed. In an instant, he'd shed his clothes, and we lay together beneath the blankets. We only dared breathe. I kissed his face, tasted the salt and snow on his lips and tongue.

I wanted this.

"You are the other half of me," Blackwood whispered. "I love you."

"I love you," I whispered back, and wrapped myself around him.

At first we murmured apologies, tried to be gentle. Blackwood kissed the tears from my cheeks and asked if I'd rather stop, but I always urged him on. I wanted him too much to turn back. Eventually, it became easier. I began to gasp with pleasure, not pain. We moved with a perfect rhythm throughout the night, and as dawn tinged the sky we fell asleep in each other's arms.

WHEN I WOKE, BLEARY-EYED, THE SUN was nearing its zenith. The gray clouds had rolled away, revealing a clear blue day. The bed beside me was empty. I could recall a kiss upon my forehead as Blackwood left, his whisper that I should rest. The entire night before had the vividness of a mad dream.

My skin tingled at the memory. A smile stretched over my face, unbidden and uncontrollable.

I sat up and caught sight of my reflection in the mirror. My unkempt hair tumbled around my shoulders. Giddiness rapidly mingled with astonishment. That person in the mirror could not be me. I got out of bed, feeling very grateful I'd given up on having a maid. I'd no idea how I would have explained, well, any of this to Lilly. I blushed as I realized I'd need to change the sheets.

As I washed, dressed, and did my hair, I tried to ignore the panicked whisperings in my mind. A lifetime of stern lectures and a childhood's worth of lessons on Eve and the apple flooded upon me all at once. *You know what happens to women who make your mistake.* It was almost as if I could hear Colegrind, my old headmaster, hissing at my ear. *You've given him exactly what he wanted.*

"Shut up," I snapped at no one. There was no reason to feel embarrassed.

But when I went downstairs, I felt as though I'd left behind an important bit of clothing and prayed no one noticed. I kept against the wall, wishing to remain invisible. Fear was eroding every sensible thought. Why had Blackwood stolen away with only a kiss? Why—

Blast and damn, Henrietta, go and see that the people have something to eat. Make yourself useful.

Breathing easier, I went straight to the great hall. Eliza was already there, distributing bowls of soup. She gave me an incredulous look.

"How could you sleep so long?"

I certainly didn't want to tell her the reason, so I took up a tray and got to work. My mind was churning as I handed out food and wrapped bandages. We seal bearers would have a meeting later on, and I'd find time to speak with Blackwood. Make certain that he, well, that he still planned to—

"There you are." Magnus appeared beside me so suddenly that I nearly stumbled. "How are you?" I struggled to think up a proper response.

"Are you all right?" might have been the first step, because he looked terrible. His eyes were swollen from lack of sleep; his stubble had grown darker.

"I'm so sorry about Dee," I finally murmured. The pain of last night, erased for those few hours with Blackwood, returned like a hammer. Taking my arm, Magnus gently walked us down the gallery. This was the long, narrow hallway filled with antique suits of armor. Every polished breastplate or gauntlet boasted the Blackwood crest, those two hands entwined in ivy.

"I want to do something for Lilly," Magnus said. The gray depths of his eyes blazed. "She would have been Dee's widow. I want her to have all the entitlements."

"She will." That I could agree to without hesitation. He nodded and seemed about to say more when his jaw trembled. Magnus turned from me, a hand over his face. When I went to touch him, he flinched.

"I can't have lost him, too. I can't have let him down like I did her." Those last words came in a stifled sob. There was no need to ask whom he was speaking of. It was obvious that his mother—and her death—was never far from his mind. Magnus muffled his cries as I laid my hand on his shoulder.

"You've never let anyone down in your life." I would not add my tears to burden him. Squeezing his arm, I said, "We won't give up on him. I swear it." At first, Magnus was hard as stone beneath my touch. Then I felt him slacken. Magnus turned around and pulled me into his arms. It wasn't romantic. We simply stood there, taking each other's burden. After a while, Magnus grew quiet. Releasing me, he didn't try to hide the tears staining his cheeks. I gave him my handkerchief.

"Thank you." He attempted a smile. "You keep my feet on the ground, Howel."

And then Blackwood came over to us, and my heart leaped into my throat.

"I've been looking for you," he said, his gaze intent on my face. That he had found me in Magnus's arms didn't seem to bother him in the slightest. Not that long ago, he'd have glared daggers at us both. Indeed, he even gave Magnus a commiserating handshake. "Let's speak today, after the meeting."

The sudden warmth Blackwood showed Magnus took us both by surprise. Magnus returned the handshake, looking a bit stunned.

"Yes. Thank you." Magnus left, and Blackwood and I were alone. I tried to keep myself calm. Perhaps Blackwood had been easy toward Magnus because he no longer wanted me and didn't care. What would he do now? Tell me what a common girl I was, break the engagement, or—

His kiss silenced the voices in my head.

"We should be married tonight," he whispered.

My knees practically gave out.

"I thought you might not want me any longer," I admitted.

"Quite the contrary. I can't get enough of you." God, how I blushed.

"Can we have everything set up by tonight?" I asked.

"Yes. First comes the ceremony in the obsidian room, then to the chapel. Then you'll be mine, utterly." His kiss was tantalizingly brief. "And tomorrow, we'll discuss the stones." For the first time in so long, I relaxed. I had given everything I had to Blackwood, and he'd accepted me. As he held me in his arms, I knew he wouldn't let me fall.

He wouldn't let England fall, either.

9

"YOU'RE GETTING MARRIED NOW? AFTER LAST night?" Eliza asked hotly. We were in her room, where she was thawing her hands after an afternoon of work in the yard. The day had gone so quickly. Blackwood and I had met with the seal bearers to discuss the previous evening, and Blackwood had announced our impending marriage. The congratulations had been sincere, if not enthusiastic. Perhaps they all thought, after the carnage of last night, that this was an odd moment for a party.

I'd expected Eliza's reaction would be similar, but I hadn't foreseen this.

"You left them alone in the woods." She sat in the chair before her fire, still shivering from the cold. "I had to send Lilly back to bed. She nearly fainted today."

Her words were like a slap. "What were we supposed to do?"

Eliza looked perfectly serious. "You're the ones who opened the barrier in the first place." She dropped her eyes. "George is like our father. He'll break anything to further his own ambition."

I couldn't speak for a moment. "Are these your words, or your mother's?"

Eliza toyed with her skirt. "You don't understand what Mamma's been through."

"On account of your father, not your brother." My voice rose, and Eliza flinched. I would have harsh words with anyone who claimed that a child's parentage determined his or her fate. I knew from experience how painful that idea could be.

"Only remember that George tried to sell me into marriage against my will." She looked up at me. "It's thanks to Julian I'm not with Foxglove today."

I felt uncomfortable. Now that I understood the, well, intimacies between a man and a woman, I felt it would be murderously criminal to force someone into a situation when they didn't want it. And my thoughts turned again to Magnus as he reminded Eliza of her own strength. He was . . .

Well, he wasn't someone I should spend too much time thinking about any longer.

"George will be steadier once we're married," I said, and Eliza looked out at the darkening sky. Bursts of vibrant red splashed across the clouds as the sun set. "I thought you wanted to be my bridesmaid."

Eliza gave a sad smile. "I did," she said. "But after what he did last night, I can't bring myself to be at this wedding."

"George is your brother. And it was my idea, not his." Not entirely true, but near enough.

Eliza studied her hands, twining a small gold band—her false engagement ring—on one white finger. "He puts no one before his pride, not even his sorcerers."

His sorcerers? "He . . . he needs to make impossible decisions as Imperator," I said at last.

Eliza frowned. "And the ordinary men who were caught in the fight? He didn't even mention them at the meeting. He mourned Valens and Dee, but not those men. Julian told me all about it. He heard it from Hawthorne. Hawthorne was *proud* of George's 'resolve,' as he called it. They don't care about the men without magic. There's always a wall between them and us."

How had we arrived at the point where I defended an Imperator's actions and *Eliza* was a revolutionary?

"Let's talk later," I said, not wanting to argue. Eliza tugged a shawl around herself and watched the fire.

"Later," she echoed.

LILLY WAS TOO ILL TO COME to the wedding. I brought her a tray before going to change and found Wolff and Lambe seated with her. They were all speaking in low, soft voices. Lilly's hair was in a plait over her shoulder, her pale face swollen. At the sight of me and the tray, Lilly burst into tears. Wolff took the tray while I held on to her, rocking her back and forth as she sobbed.

"I'm sorry I won't be there. I can't. I can't." That was all she could say. I held on to her for a while, promising her I understood, wishing I could do anything to make it better. We stayed like that until Maria knocked on the door and told me that the hour couldn't wait.

"It will be a short ceremony," Lambe said to me as Wolff got Lilly to sit down and eat a bite of stew. Lambe studied a crack in the floor. "Don't worry about that."

Back in my room, Maria helped me into the blue silk gown once more. It had been mostly repaired, only a bit stained at the hem, but I didn't mind. Sliding on my black sorcerer's robe, I looked at the engagement band on my finger. With a whisper to some blue snow-sorrows, Maria got them to weave together into a perfect crown. Witchery was remarkable.

As I looked in the mirror, I realized I resembled some pagan creature. I was rather like the stained-glass figures pictured in the Speakers' chapel: flowers at my head, a loose robe gathered about my body. Maria watched my reflection.

"I can't believe you're not going to be in the obsidian room," I said to her. Because she was not a recognized sorcerer, she could not enter such a "holy" place, or some other nonsense. She got on tiptoe and nudged the crown so that it was straight.

"I'll be at the chapel. That's all that matters. Besides, I talked with His Lordship today. He said tomorrow he'll make the announcement about me."

I breathed a sigh of relief. Of course. Now that I would have an iron-clad position in the Order, he could afford to be "generous" with Maria's own title. I fidgeted with the flower crown to make it sit evenly on my head.

The bells in the chapel tolled. My heart sped up in excitement. An hour more and the events of last night would be sanctified. Nothing to fear.

Maria embraced me and walked with me down the stairs. We crossed a long, silent corridor to the obsidian room. She deposited me at the door and hugged me once again, then left me to my fate.

I waited outside the obsidian room, my heart thudding. Porridge lay in its customary place by my side. Slowly, the doors opened. I entered to find sorcerers seated on either side of the room. Magnus sat in the group to my left but kept his eyes downcast. The doors shut, and I was in a room of night.

Ahead, one of the elder sorcerers waited at the center of the room, Blackwood standing before him.

Even though he was wearing his own sorcerer's robe, and even though I could not see the clothes he wore beneath, my breath stopped at the sight of him. We watched each other as I went to meet him, until finally the distance closed and we were together. A crown of woven ivy sat upon his head. Another ivy circlet waited on a table. Dimly, I understood. When the ceremony was complete, they would take away my crown of flowers—my own sorcerer sigil, the snow-sorrows standing in place of roses—and replace it with my husband's.

I would no longer be the Howel seal bearer. Instead, I would belong to the Blackwood house.

Part of me hated to say goodbye to my burning rose.

Blackwood took my hands in his, looking electric with

pride. We would be together in all things. We would be all right.

The ceremony began. The official held a candle above our hands, a ball of water, a stone, a feather. The four elements blessed our union.

Now there were only our vows to recite.

"I take thee into my house," Blackwood said. "Under my roof, you shall shelter. Before my hearth, you shall warm. At your breast, my children shall nourish. At your hand, my household shall sit. Let the stone bear witness to our union. Let our love be inscribed on the stone."

I felt that the earth itself rose up to bless our marriage; it had something timeless about it. Now came my turn.

"I enter into your house—" But that was as far as I got. An urgent blare of the horns outside shattered our peace.

Maria threw the door open and rushed inside. The sorcerers rose as one, shocked at having an unsanctioned member enter their holy space.

Maria shouted, "Sorcerers spotted at the barrier!"

My God. Dee and Valens. Could they have made it?

"Then we ride out at once," Blackwood said.

But elation turned to fright when Maria replied, "Lady Eliza is already on her way to the barrier. She's going to open it and let them in."

10

THE CEREMONY WAS FORGOTTEN AS THE WHOLE house of sorcerers charged out into the night.

"How can Eliza open the barrier?" I asked Blackwood as we harnessed the wind. My robe flapped behind me as we flew.

"Only a Blackwood can invite the barrier down!" he shouted. "Eliza is of the blood."

It must never have occurred to Blackwood that Eliza would take such matters into her own hands. But unlike Blackwood, she had no skills with which to fight the monsters.

We remained tight-lipped until we swept up the hill and found the Familiars surging against the barrier. They had cornered the remaining men of the squadron—I caught sight of Dee and some of the other men warding off the creatures. Magnus rode ahead, hurrying to grab Eliza. She was riding hard on horseback, her hand outstretched.

Blackwood shouted her name, but she did not stop.

She leaped off the horse and touched the barrier. In an instant, the men we thought had been lost—and a multitude of Familiars—poured through.

Magnus had Eliza by the waist and wrestled her away from

a louse Familiar. Now that the others were safely through, Magnus tried to help guide Eliza back to close the barrier. But they were beaten away by Familiars—the fiends clearly understood what Eliza's touch meant. The rest of us charged up the hill to find Dee at the head of the lost squadron, striking into the heart of the encroaching dark army. But even all of us together could not contain the monsters.

They were prepared this time. And there were so many of them.

One of the Familiars ripped into a sorcerer's back, slicing his glistening spinal column free with a meaty tear. The sorcerer—a boy, really—coughed a bright bubble of blood before falling facedown into the snow. I shot flame at the monster, at all the monsters. But there were so damn many of them.

Blackwood outpaced all of us. With his sorcerer guard around him, he managed to touch the barrier and close it. The wall went up not a moment too soon. Dozens of the monsters threw themselves against the dividing line, howling. Eliza had rescued a good many lives, but she had allowed at least thirty Familiars inside. As one of the ravens rose up into the air, its ragged wings fluttering, I unleashed a massive corkscrew of flame. My blood was up, and the threads of shadow thickened, turning my fire more black than blue. Two, three monsters fell to sizzle in the snow. I gritted my teeth and shoved one over with the toe of my boot. Its face was baked black, the stench like rotten meat.

I wrenched the crown of snow-sorrows from my head and

threw it to the earth. Feet crushed the blue flowers. Throwing my stave to the ground, I summoned a sheet of stinging ice and sent it rushing ahead to cover my enemies. I could see Magnus guarding Eliza as they made for his horse. Unfortunately, the poor beast was so terrified it galloped for the security of the stables.

A raven swooped out of the sky, aiming for me. I fell backward, dodging it as I struggled to get over to Magnus, to help with Eliza. I was running, getting closer, when one of R'hlem's skinless warriors lunged out from its hiding place behind a tree. Magnus parried the creature but lost his footing and fell. The monster prepared a killing blow with its sword while I threw out my hands with a scream, fire igniting at my fingertips. I was going to stop the beast; I had to.

Eliza didn't hesitate. She flung herself in front of Magnus. The skinless warrior ran her through with his blade in one seamless motion.

I fell to my knees. Around me, the world seemed to stop.

She crumpled on top of Magnus, trapping him momentarily. Before the beast could finish them off, I flung out my hands and let loose. My fire charred the creature to ash and barbecued fat.

Blackwood and I were beside them in a minute. One word repeated itself in my mind: *No. No, no, no.* We turned Eliza over, to see the damage.

Blood stained our hands. The thing had got her in the side. Her normally pale face was whiter now, flecked with rich crimson. Her stockings had been torn. One of her gold ear baubles had fallen loose in the fight. I noticed the strangest things in the most horrible times. Blackwood held Eliza close, as if hugging her could mend this. The stoic earl dissolved into a terrified brother.

"George. It's all right," Eliza whispered. Then she fainted.

"GET THE DOCTOR!" BLACKWOOD ROARED AS Magnus carried Eliza into the house and I followed close behind. I searched the hall in a panic, desperate for Maria. As I'd been running out after Blackwood, I'd begged her to remain behind. If the monsters got through, she'd be one last defense for the people in the house. The Blackwood family's personal surgeon appeared, fiddling with his glasses. Eliza looked waxen now, and her blood dripped onto the tiled floor as the men rushed her upstairs to her room.

She wouldn't last much longer. Where the devil was Maria?

I hurried for the stables, feeling as though my legs did not exist and that I was a head being carried from one room to the next. The faces and furnishings around me blended. Time dripped away, as surely as blood. Eliza's blood.

Through the chaos, I glimpsed Lilly and Dee standing by the entrance. He had her lifted up in his one good arm while she sobbed against his neck. Despite the horror around them, Dee looked as if he'd been ushered into paradise itself.

"Where's Maria?" I gasped as I came up beside them. Lilly dropped back to the ground.

"What is it?" Dee asked.

"Eliza." That was all I needed to say. Lilly raced past us at once, heading for the stairs.

Dee gripped my shoulder. "I saw Maria head upstairs when you were all coming down the hill."

If Maria was already with Eliza, then we had a chance. I followed Lilly, praying to every god in existence as I went.

In Eliza's bedroom, I found the doctor and Maria toe to toe.

"I will not take orders from some chit of a girl!" the surgeon bellowed, the veins in his neck popping. He whipped off his glasses to make his point. Maria eyed the man with pure dislike.

"So you'd bleed her, then? Has she not yet been drained enough for you?"

Eliza lay on her bed, the mattress grown slippery with blood. They'd got her dress and corset off, and she was in only a stained shift. Blackwood looked between the doctor and Maria like he did not know which way to turn.

"My lord, you decide," the doctor spit.

Blackwood gripped his sister's hand. She was fading fast.

"Let her do it," I said to Blackwood. The doctor muttered something about women while Blackwood held up a hand.

"Maria. Proceed." He sounded ill.

The doctor stormed out of the room as Maria pulled up Eliza's shift to study the wound. She began firing off orders.

"I'll need hot water. Lots of it. Cloth bandages, needles, thread, and the kit from my room. There's yarrow on my shelves, along with agrimony, rose, and lemon peel. Get them all. They'll help with clotting. Go now." She barked these orders at one of the servants, who fled the room. Maria's hand remained on Eliza's wound, keeping in the blood. Magnus entered, and his eyes trained on the bed at once. He made a noise as though he'd been hit.

"We should wait outside," I told him. "Come on. George!" But Blackwood wouldn't leave his sister. I pushed Magnus out the door to wait in the hall. His gaze appeared unfocused.

"Eliza won't die," I whispered, trying to convince us both. Magnus slumped against the wall. He was chilled from the outdoors, melting on the spot. He smelled of the pine woods, of sweat and blood.

His eyes found mine. "I should have protected her better."

"Right now, we may only wait," I said. And we did, waiting as the servant hurried past us with Maria's things. Waited and prayed until Blackwood gave a great cry. Heart in my throat, I pulled open the door.

The mattress and sheets were ruined with gore. Maria wiped dried blood from Eliza's face. Blackwood had his back to the wall, hand before his mouth. Eliza was pale as death.

God, no.

But then her lashes fluttered. She opened her eyes and breathed. Maria wrung out another cloth in a basin of hot water.

"She'll be all right." She winked at me. "I'd best get something to bolster her." With that, she exited.

The three of us crowded Eliza at once. She tutted, weakly waving one hand.

"George. Honestly. You'll kill me for want of air," she whispered. Her brother kissed her hand several times.

"I'm sorry," he breathed. "Sorry for everything. Foxglove. All of it."

"You wanted to protect me." She gave a short laugh. "Considering I've been speared through the side, you may have had a point."

Blackwood tried to laugh but remained on the verge of tears. "I'd this horrible feeling that you would go, and everything would go with you." It sounded now as though he were talking nonsense.

Already, some color was returning to Eliza's cheeks. With one of Maria's brews she'd be strong in no time. Maria returned, stirring a steaming potion in a wooden cup.

"All right. Drink this down." She seated herself beside her patient.

Eliza drained the cup while Blackwood came to my side. We both looked at my stained wedding dress.

"Perhaps we might find a new gown," I said lightly. He laughed while Magnus went to sit and speak with Maria and Eliza. The now-empty cup went to the bedside table while Blackwood and I headed into the hall for a moment of peace.

"That's twice you've brought me to the altar," he said, taking my hand in his. His flesh was cold, but so was mine. "We never manage to go all the way." Lord, was he joking?

Good. We needed some humor.

"I hear that magic often comes in groups of three. The third time will come out right. Tomorrow?" I asked.

"This time, we'll finish the vows even if R'hlem burns the place down." He kissed me. "It will be worth it, my love."

I couldn't help thinking of the others belowstairs, the wives and children of the men who had been lost. At least we'd rescued another few from R'hlem's sacrificial maw.

I kissed him back.

And then the screams began.

The bedroom door flung open to reveal an ashen-faced Magnus. "Call the doctor back!" He raced down the carpeted hall.

Blackwood and I rushed inside the room to find Maria standing next to Eliza, a look of horror etched on her face.

"I don't understand!" she cried over and over again. Eliza bucked and thrashed, tearing at the bloodstained sheets.

She was foaming at the mouth, her eyes bulging from their sockets. Her head snapped back, her spine bending at an unnatural angle. I grabbed a wooden comb and jammed it between her teeth, and Blackwood helped turn her on her side. He was shouting her name. Eliza gripped at the sheets, her fists tightening and jerking spastically. She made a terrified sound, much like a wounded dog.

Maria, for the first time, looked as if she did not know what to do.

"Stand back!" The doctor pushed us aside and grabbed

Eliza by the shoulders. "Breathe!" Eliza vomited a foaming torrent of blood. She collapsed against the pillow and went horribly still. Her face slackened. A thin whisper of noise escaped her throat.

Blackwood screamed his sister's name while the doctor felt at Eliza's wrist and neck. Finally, he looked up at us, his glasses glinting owlishly in the candlelight.

"She's dead," he announced.

11

SILENCE REIGNED, SAVE FOR MARIA'S HARRIED breathing. She held her hands before her face, and I noticed, numbly, that her left hand balled itself into a fist.

Blackwood would not let go of Eliza. He touched her face, a look of dawning horror spreading over his own.

Eliza couldn't be dead. Not like this, and in such agony.

"We couldn't save her," Blackwood said.

The doctor spied Maria's wooden cup. He took it up and sniffed the dregs. "Who gave her this?"

"Why?" I drew nearer.

"A wound doesn't have that effect upon a person. Poison does." He dipped his handkerchief in the remains of the drink and sniffed again. His entire face contorted. "My God. It's pure belladonna."

Nightshade. Maria had . . . poisoned Eliza?

"It was a mistake," I said automatically. No. No, I wasn't going to allow these thoughts. But Maria was beginning to cry.

"This drink is *pure* poison. There was no mistake." The doctor threw the cup to the floor.

No. Maria was our chosen one, our savior. She did not go

about murdering young women. But Blackwood had roused himself from his stupor and turned to Maria with a hellish light in his eyes.

"Get her out of here," he said.

We'd already lost Eliza. I couldn't bear any more.

"We don't know what happened!" I cried, blocking the doorway. Magnus, who had returned, merely knelt beside Eliza's body. Men knocked into me from behind, swarming around Maria. She didn't fight. She did nothing but weep as she beheld Eliza's corpse and the men dragged her from the room.

"Stop this!" I shouted, fire rippling over my hands. My vision swam. It seemed that the light in the room had begun to dim, that the shadows crept across the carpet to me.

I was using Rook's shadow powers. Stunned, I felt my fire extinguish, and the room returned to normal.

"Put her away." Maria wept so hard, her words were almost unintelligible. "Chain her up. Quickly."

The men knocked me against the wall as they passed. Blackwood followed at their heels.

"Put her in the old dungeons, on the Faerie grounds! Bind her in iron! Don't let her out!" he bellowed. Then he was gone, his shouts mingling with Maria's sobs. The doctor tilted Eliza's chin this way and that, a look on his face pitched between genuine sadness and smug condescension.

"If you'd kept me here, she'd still be alive," he said.

"She would have died of her wounds instead," I snapped. He raised an eyebrow.

"Would that have been less painful?"

Magnus grabbed the man by his vest. The doctor whimpered as Magnus brought them nose to nose.

"Why don't you walk me through exactly what happened?" Magnus growled.

I went to the bed. The squelch of blood beneath my shoes didn't stop me. Eliza's green eyes were glassy. I thought back to the first day we'd met, in Madame Voltiana's shop. She'd made me laugh. She'd been the bubbling life of any room. Now . . .

Her hand was cold and waxen. My whole body shook, and I fled the room. I couldn't stand to look any longer, and Blackwood needed help. Someone would have to tell his mother. And Maria . . . I had to understand what had happened. Because I knew, beyond any doubt, that it had been an accident. She had rushed. She had grabbed the wrong vial. Something trivial had led to something catastrophic. Beyond anything, I knew she had not meant to do it.

Downstairs, the place was in an uproar. Head spinning, I asked to be directed to Blackwood. Soon I found him in the smaller parlor, the one nearest the divide between the west wing and the ancient Faerie estate. This room functioned as a second library, and a painted wooden globe stood by the window. I closed the door behind me, muting the voices in the hall. Blackwood sat in a chair before the fire, face in his hands. He cast a warped shadow over the carpet.

Above the fire hung the great portrait of Charles Blackwood. It gazed down upon us with a look of unruffled calm.

But with all I knew of him, I could only see a smug and callous expression. Dark mirth glinted in his eyes.

The sight of that wicked bastard gazing down on his grief-wracked son made me want to set the damn thing on fire.

Blackwood didn't move as I approached.

"I'm sorry." My tongue felt clumsy in my mouth. There were no words for what he was facing. He stayed still, his long, pale fingers hiding his face.

"She was . . . ," he said, and stopped. He didn't appear to notice me as he stood and walked to the fire. His shadow danced erratically as he placed one hand on the wall. "After the war came, she was the only source of light."

He bent over, an invisible weight pressing between his shoulder blades.

"I imagined I put all my fine qualities into her, like a memory box. She was everything about me that was right. Everything that was good." He couldn't speak the final word. He mouthed it, like it had been snatched from his lips. "What am I now? A hollow man with a title."

His voice was brittle. When I held him, he collapsed against me like a puppet with its strings cut.

"I'm sorry," I whispered again and again.

He shoved me away, and I tumbled backward into a chair.

Blackwood's eyes gleamed with a cruel light. "You forced me to bring that witch with us."

"What?" I couldn't have understood him. "Maria is the chosen one."

"I took your word on it." He paced back and forth, a wild cat edging its way toward a kill. "You seduced me into believing it."

Seduced him? I stiffened. "Lashing out isn't going to bring her back."

He kicked over a table, sending the objects set upon it to smash on the floor. A porcelain clock lay in pieces. Blackwood stalked toward me.

"How do I know you haven't been working for R'hlem all this time? Such an obedient daughter," he spit. Dear God, he was losing his mind.

"You know I'm not working with him," I snapped. He kept coming, though. My body tensed as the flames murmured under my skin. "Eliza wouldn't want this."

"Don't say her name!" he howled, a sound of pure suffering. "You . . . slut!"

My whole body lit on fire, blasting him to the floor. That word latched its claws into my back, but I couldn't feel the pain yet. He looked up, grief and hatred in his face.

"If you ever speak that way to me again, I will kill you." I extinguished and left the room.

It wasn't until I was halfway up the stairs that the wind rushed out of me and I slid down onto a stair. I burst into tears, my skirts a tangled mess on the staircase. Blood still spattered my gown. Eliza's blood.

That would send me over the edge all over again.

Think calmly. Think. That cold, practical voice that had led me this far whispered in my mind, and I took sucking breaths of air.

Blackwood was wrong about Maria. She could have unleashed the full force of her powers on us. She could have evaded capture as easily as a cat can hop onto a ledge, but she'd let herself be taken away. She'd wanted them to take her.

Chain her up. Those had been her words. Not *Chain me up* or *I'm to blame.* She'd said *her.* But who the devil was *her?*

I had to find Maria. I had to set this right somehow. Though I knew, even as I made my way back down the stairs, that it could never be right again. All the king's horses and all the king's men . . .

I found my way to where Magnus was staying, in one of the smaller, darker rooms that looked out onto the snowy yard. He sat on the sill, gazing at the world beyond. In his arms, he held a bundle I quickly identified as Valens's baby, Georgiana.

There was only one reason that Magnus, not Valens, would be holding her right now.

"Valens is gone" was all I could think to say. Magnus looked down to the swaddled child as she raised a chubby fist.

"Leticia collapsed. She needs rest, and since I'm the godfather . . ." He looked up at me, dazed. "Richard made me godfather. Stupid idea. I can barely look after my own boots."

"No. He made a wise choice," I whispered. Magnus grunted in what could pass for laughter and held the child closer. He looked into her face with a wondering expression.

"They're so small." He blinked. "Not the most profound

thought I've ever had." He held out one finger to the baby, and she took it, wrapping it in her tiny fist. Then, "I failed her."

"Eliza made her own choice. She brought Dee and the others home."

"Howel, I can't do this." He sounded so young and afraid. I sat beside him as he budged over to make room. The baby had fallen asleep, secure in the crook of Magnus's arm.

Infants were wonderful. They could sleep through the fall of civilization, dream during the death of thousands. So long as they were warm and loved, nothing else mattered.

Loved.

You . . . slut.

Stifling a sob, I leaned against the window.

"It's all right. I know," Magnus whispered. Except that he did not know, and I couldn't tell him.

"What are we going to do about Maria?" I asked, my voice lifeless. I couldn't allow Blackwood to drag me down. If nothing else, Maria needed me more than ever.

"I don't believe she did it on purpose." Magnus sounded resolute. I could have kissed him. In the back of my mind, I'd worried that I was desperate to believe anything but the truth: that Maria was a murderer. But if Magnus believed, then I was not alone, and not mad.

"Could it have been a trick? Perhaps there's an enemy within our ranks." It might even be one of the people we'd let into the grounds, working for R'hlem. My stomach knotted at the idea. "Did anyone come with you whom you thought odd?"

"No." He followed my meaning at once. "I'd put my life in the hands of every single man, woman, and child I brought with me. Well." He calculated. "Perhaps not child. Babies make rather bad protectors." As if to illustrate, Georgiana began to cry. Magnus hefted her up onto his shoulder. Then, as rapidly as it had appeared, his smile vanished. "Howel, what am I going to do?"

I laid a hand on his. He looked down at it in surprise.

"Lead them. You're incredible at it."

Magnus gave a huff of disbelief. "I used to be incredible at playing cards and parading about like some kind of stuffed peacock." He paused. "I mean, I was quite good at it. Best around, in fact. Do stuffed creatures parade? Or does that all end once you're stuffed and mounted?"

"I wouldn't know." I dissolved into a quick, hiccupping fit of laughter. Magnus squeezed my fingers, and squeezed tighter when I began to cry as well. "I think I'm going mad tonight."

"Too much for any one person to handle." Magnus leaned close. "But you're strong, Howel. Stronger than the lot of us combined. You'll see it through."

I didn't believe him, but I was so grateful that he'd said it. For that one, small moment I was so glad to be seated in this room, a baby gurgling up at us. It felt human, but it couldn't last. Good things never did.

"I need to see Maria." I smoothed my hands down the still-bloodied front of my gown. "Don't tell anyone where I've gone."

Magnus nodded. "If anyone asks, you went to your room."

I left Magnus and the child and went into the Faerie side of the house.

The stately marble pillars and tiled floors gave way to those uneven flagstones beneath my feet. Silk-papered walls and family portraits became narrowed hallways and growths of ivy and moss. It smelled of earth here. Bright flashes of light appeared and vanished, probably faerie lights meant to lead me onto a wrong path. Soon I came to a spiraling set of steps and went down.

The dungeon had no bars or cells. It was one circular room of stone, thirty feet wide. They'd left Maria in the center of the floor, chained by her neck. There were two entrances into the dungeon, and I took the one from the west. As I crept down the steps, I listened to Maria's echoing cries. I perched in the doorway, hidden by shadow, and watched her. She was on her knees, sobbing fit to break her own heart.

"Why?" she keened. "I didn't want to hurt her. *Why?*"

Her left hand formed a fist, relaxed, and formed a fist again in a pulsing beat. When she sat up, the look in her eyes was vacant. She traced her tongue along her lips.

"That's better," she said, but it was not her voice. I'd heard that voice many times, though. The voice of Maria's "imaginary" friend, the one she'd created as a child. Willie. But the look on Maria's face now was alien. It didn't belong to her.

It was as if she'd become another person entirely.

I had heard stories of spirits that entered the body of an unsuspecting person, tales told on dark winter nights around the fire at Brimthorn. This was like that, and yet . . .

"Willie" stood, wobbling unsteadily before finding her feet. She stretched her arms overhead and cracked her back. "Hush your crying, ungrateful child. You think it's been pleasant, riding in your simpering head?"

Willie made a coughing noise and then struck herself in the face with her own left hand. I clenched my teeth; it was still Maria's body, even if it was taken over by an outsider.

"Shut up! I don't want to listen to your cringing any longer. You little ginger filth," the voice barked. I stepped into the light, and Maria—or the thing pretending to be Maria—stopped.

"Who are you?" I asked. "Willie" chuckled, crouched on her heels.

"Should've known you'd be down, with your simpering and sanctimony." She chattered her teeth idly. "Never knew William Howel, but I've heard you've the look of him. If only I'd stayed home when that prig Lord Blackwood asked for my help. Aye. 'Twould have been an easier thing for all of us."

For a second, I thought she meant George. But then a creeping realization came over me.

"Charles Blackwood?"

"Oh, it begins to understand," she cooed. "Willie" tugged at her hair, and her eyes watered. "Abusing this piglet's going to come at a price now. I can feel what she feels."

"Who the bloody hell are you?" Was Maria still in there? It

was her face, but the monster behind her eyes was not Maria. "Why did you kill Lady Eliza?"

"Lord, she'll have all my secrets before the night is through," the creature wheedled. She lay back, legs crossed at the knee before her. "I admit, killing that Blackwood bitch was a pleasure fit to rival the most luxurious—"

Like a mask falling away, the real Maria showed herself. She shrieked in terror before falling back.

It was like a shutter flung open in my mind. Charles Blackwood, Howard Mickelmas, and . . . Mary Willoughby. The sorcerer, magician, and witch who brought the Ancients down upon England.

"Mary," I said softly. "What have you done?"

She sat upright and grinned. "Took you long enough, you lanky thing. Of course, you're not much of a brain, are you?" She spit at my feet. I resisted the urge to strike her. She was inside Maria, after all.

"How?" I rested one hand on the top of Porridge. She stared at the stave and made a face.

"I recall being taken up to a hilltop as the sun crested the horizon. They tied me to a stake and carted screaming women to stand alongside me. In the crowd of onlookers, I saw a girl no more than five years old, howling for her mam." Willoughby licked her lips again, a serpent-like movement. "She needed a warm, caring woman in her life." Willoughby snorted. "The sorcerers thought I was swearin' while they lit the pyres. But there was quite a lot of death to go around that day. They paid no mind to my incantations." She knocked her left hand onto Maria's head.

"So you became Maria," I whispered.

She shook her head. "The magic was enough to bond me with the child. But greater, darker magic was needed to give me control. Blood and death magic: the two talents witches dislike immensely. Blood magic's bad enough; you can stop a person's heart with enough willpower. Death magic, though, the taking of an innocent human life?" Willoughby gave a whistle. "That's the only force strong enough to separate a human soul from its body. I knew that, and figured once I had Maria loose in the saddle, I could take over permanently. But Maria?" Willoughby sneered. "She was too good. Anytime I'd plant the suggestion in her mind, she'd bat it away. So I had to stay vigilant. And when the house was all a-rushin', and she was makin' up that quick potion, I used my influence. I made her take the wrong bottle. And there." She clapped her hands. "One dead girl, and a Blackwood to boot. Could not have been more perfectly planned."

I pictured this woman waiting in the corners of Maria's mind like a fat gray spider. My fists clenched.

"Let her go."

Willoughby spit and wiped her mouth. "Does that ever work, poppet? Askin' a person to give up on their plots and schemes? Soon I'll have a body again, much bonnier than before. Even with the ginger hair." She looked me in the eye. "And I know your secrets, girl. Your da wants to tear this world asunder. Well." She winked one dark eye. "He's welcome to it. Perhaps I'll aid 'im."

"Maria," I whispered. "Fight."

For a moment, it seemed my words had no effect. Then, like a snake shedding its skin, Maria emerged from the witch's grip. She sobbed, shying away as I approached.

"I can feel her." Maria cradled her head. "If they burn me, it'll be a blessing."

"No. You're the bloody chosen one." I forced her to look at me. "I won't let them harm you. I swore that before, and I hold to it."

"But I'm a m-murderer." She could barely get the word out.

"Willoughby is, not you." It didn't matter what Maria had been involved in, or what kind of monster currently claimed her soul. She was the one foretold. She was the one to save us, and if it meant battling Blackwood or his men, I would do it. Because she was *our* savior.

And more than that, she was my friend.

12

I HAD JUST RETURNED TO THE MAIN HOUSE, STILL trying to figure out how to help Maria, when a messenger ran to meet me. This was one of the young boys we'd rescued, scarecrow-thin and dark-eyed.

"M'lady." He pressed paper into my hand and scampered off. I didn't correct him and say that he shouldn't call me a lady. After what Blackwood had said, I didn't believe I would ever be a lady. Not his, at any rate.

My stomach dropped as I thought Blackwood might have sent the note. But instead, a looping, dreamy handwriting spoke one word: *chapel*.

It was Lambe.

Wolff awaited me at the chapel door, snow eddying about his feet.

"Howel." His voice sounded thick with tears. I squeezed his shoulder as he ground the heel of his hand into his eye.

He didn't have to say more. We entered the chapel and passed the sleeping Speakers, discovering Lambe in his customary place before the altar. His shirt was stuck to his emaciated frame in thin, transparent patches. I could pick out his ribs underneath the cloth. He scratched his arms, leaving long, red marks.

"Damn them all," Wolff muttered.

Lambe extended his hand. "Valens. Lady Eliza." Was he asking me if their deaths were true?

"I'm so sorry. They—"

"The lady has spilled blood. There's no going back now. You've got to get them all out of here." He raked up his sleeves even higher, revealing scabs that began to bleed afresh. I grabbed his hands to still them. "The lady will start the fire in the wood. Save as many as you can."

More of his prophecies.

"When did you last eat?" I whispered. Lambe looked out at the rows of immobile Speakers, the drug perfume hanging in the air like a canopy.

"It's all useless!" he cried, before sliding to the floor. Wolff picked him up like a sack of flour.

"What's this about a lady?" he whispered to me.

"He's been mentioning her for months now." Whenever Lambe declared something was going to happen, it would. Eliza dead, Blackwood against me, and now this? How could the entire world fall apart in one night?

"You know whatever he predicts will happen." Wolff looked as weary of this as I felt. "Maybe not in the way you'd expect, but it will. Do you suppose Blackwood will let us all go?"

"He won't let any of us out of Sorrow-Fell after tonight, least of all the queen." My thoughts went to her at once. If she were to be lost, or harmed, the war would truly be at an end. "You couldn't blame him, really. Who would want to move sick people and small children when they're already safe?" But Willoughby's plot had kicked Lambe's hypothetical outcome into reality. Because of her, Sorrow-Fell was now the least safe place in the kingdom. "I could try to persuade Blackwood, but . . ." I stopped there, because I could not finish aloud the thought that Blackwood now despised me.

Wolff kissed Lambe's cheek. Love enveloped them. The world was tearing itself to pieces around them, but at least they'd found this contentment.

I left hoping for their happiness, and a happy day for all of us.

I doubted it would come.

THE HOUSE FELT LIKE A TOMB. Only a few lamps had been lit, both to save oil and out of respect for Eliza. As I stepped along the carpeted hall, I kept an eye on my shadow. It remained small and normal. I prayed it continued that way. I could sense that Eliza's death had spurred the darkness inside me to emerge.

How was I to get everyone out of Sorrow-Fell? How could I get Blackwood to listen to reason?

A strangled cry halted me. Muffled sobbing sounded from behind Lady Blackwood's door, the most human noise I had heard so far tonight. My heart sank as I listened, and I cracked open her door. The crying stopped.

"Hello?" I felt like an idiot, but Lady Blackwood answered.

"Come here, girl." Too late to turn back now.

I slipped inside to close the door behind me. The room was nearly pitch black, so I nurtured a small flame in my hand by which to see. I discovered Lady Blackwood out of bed, standing with her back to me, weeping over a dark shape laid out upon a table.

She was standing over Eliza's body.

They had dressed her in a delicate white-lace gown. The blood had been washed away, and her hands lay folded over her chest. Blue snow-sorrows were braided in her dark hair, and a single bloom had been placed beneath her hands. The same flowers used for a wedding would now be for a funeral. She was so perfect with her thick lashes fanned over her cheeks that I half expected her to open her eyes and make comments about how dark the room was.

She would never speak again, and that thought pierced me. Impulsively, I kissed her forehead. It was cold as clay.

"She was so perfect." Lady Blackwood's voice was lifeless. "All that made this empty life bearable."

"My lady? I'm so very sorry," I whispered, brushing my tears away. She did not turn her face. "How may I help you?"

"Leave this place," she croaked.

"I cannot. I have a duty."

"Duty? Was it your duty to bring us the witch who killed my daughter?" Now her voice warmed, and she turned to me. "Bring your fire closer," she whispered. "I want you to see."

It was the last thing on earth I wanted, but how could I

refuse her? Lady Blackwood leaned toward me as I summoned more fire to my hand. I choked on a scream.

I had seen the faces of cadavers lying in coffins. The woman before me looked as though she had rotted aboveground for some time. She'd no nose, merely a socket where that nose should have been. Patches of raw, exposed flesh dotted her gaunt cheeks and blistered lips. When she spoke, I glimpsed a mouth with only a few teeth remaining—they were yellow and rotted. Saliva dribbled out the side of her mouth.

"Before he died in battle, my husband delivered one parting gift to me." Lady Blackwood made a rumbling noise in her chest and began to give a hacking cough. "He was such an adventurer, you know. When he wasn't trying magic, he was trying women. One of them gifted him a disease that he passed to me. Had the Skinless Man not killed him, this would have." She coughed again.

I couldn't take my eyes from her. Her hair was white and brittle, with bald spots decorating her scalp. She picked at the collar of her rotted nightgown.

"Charles had a quick death. Far quicker than he deserved." Though I didn't consider being flayed alive a merciful end, I stayed silent. "I told you to run away, but you stayed with your *prince*. You thought him so good and strong? Well. George is a Blackwood." The lady blinked at me. One eye was milky white with blindness. "He never had a scrap of tenderness in his entire being. Not like his sister." At the mention of her daughter, the lady's harshness melted. "Eliza was the joy of this family. George?" She gave a hacking laugh. "I know what wickedness you pair have done. I'm sure he'll shun you now, like the coward he is. He can't help it. His soul is defective."

My feelings warred inside me. I felt pity for this woman, sorrow for her loss, and anger for her attitude toward her son. Even after what had happened between us, I knew the pain he had suffered. Now I'd a better idea of whom to blame for it. Blackwood's need for control, in love and in all things, had its roots here. Lady Blackwood deserved sympathy for what her husband had done to her. She deserved none for what she'd done to her son.

"You've wronged George, my lady."

"You take his side. But he's already proven his heart to you, and it is ice." She leaned back over her daughter's body. "You're bound to him now. You'll never be free of this fate." She looked at me again, my fire playing on the ruins of her face. "The same as me."

The door slammed open, and I dropped my flame. Blackwood stood outlined against the light of the hall.

"You took her body. How could you?" He stared at his mother, the anger between them hot enough to burn. "Leave," he ordered me.

Even now, I pitied him. There was no one to comfort him any longer. They'd all been taken, or he'd driven them away, or they'd raised him while whispering poison in his ear. "Let me stay," I said.

He looked me in the eye, his gaze acid and loathing. "I don't need you."

Lady Blackwood coughed. "Do leave us, Miss Howel. This is a time for *family*." I wanted to scream at both of them, or to cry. Instead, I gave them what they both deserved: each other. Blackwood did not move a muscle as I left. As soon as I'd exited, the door slammed behind me on a gust of wind.

I heard the rasping of Lady Blackwood's voice and . . . what might have been crying. The tears were not hers.

Hastily, I returned to my room. I sat in bed at least an hour, until the chapel bells chimed midnight. The guard changed below my window, and I went to look out at the moon-colored field. Last night, everything had been wonderful, sweetness mixed with the bitter. Now the world was ash.

Below me, a lone figure waited by the ivy-covered wall, face visible in the light. He was wrapped in his cloak, a charcoal smudge against the wall.

Blackwood watched my window.

I looked away.

BLACKWOOD WOULD NOT MEET WITH ME the following day, but Lambe's message reverberated in my head. We all had to evacuate. The fire was coming.

I had to save Maria, and I had to get everyone out of the estate. How the hell I was to manage this, I could not say.

Even with snow on the ground, we were able to give Eliza and the rest of the fighters a decent burial. The men were laid beneath a tall tree that would be beautiful in high summer. Eliza went to the family burial yard, a cloistered section of the grounds. It was sheltered by two stone walls, with only the barest markers to indicate where the dead slumbered.

Until they lowered Eliza's silk-clad body into the grave, I did not truly believe she was gone. The same for Valens, who received a memorial stone while his widow clutched her baby and sobbed. Eliza and Valens, vanished from the earth. How these young, strong people could now be silent forever was a puzzle I could not solve.

After the funeral rites, Blackwood returned to the isolation of his study. I'd watched him across the open grave, his face white as his sister's body disappeared into the earth. I'd gone to him as soon as the ceremony ended, but he'd brushed past me. Now I stood by Eliza's grave, staring at the quiet earth. How was I to do this? How?

Magnus also remained. His eyes were red, and he seemed a closed fist poised to strike out at the nearest target. He laid a blue snow-sorrow on the earth, near where the headstone would one day stand. That flower would remain in perfect bloom throughout the cold winter. Neither of us spoke as he walked away. Only then, like a burst of divine light, did I realize what was to be done.

I followed him back to the barracks yard, where his squadron gathered around him. Rings of the ordinary men they'd saved joined the sorcerers. Magnus was speaking softly, and I caught some of his words as I came nearer.

"Richard Valens was a better man than I could ever be. I swear I'll try to lead as he did. If you find I'm failing at the job, tell me. Lord knows Valens would." A small ripple of laughter at that.

Magnus held the attention of every man and woman, magic and non-magic alike. Yes. He was the perfect person to help me. I waited until his speech had ended and he'd sent them all to the house, or to wait in the yard so that they might have a sparring match.

"I need to talk to you." I caught up as he walked back toward the stable.

"And I want to listen to you. It's wonderful when things work out so neatly." We walked into the stables, which now stood nearly empty. The injured had all been moved to the great house. There were still a few horses in here, and they blustered as they moved in their stalls. The sweet scent of hay and grain met me. This all reminded me so much of Rook.

And of Magnus's promise to kill him.

"What is it?" Magnus asked.

"Lambe told me we were in danger."

"Oh?" His eyebrows lifted. "Is this another psychic flutter he picked up?"

"When you put it like that, it sounds rather foolish." I smiled weakly; he did not. "He says Sorrow-Fell will burn. We need to get everyone out." I waited to see if he would scoff, but he did not.

"You believe him?"

"Absolutely."

Magnus took up a handful of grain and fed it to the horse behind us. "All right." He turned back to me. "What shall we do?"

Having him ready to follow my plans felt wonderfully different. "Blackwood will never let the queen go."

"Not even if she orders him?" His eyes narrowed. "That sounds like treason, Howel."

"Trust me. Blackwood's let the power of being Imperator overwhelm him. Having the queen under his authority grants him total control. He wouldn't give it up even if he believed Lambe."

Magnus nodded. "What do you propose?"

"I've an idea about how to free the queen, but I'll need you to do something rather dangerous." I bit my lip. "And we'll need help from an unusual source."

"Who?" He frowned. I told him my plan. "Howel. You always were a madman."

"You want to leave?" Blackwood steepled his fingers as he sat behind his father's desk. The crisp morning light illuminated dust motes that floated in the air. For this meeting, Magnus had worn his soldier's livery. He'd even combed his hair and shaved. He looked respectable, no longer the wild figure charging up the hillside to certain doom.

I'd given Blackwood a chance to do the right thing and

told him the entire truth of Lambe's vision. He knew as well as Magnus and I that these prophecies could not be ignored. However, he'd listened to me without hearing. He would not be swayed.

"We should at least get the queen out." I waited, hoping he'd agree and make this easy.

"Absolutely not. Her Majesty is safer with me."

Under your control, you mean.

"Lambe's premonitions should be taken seriously," Magnus replied. Blackwood scoffed.

"The Speakers also said that a chosen one would save us all. But I've yet to be convinced." I bit the inside of my cheek to avoid shouting at him.

"At least let Magnus and his squadron take the people away. Perhaps there's some residual protection at the priory in Northumberland," I said. Blackwood pushed back from his desk.

"Considering it's been pulled down to the roots of its foundation, likely not. But you've always been an optimist," he told me. Then, "Magnus, you may go. My sister has barely been laid to rest, and you already wish to be away." His voice faltered at mention of Eliza. "If you hadn't pulled that ridiculous stunt at her debut, she'd be married to Foxglove and alive today."

"Eliza was never your pawn," Magnus returned.

I had to stop this at once. "Please listen to Lambe before disaster strikes," I said.

"Disaster will *not* strike." Blackwood sat back down. "I will make damned sure of that." The *optiaethis* rested by his right hand. He stared at it, cracking his knuckles idly. "The queen stays. As do you, Howel." So I was Howel again. Not Henrietta.

I left with Magnus, struggling to contain my tongue. But at least our plan would continue uninterrupted.

"You know what to do," Magnus whispered before departing. So I went looking for Alice. We would have only so much time to get this right.

Alice was delighted to be a part of my plan and transformed neatly into a mouse. She had taken the effort to make herself rather adorable, with brown and white spots and quivering whiskers. I carried her in my pocket up the steps to the queen's tower. Her Majesty was working at her desk when we entered. Two guards remained by her door, even when I asked them to leave.

"Lord Blackwood's orders. We're to make certain no harm comes to Her Majesty," Virgil said. Ah yes, no harm could come to the queen, and the queen could do no harm by leaving.

"May we at least close the door?" the queen asked. She looked tired. The guards obliged us. Once we were alone, I took Alice out of my pocket.

"This is for you, Majesty."

"Is this a joke, Howel?" When the mouse became Alice, well, that erased her exhaustion. "The devil?" The queen rose to her feet.

"Well, I *am* a magician, Your Majesty. There are some as would call me that," Alice said dryly. I nudged her.

"Majesty, it's essential that we get you out of Sorrow-Fell, but Lord Blackwood will not let you leave," I murmured. "I've a plan in mind to help you escape."

"With this . . . magician?" Queen Victoria gaped at Alice. "How?"

I waited while Alice stroked her chin and studied the queen, walking around her in circles. When Queen Victoria tried turning with her, Alice held up a hand. "If you please, Majesty, I've got to get the correct proportions. Magic's a science as well as an art."

The queen looked ready to ask what the hell we thought we were doing, when Alice snapped her fingers. Her face morphed; her eyes grew lighter, her nose smaller and more upturned. She shrank several inches and grew rounder in certain areas. By the time she'd finished, I was staring at two Queen Victorias, not one.

The only difference was that one of them wore threadbare clothes that were too large for her frame. Alice grinned.

"Her Majesty has lovely little hands. I'm quite envious."

"Oh. Oh my." The queen sounded frightened . . . and amazed.

"Care to hear the rest of my plan?" I asked.

"COMPANY, PREPARE," MAGNUS CALLED AS MEN and women, commoners and sorcerers gathered together. They flanked wagons that contained the sick, the injured, and those too delicate for intense travel. It was so odd, and felt so wrong, to put the ill on the road. But when Lambe's vision came true, these people would be safer far away from here.

Horrible, that I shouldn't consider Sorrow-Fell safe.

Magnus rode to the head of the army. Dee rode alongside him, with Lilly in one of the wagons.

As I'd loaded supplies, I'd overheard Dee speaking with Magnus before they left.

"So. Captain." Dee had clapped Magnus on the shoulder. "You should be proud."

"I shouldn't be the one they're looking to. They need someone like Blackwood, eh?"

"You're the right man for the job. All you need now is to *become* a man." Dee had laughed, but Magnus had not.

"Perhaps you're right" was all he'd said. Now he was at the head of his "band of brothers," a Shakespearean phrase he would have relished, looking every inch the commanding warrior. The troops were pointed toward the barrier. We'd had the area scouted, and there was a patch of woods to the east that was clear. If the troops moved quickly, they could get out without a fight.

I wished I could go with them. If Maria had been free, I might have. But I could go nowhere without her. I hurried over to Lilly to say goodbye one last time. She saw me, and we clasped hands.

"Do you have everything you need?" I asked. She patted a bundle of blankets beside her. The bundle shifted a tiny bit.

"We're all ready. Take care." She kissed my cheek. The horses started, and Magnus led the charge up the hill. Blackwood was at the barrier already, waiting to let them pass.

The ground trembled as the army thundered ahead. In the air above, I tracked a sparrow hawk as it winged its way toward the barrier, and smiled. The sounds of the army grew fainter. I waited and waited, until finally I could bear it no longer and flew up to the edge of the barrier, beside Blackwood. He and his men were watching the now-clear area beyond.

"Well?" I asked. Blackwood turned his eyes to me, and for an irritating second I thought he'd shut me out.

But instead, he replied, "They made it through."

Excellent. We did not speak on the walk back, but once home he summoned me to his study.

I seated myself on the chaise while he sat opposite me in a claw-footed chair. The walls were papered a dark gray, with a large oil painting beside the door. The painting celebrated sorcerers parting the sea in ancient Greece, all of the men robed in white with their hands stretched to the horizon. It was such a colorful, hopeful image; to have it in this room felt sad.

"We need to talk about Maria," I told him.

"She's going to be burned. I've told the men that she is a witch," he replied evenly. Surely I couldn't have heard him right.

"How could you do something so vile?" I hissed.

"She murdered my sister." Hatred radiated from him.

Finally, I had the freedom to speak.

"Maria didn't kill Eliza. It was Mary Willoughby."

He paled but stayed mercifully silent as I told him what I'd witnessed. By the time I'd finished my explanation, he had his head in his hands.

"Then you've given me more reason to have her exterminated. If she's carrying that monster inside herself—"

"That *monster* worked with your father to summon the Ancients, and then he murdered her to cover his tracks!"

Blackwood sprang to his feet.

"Keep your bloody voice down!" he snapped. "If you're to be my wife, you'll keep a civil tongue." I laughed at that.

"You think we'll be happily married after what you've said to me?"

"Not happily." He turned his eyes away. "But I'm a man of honor. The fact you think there is *any* option beyond marrying me is disgraceful."

"I'm not going to marry anyone out of charity."

"It's not charity. I still want you," he whispered, his face contorting as he spoke. That shocked me into silence. "God help me, I thought my feelings would die with Eliza. They did not."

I knew I should say I didn't feel anything for him now. But the words didn't come.

"Now," Blackwood said. "Maria will die tomorrow. I will not hear another word about it," he added, raising a hand as I started to argue. "We must begin our study of that stone circle. First, the queen will want her report."

He said it mockingly.

I decided to accompany him. We walked through the east wing, up the tower steps, and passed the guards by Her Majesty's door. When we entered the queen's chamber, Blackwood looked about in confusion. The bed was made. The room was empty. Comically, he looked ready to open the closet door and rifle through the drawers to find our monarch.

"Where is the queen?" Blackwood asked the nearest guard. The poor fellow looked white with confusion.

"Beg pardon, m'lord, but Her Majesty never left." The boy's bewilderment was not feigned. I, however, could not conceal a small grin of triumph. Blackwood regarded me with amazement, as though I'd turned bright green. He blocked my path.

"Where is she?" He clenched his jaw.

"With Magnus."

"How?"

It hadn't been too difficult, really. A few hours before the army left, Alice had morphed into the queen, remaining as a decoy while I flew the real Victoria out the window. With Lilly's help, it had been easy to hide the queen in a wagon under those blankets. Alice had remained in the room until the army began to move, at which point she'd transformed into a sparrow hawk and followed out the window.

Finishing my tale, I added, "I didn't think it right to keep our monarch a prisoner."

"You. Didn't think." Blackwood appeared almost proud, as if he were glad to have been outwitted. The pride lasted about as long as a snowflake before a fire. "Bring my squadron," he told the servant. My stomach dropped, but I was not going to appear frightened of him. Once the boy had left, Blackwood and I had a moment alone.

"Can't you see what's happening to you?" I asked. He went to the window to look anywhere but at me.

"How much more can you take from me? My sister. My peace." He came to me then, as lithe as a snake striking. I gusted into fire, just as a warning. "I didn't know pain like this until I met you. I swore to myself I'd never be weak like my father, but see what you've done?"

"Your weakness is not my fault."

"But in its own way, it was fate." He touched the handle of his stave, and I could glimpse the carved ivy leaves upon it, identical to my own. "Why do you have this hold upon me?" He came close enough to graze his lips along my ear. "Why are we destined for this?"

Even now, after all he had done, my body still gravitated to his. When he touched me, there was a mixture of pain and pleasure, revulsion and desire. I felt an urge to run from him, and twisted with that, the yearning to be consumed by him.

"You're my prison," I told him, but I could not make myself hate the words.

"And you're mine. But God help me, I don't want to be set free." He sounded miserable. My whole being hummed to kiss him, to let go of every reality but his hands and his lips. Had my thoughts always been this unchaste?

Footsteps announced the arrival of Blackwood's guard. To

them, he said, "Howel's to remain in this room. I'll have her meals sent up. Two men will be posted at the door, and two at the first landing, day and night."

I didn't resist. When Blackwood held out his hand for Porridge, I unbuckled the sheath and gave it over. I trembled as the stave left my hand—it was like giving away a cherished pet. Blackwood wouldn't do anything to hurt it, at least.

But I'd need it back.

"For how long?" I asked as he slipped Porridge into his coat.

"For as long as it pleases me." He left. The two sorcerers regarded me with heavy-lidded eyes. I went to close the door. One of them stopped it with his hand.

"You must think we're rather stupid. You've your magician trickery, after all." So. The door would remain open, then. Anger flared in my mind. I sat back on the queen's bed and gazed out the window. Already, men were assembling a pyre, setting the stage for Maria's demise. My stomach quailed at the image.

Magnus and the others were safe now, but Maria's time was running out. If I wanted to save her, I would have to act soon.

Mercifully, I still had my plan.

13

A FEW HOURS LATER, THE SKY HAD DARKENED. AS I'D run over the plan again and again that afternoon, searching for flaws, I'd watched them finish constructing the pyre. It was rather simple, a crude wooden platform with a large stake in the center. Kindling had been placed in the open space beneath the platform. The fire would rise high and well in this cold air.

The image of Maria tied to the stake, her red hair turning to actual flame, spurred me on. I'd an idea, but I would need privacy to try it. And there was only one way I could see that the men would allow me to close the door.

I began casually undoing my dress, bringing out a line of cloth from the cupboard. Both of the guards startled.

"I have, er, feminine business to attend." My monthly courses were not due for three weeks or so, but that certainly did the trick. Both men looked as if I'd threatened to murder a kitten in front of them. "If you'd do me the courtesy of privacy?"

One of the soldiers pulled at the door as though it were his protection against death itself. "Three minutes. No more," the other man warned.

Finally. I fast buttoned myself up and turned toward the window. They'd taken Porridge from me, which meant controlling the wind would not be so simple. But if Rook's shadow powers would serve me . . . just this once, of course.

I shuddered to think of doing it, but there were no other options.

I pushed the window open, facing the cruel bite of the wind. *Like a princess escaping a tower where a horrid witch has confined her,* I thought. *Or a monstrous king.* A part of Blackwood had relished imprisoning me. I knew that he loved my strength— he'd told me so, once—but there was another part of him that wanted to see such strength submit to him.

He would get no such submission today.

Right. How did I go about this? I recalled Rook lifting his hand and summoning shadows from every crevice and corner. He had worn the darkness like a cloak, used it to transform and steal through the tiniest cracks and keyholes. I did not want to access that ability—it frightened me. But if I used it just this once, I might be all right. Closing my eyes, I willed the shadows to cover me.

A small, excited voice whispered an unknown language in my mind. The wounds at my shoulder throbbed so terribly that my head pounded in reply.

I tasted fear on my tongue.

I needed to move. The men would soon open the door.

Slowly, I stretched out my hand. This time, the voice in my mind grew louder. Something rustled in the corner of the room, silk gliding across stone. Then a wash of cool overcame me. The pain at my shoulder disappeared for the first time in months. I felt divine.

When I opened my eyes, there was only pitch black. Yet I felt no fear; I could see perfectly. Once, I'd needed my fire to pierce Rook's shadow, but now it seemed that the darkness had taken root in my skin. It was a part of me.

I was one with the dark. Shadow flowed through my veins, or rather my veins dissipated and became shadow. The weight of my human body was gone; only darkness remained. It was such glorious power. I felt I could travel the world in a single instant, meld into every nook and cranny of the earth. My human mind threatened to vanish . . . no.

I forced myself to slow. Now in the form of a shadow, I tipped over the windowsill and slid down the ivy—I had never floated so comfortably, even upon the back of the wind. Once on the ground, I shed the shadow as quickly as possible. The dull heaviness of my human body, my arms and legs and head, returned. The pain at my shoulder flared once more, but I welcomed it. I never wanted to use that power again.

Sorcerers strolled past me, heading for the yard. I pressed against the building to hide myself, already regretting not bringing a damned cloak. My teeth chattered. I stole over the snowy grounds, headed for the kitchens.

Thank God, there was no one in the servants' hall. I went up the stairs and headed to the right. Soon I'd made it back to the Faerie grounds, with no one around to discover me.

My heart thudded as I ran down the winding corridors. I found the spiraling steps and hurried toward the dungeon.

Maria was alone, still chained by the neck and lying on her side. Her red hair spilled out around her head, looking like the coppery sheen of blood in the slanting moonlight. I shook her awake. When she sat up, I waited to see if she was Willoughby. But her frightened eyes told me that Maria had won, for now.

"What are you doing here?" she whispered.

I hushed her as I began to melt the chain at her neck. After the void and chill of shadow, the fire nearly hurt my hands.

"I'm getting you out," I said. The links broke, and I helped her to her feet. Maria tugged at the metal collar that still circled her neck. I couldn't melt that without hurting her.

I wasn't certain how we would get past the guards in the yard; my imagination had always failed there. Normally that would have driven me mad, but tonight all I cared about was getting out of here. If we could find some warm clothes, a cloak perhaps, that would be so much the better. I wasn't certain how far we'd make it otherwise. My fire could only hold for so long.

If I could get Maria out, perhaps Lambe's vision would not come true. We had gotten many of the sorcerers and regular folk out of here—but not all. I wanted to spare them . . . and Blackwood, if I could.

"Where are we going?" Maria stumbled against me. I'd never seen her so fragile. Fighting off Willoughby's influence had to be a tremendous drain.

"Up the stairs. If we can reach the ground level, we'll head out the back door and—"

We weren't going to reach the ground level or the back door, because a large group of men awaited us at the mouth of the exit. Blackwood stood at the front of them. I wrapped an arm around Maria's waist and turned us, only to find another group standing in the opposite doorway. No way out.

"That was a clever escape, Henrietta," Blackwood said. I noticed Porridge hanging in the sheath by his belt. If I could snatch it . . .

"Please. Let us pass." I could feel my knees giving out beneath me. Between the two of us, Maria and I were not going to put up any real fight. Blackwood grinned, a mirthless expression.

"Release the witch," he said. My temper boiled over.

"Half witch. You conveniently forgot the sorcerer half, didn't you?" I snapped. His eyes flashed a warning, but I spoke to the men. "This is Cornelius Agrippa's daughter. Look at her eyes and you'll know the truth."

A confused murmur broke out. Hawthorne examined Maria with growing astonishment.

"Uncanny." He looked at Blackwood. "My lord, did you know?"

Maria's left hand began to clench into a fist—blast, Willoughby must be coming out. We were in such dire straits, I couldn't tell if Willoughby's arrival would make this better or worse. Based on our luck thus far, I was betting on worse.

"This girl murdered my sister. Nothing else matters," Blackwood said.

"Oh, but it wasn't poor, sweet Maria that murdered the brat." Maria threw off my arm and stood on her own two feet now. Or rather, Willoughby did. "That would be I, Lord Blackwood. Son of the man who brought down ruin on this country." She grinned.

Blackwood's entire body went rigid with fear. Well, I'd bloody well tried to warn him.

Hawthorne appeared baffled. Willoughby winked a dark eye at him.

"You all burned my kind, but we're hardier than you supposed." She sidestepped away from me, keeping the focus of all the men. "Twelve years ago, I helped Howard Mickelmas open a portal to another realm. And the sky became black, and the world was set afire."

"Mary Willoughby?" That was one of the younger men, who scoffed as he said it. I could feel the disbelief growing. They thought this was a bad attempt on Maria's part to save her skin.

I could feel something invisible and horrible rushing toward us. Something was going to happen, and soon.

"Let us pass. Now," I said to Blackwood. He did not respond to me.

"The witch is lying," he said to the men. "This is a ploy."

But Willoughby was not done yet.

"I *thought* I recognized you," Willoughby said to Hawthorne. "You were among the men gathered by Charles Black-wood to ride out and, ah, apprehend me and Mickelmas. He got away, tricky bastard that he was, but I wasn't so fortunate. What did I say to you, when you found me?" She pretended to think, then held up a finger. "Ah yes." Then she let out such a string of curse words that the walls would have blushed if they could. Hawthorne looked ashen. "You said you'd never heard such a tongue on a woman in all your life. You tutted about it. Yes, sir." She wagged a finger. "You tutted."

By the look on the man's face, I knew that Willoughby had spoken true. The men believed Hawthorne's reaction, and so they began to believe her.

"Blackwood, let us go," I said. He paled considerably but did not flinch.

"You went to the nearest coven, once you'd had approval from your blasted Order. You kicked their doors in, murdered the men where they stood, dragged the women to your carts, then took them to the pyres and burned them alive." Willough-by's eyes sparked. "All you missed was a small girl. Do you re-member now, sorcerer? You should have slaughtered her with the rest of her people."

"My God," Hawthorne whispered. My mouth felt dry.

"Bind this witch and take her outside," Blackwood barked. But no one was listening to him any longer.

"Are you sure you're the one to be giving orders, Your Lord-ship?" She swirled her skirt as she walked to him. Willoughby gave Maria's hips a swivel that the girl herself never possessed.

"Considering it was your own dear daddy who helped call down those ancient monstrosities?"

I summoned a gust of wind in warning, but Willoughby threw open her hands . . . and the wind blasted back in my face. Willoughby had access even to Maria's elemental powers.

Blackwood did not try to make excuses. Perhaps it was madness, but he seemed to deflate with relief.

Already, the power in the room was turning. It might end well for me, or terribly, but I did not know which.

"You sorcerers want to know why you're all crammed into one bloody estate? Why your homes and families were stolen from you?" Willoughby looked at the men, hatred burning in her eyes. "It's because the great Charles Blackwood took me and Mickelmas to an isolated place. All three together, we opened that blasted circle and let those hellish demons through. Your dear departed Charlie Blackwood decided to shirk his share of responsibility. Mickelmas and me, we paid the price. And you all reveled in it, didn't you?" She paced like an animal. "Was there never a seed of doubt, you older gentlemen? When Lord Blackwood gave you his news, did you never entertain the idea that he was perhaps involved?" She chuckled. "Or was it a reason at long last to allow your hatred for magicians and witches to flow?"

The gleeful way Willoughby was grinning, the relish she took in her performance, seemed excessive even for her. Was she buying time?

"Something is wrong," I murmured, but the men were not

listening to me. Blackwood stood straighter than ever, a man waiting stoic on the beach as a tidal wave roared into view.

"So you burned and you tortured and you ravaged us, witches and magicians, too. And you let the monsters stampede about this filthy country, with its filthy people. But did you ever know that your great Earl of Sorrow-Fell was responsible? And did you know that his son knew all about his father's sins?"

"Liar!" I shouted. It wasn't a lie at all, but I had to protect Blackwood. When he looked at me, for one moment the anger dissolved between us. Willoughby turned on me.

"Don't go pointing out liars, my girl. Not unless you've a wish to be named in their ranks." Her gaze was all the threat I needed. She knew about R'hlem.

"Is it true?" Hawthorne asked Blackwood. The earl seemed smaller and younger than I had ever known him. With a few words, Willoughby had stripped him bare. If he'd lied boisterously, he might have convinced them. Who would want to believe such a thing, after all? But Blackwood had never been as comfortable with falsehoods as I had. His silence was all the confirmation needed.

"Then I take it upon myself," Hawthorne said, "to strip you of your titles and privileges pending a thorough investigation."

Blackwood's eyes widened, and I felt a kind of uneasy *shifting* in the air.

"You fool. Don't you know what you're doing?" Blackwood cried as the men seized him. Willoughby began to giggle. God, I wanted to strike her.

"What is it?" I asked Blackwood as the men grabbed his stave.

"If you strip me of my title, the Blackwood family does not control this estate! That means that the barrier—"

He didn't need to say anything more, because at that moment a great, screaming boom shattered the air. My bones rattled to hear it, and Willoughby kicked up her heels with triumph.

I felt him as soon as the barrier came down. He had lurked in the shadows for such a long time, waiting patiently as a coiled serpent. As soon as he set foot onto the land, my blood screamed in recognition.

R'hlem had come to Sorrow-Fell.

My father was here.

14

HAD WILLOUGHBY PLANNED IT? R'HLEM COULD visit people across the astral plane, pop into one head and then out of another. Perhaps they'd concocted this together, once Willoughby was in control of Maria's body. Indeed, seeing the way that horrible woman celebrated stoked the fury within me. Had she not worn Maria's face, I'd have burned her on the spot.

"Fools!" Blackwood shouted as the men looked about in shock.

I burst into angry flames, which turned out to be the stupidest thing I'd done yet.

Willoughby summoned my fire to her hand and shoved past the men in the doorway. She raced upstairs, trailing sparks as she went.

I needed my stave. Taking advantage of the bewildered men, I snatched Porridge back from Blackwood.

We looked at each other, understanding stretched between us. His lifetime of hiding had ended.

"Give him his authority back!" one of the men shouted. But that would do only so much good now. Still, we might succeed.

So long as the essence of Sorrow-Fell remained intact, so long as . . .

So long as the house did not burn.

Lambe had warned me of the lady burning in the wood.

I went after the witch. The men followed, their voices a confused cacophony as we emerged into the hall to find the place engulfed in rippling flame.

The rooms of the faerie castle were made of stone, so very little was burning save a few moth-eaten tapestries. But the halls of the main house were polished wood. The place had gone up as neat as a log in a fire. The portraits of ancestors blackened and curled, youthful foreheads wrinkling, pale faces flaking off in bits of ash. The carpets, the wooden furniture, the wooden banisters were all ablaze. It was hot as hell, and the smoke made my eyes water. In the center, Willoughby crowed as she unfurled fiery blast after blast at whatever she could touch.

Blackwood and the men dashed around me, summoning snow and water from outside to put out the flames. Servants poured out the front door, screaming for their lives.

I moved quickly. Though the flames could not harm me, the smoke would. We would all choke to death if it got much worse.

A cry turned my head. At the top of the staircase, standing in her long white nightgown, was Lady Blackwood. Her gray, thin hair hung in her face in strings. She had not put on her veil. In the bright light of the fire, she resembled some ancestral ghost made garishly visible. Extending her thin arms to either side, she cackled.

"Look at it, Charles! Look!" She clapped her hands like a gleeful child.

Oh no.

"My lady, stay there!" I passed through fire without any fear. With a swipe of Porridge, wind buffeted upward to push her back to safety. "I'll come get you!"

But a piece of fiery timber collapsed in front of me. Before I could catch her, Lady Blackwood deliberately stepped over the edge and plunged into the fire below.

Now sorcerers blasted water onto the ever-increasing expanse of fire, but it was a losing battle. Billows of black smoke flooded the place.

Familiars stormed in over the threshold. They ran a few sorcerers through with their claws and daggers. I found Willoughby dancing closer and closer to the fire. She didn't care if she and Maria died or not.

I would not let her take my friend.

Screaming, I threw myself into Willoughby, knocking her to the floor. Willoughby tried to strike me, but I slapped her face—Maria's face—again and again. The heat was atrocious. I was dripping sweat.

"Maria!" I drew a ward around us, just in time. Another piece of flaming timber fell and shattered on my ward. I gripped her left hand, now balled in a fist. Something about how tight it was made me think that if I loosened it, it might call Maria back. Slowly I straightened her fingers, shaking with the effort. "Let her go," I said through my teeth.

And then, through what must have been superhuman effort, Maria sloughed off Willoughby and returned. She looked up at me, her face white and wan.

"I c-can't stand up," she said.

I would stand for her. We got to our feet, the front door directly ahead. Fire ate the velvet curtains by the windows. We left the men fighting and screaming around us. Two sorcerers who had come in from the cold lay at our feet, throats slashed and blood spread along the marble floor. Flakes of snow and ice still hung in their hair. I ripped the cloaks from their bodies, draping them around Maria and myself. Guilt pained me, but the men wouldn't need these anymore. We did.

"Henrietta!"

Blackwood was surrounded on all sides by creatures. A louse Familiar leaped for him, and Blackwood cut the monster down with one swift stroke of his blade. He spun his stave in an expert fashion, raining fire down upon the monsters. His every move was elegant and powerful, each muscle honed to this task. He looked to me, his expression twisted in pain. I was abandoning him, and we both knew it.

I had to, for Maria's sake.

A Familiar rose up behind him. I guided a stream of fire to kill the thing. The last help I could give Blackwood. I prayed it would be enough.

"Let's go," I whispered to Maria as we shoved our way out

into the snow. I looked about in terror, in case my father should appear. As the sorcerers screamed behind us, I forced myself to leave. I could not even stop to look for Wolff or Lambe, to try to help the Speakers. Selfish as it was, Maria was my sole concern. The blazing heat of the fire at my back, I didn't yet feel how shattering the winter cold was, though I would soon enough. Through the night, monsters were arriving.

Besides the swarm of Familiars, I recognized the large, disgusting forms of a few Ancients. We were exposed here in the open, and I gathered the shadows around me with a murmur halfway between a spell and a prayer. The dark whispered in around us. Thus shielded from the Ancients' sight, Maria and I paused to watch the creatures approach.

There was Zem, the enormous lizard crawling across the ground toward the house, his tail swinging lazily, forked tongue jabbing out of his mouth. Molochoron rolled behind the serpent, pulsing with disease. The moonlight glistened on his gelatinous surface. Before I could do anything, he rolled atop a young sorcerer lying in the snow. The boy screamed as the blob sucked him up inside his monstrous body. I glimpsed the boy thrashing, until he went horribly still.

Though my first instinct had to be to protect Maria, reason abandoned me for one brief moment. Porridge in hand, I wanted to fight. But then all my courage deserted me.

R'hlem came striding up the path.

My father had not changed since I'd last seen him in London. His flayed face was as disgusting as ever, the single eye in his forehead a terror. He wore a fine winter coat, the collar trimmed in fur. He strolled behind his monstrosities as though taking them on a pleasant walk.

I couldn't let him get hold of Maria. Or me.

Shaking, I dragged her over the yard and into the trees. We went up the hill, losing ourselves in the densest part of the forest. There, I could breathe and let Maria rest against a tree. Retching, she sank to her knees while I paced back and forth.

"We can't stop them," she muttered, looking back at the estate. The flickering red and orange of the fire illuminated the night sky.

"No. Not yet. We have to push north and find help."

Together we made our way through the dark forest. After I had been allowed to pass into the druid lands, it was almost as if I could feel Sorrow-Fell around me, like a living thing. As the Ancients rampaged, I could sense the place withdrawing into itself to hibernate. The Fae magic of the estate, smashed when Blackwood had been dethroned, shriveled around us. Lines of those luminescent toadstools that had marked pathways flickered and died.

Ahead, there was movement as a snow-white stag caught my eye. It stepped so lightly over the ground that it did not leave prints. Blackwood had told me once the white stags were the most magical creatures on this estate. I marveled at the animal, the silky sheen of its coat, the delicate hooves, the soft muzzle. Its black eyes beheld me, and I glimpsed a human intelligence within them. Then the stag turned and bounded away, drawing the magic of the area behind it like an invisible cloak.

Sorrow-Fell was going to sleep.

Cursing, Maria and I made our way out of the estate. It was a ten-minute walk to the barrier, and we could not risk flying. Behind us, the place smoldered, the park littered with the bodies of the dead. Maria dropped to her knees at the barrier, vomiting all over the snow. I held her hair away from her face. Her skin was hot to the touch.

"I'll be all right," she gasped. "She doesn't have me now."

If Maria could hold Willoughby off for good, that would be too wonderful. But it had been mere days since her possession had started, and she already looked drained of life.

I thought of the druid lands beyond the house, the stone circle and the runes. Soon R'hlem would go there to prepare the beginning of the end of our kingdom. The sorcerers had defeated themselves in their rush to condemn Blackwood and his father. The irony was almost too much to bear.

Blackwood was surely dead. How on earth could he stand against R'hlem? It felt as though I were sinking deep beneath the surface of a frozen pond, watching the light fade from above. Our country's future was gone.

Sorrow-Fell belonged to the Ancients now.

15

I HAD ALWAYS FANCIED MYSELF A SURVIVOR. AFTER all, I had overcome hunger and abuse at Brimthorn. I had faced the most magical men in London. I had destroyed a bloody Ancient. But all of that glory paled in comparison to trying to catch a rabbit.

"See? You've only to loop it like so." Maria's hands took over, turning a clumsy muddle of rope to something secure. She had her wild tumult of hair back in a low bun, a stray wisp or two falling into her face as she worked. "Then we'll tie it to that little bar of the trap I made." She gestured to the small contraption she'd hammered together from a few sticks. "It'll hang there, and we force the rabbit through. Roast rabbit's the best thing for winter."

"Any food at all's the best thing for winter." My stomach felt like someone had trod on it till it was flat.

"Least we'll never run out of fire," she said, giving me a hopeful smile. Since we'd left Sorrow-Fell five days before, Maria had not broken down. She'd woken cheerful every day, digging us out of whatever burrow we'd made for shelter. I could provide fire, but she knew how to set up the camp. She knew how to read tracks to find animals for hunting. She knew how to avoid stepping into deep pockets of snow, which could drench and freeze a person. Maria knew every step of the land as if it were a part of her own body.

And I? Well, I could provide fire. I would stand there in the snow, a thin layer of blue flame covering my body, while Maria warmed her hands and cooed words of encouragement. "You've such a pretty flame" and "Nice and warm" were two of her polite endearments.

Maria set the hanging snare and huddled beside me. I tried offering a bit of fire, just to be useful, but she made me put it out. "Don't want to frighten anything off," she whispered. Before too long, a brown rabbit hopped along the snowy path. Maria had set up something of a blockade, fallen branches and the like that forced the little creature to hop where we wanted it to go. Within minutes, the rabbit was hanging in the snare. Maria took out her knife, and the end was swift. I kept a hand over my eyes all the same.

"You eat meat, for pity's sake. You know where it comes from," she tsked as she skinned the creature. "Now then. Light us a fire, if you please."

My hands shook as I held them over a pile of kindling. I'd never known a human could survive such cold. I'd never known hunger like this, either, and now wanted to go back to my childhood and shake myself for when I'd complained of a meager supper at Brimthorn. At least there had *been* supper.

"What should we do?" Maria asked as we ate the thin

rabbit. Her eyes were sunken, and dark circles like bruises had formed underneath them. The battle against Willoughby was ongoing, though she never complained.

"Magnus took his squadron north, though I don't know where. What about the witches?" And the magicians as well. Perhaps I could melt some snow for a scrying mirror.

"Not sure how many of the covens remain. Witches are tribal by nature. Territorial. Could be they've all grown accustomed to warring among themselves." Maria sighed, gnawing at a bone. "Even if we find them, gettin' them to all agree to come fight for the bloody sorcerers seems a tall order."

Well, perhaps once we convinced them how bloody urgent it was, they'd fall into line. That was likely a fanciful dream, but one to which I clung. We packed up the camp and doused the fire, making sure there was nothing R'hlem could use to track us. As we walked, Maria pulled up her collar. "You did well grabbing these coats when we ran." She beamed. "I wouldn'a thought of it, and we'd have frozen to death."

"You're trying to make me feel less useless, aren't you?"

"Not at all," she said too quickly. For the first time in two days, we laughed. As we walked, she sighed. "Truly, though, I miss the bonny cloak that you gave me. And my ax," she added with a wistful sigh. "Imagine they burnt in the fire."

"Perhaps R'hlem kept them. I imagine he's wearing your blue cloak right now, vain devil that he is. We'll get them back." I took her arm in mine. "You'll see."

"Know any good songs?" she asked as the sun vanished behind a cloud. "It makes the cold hurt less."

"I'm a poor singer."

Maria was not a poor singer. Her voice was throaty and strong, and she sang "Black Is the Color of My True Love's Hair."

"The winter's passed and the leaves are green
The time is passed that we have seen
But still I hope the time will come
When you and I shall be as one."

On that last line, a different, more womanly voice took over. I grabbed Porridge, but Maria held up her hand.

"I'm all right. She's gone." She staggered a step or two. When I went to catch her, she held me off. "Please, Henrietta. I must find my own feet."

We walked apart for a while, and Maria did not sing again.

That night we found an overhang of rock and huddled together beneath our cloaks. While Maria slept fitfully and the winter wind roared outside, I tried to think of a plan. The only thing we had on our side now was time. R'hlem likely could not open that portal before the spring equinox. That was the good news.

The bad news: the spring equinox was mere weeks away. If we wanted any hope of stopping R'hlem, we needed to find enough manpower to ride back to Sorrow-Fell and wrest the portal from him. How we were to deal with all the Ancients and Familiars, I'd no idea.

One step at a time.

We could still prepare. I needed to believe that. Grunting, I unlaced my boot and touched snow to my blistered feet. Every step now was like a gunshot in my mind, but we couldn't stop until we'd entered Scotland and found help.

Then Maria began laughing.

I froze. That might be Willoughby claiming the girl again, but I didn't think it was. After the scare with the song earlier, Maria and I had agreed that when she felt Willoughby overpowering her, she was to say "lady in the wood." Then I was to knock her senseless.

It wasn't a perfect plan.

She hadn't uttered the words of warning. Slowly, I turned to her. The laugh sounded again . . . but with an unusual edge to it. With mingled relief and concern, I realized that Maria wasn't laughing.

She was *sobbing*.

I'd never heard such a sound from her before, like a wounded animal. Arms wrapped around her body, she shuddered as she strained for breath. I touched her shoulder, but she shied away and bunched farther into a ball. With nowhere else for her to go, I rested my hand on her shoulder again and waited for her to tell me the matter.

"I'm alone." Maria's voice was muffled.

"No," I murmured. It was all I could think to say.

Maria pushed her tangled hair away. "I thought . . . I thought she cared about me." Her face twisted, and I knew the subject was Willoughby. "After Mam died, the world was hell. The workhouse . . . all the screams and struggles in the dark, all the horror I didn't dare name. Thought I'd die there. Then when I finally escaped, I ran back to my grandmother's coven, and she . . . she cast me out." Tears fell into her lap. "Told me it was my fault Mam died."

"That's a lie," I said, appalled. What kind of monster could say such a thing?

"Willie was all I had." Maria pulled her knees to her chest and hid her face. "And she was usin' me. Only person that ever loved me was my mother, and they burned her." These last words were lost in a great, low wail. Her body rocked with her sobs.

I wound my arms around her. She was tense at first but yielded bit by bit. I whispered, "I swore I'd never let anyone harm you. *I* love you, and I won't let her take you."

She kept crying but relaxed against me. After a while, the sobs stopped, and we both grew heavy with exhaustion. The hours were cold and dark, and our hunger still had teeth. After a long silence, she spoke.

"You truly think your da likes parading about in my peacock cloak?"

For some reason, I found that image hysterical. "One day, we'll make him give it back," I promised, between giggling fits.

"One day. Like the sound of that," she said. Nudging her elbow against my arm, she added, "And 'we.' Like the sound of that, too."

THE NEXT DAY, MARIA SEEMED TO have improved marvelously. At least one of us felt better. I'd woken with what seemed a wild animal tearing the inside of my skull. My shoulder wounds burned in a way I'd never known them to before, like bee stings with boiling oil poured over them. A new blanket of snow had fallen the night before, and the world around us was pristine as a painting, and cold as the lowest level of Dante's hell.

Apparently, we'd passed into Scotland the day before. I'd never been this far north, and recalled Miss Morris, our head teacher, and her tales of barbaric kilted Scotsmen who roamed the land and drank the blood of maidens to satisfy ancient clan rites. I secretly felt she'd mashed up a copy of Sir Walter Scott with the vampires from a penny dreadful.

The trees began to thin around us as we neared the edge of the forest.

"Look at that," Maria said, her breath a cloud of white. "It's grand, is it not?"

Snow-covered hills appeared in the distance.

The air tasted clean, as if it had been scrubbed and proudly set shining on display. My skirts were sodden, though, and I lit the hem on fire to dry myself. Maria warmed her hands by my flame.

"Do you think we might come upon a free town soon?" I asked her as we trudged along.

"I'm afraid independent towns might be scarce just across the border," she replied, jumping over a fallen log in our path. She looked back at me, a strange expression on her face. "Do you truly think I'm your chosen one?"

"What?" The question was so startling I tripped on the log and nearly tumbled face first into the snow. "Of course you are. Why on earth would you think you're not?"

"I killed . . . that is, Willoughby killed Eliza." At mention of the girl's name, Maria hung her head. "And the whole of Sorrow-Fell burned. Seems I've caused more harm than good to our side."

"That's ridiculous," I said, reflecting again on that prophecy tapestry. Part of me wanted to strangle the Speakers for how damned opaque they'd been about the whole thing. But then, as I dwelt again on the prophecy, I frowned.

That third line . . . *Sorrow falls unto the fierce army of the Blooded Man*. Originally, we'd all assumed that meant that sadness and loss would come to R'hlem and his army. But . . . sorrow falls . . . sorrow-*fell*.

Unto the fierce army of the Blooded Man.

Perhaps . . . perhaps Maria was not entirely wrong.

"What are you thinking?" she asked. I hastened to change the topic, but even as we discussed how to forage for supper, my mind turned the question over.

Perhaps the prophecy revealed that R'hlem would conquer Sorrow-Fell. But if that were the case, then surely that meant good things could come. After all, if Maria burned in the heart of the black forest . . .

For the first time since realizing Maria's destiny, fear truly gripped me. For now that I had begun thinking, I could not stop. *Black forest* could also equal *black wood.*

Or Blackwood.

Burning in the heart of Blackwood could mean the destruction of Sorrow-Fell. It could mean the destruction of the Blackwood line in general. And Maria, even inadvertently, had already caused Eliza's death, and Lady Blackwood's as well.

Perhaps I was inventing all of this. Perhaps none of it was true. But the more I shifted the ideas, the more I began to see how many different ways that prophecy could be interpreted.

The tapestry had never specified a chosen one. It had never even truly explained what she would do. The ending line had read something about triumph reigning in England, but suppose that simply meant one side winning this war? Suppose it indicated *R'hlem's* side?

What if we had wasted years of everyone's time and countless lives in pursuit of a prophecy that had been incorrectly read and a chosen one who did not exist?

Or worse, what if Maria had been meant to bring about our downfall? She walked ahead of me, mercifully oblivious to my thoughts. She herself was truer than any other person I had ever known. But the woman inside her, the wolf howling at the door . . . *she* could not be trusted.

And what if she won the battle for Maria's soul?

"What is it?" Maria noticed that I had stopped. My animal instinct shouted to get away from her.

No. That was madness. She was terrified enough as it was, and what I was thinking couldn't be true.

"My shoulder's getting worse," I said, which wasn't a complete lie. She made me rest against a tree while she pressed at it, which brought tears to my eyes. I might also have cursed at her. I didn't mean what I said. Much.

"You're a great baby sometimes," she muttered. While she attended me, I gazed into the distance to take my mind off the pain and the prophecy.

I noticed that the twilight was coming on far too soon. True, we'd only had a few hours of daylight this time of year, but I was certain the sun had only just risen. All around us, the forest and hills darkened. Ahead, on the horizon, the darkness seemed to congeal. It wasn't night. It wasn't a collection of clouds, or shadows. It was more on the ground, a movement of pure blackness. It . . .

"An army," I gasped.

"Not the one we want, either," Maria muttered.

No, not at all. It was R'hlem's army, and it was heading straight for us.

16

AT FIRST I THOUGHT WE MIGHT FIND SHELTER deeper in the forest, but the swarm could not be outrun. They'd stumble upon us no matter what we did. We needed a way to survive within their ranks.

Maria and I huddled together behind a tree to watch the approaching tide. God, my shoulder *blazed*. A wish reverberated in my mind over and over, to find shelter, to find shelter, to find shelter.

"By the mother," Maria whispered. I opened my eyes to discover the lengthening winter shadows crawling toward us like ink over the snow. My entire shoulder went blissfully numb.

We were in darkness now, and I held up a tiny ball of fire to pierce it for Maria. For myself, I could still see perfectly. We were now covered in shadow, invisible to the casual eye. If anyone glanced at us, I was certain we resembled nothing more than the lengthening winter darkness. As much as I hated to use these powers, this was the only way we were getting out alive and uncaught.

We listened as the army enveloped us, the fetid stench of the monsters surrounding us like a wall. Maria and I moved with the creatures, passing through the last of the forest and out into a wide glen. There we stopped. All around us, the creatures dragged wagons or set up tents. The camp swelled, running on either side of us in such a direction that I could not see the end of it.

For the time being, we were stuck.

"What do we do now?" Maria whispered as we walked through the rows of monsters. My shadow continued to cloak us from sight, but I wouldn't be able to stay like this much longer. Not without the risk of losing myself, like Rook.

"See if we can find a way through," I replied.

Up ahead, the Familiars were detaching horses from their wagons. It was almost bizarre to see these feral, mindless monsters doing anything as mundane as taking off a harness or brushing down a horse. The Familiars had formed a circle of wagons. We might be safe and hidden from view in the center, and I hurried us toward it.

We passed actual people, not merely the transformed Familiars. These men and women wandered freely through the camp, their clothes patched, their faces dirty. In fact, they appeared quite fanatical. We dodged about them as they began a kind of capering dance in a circle. Joining hands, they chanted to the sky. The women wore their hair long, while the men had collars of bone with iron bells attached to their necks. One of them, a tall, gangly fellow with a shaved head and startling handprints of blood decorating his chest and throat, barked at his group in an unknown tongue. The people knelt at his feet, arms raised to the heavens as they shouted praise in that ancient and terrifying language. I caught the names of the Ancients, and one in particular, R'hlem, was shouted over and over again.

So my father had people worshipping him now. That was bound to please him.

I realized that if Maria and I copied them, we might have a better chance of blending in. I undid my simple chignon, letting my brown hair fall about my face. I shook it up for good measure, then smeared mud across my cheeks.

"Have you gone mad?" Maria asked.

"It'd be so much easier to bear all of this if I had." I helped her dirty her face—her hair didn't need the help. Letting the shadow cloak fall away, we moved together toward the wagons. If a Familiar glanced at us, we praised R'hlem, calling his name over and over with our hands to the sky. This appeared to satisfy every monster we met.

I was better at faking the wild prayers than Maria. Then again, deception didn't come as naturally to her as it did to me.

"See if we can't find a supply wagon," I whispered. Even with Maria's foraging skills, it was clear that we were going to starve if we couldn't find a full meal.

We approached a circle of wagons, searching for one laden with sacks of grain. Unfortunately, these wagons looked like the type meant to contain wild animals in a traveling circus. Metal cages displayed clusters of moaning, dirty people.

We'd happened upon their prisoners.

Maria and I slipped inside the circle, finding our way to the center. Cages were on every side of us, but we were hidden from any Familiar that might pass by. I peered into one cage after another; the people inside looked wasted and gray. One woman lay on her side, shivering beneath a blanket. The sight was heartrending. I brushed close to the bars of one cage . . . and felt a hand grab my arm.

"Stay back!" Maria cried. The man released me, and I noted his bright black eyes, his dark skin and graying beard. . . .

Dear God. Mickelmas.

His bottom lip was swollen and his right eye nearly closed from a recent beating. He held a finger to his lips for silence and waved us nearer.

"Of all the places in this whole blasted world, of course I'd run into the pair of you in a death camp." He said it with a tinge of pride. "You never were one for staying home and doing needlework, pigeon. Though you'd probably live longer if you did. Besides, needlework pays a good wage, and I could use a new handkerchief. . . ."

He was talking feverish nonsense. He cupped a hand around his mouth.

"My companion isn't well," he said in a theatrical whisper. I looked inside the cage, taking in the wretched fellow huddled in a corner. His dirty features appeared familiar.

Recognition burst in my mind. The life had drained from his once-lively brown eyes, but I knew him to be Master Agrippa.

I looked at his hands. The stump of the right one—he'd chopped it off to keep me from being taken to God knows where along with him—had been wrapped in linen strips. Someone had cruelly jammed twigs into the stump, the mockery of a replacement hand. Agrippa lay with his head back against the bars, his mouth open.

"Surprised, I take it," Mickelmas said, grunting as he came closer to the cage. "He's rather a boring conversationalist. Hasn't spoken a word these last two weeks. I rather think R'hlem hoped we'd turn on one another. Wasn't he disappointed?"

Agrippa grumbled, blinking as though awaking from a dream.

"Sir? Do you know me?" I gripped the bars, but Agrippa's eyes remained glazed. Mickelmas helped prop the man up.

"He's been dead to the world since his fever." Mickelmas shook his head. "Get a handful of nonsense once in a while, but that's all."

Maria moved closer, touching the bars. She cocked an eyebrow as she studied Agrippa. "Your old Master," she said, her voice lifeless. She'd seen Agrippa's portrait several months earlier. She now knew he was her father.

"Yes," I said. Then, "Are you all right, Maria?"

She looked hard at the man in the cage. I expected tears, or curses. Perhaps I thought she'd spit upon him. Instead, she shoved away and went to the other side of the circle. She crouched down, arms wrapped about her knees. I could only guess at her thoughts.

"What've you been up to since last we met?" Mickelmas sounded like we were old friends having a chat in a tearoom. He leaned against the bars, one arm dangling languidly. "Making stirring speeches on the nature of friendship? Found another boy to moon over? Didn't you have six different fellows going at one point?"

"Are you quite done?"

"Never, so I'd suggest you broach a new topic."

"Very well. Sorrow-Fell's been taken by R'hlem. What do you say to that?"

"Ouch. Does that suffice?"

"There's more, and worse. I found a stone circle there—"

"Let me guess. The one used by Wild Mordecai and Ralph Strangeways to pull those beasts in and out of the other world?" he drawled. My gut tightened.

"You knew?" I inspected the cage, trying to figure a way to break it open without drawing too much attention. "Did you tell R'hlem after he captured you?"

"Why, my dear little apprentice, you truly think I would give such an important piece of information to our enemy?" He placed a hand over his heart in mock outrage.

"Are you saying you didn't?"

"No, I *did*. Of course I did. Told him whatever he asked. I didn't relish the thought of walking around without a face, you know. Most uncomfortable." Fire washed over my body, and it took all my willpower to dash it out. Mickelmas reclined against the bundle of straw on the floor, a finger over his lips. "We don't want the whole cavalry descending on you, my little bonfire. You'd make a nice trophy."

"You told R'hlem about the circle, you miserable—"

"Don't go flinging nasty words about, girl." Mickelmas crossed his arms. "I told R'hlem that I knew the circle existed, but I didn't know it resided in Sorrow-Fell. Wonderful bit of irony, that. The Blackwoods were searching for an answer that was right there, practically in their own house."

"But R'hlem knows what the circle does? How to use it?"

"He captured me at the most opportune moment." Mickelmas said this to the air, not really to me. He held out his dark hands as if setting the scene. "As if he knew when I'd have the information. R'hlem snatched me just after I'd made the most wonderful progress."

After London had fallen, Mickelmas had told me he planned to search the country for the way to rid ourselves of the Ancients once and for all. "You went looking for the answer, and you found it?"

"Spent some time reading magical texts at Oxford. The Ancients didn't bother with burning books, which was so bloody helpful. Oxford houses the greatest selection of Wild Mordecai's teachings, which is where I learned about that stone circle. Though of course I didn't know where the circle was—Wild

Mordecai wasn't a man for specifics. Poor, crazy bugger." He gave a mirthless laugh. "To think, it was with you all along. If only I'd managed to avoid capture. After I left Oxford, I was on my way to find you when—"

I couldn't quiet my anger. "Why haven't you escaped from here? You can fold yourself up into the slightest bit of space, so getting through these bars should be nothing at all."

"Ah. My fabulous magical ability," Mickelmas said with a mocking flourish of his hand. "These cages are charmed, I'm afraid. Those trapped within find their magical talents utterly bound. R'hlem employs his old magician tricks with such fabulous cunning."

"You should have let R'hlem kill you," I snapped.

"You're very cavalier with other people's lives, you cheeky thing." Drawing himself to his feet, he looked down on me. "Also, you seem to think I told R'hlem everything I know. Once he had the basic answer, he thought I'd merely serve as an object for his torturous rage. He never asked for anything more." Mickelmas smirked and pulled at his beard. "That was always William's weakness. He'd no love for detail."

"You've other information?" I asked. Maria came over and squeezed my arm so tightly I told her to stop.

" 'Lady in the wood.' " The words had barely left her mouth when I heard the warm, poisonously honeyed laugh of Willoughby.

"Let go my arm, or I'll set you on fire," I warned.

"Not very kind, are you?" she purred, and sauntered past me to the cage. Agrippa continued to stare at the ceiling. Mickelmas, though, watched the girl with a wary expression.

"I have the uncanny feeling we've met before," he said, squatting to peer into Maria's face. "Got that sensation the first time I met this girl. Tell me. What presence has taken root in this poor child's mind?"

"Howard, you ought to recognize me." Willoughby ran a tongue along her teeth. "After all, you're the one who left me in the meeting place." Mickelmas looked horrified.

"Mary. Frankly, I never thought I'd meet you again in this life," he said.

She spit, hitting him right in the face. He calmly wiped the spittle away.

"Thanks to you, I'd barely any life to cling to," she barked. I hushed her. If any of the monsters or fanatics caught us here now, it would go badly.

"I had to leave. The Order would have found me." Mickelmas frowned. "I tried to warn you, for God's sake. Besides, what fugitive in their right mind waits in one place for more than seven hours?"

Now they sounded like a pair of old school chums who'd fallen out. I hushed Willoughby again when she grunted at him.

"Don't quiet me, traitor's girl. I'll have the hounds and beasts upon you," she snarled.

"Then may I remind you, they'll only take me hostage, being the traitor's girl and all," I snapped. I wasn't sure how my father would handle seeing me again, but I doubted he'd kill me. "You, on the other hand, will be torn limb from limb."

"R'hlem wouldn't," she said proudly.

"Would you gamble your life on his consistency and compassion?" I asked. To her credit, she didn't reply. "Now. How do I get you out of here?" I whispered to Mickelmas.

"It might be difficult. Though there is one person you could try."

A scream sounded in the air above us. Cursing, I dragged Maria, or rather, Willoughby, beneath the wagon to hide with me. I winced as the great flap of wings overhead kicked up snow. From my hiding place, I could see that the fanatics were dragging a line of ten men and two women toward the wagon circle. The people's hands and feet were chained. Fanatics dipped their fingers into wooden bowls and painted the captives' foreheads with blood. One of the Familiars, a flayed warrior of R'hlem, signaled overhead.

On-Tez the Vulture Woman descended from the air, her great claws raking the snow as she settled. The Vulture stretched her wings to their full span, the stench of rot and bones emanating from her. She watched the line of prisoners over her hooked nose. Gnashing her sharp black teeth, she hopped back and forth in a manner entirely too birdlike.

"You have a choice," the Familiar said to the prisoners now on their knees. "Give yourselves to the bloody king's army, or die."

The first man shook his head. "Never. Kill me if you will."

The Familiar did not ask again. He merely unsheathed a sword of ridged, twisting bone and sliced the man's throat where he knelt. The wide-eyed fellow collapsed into the dirt, bucking as his life bled away.

The Familiar did the same to the next man, until the third, with tears in his eyes, nodded. "I'll serve the bloody king."

"Wise decision." The Familiar unshackled the man and shoved him forward. On-Tez waddled toward him, clacking her teeth with fiendish excitement. The man screamed as she pinned him to the ground with one of her clawed feet. On-Tez leaned over the man and breathed into his face. Black sparkling mist wafted over him. As the man inhaled it, the flesh on his face bubbled. I bit down on my fist to avoid screaming. His hair dissolved, and when he stood, his nose sharpened like a beak; black feathers sprouted on the crown of his head and along his arms. The new Familiar followed his master, while one of the women clawed at her face in terror. From the way she screamed the man's name, I got the feeling they were married.

So this was how R'hlem expanded his army, why I'd come across so many ghostly villages in Cornwall or Kent. Why hadn't I aimed just a little bit higher when I'd stabbed him in his chest? Why had I shown the slightest hint of mercy?

To turn someone into a servant of something so evil was . . . was . . .

Master

The thought flicked through my mind for one second and then vanished.

"What is it?" Willoughby asked as I began to cough. It was as if I'd forgotten how to speak. The world around me seemed to dissolve into darkness, except that I wasn't calling the shadows to me. I felt flame spark in my hand but couldn't see it. God in heaven, was I going blind? How? Why?

Master

There it was again, that word. God, it made me *hungry,* that word, an ache in the pit of my stomach. The images of everything ahead of me threaded with fire. The dark itself was light.

"Henrietta." Maria had returned to herself and shook my shoulder. I was going to rip her bloody throat out if she bothered me, if she took me away from . . .

Him.

He strode toward the last four prisoners in line. The skinned Familiar bowed to him as he made his way, shadows undulating over his skin like folds of drapery.

Rook. Korozoth. The Shadow and Fog.

My *master.*

17

AS ROOK INSPECTED THE REMAINING CAPTIVES, I fought against the animal cry welling up inside me. Dimly, I recalled the day the shadowy Familiars had discovered us on the hillside near Brimthorn, the same day Agrippa discovered my magical abilities. Rook had tried sheltering me from the attacking Familiars, but his eyes had gone pure black, and he'd screamed like a demon.

Briefly, he'd been their slave.

No. I would not give in to that mania. I would not go to him, worship him. Though I wanted to. Lord, how I wanted to.

"You've dealt with the others?" Rook asked the Familiar, kicking the three bodies now lying at his feet.

"Yes, lord. I'm about to see to these," the Familiar replied, holding his bone sword before him in a sign of respect. Blood dripped from the edge of the blade. Rook dismissed the skinless creature.

"My own followers have been severely depleted, and I require new recruits. Leave these to me." His voice was deeper than I'd ever known it in life. That voice was not Rook's. It did not have his Yorkshire accent, and the words . . . they were not words he would use.

"Indeed, lord." The servant bowed and left. Rook stood before the prisoners, flexing his clawed hands.

His hair was still flaxen, bright against the darkness. His eyes were pure black, and the bones of his face longer and sharper. Fangs hooked over his soft lower lip. His shirt was open at the front, revealing a chest still riddled with red and circular scars. His hands, now tipped with claws, cupped one woman's chin. He brought his face close to hers as she regarded him with swollen eyes.

A bolt of fury tore through me. He shouldn't touch her, and he shouldn't touch anyone else, not anyone, not

MASTER

Biting my lip, I buried my face in my arm. Every breath was like fire. Control returned slowly. I wouldn't watch Rook slice these people's throats, or transform them. I couldn't think of the boy I'd loved ruining the souls of innocent people.

"Look," Maria whispered.

Growling, I glanced over to find Rook . . . slicing the people's chains.

The women and four remaining men got to their feet. The woman who'd seen her husband transform began to sob anew. Rook stepped away from them and glanced over his shoulder. It was a nervous gesture.

A human gesture.

"Go now. When you reach the edge of the camp, run. Don't look back." He waited while the prisoners stared in astonishment. Flashing his fangs, he snarled, "Leave, or I'll kill you all myself." They needed no further encouragement and hurried away.

"He let them go," Maria murmured.

Human. Rook looked human, or at least, more human than he had before. He acted human. Alone, he knelt on the ground. I wanted to touch him. I wanted to kneel at his feet, to wrap my arms around his legs. He was so beautiful, so perfect, so wonderful, so . . .

MASTER

There was nothing left for me, nothing but the darkness and the promise of a place by his side. I wanted to call out for him. Someone caught at me, perhaps Maria, probably Maria, and I struck her. I barely felt her face beneath my hand, it was so unimportant, and then I was crawling over the earth. My skirts, my corset got in my way, and I wished I could shed them. They were like a serpent's dead skin that I could shuck off and crawl, glide, slither toward my master, my master.

The blinding pain in my shoulder became white-hot and then cool. It was as if my entire body had been dipped in a fresh spring.

He looked on me with astonishment as I clawed at his feet. Rook's eyes held recognition.

He watched me with horror.

Inside my head, a small voice screamed to be let out, tiny

fists beating against the walls of my skull. The voice wanted this to stop. But how could I stop it?

There were people all around me now, creatures of every shade and variety of Familiar. Surrounding me was a nightmarish assortment of fangs and slitted nostrils, of yellow eyes and melted flesh. They wanted to make me one of them.

No.

I squeezed my eyes shut. Feeling returned to me, a tingling that became a hot wave of pain as my shoulder ached. But I was myself, surrounded by monsters.

And then all the beasts broke apart as someone came stalking through the crowd. She was a woman, a very tall woman, with black skirts that swept briskly over the ground.

I would have known that way of walking anywhere.

"Korozoth. You've summoned my niece," Aunt Agnes said, looking me over with an appraising eye. "Her father will be pleased."

Her face was long, her skin as olive as my own. Her brown hair was parted severely down the middle, now threaded with gray that had not existed before. Severe lines framed her unsmiling mouth.

Aunt Agnes, the woman who had abandoned me at Brimthorn, who had called me a horrid child, now stood before me with the air of superiority. She wore a black gown, as always, but the fabric was fine. The lace at the sleeves and neckline was ornate and expensive. Being the sister of the bloody king had indeed done wonders for her.

Screaming, I tried to strike her, but my hands remained clumsy. She nodded to Rook.

"I'll take her, Korozoth. I'm certain her father will desire a special audience."

She looked at me with no pity. She would deliver me to R'hlem herself, on a platter. The darkness that had clouded my mind was dissipating, and horror—nay, terror—rushed to take its place. I wanted to cry out for Maria or Mickelmas but didn't dare draw attention to them. Instead, I caught Rook's eye. He placed a hand on my shoulder. His touch was gentle.

"She won't harm you. Go," he said, his voice thick. A twinge of delight went through me, to have been given an order by my master.

I shut the door on that thought and allowed my wretched aunt to lead me away.

I forced myself not to look behind for the others.

If I was to meet my father again, I didn't want to worry about anything other than being in his presence.

MY AUNT LED ME ACROSS THE camp and into the hills themselves. A tunnel led into the earth, and we entered a snaking corridor lit on either side by torches. The air was close in here. How long had it taken to dig all of these tunnels?

Eventually we entered a high-ceilinged cavern, with a lantern over our heads and a table and chairs waiting in the center. Aunt Agnes deposited me in a chair without a word. What should I have done when she bade me sit? Should I have refused and shouted at her? No, because even after all of this time I was that five-year-old child, watching with wide eyes as her carriage rolled out of the Brimthorn gate and out of my life.

"Wait here." She exited down an echoing corridor. I took the opportunity to study my new prison and noted that it was laid out to be rather fashionable. A rug decorated the ground, and the ceiling dripped onto the surface of a polished wood table. The drips made sense, considering we were in a cave. In point of fact, *cave* was a rather small word for where I was.

So R'hlem had formed his permanent base in the heart of a great set of rolling hills. No wonder finding him had been so difficult all these years.

This was a set of rather homey chambers, all things being equal. In one room, I glimpsed a brass four-poster bed, with lush pillows and a quilted blanket. Truly, this was made for comfort.

Well, apart from the dripping, and the earthen walls on every side of me.

How was I to escape? How was I to free Mickelmas and find Maria?

I put these thoughts aside as my aunt reentered, my father behind her.

I gripped the arms of my chair and glanced down at my hands. My engagement band shone in the dim light.

All these months later, and the shock of seeing R'hlem had not worn off. My father was tall enough that he had to bend slightly to make his way through the entrance. He strode to the table, placing his hands on the back of a velvet-lined chair.

He had fully recovered from the wound I'd given him months ago. He still dressed in fine clothes, tan breeches tailored to his legs. I wondered if he'd kidnapped some poor seamstress and forced her to do his bidding. Already, blotches of blood had sprouted all over his trousers, like garish dabs of paint. Pulling out a chair, he sat beside me.

"My prodigal daughter returns," he said. My aunt remained standing. She kept her black-gloved hands folded before her.

"What are you doing back in Scotland? I'd have thought you'd remain at Sorrow-Fell now," I said, with more confidence than I felt.

"Are you disappointed? Or is this artless fishing a ploy to discover whether your friends are still alive? Lord Blackwood in particular." He spread a linen napkin over his lap. It seemed we were about to dine. My stomach rippled at the thought.

"My friends? Are they all right? What have you done to them?"

R'hlem grinned. "Your Lord Blackwood is notoriously difficult to keep in one's grasp. Unlike his father, he turned tail and fled with his remaining sorcerers upon my arrival." My father licked his fleshless lips, a distressing sight. "I'll give Charles this: he was no coward. His son didn't even inherit that admirable quality."

"He's wiser than his father," I said, more hotly than I'd anticipated. R'hlem did not smile.

"You are engaged to him." He didn't make it a question.

"Why do you say that?" All the hair on my arms stood on end.

"The sorcerers I captured were happy to tell me anything I wished to know about you. Besides, there's the ring you wear. I saw it on Charles's wife, the few times we met." He nodded at my hand, where the silver and pearl rested. My cheeks burning, I hid it beneath the table. "After everything you knew about our families, you still would have married that treacherous bastard. You have no shame."

There was no love in his eye when he studied me. Well. I had been the one to stab him in the heart, after all.

"George is not his father. Am I such a stunning reflection of you?" I snapped. Aunt Agnes shifted slightly, lowering her head. She'd seated herself in a corner and was sewing dutifully, mending some garment.

"Sadly, no. You're not even a shadow." His eye trained upon my shoulder. Had that been a bad joke? "I've grown accustomed to your callousness toward me. But after what the Blackwood family did to your mother, your defection to them is a sin you'll never wash away." He spoke every word with such clear precision that it was obvious he was masking deep anger.

"My mother?" He had mentioned this once before, the last time we'd spoken on the astral plane. I'd assumed it was a dramatic flourish of his. "What happened to her?"

This appeared to mollify him. "You never told her, Agnes?" His voice was dangerously soft.

"I haven't seen her since she was a child. Howard wouldn't tell her anything like that." Agnes never looked up from her needlework.

What the bloody hell was everyone talking about?

"You still believe your mother died in childbirth, don't you?" R'hlem's tone was no longer harsh.

Perhaps I truly didn't want to know, but I couldn't stop myself.

"You told me it was a broken heart," I said to my aunt.

"Oh, it was more than that. Much more." R'hlem threw his napkin to the table. Fingerprints of blood stood out on the white linen. "Your mother was murdered by the sorcerers' Order."

Now this felt like madness. Above all else I was tired of being lied to, manipulated, given one piece of information only for it to be contradicted by another.

"Is this another trick?" My heart beat faster.

"Do you believe I would have spent a decade ripping this country apart for my own petty grievances?" He now sounded stunned, as though he finally realized exactly how little I thought of him. "I wouldn't do it without the greatest possible reason."

"What did they do to her?" I whispered.

He curled his fleshless lip. "No. No, I won't give you what you want. Perhaps another day, when the idea has had enough time to fester." He glanced at two fanatic serving girls as they entered with trays of dinner. Despite my fear and confusion, I was starving. They placed some mutton before me, and it took all my control not to tear into it. R'hlem didn't touch his meal, and Aunt Agnes didn't sit with us. In fact, she did not eat. I sat up straight and cut my meat. R'hlem laughed at that.

"Still trying to be a lady." But he said it with seeming fondness. The girls left, and I used that small opening he'd provided.

"What are you planning to do with Sorrow-Fell?"

R'hlem chuckled. "You know perfectly well. Playing the idiot doesn't suit you." He took a slice of potato and popped it in his mouth. Watching his muscles strain as he chewed nearly made me lose my appetite. "The Kindly Emperor will come, and he will bring with him all the horror that this dying world can stomach. That, and more."

"Please don't do this." It was all I could think to say. "Your hatred of the sorcerers is valid. The more I learn about them from you, the more I see that." Perhaps if I flattered him, I could change his mind. "Your cause is . . . nobler than I'd thought. But if you open that portal, you'll destroy everything you've worked to build. That's not how a leader behaves."

"A leader. Is that how you see me?" he asked. My stomach cramped to hear that pitying tone.

"They call you the bloody king."

"Once, I had no mind to be a king. All I wanted was the overthrow of the Order. That was it. That was all of it." He pulled apart a section of meat, scowling as he did so. "When the girl queen took her throne, I felt that I could mold her to my way of thinking. I might even have let her keep her kingdom. All she had to do was denounce the sorcerers and raise the interests of magicians." He looked at me, his one eye filled with rage and regret. "Until I knew you lived. That changed everything. But through your mindless devotion to the sorcerers, you proved how deep and cancerous the Order's hold has become. There is no extricating this country or its people from sorcery's grip. The best way to save it now is to destroy it."

"That's my fault. Punish me, but leave England alone." Once, my pleas and wide eyes might have excited his compassion. Once, before I stabbed him in the heart.

R'hlem threw down his napkin, got up, and beckoned me. Aunt Agnes continued to sew as I followed after him down an earthen corridor lit by torches in wall sconces. Soon we arrived at another chamber. Inside, I discovered what appeared to be a comfortable bedroom.

A large brass bed had been placed near the back of the room. "I would have stationed it in the center, but a ceiling drip warped the blanket," R'hlem said conversationally.

Indeed, the bed had a down quilt of fresh pink. A vanity with a washbasin and a mirror sat to the other side of the cavern. Near the entrance, a dressmaker's dummy sported a beautiful lavender gown, with pairs of dainty ribboned shoes lined around it. A doll's house painted a fresh pink and white had been set on a table near the foot of the bed. I felt numb as I touched the toy windows, the miniature doorways.

"I'm too old for dolls."

"Of course." He moved across the room, regarding me from every angle. At my feet, I discovered a collection of six or seven parasols. Some were pale green or pink satin. Bemused, I selected one . . . and found my fingers sticky with blood. Gore had spattered these parasols. I dropped it quickly, biting back a scream and fast wiping the blood from my hand.

"I've heard that young ladies like parasols," R'hlem said. "Once the Kindly Emperor comes, I will protect you from his wrath. Then, when this country is barren and free once more, we can rebuild it as we choose." He smiled. "You could have the entire city of London as your own. Think of that. The new queen."

I kept my eyes to the floor and said nothing. I needed time and space to think, which I would only have when he left me alone.

R'hlem did not approach me further. "Rest. We'll talk in the morning."

He left, his footsteps quiet on the floor. I found myself alone, beneath a hollow hill teeming with monsters. Maria was somewhere outside, weak in Willoughby's influence. I had to find her, leaving me with one great problem.

How was I to escape?

18

"WAKE UP," A FAMILIAR VOICE SAID. I WAS STILL dressed, and lying on top of my bed. Blinking, I discovered Aunt Agnes standing over me, a tray in her hands. It was remarkable how her unsmiling expression hadn't changed since my childhood. She placed the tray on my lap as I sat up. "You must eat."

Was that all she'd say to me? Twelve years of silence, and now a simple "You must eat"? I forced a bite of toast. I wasn't hungry, but I would do anything to get her to leave. Still she remained, glaring down at me.

After I'd learned that Aunt Agnes had taken me to Yorkshire at Mickelmas's request, I'd changed my opinion of her somewhat. It had softened my memory of her saying that I was unlovable. She'd been trying to prevent any contact between us.

But then she'd gone to my father's side. It made little sense.

"How did you come to be here?" I sipped the tea and hated that it was excellent.

"Upon his . . . arrival . . . your father allowed me to live in my cottage in Devon." I remembered Devon and the cottage.

The memory pained me now. "I stayed there until recently, when he requested that I join him here."

"Why?" I asked.

She didn't blink. "Because he discovered you were still alive."

She said it with no anger or blame, but I flinched.

"At least he's treated you well," I muttered. She was wearing fine clothes and moving about my father's camps with absolute freedom.

"In a fashion," Agnes said, and removed her right glove.

She slid out a hand wrapped tightly in bleeding bandages. The tray slid off my lap and crashed to the floor, the porcelain shattering. I got up from the bed and backed away. She returned her glove with an ease that belied how terrible the agony must have been.

"He never allows it to heal. You are fortunate," she told me. "He might have stripped a piece of flesh from you as punishment. But even the great bloody king can't harm his own child."

I sat back on the bed, my stomach churning. Aunt Agnes walked over to my vanity, upon which she'd placed some clothes.

"Here. I made you a new petticoat myself; your old one is simply too filthy to be saved." Indeed, I was covered in mud and blood. She laid the garments on the bed. One was a simple black gown and one a linen petticoat. Something glinted at the edges of the petticoat.

She'd sewn letters into the hemline. No, not letters, rather . . . runes. Golden runes, much like I'd once seen on the edges of Mickelmas's multicolored coat. Hadn't he told me that my aunt had sewn that marvelous garment? Agnes's eyes were steel, as was her voice.

"Put it on," she said, glancing over her shoulder. "We'll talk further." Then she left the room.

I fumbled out of my soiled clothes. There was some hot water and soap for a wash, so I scrubbed my skin until it was red and tingling. I skirted instinctively around the angry wounds at my shoulder, though I realized that they did not pain me as much. Not since I'd seen Rook, at any rate.

I put on my shift, corset, and petticoat, the golden runes gleaming in the dim cavern light. Once I'd pulled on my gown, I called Aunt Agnes back. She evaluated me carefully. I lifted the skirt to show her handiwork, which pleased her.

"Good. Now I want you to transport yourself back to Mickelmas's cage. Do you know how to do that?"

"All I have to do is think of a place and go."

"Careful. Runes carved into a floor are sturdier. With runes in your clothing, it will be like balancing on one foot atop a galloping horse. You must be absolutely certain you know where you're transporting, and it can't be too far away. If you aren't careful, you could end up trapped inside the very walls of this mountain," she said.

Well. Good thing I hadn't tried taking off at once.

"Picture the place in your mind. Find at least three things— unrelated to people—that define that particular space. Then wish yourself there." Aunt Agnes nodded. "While wearing this, you must be careful with how you think. Daydreaming could trigger the runes."

Wonderful. So they were fantastically dangerous. But what mattered now was freeing Mickelmas and finding Maria.

"Can you open the cage door?" I asked her.

"Yes." My aunt tugged on a ring of keys hung about her waist. "Now, let's waste no time." She hooked arms with me, coming along for the ride. Well, this was further encouragement not to foul anything up.

Three things. I remembered the cruel shape of the cages. There had been a patch of hard, dry earth beneath Mickelmas's cage. And I couldn't be positive, but I recalled a great towering pine tree thirty feet or so away.

There was no time to dally. I thought of these things, then wished myself to them.

It felt as though my body were hurtling off a cliff while also remaining still. Agnes had been right; it felt terrifying. Unlike the floor porter runes, this skirt gave the sensation of tipping end over end.

In the half space between one breath and the other, we arrived. The sunlight was shocking after time in the hill. Mickelmas sprang to his feet.

"I'd begun to think you had joined your lovely brother's side," he said to Agnes, sounding relieved. She took her ring of keys and began to fit one into the cage's lock.

"Where's Maria?" I looked about but caught no trace of her. My stomach contracted in fear. God, could they have taken her? Had Willoughby assumed control?

"Here," said a voice from beneath the cage. She crawled out from under the wagon, dirt streaked on her face. Her red curls were flattened with mud. "Had to hide when the guards came for an inspection."

Agnes got the cage open, and Mickelmas leaped to the ground. Together, he and I helped Agrippa out as well, though he came at a slower pace. His body felt fragile as glass. I remembered the man who had played games of chess with me, who had wept with pride when I mastered my magic. This shell could not be him. Agrippa turned his eyes skyward and uttered some nonsense syllables.

"Be careful, sir," I whispered.

Maria did not attempt to help. She avoided my eyes, purposefully staring at the ground. I could read the fierce set of her jaw and knew she was angry. Maybe not at me, but at the situation.

Of course, this was the man who had murdered her mother. None of it was easy. Agrippa slumped forward, and Mickelmas grunted as he helped carry the weight.

"He might be more trouble to bring than he's worth," Mickelmas muttered, though he kept Agrippa walking. "I assume you've a porter circle of your own now, chickling."

I lifted my skirt to show him the edge of the petticoat.

Mickelmas sighed, probably in fond remembrance of his own colorful coat.

"If only I'd remembered the porter runes. It would have saved us a great deal of time in captivity," he said.

"I warned you to memorize them." Agnes shook her head. As one, we gathered at the edge of the wagon circle. The area beyond teemed with Familiars, so I closed my eyes and summoned the shadows.

I hated how natural it felt to call them, and how quickly they now answered. Thus protected by the darkness, our group continued toward the forest. Once the trees hid us, I could remove the shadows.

"Are you sure we can't leave now? Everyone could grab hold of my dress," I whispered, but Aunt Agnes shook her head.

"I don't know that we can go together on the strength of one petticoat. Anyone left behind could suffer an unusually cruel fate."

In that case, we would wait to get to the trees.

I moved first into the forest. Mickelmas and a sluggish Agrippa followed, then Maria and my aunt. All together at last, I lifted my skirt to show off the gleaming runes. "We should write them into the snow. That would be powerful enough, wouldn't it?" I asked Agnes. To my relief, she nodded. I stood there while everyone crouched down to read my runes and worked together to write them into the ground. "Where should I send us?" I whispered to my aunt.

"It's dangerous to ask for a place you haven't seen. But the places you have seen—"

"Are more dangerous than any other," I agreed. Sorrow-Fell and London were both overwhelmed by R'hlem's forces. With a pang of horror, I realized that Brimthorn was still a mere ten miles from Sorrow-Fell. I should have begged Blackwood to evacuate the children. I should have . . .

"What about deeper into Scotland?" Maria asked. "There might be covens still roaming the highlands, especially now. R'hlem's eye's fixed on the south of the border, and the sorcerers are no longer a threat. The witches'll be growing bold."

And we would need an army to return and take Sorrow-Fell. "All right. Tell me about a place in the highlands. One that you specifically know." Maria pondered it.

"Whatever we do, we must do it soon. Dear Cornelius is making it difficult to hang on," Mickelmas grunted, trying to prop Agrippa up against a tree.

There was a pulse in my mind, as gentle as a fleeting thought. But the word was laced with poison.

Master

I dropped my skirt and turned about, searching the shadows. I looked at the camp beyond the trees, my pulse racing.

"You know, if you're not going to write the runes, the least you could do is be still," Mickelmas grumbled.

"What is it?" Maria asked.

Master

My eyes widened. "No," I whispered.

Shadows surged toward us. The others backed away in fear, but I did not move. It was no use.

"Give us your fire," Mickelmas snapped. Then, with a cry, Maria was yanked away from the group. My stomach fell as Rook materialized out of the darkness, his clawed white hands at Maria's throat. He bared his fangs.

"We must talk, Nettie," he said.

19

AS ROOK TIGHTENED HIS GRIP ON MARIA, I HELD UP my hand in warning. Flame sparked on my fingers, the threads of blackness still woven through my fire. Rook smirked to see it.

My head whirled, trying to make sense of everything. I'd seen him release those prisoners, yes, but now he was threatening Maria. If he tried to take her away, I would kill them both. Even if firing on him meant harming her, I'd do it. She'd do the same for me, after all.

My gut went cold as I realized that, not so long ago, I'd had the same thoughts about Rook, when he'd landed in the clutches of the shadow Familiars at Brimthorn. Perhaps if I'd opened fire that day, I'd have saved us all pain. . . .

Dimly, I realized that I was having an easier time resisting the urge to call him master and fall at his feet. Even if the desire was still there, it didn't rule me. Had I become stronger?

Looking at Rook, his fingers tipped with claws and his mouth sharp with fangs, my heart twisted.

I failed you. The words were on my lips, but I couldn't speak them.

"We must talk," he repeated, and the words slithered over

my skin. The strength I'd had in resisting his pull weakened. I started to fall at his feet. *No.* I was no one's servant.

"Talk of the people you've murdered and mutilated?" But of course, I'd made it possible for him to do all that. I hadn't alerted the Order to his condition, even when I should have. I'd dragged Maria into the entire mess, which had led to Sorrow-Fell's destruction. In every way, I could see my mistakes as falling dominoes, one striking the other to form an image of chaos.

"Do you hear how I speak, Nettie? I'm human again. Or at least," he admitted, easing his grip on Maria, "more human than before."

It was true. The fact he could speak was itself a miracle.

"How?" I asked as Mickelmas and my aunt edged closer to me.

"I believe it is our connection. Once I'd . . . marked you." He looked down at the ground as he said it. That was a human gesture, rich with embarrassment. It was a gesture Rook would have made.

"Perhaps." I drew one step closer to him. "I saw you in the visions. Stephen."

His mouth relaxed into a smile. "Yes. I saw my family again. My brothers had been lost to me for so long." Pain seized his features, though he let Maria go. She backed away to join Mickelmas and Agnes. "And look at how *you're* speaking, Nettie. I'm forcing myself not to control you." He winced, as if in concentration. "It's harder than I would have thought. My very nature screams out to dominate you."

"But you won't," I whispered, warm with relief.

He shook his head. "Not if I can help it."

Maria and the others were looking between us. They'd be safer if we had this conversation in private. I reached out to put my hands on Rook, and pictured the cavern, and my room within it. The bed, the dollhouse, the bloody collection of parasols. I didn't relish the thought of a trip back, but it was the only nearby place that I knew absolutely. That feeling of suspension and plummeting washed over me at once, and then we were alone together, holding on to each other in the cavern. The air was chill on my skin, and the place smelled of stagnant water. But we were away from the others . . . should something happen, they would not be harmed. Nor would Rook.

"Privacy is a fine idea," Rook mused as I released him.

"Help me save you." Now that I'd seen and spoken to him again, I couldn't abandon him. Rook lowered his head.

"I cannot stay in this place any longer. The Skinless Man drives me to despair." He looked at me with what seemed like hope. "I will follow you from a distance, if I may. A fair distance, so I don't overpower you, but enough that I may help you. And," he added in a softer voice, "so that you may free me when the time comes."

Yes. Yes, I'd find a way to release him from this curse. Rook took my hand in his. His claws traced across the thin skin of my wrist, but he was Rook again.

"Then follow me," I said. "Let me go back to the others,

and we'll be off." I was on the verge of picturing that spot in the woods again when Rook held up his hand.

"There's something you need first," he whispered. "You must trust me."

Trust. Even though it was Rook, I still hesitated.

Rook touched my hand, and for a heartbeat the world around us was pitch black and somehow also brilliant with light. Memories crowded about me. Memories, I realized, of our life together. The time we'd found our own private hiding space out in the heather. When I'd nursed him through one of his fevers, bringing him hot broth and begging the cook to keep the fire lit in his corner. The memories bubbled up and then evaporated.

When I'd been inside Korozoth, all those months ago, I had seen visions much like these.

Korozoth and Rook were not mere creatures of darkness. They were creatures of memory and time, of the darkest recesses of the human mind and soul.

Rook had shown me our past to remind me that I could trust him.

I released his hand, and the memories ceased. Putting a finger to his lips, Rook slipped away to the dark corner of the room. "I'll return soon," he said, and vanished into shadow.

I waited by the dollhouse, wanting nothing so much as to shove the thing to the ground and watch it break. Seconds later, Rook materialized holding a small figure in his arms. He set the being down on the ground to face me.

I didn't recognize him at first without the ears, but I soon realized the little hobgoblin in front of me could be no one else.

"Fenswick!" I swept my friend into my arms without hesitation. Back in the faerie realm, Fenswick had attacked a bog troll in order to save our lives. I was certain he'd been killed, but here he was, although dressed in filthy roughspun rather than his customary well-tailored suit. But he'd his four little arms, his bat-turned nose . . .

And he was missing his ears. They had been beautiful, as large and full as a wild hare's. Now two stumps were all that remained. Someone had hacked them from his head. He reached one of his four hands up to touch an ear—a gesture he'd been fond of—but flinched when he realized its absence.

"Punishment, you see," he told me in that high-pitched voice I thought I'd never hear again.

"Show her what you have," Rook whispered. Then, to me, "He wouldn't give it to anyone but you."

Fenswick rummaged in a pocket of his shirt, pulled out something small, and laid it in my hands. It was the bone whistle I'd taken from Ralph Strangewayes's house in Cornwall. A few mere inches of hollowed-out bone with some crude holes drilled along the length, this was the whistle that had allowed me to subdue Callax, the Child Eater, if only for a moment.

"How did you get this?" I breathed. It was still tied upon a string, and I placed it around my neck. I tucked the whistle down the collar of my gown for safekeeping.

"You left it behind in the Fae tunnels. I felt I should secret it away before someone less savory picked it up," Fenswick replied. He shuffled his small feet.

"You must come with us," I said at once. We would need a doctor, and besides, I couldn't bear the thought of leaving him behind in this hellish place.

"I don't believe the Order would welcome me after what I did." It was true: he'd conspired in Queen Mab's elimination of our forces on those cursed Faerie roads. "And I don't believe you would want me along, considering what I did to our young friend." His black eyes darted to Rook. Fenswick's poison had helped lead to Rook's transformation.

"You shouldn't blame yourself." Rook was gentle. "I was past saving."

No. Never past saving.

"You're coming with me," I said, holding out my hand for Fenswick. "Now. We need to move quickly."

"Are you certain you can make it?" Rook asked.

"I can try."

"Then—"

"What a delectable surprise," a woman said, her voice bright with false cheer. Another creature shuffled into my bedchamber. "My little hobgoblin, sniffing out such *nasty* company."

The woman before me was short and utterly bald, her face shriveled as an old tomato. She'd pointed ears, which twitched as she beheld me, and her entire body was deformed with scarring. But the voice guided me to her identity.

Queen Mab.

20

HAD FENSWICK BETRAYED ME? OR ROOK? I WAS ready to mentally vault myself out of the chamber, alone. But Rook and Fenswick stepped in front of me protectively.

"You will not have her," Rook growled at Mab. The faerie queen hissed with laughter.

"Oh, I think I might. This little beast has been aching for my special attentions," Mab cooed, sounding as sickeningly sweet as ever. Rook's shadows flared at his feet. He was growing angry, and I began to fall into that mass of darkness, giving myself utterly to it.

"Don't," I choked out, steadying myself with a hand against the wall. Mercifully, the tightening invisible line between us slackened; Rook had understood.

With the speed of a spider descending upon a fly, Mab snatched up Fenswick. She pulled one of his arms behind his back, twisting it at a cruel angle. The little hobgoblin keened as she ripped into his flesh.

"You marked me like *this* for all eternity." She chattered her teeth at me. "I can't hurt you. Your illustrious father would have me flayed from head to toe, and *that* would be even harder to live with. But allow this," she spit, wrenching Fenswick's arm to a more unnatural angle, "to serve as payment."

Porridge was in my hand immediately.

"If you don't put him down, I'll kill you." My voice was clear and cold. Unheeding, Mab bit into Fenswick's neck and spit blood at my feet.

"Mmm, perhaps I *will* break a few of your less essential bones. I can always tell your father I'd no choice," she snarled. But the shadows rose up behind her—Rook had moved. She dropped Fenswick as I warded a blade.

"Stop now," I ordered. In reply, Mab punted Fenswick across the floor while he howled. I heard the snap of bone and had no time to react as she threw herself at me.

Rook's shadows blinded her. She flailed in the darkness, and with one swift move I sliced the faerie queen's head from her shoulders. The body collapsed to the floor in front of me, and the head rolled away into the corner. *A head for a head,* I thought, recalling Whitechurch. Mab had killed him in a similar fashion, and in a similar place. Hands trembling, I slid Porridge back in its sheath and picked up Fenswick, who mewled like a pained cat.

"She broke my arm." Fenswick clutched at the front of my gown.

"Rook. I'm leaving," I whispered. He touched my shoulder. I thought again of the spot in the forest where we'd left our friends, and we were spit back into the dim light of the glen.

We were not alone.

A ring of at least ten shadowy figures surrounded my group. The Familiars hissed at them, then turned to face us. Maria and Agnes stood in front of the men, hands out in case the Familiars charged.

"Come now, my dears. Let these people pass," Rook said, his voice soothing as he outstretched his hands to the creatures. The shadow Familiars turned to him like trained pets to a beloved owner. Shuddering, I glanced over at my friends. They'd carved most of the porter runes but hadn't finished yet. Maria waved me closer as I inched toward them.

"Go on ahead." Rook's voice was calm, and he kept his eyes on his "children." "I'll follow you."

"Not sure about the following bit, but I *love* the part where he told us to leave." Mickelmas was sweating under Agrippa's weight. "Let's finish the blasted circle."

My body grew cold as drums began to sound all across the camp. They started deep in the heart of the hill, a steady tattoo. Someone had likely discovered Mab's body and my disappearance. Our time had run out.

Mickelmas let out a blistering string of curses as I rushed inside the unfinished circle.

Everything happened at once.

The shadow creatures rushed me; even Rook could not hold them back. There was no time to finish writing. We would have to make do with my petticoat.

"Grab on!" I shouted, and my friends snatched my skirts.

Mickelmas, Agrippa, and Maria touched me, and I kept Fenswick clutched to my chest. We were all nearly together. Aunt Agnes, who'd been working on the circle, ran to meet us.

A shrieking Familiar grabbed my aunt and dragged her down. Agnes fought but was not strong enough. She looked up at me, showing the acceptance in her eyes. More Familiars swarmed toward us through the trees, bearing clubs and daggers. There was no time.

I couldn't save us all.

"Henrietta!" My aunt shouted something I could not understand, though I caught the word *pocket*. My thoughts shattered as the darkness swept us away. Above the chaos, I could have sworn I heard my father's outraged cry, until it, too, was gone.

Where were we going? I forced myself not to think of Sorrow-Fell, or London, or Brimthorn. All I could think of was the wilderness of Scotland, a half-fanciful idea of a place I did not know. I could feel Maria and the others hanging off me, as though suspended above a bottomless cavern. I feared that if I did not choose a place soon, they might let go and be lost.

I thought of Magnus and his charge against the barrier with his army.

I thought of safety.

We sprawled in a mass of arms and legs. I lay facedown in the snow, the sting returning me to myself. It was night, and so cold. Mickelmas swiped at his coat. Cursing, he shoved his hands into the snow, yelling nonsense words. At first I thought he'd gone mad, but then the snow began to roll up, as though by a giant, unseen hand. Crude walls were erected, a glittering roof smoothed on top. There was a doorway. In a matter of seconds, a house had formed out of snow and ice.

I was dumb at the sight of it.

"Don't thank me, of course." Getting to his feet, Mickelmas slung Agrippa's arm over his shoulder and hobbled the pair of them indoors. "Gratitude's far too much to expect around here."

Fenswick trotted after him, alongside Maria. She called at me to come inside.

But I kept picturing my aunt's face as I left her to whatever twisted fate my father could devise. I had seen the flayed hand he'd gifted her. What other, more horrible pain could he imagine?

I began to shake, and not with the cold.

"If you don't mind, we could use some fire," Mickelmas called, poking his head out the door. "Though the house might melt."

I went to help them, my heart numb.

A FEW HOURS LATER, I KEPT watch while the others slept. I fashioned tongues of flame to hover above each of my friends as they rested, providing warmth that would not melt the walls. Agrippa lay bundled in his cloak; Mickelmas snored close beside him; Fenswick curled into a ball between them. I'd swaddled him round the middle with a strip from my dress, to help with his ribs. Maria was the only one to stay awake with me. She stared at the unmoving shape of her father, her left hand opening and closing.

"'Lady in the wood'?" I ventured.

"She's not taken over," Maria replied.

I pulled my cloak tighter about me and slid my hand down my skirt. Something crinkled, and I reached into the pocket and took out a letter. Of course. My aunt had said something about a pocket. I recognized her formal handwriting, opened it, and read.

Dearest Nettie,

I am not in the habit of presenting my emotions plainly. Forgive me. I am writing this to tell you the truth.

First, you must know our family history in order to understand the full scope of your father's war. It is true that Charles Blackwood sent your father to that netherworld—Mickelmas informed me of it, though we kept the secret from your mother. She was newly pregnant, and we feared what knowledge of your father's fate would do to her. We should have been honest. I see that now.

Soon after you were born, your mother went to London to petition the Order to look into the matter of William's supposed drowning. Your mother had a courageous spirit, one of the things I admired—nay, loved—about her. Unfortunately, Lord Blackwood did not appreciate her meddling. So after she dared to name him as responsible, he had her committed to Lockskill Prison.

You may be unaware, but under English law all magical matters—and citizens—are subject to the royal sorcerers' Order. Though she'd been born without magic, as a magician's wife your mother was counted as one of us. I believe Lord Blackwood cited female hysteria as her problem—easily believed, especially by those know-nothing London physicians. Thus he kept her in Lockskill, which has far more in common with a medieval inquisitor's palace than an actual prison.

I'm sorry, but I must tell you all. I brought you to see her once before she died in that hell. You were an infant, too young to know her or what fate had befallen her. I shall never forget. Helena's hair had been shorn close to the scalp. There were horrid scars all along her head—it was clear they'd operated in some awful way. She could no longer speak, or move. Lord Blackwood ensured your mother's silence.

William might have shown mercy to a country that treated magicians as inferior. He might have forgiven them for driving our brother Henry, an active voice in the struggle to free our race, to despair and suicide. William might even have forgiven the Order for not caring what became of him all the long years he suffered in that hellish world.

But he could never forgive what they did to your mother.

The second thing that I wished to tell you is this: Howard came to our house in Devon straightaway after he'd let William back into the world. He told me that William would come soon to find his wife and child and that I should hide you. I took you to Brimthorn. I paid your tuition in full so that there would never be letters by which to trace you. I told you I did not love you, so that you would never write.

I have always loved you, Nettie. Those few years spent raising you were the happiest of my life. I fear that, now you've finally come home to your father, I will be gone too soon to tell you. Because of course I will help you escape.

Should I not survive, I wanted you to have the truth. Forgive the lies I told. Forgive your father, if you can, and forgive me.

With love always,

Aunt Agnes

I could barely see the last lines through my tears.

"Is it bad?" Maria whispered. I handed her the letter, put on my cloak, and left the house. The cold bit, but I barely felt it. It was as though I'd placed a shell around myself from a young age to protect me from the world. Now that I had the truth, my protective layer was ripped away. I stood raw and naked against the world.

A glowing light appeared on the edge of the wood. Numbly, I watched a slow procession of creatures as they walked out of the forest. They were both human and decidedly not, with elongated limbs and hair that streamed stardust.

At the head of the procession came a woman, her bare feet treading across the snow as if she did not feel the cold. Her footprints left behind shimmering outlines in the frost, and luminescent buds of flowers sprang up, only to wither and die without this godlike woman's touch.

When I blinked, the tall woman appeared before me.

The world around me, and the dark of the night, disappeared as a beam of searing white light enveloped me. I fell to my knees, as if in worship of this goddess before me. Her neck was too long and slender, the hollow at her throat deep enough to hold an egg. Her face was oval, startling in its perfect symmetry. Her eyes were a shattering blue, and her long, terrifying fingers reached out to touch my face. She stopped inches from contact, and I knew that her touch would burn me through like a moth's wing in a candle.

She was light, in its most base and terrifying form. Her movements were imitations of human movements. She was not one of us and did not mind that at all. Mab at least had aped human behavior.

I knew this was Titania, queen of the light Fae, and she was a thousandfold more beautiful and terrifying than her sister had been.

"My sister met her end this evening." Titania's lilting voice cut my soul. "The blood spoke. The blood told me of the hand that had spilled it. Your hand, mortal child."

I could not panic. How could I, confronted by so much beauty? "Queen Mab attacked me."

"She had a hobgoblin in her clutches, child, not you."

"Anyone who attacks my friend attacks me."

Titania did not move. I got the sense that she would be comfortable not moving for centuries on end. It made me want to scream.

"Custom demands that I seek your head in exchange for hers." Titania blinked, just once. That action took nearly a minute to complete. "What have you to say in response?"

"I am—"

"Do not lie and call yourself the sorcerers' prophecy. The true chosen one sits over in that house of ice and snow." The faerie queen touched a hand to her moonlit gown. "You are, however, the Blackwood bride. And you have made the correct sacrifice."

My body chilled at her words. Lady Blackwood had ranted about the curse and a Blackwood bride, but I'd been certain it was part of her own warped imagination. "I beg your pardon?"

"Hundreds of years ago, I laid a curse upon the Blackwood line, to be broken once they delivered my proper sacrifice." A small, terrifying smile graced her mouth. "I have always despised my sister."

I blinked. "Do you mean that this Blackwood curse, as you call it, is gone because I killed Queen Mab?"

"You humans have a terrible habit of needing the same questions answered several times. Yes."

"You might have told the Blackwoods this," I said through gritted teeth.

"But what amusement would I find in that? Far better to watch you stumble through your brief, mortal lives in confusion."

I wondered if I could burn Queen Titania as I had Mab. Then I decided not to push my luck.

"What boon would you ask of me?" The queen smiled. "I shall give a gift of your choosing."

Despite the fact that I was almost numb with rage, I kept my head. "Bring your armies to the sorcerers' cause in this war."

She answered immediately. "No. That is dull. Ask another."

"But that's what I want!" It was like debating the wind on why it should not blow. "Besides, R'hlem wants to destroy England from roots to crown. He'll destroy you with it," I said. The faerie blinked again.

"Death is change. I rather envy my sister, as she now undertakes a greater voyage than I imagine I ever shall." Titania put a hand to my throat, and the touch was awful and splendid beyond anything I'd known. I could hear myself screaming, as though I were standing right beside my own body.

Then she released me, and I felt emptied like a cup.

"Perhaps, mortal child, I shall give you something else you

might want." She traced the tip of a finger through the air, and a glowing image appeared. It looked rather like an *M*, only with curling lines at the bottom and three slashes through the middle.

The image disappeared, but I could see it behind my eyelids as I blinked. Indeed, I would never forget it; it felt branded into the fissures of my mind.

"What is it?" I croaked.

"As I've said. It is more fun to watch you stumble for the answer."

This woman was a beautiful nightmare.

"Thank you," I said slowly. "But I still request Your Majesty bring her armies to our side."

"Take my gift, or I will claim your head," the queen answered.

"Well, in that case, you've given me the loveliest warped *M* I have ever seen in my life," I snapped.

"You're welcome." She smiled now, showing her teeth. They were the white of an exploding star. "I thank you for your service, Henrietta Howel."

The queen vanished. I found I was kneeling in the snow, and the cold rushed in over me like a wave. Warm. I needed to get warm.

Thankfully, fire was my specialty.

Heat washed over my skin, and my body relaxed.

Then, dotted along the distant horizon, I caught the glimmer of torches and extinguished myself. Bloody hell, we'd been spotted. Had my fire alerted them? The persistent beat of drums met my ears and grew louder. They were coming closer.

Maria raced up beside me.

"R'hlem?" she whispered. Damn, we had to get out of here.

Joining hands, we hurried for the house. Mickelmas stood in the doorway, blinking sleepily at the world and the attackers. His untied hair formed a brilliant white and gray cloud. Before he could speak, a group of riders stampeded out of the surrounding tree line, heading for us.

We'd been surrounded.

"Grab on to me!" I cried, but one of the riders blocked our path, trapping Mickelmas inside the house. Bother it; at least I could jump about now with my petticoat. I thought about the house, about safety, and vanished . . . only to pop up in the thick of the riders.

Why couldn't I master these blasted runes?

"Whoa!" a man cried. His horse pawed the air. I let up a burst of fire, and the animal cantered away. Her rider cursed as he got his mount back under control. I readied myself for another fiery blow.

"Henrietta?" The man wheeled his horse around.

Magnus.

21

I SAT ON A THIN ARMY COT WITH A BLANKET DRAPED over my shoulders. The mug of broth in my hands tickled my throat as I drank. My luck could not have been better, and I vaguely wondered if Titania had aided us in some way. Perhaps she had known where to find our allies. We had made our house of snow a mere half mile from Magnus and his army. The torches in the distance had indeed been R'hlem's men, but with the army's help we'd got away before the Ancients could catch up.

I'd been placed in this tent and told to wait for the captain to see me. Well, having drained my mug, I'd had quite enough of waiting. I wanted to know where the others were; we'd been separated upon arrival. I left my tent and walked into the yard. We'd arrived in darkness, so I hadn't seen much of anything. Dawn was breaking, and before me I found a virtual city.

Rows of clustered tents spread on every side of me. The white smoke of multiple cooking fires rose into the air. People carted food or carried bundles. Children's gleeful voices rang out. I watched them as they raced through the snow, laughing.

I hadn't heard anything as wonderful as children's laughter in so long.

I set myself to walk up the hill to the largest tent—the captain's, I'd been told. I expected to be stopped at the entrance but found it unguarded. Perhaps they were changing their post. I slipped inside.

They'd laid rugs over the ground for added comfort. Near the center of the tent, a large table supported a map. Several red and blue painted figures were scattered about the sketch of England. A neatly made cot resided to the far left of the tent.

Magnus's voice halted me in my tracks. He stood beside the table with his back to me.

"How wise," he said. At first I thought he was speaking to me, until I heard a gurgling coo. He spoke to a bundle in his arms. "Yes, yes, very sound advice. Put the pants on the asparagus, and toy trains for everyone. Mmm, you're an excellent leader." The baby giggled as he swept her up over his head. "Wait a minute! Pants on the asparagus? Who put you in command? You're a baby! You're insane!"

I laughed. Magnus brought Georgiana down to rest against his shoulder and faced me with a smile.

"Howel. Do you ever tire of being exactly on time?"

There were a dozen ways I could have answered him, but all possible words fled my mind. Magnus was . . . different. Not to say that he'd grown taller, that his voice or features had shifted. All I could do was compare him to, well, himself.

In London, I'd known him as a smiling, foolhardy boy.

After his mother's death, he'd grown even more reckless than before. At Sorrow-Fell, he'd been broken, and looking to break things in return.

Now his mass of auburn curls had been cut, military style. His square jaw was clean-shaven. He'd found a tailored uniform that properly fit the great width of his shoulders. His brass buttons gleamed from attentive polish, same as his boots. He had always been tall, but I had never before noticed how straight he could stand. Magnus's gray eyes warmed as he beheld me, but there was hard-bitten knowledge in his gaze as well. Those were *his* maps on the table, the wooden figures placed by his strategic hand. He held Georgiana with the air of an expert. This was the captain's tent, and he inhabited it fully.

I understood what about him had stolen my breath away: Magnus the boy had been charming and handsome; Magnus the man was a force all his own.

"Howel? Are you well?" He appeared concerned by my silence.

Clearing my throat, I managed to make a reply. "I'm afraid war makes punctuality a necessity."

"There. I knew you'd put me in my place with a single word." He gave a sly wink, and my cheeks flamed. But I felt a rising excitement as well, as though someone were leading me into a dance that I loved.

"Don't sell yourself short. It took more than one word." I calculated. "Seven, I believe."

Magnus laughed, which made Georgiana squirm. He held the baby out to me.

"This one believes toffees will solve all our problems. What I get for making an infant my chief of staff."

I gave Georgiana my finger, which she took in a tight-fisted grip.

"I'd ask to see the magical petticoat, but I believe that's improper conduct." Magnus placed Georgiana in a makeshift cradle near his desk. "Awful good luck to come upon you when we did."

"Yes." I wasn't certain it was luck, though. It seemed too great a coincidence that I'd thought of Magnus and arrived mere minutes from his door.

I decided not to tell him this. It mightn't be, well, proper.

"Did you see them out there?" Magnus strode to the entrance and opened the tent flap, gesturing out at the crowds. "They're flocking to us now. We found some more coming from the north and took them in. You know sorcery's great defect?" He closed the flap. "We've believed ordinary men and women to be useless. At best, they're merely in the way, at worst they're cattle for us to rescue." He shook his head. "They're the foundation of our society. We sorcerers are not engineers, or farmers, or tradesmen. We've sat back upon our magic for so long, we've ignored the more modern aspects of the age."

I nodded, understanding what he meant. While the sorcerers had hid behind a ward, or the magicians had congregated to commiserate and lick their wounds, the common people had been working to survive. They'd fed and shod and clothed one another, fixed wagons, created weapons. What had we to offer in return? Wind and rain. The warping of a ray of sunshine. A tongue of fire to warm the night.

Sorcery was not the future of England. Perhaps it never had been.

"Now tell me," Magnus said, guiding us toward the table. "Where is Blackwood? What's happened at Sorrow-Fell?"

My heart sank at his blissful ignorance.

"R'hlem's taken it," I murmured. By the time I'd finished relaying the story, I was on the verge of throwing up. The memory of R'hlem striding up that path was too much.

"Why didn't Blackwood escape with you?" Magnus seemed genuinely puzzled. Face burning, I looked at my hands.

"We were separated. Besides, we had a falling-out."

"Why? I thought he was poetically, madly in love." Magnus leaned back in his chair, frowning. "Something terrible must have happened."

Unfortunately, I could not think of how to lie. So I told the truth.

"He blamed me for bringing Maria to Sorrow-Fell." At that, Magnus's eyes narrowed. "We had a rather . . . painful conversation."

"Why are you fidgeting like this?" Magnus laid his hand on top of mine. "Howel, what happened?"

I readied myself, but when the words came they were a stutter. "He c-called me a slut." I whispered the last word, but Magnus understood. He rose to his feet.

"Why would he say that to you?"

"Please don't make me go through the bloody details."

I could see that Magnus understood my meaning. He went to study a map on the table, more as an excuse to look away from me than anything else. My face burned. Well, if he couldn't stand my presence any longer, then I shouldn't care for his good opinion.

"So we must assemble an army," I said. "We have to take Sorrow-Fell back before the equinox."

"Of course." He sounded distracted. I gritted my teeth.

"I assure you, I'm still capable of being looked at."

"What?" He turned, surprised. "Howel, I'm not angry at you. I want to *kill* Blackwood." Indeed, a muscle pulsed in the side of his neck as he spoke.

"Then I don't disgust you?"

"Disgust me?" He appeared horrified by the words. "I think I'm the last person on earth to judge you for something like that. This insipid idea that a woman's worth is based on something so . . . insignificant." I laughed because I feared I'd cry otherwise.

"May I see the queen?" I asked, changing the subject. There was more to do, and more plans to make. We needed to begin as soon as possible.

"Of course. She's anxious to meet with you. You know, she's

quite a bit stronger than I'd have imagined, given her upbringing. She can outride—" Magnus's voice and smile died. "Howel. Something's happening with the shadows."

Oh God. No.

From the corners of the tent, the darkness crept forward. I felt that tug again at the back of my mind, the whisper of the word *master*. Rook began to unfurl himself, one tendril at a time. He'd tracked me, as he'd said he would. I was so relieved to see him unharmed, but he was appearing in Magnus's tent . . .

And Magnus had promised that one of them would die.

"It's just my shadow abilities," I said, trying to stand in front of Rook. "Sometimes, I . . ." But I stopped, because I couldn't lie to Magnus. Not after everything that had happened. "I'm sorry," I amended, shielding Rook with my body. "We found him in the enemy's camp. He's changed, Magnus. He's not the same as the night when—"

Magnus whipped out his stave, his features tightening with hate.

"You." The word was venomous. He cut a blade with one thought. Rook finished forming, remaining crumpled on his knees.

"I beg for mercy," he whispered, gazing up at Magnus with mournful dark eyes.

"Denied." Magnus gave a fearsome cry and attacked.

22

ROOK DISSOLVED INTO SHADOW AS MAGNUS SWUNG his stave. Magnus pivoted expertly, snatching fire from the candles upon his desk and hurling them at Rook. The flame sprayed over Rook's protective black cloak. Georgiana sobbed in her cradle, throwing Magnus off balance for a brief moment.

Rook returned to his human form. Holding out his hands, he said, "I have no desire to fight."

Magnus responded with a burst of fire, flattening him on the ground.

"Stop!" I cried, placing myself between the two.

Magnus bared his teeth. The kind, understanding young man had vanished before my eyes. "How could you bring him here?"

"It wasn't his fault, Magnus."

"How do you figure that?" Magnus tried to step around me to get at Rook.

"My father was controlling him!" There.

Magnus froze. "Your father?" he asked, bewildered.

Rook lay there, his hands up to Magnus. Dried blood darkened the lines of his palms.

"Please," he whispered, but his voice focused Magnus on the task at hand. With a sweep of his stave, he shot more fire. The blow landed, and Rook hissed in pain. *My master, my master is hurt. The bastard has struck him. The fiend!* Darkness closed over my mind, and my instincts were animal.

Snarling, I pounced upon Magnus, who tossed me to the earth rather easily. In response, I set my flames on him. Magnus backed away with a curse. Rook placed himself before me and loosened his invisible hold on my mind. Blinking, I felt myself fall back under control.

"Please," Rook gasped. "I won't be able to keep her from fighting you."

"Because you've made her your slave!" Magnus roared. I placed my arms about Rook's neck. I felt the tension in his shoulders, the throbbing heat of a scar below my hand. Magnus looked the picture of righteous fury.

"If you want to take your revenge," Rook said gently, "I will not stop you."

Both Magnus and I stilled.

"In fact, you'd be doing me the greatest favor," Rook breathed, loosening my hands. He stayed on his knees before Magnus. "No mortal man should bear this burden. I hate what I am." His voice wavered. "After I changed at Lady Eliza's party, I had no control over my actions, but I saw everything. It was a living nightmare, what I did to your mother." He lowered his head. "You've more a right to kill me than anyone."

"You don't know what you're saying," I said, gripping his arm. Magnus advanced upon Rook.

"This is a trick." He'd summoned more flame, which he balanced on the tips of his fingers. Rook did not move.

"Please. If you wish to end me, do so now. Every moment, I feel my mind unraveling. R'hlem calls me. Even my connection with Nettie cannot change that."

Magnus stalked forward. "No. Fight back, you . . . you monster." But Rook dropped his chin to his chest.

"I won't."

Magnus stood over Rook with the fire burning in his hand. I was prepared to do battle, but Rook held up his clawed hand to stop me. My muscles tensed as I obeyed.

Magnus extinguished the fire. He strode over to the table, breathing heavily, and threw one of the chairs to the ground. The chair splintered, and Magnus stalked out of the tent.

"I am sorry." Rook laid his head briefly upon my knee. I smoothed his fine flaxen hair. There, now. We were safe and together, my master and I. Then, in a low voice, he said, "The one to kill me, Nettie, will have to be you."

I was so shocked that I stood. Rook gazed up at me. "What do you mean?"

"Exactly what I say. You're the one with the power to do it." His clawed hand touched mine. "You promised, Nettie. You promised to save me."

I was fully myself now, and amazed that he could suggest such a thing. "Rook, no. You're tired. You don't know what you're saying." I took his face in my hands. His cheeks were ice cold beneath my touch. "You need to hold on for just a little while longer. Mickelmas and I will find a way back. Don't worry." Kneeling down, I kissed his cold forehead.

Rook sighed and pushed me away. "I knew you would not listen."

"I'll listen to reason," I said, growing crosser by the minute. "No more talk of killing. Do you understand?"

"Very well." Rook sounded resigned as he stood. "Till later, then." Soundlessly, he disappeared into the shadow of the tent. As he vanished, I felt the final pressure on my mind dissipate. I was all right now.

Honestly, I couldn't believe what Rook had asked. It was madness to even consider.

Dazed, I followed Magnus outside. He remained in front of the tent with his hands plunged in the pockets of his coat.

"Thank you," I murmured. "I didn't think he'd, well, turn up like that."

"I know," he growled, closing his eyes. Then, "What did you mean about your father?"

There were a million subtle and intricate ways to begin, but the simplest answer came tumbling out. "R'hlem is my father." He gave me his full attention. "I know you may not believe—"

"No, I do. Strangely, it makes sense." His expression remained inscrutable, but he opened the tent flap once more and ushered me inside. We moved back to the table. I sat on a stool, and Magnus righted the splintered chair and sat across from me, wincing when the broken thing groaned. "Remind me not to break furniture in the future. Well, then. Go on." He gestured for me to continue.

"Would you like the full story?"

"That would be a fine place to start," he said, not unkindly. As I told him, he listened, only stopping to ask for clarity. There was no judgment and no disgust. He was curious, and above all, he was sympathetic.

"You never run out of surprises, Howel." Leaning back, he smiled. "What do you propose we do now?"

"The only way back to Sorrow-Fell is with an army. Witches and magicians will be the strongest magical resources we have now." Indeed, sorcerers were practically an extinct species. "Any news on possible covens?"

"There are supposed to be groups of wild women that roam the highlands." He helped me to my feet and placed my cloak around me. "Some of the men we've picked up have told of ladies who dance naked by moonlight and ride the wind on pine branches. I've had the forests scouted, but no one's returned with anything substantive. As for magicians, there's that Alice girl you used to save the queen." He smiled. "She's been a great help. Shifting is a marvelous talent, don't you think? We've used her to locate a few other magicians. One of them's a lady with a bottle for a leg. Most ingenious. As for getting more, I suppose we might ask Mickelmas. He's got his own tent farther into camp. Apparently, he's a bit of a troublemaker."

"How unusual," I said flatly. "Perhaps I should speak with him."

"That was my very thought."

It occurred to me as Magnus and I walked out of the tent (after calling for Georgiana's nurse, of course) that he hadn't negotiated who was to do what. He hadn't asked me to stand behind him, or stay silent. My involving myself with his plans didn't seem to bother Magnus in the slightest.

It was rather welcome, actually.

We walked through the camp. To my vast relief, I caught sight of Lilly as she went from tent to tent. She carried a tray laden with bandages, and when she saw me she threw the thing aside. We embraced, and her arms crushed the breath from my body. Lord, for such a little thing she was absurdly strong.

"Arthur told me you'd been found. I couldn't believe it." She squeezed tighter.

"I'm difficult to kill." Though if Lilly kept hugging me like this, she might manage it. When she let me go, she stooped to pick up the fallen bandages.

"Was about to go up to the tent and get you. That funny magician's looking for you," she told me.

"Indeed, it would appear the funny magician's now located you." Mickelmas swept out of his tent, unfurling himself like a velvet cloak taken out for the winter. He wore a dirty jacket with a spotted shirt underneath but fussed with the sleeves as though they were the most elegant attire. "I believe I've something you could use, my cheerful duck." He crooked a finger. "Follow me. We'll need space for this trick."

"More tricks," Magnus sighed, shaking his head. "So long as he doesn't turn anyone into a talking horse." He paused. "I mean, if he turned someone into a talking horse I'd laugh. Then I'd ride it around a bit. Then dress it in several hats. Then I'd get him to turn it back to a person."

"It worries me that you've put so much thought into this," I said.

We followed Mickelmas past the tent city and into the wilderness. My teeth chattered as a freezing wind sliced by. Mickelmas snapped his fingers.

"Bit cold, don't you find? If you could set a cozy fire, it might help."

Grumbling, I did as he asked, circling flame all about us.

"Much better. Now, time for a pinch of magic. I managed to keep this safe from old . . . well, from R'hlem," Mickelmas said, eyeing Magnus carefully. He was trying to be cautious, which I appreciated. Unfolding a paper he'd tucked into a tiny, tiny pocket of his jacket—I'd have asked how but remembered his remarkable powers for molding himself into the smallest of places—Mickelmas handed it to me. "Be a lamb and hold this open while I work."

It was a circle of runes, so complicated and intricate that my mind boggled the first moment I beheld it. It resembled a labyrinth of ink scratches and nonsense letters. There were squiggles, and wobbly arrows, spirals and dots. Magnus and I guided Mickelmas as he carved the runes into the snow. It was tricky. The spirals dipped into swirls, and jagged, crawling lines gave way to graceful arabesques. Finally, Mickelmas finished his writing, and we stood back to stare at the circle.

"Don't we need a solstice or an equinox to open a portal?" I asked. Mickelmas shook his head as he rolled his sleeves.

"For greater phenomena, such as tearing open the fabric of reality and letting monstrosities through, solstices and equinoxes are lovely. But for mere summonings, any old time will do. So long as you've got an unused spurt of blood lying about, that is. That's the stuff with which people are always reluctant to part, but you can't make pudding without opening a vein."

"Is that how it goes?" Magnus walked about the circle and whistled in admiration. "Sir, you're quite brilliant."

"Well, it was either be brilliant or work very hard. Brilliance takes less effort." Mickelmas ushered both of us to one side. "I should warn you, I've only the faintest idea of what's about to happen."

"Marvelously reassuring," I said.

"Shut up."

He wasn't going to answer the unspoken question. "What exactly are we summoning? And what do you want to happen?"

"I'm summoning a famous figure in magical history," he replied. "Hopefully, he'll have some useful information. As for what I'd like to have happen: If a terrifying creature lands in the circle, we're fine. If a terrifying creature lands outside the circle, we're dead."

Magnus and I took a step away from him.

Mickelmas picked a dagger from a pocket, then sliced his hand in one swift movement. He flung the droplets of dark blood to stain the snow, and waited.

The ground hissed. It was much like what had happened in the vision he'd shown me, of when he and Charles Blackwood and my father had ripped open that hole into another world. My stomach tightened in fear, and I grabbed Magnus's arm. He twined his fingers through mine, as the sky above the circle swirled like a whirlpool of water.

"No, it's going to crack open!" I cried, but stopped when the "spout" of the whirling air touched down in the snow. With a wet, popping sound, a creature appeared before us. The thing was the vibrant blue of a summer sky. Bright, shining wings much like a dragonfly's sprouted from its back. The mouth was human-shaped, but the eyes were bulbous and glittering as an insect's.

I realized that I had seen this creature's image hanging upon Ralph Strangewayes's walls. This was . . . what was the demon's name? Azrael, Azureus. Yes, Azureus: Latin for "blue." He had been Strangewayes's pet, famous enough to have his portrait painted by the great artist Holbein.

The thing opened a mouth full of needle teeth and spoke in a low, guttural tongue. It was impossible to decipher the words.

Azureus spoke again, this time in a dialect that sounded like a pocketful of jingling coins.

At last, he said, "Are you from the summer isle? Is this the land of the thin-cheeked queen?"

Perfect English.

"There is a queen, though not, I think, the one you recall," Mickelmas said to the being. "Thank you for answering my summons."

"A request one cannot refuse is not quite an answer," Azureus snapped, crawling up to the edge of the circle. The voice was disconcerting; it sounded rather like the thin space between two voices speaking in unison. "It is an imprisonment. You, magician—I smell the bastard Strangewayes's taint within your blood—are no better than he was."

Apparently Azureus had not cared for Strangewayes. I recalled that cage back in Cornwall with the mutilated metal bars, and Strangewayes's skeletal body sprawled across the floor. I wondered if Azureus had been the entity to finish the father of magicians off. His tail—for he did indeed have a lizard-like tail—whipped back and forth across the snow.

"What are these children doing here?" he asked.

Magnus and I were far off to the side. But then again, the creature had insect eyes. He could likely see in every direction at once.

"We're in a great deal of trouble," I told Azureus, approaching cautiously. Then I gave a small curtsy. "Sir."

"The females of your species are more polite than the males. Perhaps she might kindly wipe away the barrier's divide and release me."

Again, I imagined Strangewayes's skeleton. "No, I believe that wouldn't be comfortable," I said. The creature snickered, a buzz like a plague of locusts.

"Azureus, if you were to assist us, I'd be happy to tear this document." Strangewayes held up the paper with Azureus's summoning runes written upon it. The creature fluttered his wings; clearly, he was interested. "What say you?"

"I would not be trapped in a circle ever again?" Azureus muttered darkly.

"How long did Ralph Strangewayes hold you?" I asked.

"Many years. The bastard chained me." Azureus crawled back to the edge of the rune circle.

"Answer my questions, and you will be forever free. I give you my word," Mickelmas said. Azureus clawed at the snow, leaving deep furrows. Then he sat back on his haunches, his tail curled around his leg.

"Ask."

"Do you know of a man from our world who arrived in yours? A man called R'hlem?" Mickelmas asked. I shivered.

"Oh, I remember a man who fell into the realm of the Kindly One. At first, he bleated like a wounded animal. Send him home, he begged, even though he would be leaving behind the mountains of cloud, the boiling rivers, the great deserts that spanned to the edge of reason, the palaces of incredible size that could fit within a child's pocket. He would have left all that behind for some mewling woman. To the children beyond time, his sobs were insults. In fact, he was lucky to have met me. Having been transported to this cold, lifeless world for so long, I was the only one that understood his pitiful tongue."

"You knew R'hlem?" I whispered. Now I crouched next to the circle, despite Magnus's warnings. "How did he become what he is?"

"You mean, how did he lose his outer shell?" Azureus's nostrils, formed much like an ape's, sniffed at me. He was mere inches from my face. "You smell like him. You must be the child he kept weeping about."

Even after everything R'hlem had done, my heart broke to think of that.

"To hide from the Kindly Emperor, the man lived on the edge of the river lands. He could not drink the liquid within those rivers, as the water would melt the flesh off any living creature. I took pity on him. Yes, I, I who hated magicians with such a passion. I brought him to my cavern, the one with walls of glittering eyes. I taught him that his power as a magician, whatever little ability he possessed, came from my race.

"You magicians are descendants of my kind, the most potent realization of our brilliance in this colorless world you inhabit. However, all your so-called magic comes from the world beyond time. Witch, sorcerer, magician: you all belong to us. We are always with you, moving alongside you, the tissue and blood beneath the thin layer of skin." Azureus smiled at me.

"Your father learned the importance of unbuttoning that skin, child."

I fought to keep myself calm. "We found a stone circle in Sorrow-Fell. There were twelve stones with runes written upon them."

"Mmm. The first portal. The oldest, most powerful doorway of them all."

"We know that Ralph Strangewayes used it to send Ancients—er, to send your people home. We know he used one member of each magical race to do it. How do we make it work? Do you know?"

"Millennia ago, explorers from my own world entered yours. They taught your people magic and even mated with some of them. Their offspring are the creatures you call Fae." Azureus grinned, a dreadful sight. "Your people worshipped my people as gods; how times do change. The explorers could not stay, but in their misguided love for you common and insignificant creatures, they created that portal. It was meant to be a doorway that opened a mere crack. Only so much that it would allow the air of our world to touch yours. In this way, magic flooded the world. It enriched the people around you. Pull the circle down, and you would end magic in your realm forever."

A world without magic did not seem possible.

"R'hlem's going to abuse that circle to destroy this world." I leaned as close as I dared. "How can we stop him?"

"That portal could ruin this country, but it is also the only true means of saving it." Azureus rose up on his hind legs, which were bent rather like a dog's. "You will need one of every magical race to control the circle."

"Yes. How would we go about that?" Mickelmas sounded calm, but I detected tension in his voice.

Now Azureus smiled. "I might keep that little tidbit to myself."

"You damn, stupid—" Mickelmas stopped himself, and I tried once more, my heart pounding.

"Please, sir. So that we may release you more quickly."

"You speak as though it's my fault you're holding me," Azureus sneered, his tail swishing. "Because your female asks sweetly, I will comply. When the sun is at its height on the equinox, splash blood upon the runes to open the portal. With three of you standing by, one from each race, you will be able to control the opening. Summon my brethren to you, have them enter into the circle, and then send them home." Azureus picked at his needle teeth. "Does that satisfy your curiosity?"

"But how should we summon the Ancients to the circle in the first place?" Magnus crossed his arms.

"By the teeth of the Emperor himself, how should I know?"

"Sir," I said, and the creature's wings fluttered. "Thank you for the gift of this knowledge."

"True, I have given you much. I am far kinder than Strangewayes ever was, with his endless raids upon my world. He murdered us, stuffed and hung us upon his walls. The bastard. The fiend!"

"Is that why you helped my father?" I asked. "To prepare a weapon against this world?"

"No, sweet and stupid child. I wanted to torture your father," the creature replied with ease. "I stripped the skin from his bones to massage greater magic into his muscles. I hung him by his wrists and ankles in a crystal cave, filled with the preserved screams of the damned. His cries solidified into fat, glistening stalactites. He begged me to stop. No, I told him, I'm making you better. Stronger. You will see farther than others, infiltrate minds as gracefully as stepping through a door. You will be a king of the beasts. Keeping a flayed man alive is a difficult trick. You've never heard anyone weep so profoundly."

A white-hot flash of hatred went through me.

"Henrietta, no!" Mickelmas cried. Magnus grabbed me, but not before I'd fired at Azureus. The monster dodged the fireball.

"You're the reason for all of this!" I shouted.

"I'm the reason your father has the power he does, but I am not the reason he went to my world. Your Lord Blackwood, whom he told me about, is the reason. Your mother, and you, the reason R'hlem chose to traffic in such dangerous magic to begin with. Your kings and queens, the reason magicians are so downtrodden. Ralph Strangewayes, the reason your kind exist at all. The reason I hate you so. There are as many reasons for things as there are stars in your cold, lifeless sky. Move past reasons, if you want my advice, R'hlem's daughter. Only seek truth."

It occurred to me then that the bone whistle might play

the monster into submission. I took it with fumbling hands and blew, my fingers moving up and down the holes along its length. Azureus cocked his head to listen.

But as I played, he said, "My own magic has no effect upon me. Look, child." He turned around, and I noticed that bony spines protruded along his back, much like a porcupine's quills. I realized that one spine was missing, and stopped playing.

God, I'd been putting something of this creature's body into my mouth. I nearly spit into the snow.

"So you see, that magic will work upon most any other creature. That, and the soul sieve." He licked his sharp teeth. "The lantern. Do you have it?"

I did not, but Blackwood had. "Why?"

"The lantern was Strangewayes's greatest gift from my world. The light within it is a creature itself. Did you realize?" Azureus fluttered his wings, as if to punctuate the revelation.

"The *optiaethis*?" I asked.

"So. You know its name." That appeared to please the creature. "Strangewayes called it a 'soul-sucker.' An apt description, I think. The *optiaethis* grants its user enormous power. Open the cage, and it will beacon every single creature—or Ancient, as you call them—within one thousand miles. But that power comes at a terrible price, child. The *optiaethis* drains the very soul out of whosoever wields it. Take my advice: if you can accomplish your mission without that artifact, do so."

"You're very kind," I murmured, lost in thought. If Blackwood was still alive, I prayed he hadn't used the lantern.

"This is not the first time I sold out my own brethren to help a magician." The creature snarled. "Killing that bastard Strangewayes was the greatest thrill of my life. There. Is that all?"

"One last question, if I may. I'm curious. What exactly is the Kindly Emperor?" Mickelmas asked. Azureus fell silent.

"If you are fortunate, you will never witness his smile." Azureus looked to me; he'd given up talking to Mickelmas. "I have kept my bargain. I have given you answers. Will you keep your bargain, child? Or will you imprison me as Strangewayes did?"

"We might keep him about, just in case," Mickelmas muttered. Azureus's shoulders hunched, and I saw then that he had expected this. He had expected to be lied to. I would not affirm his low opinion of humanity.

"If we have nothing left to ask, we will release him," I said. With a sigh, Mickelmas nodded.

"That is kindness, R'hlem's daughter." Azureus clicked his teeth. "I know you are angry for what became of your father, but I gave him the power that he craved. I did not string him up in that cavern against his wishes. When I plucked out his human eyes to grant him an all-seeing one, it was at his request. He is not innocent."

None of us were, but that did not mean we should be tortured for it. I took the paper from Mickelmas. As Azureus watched, I set it alight in my hand.

"Never return to this place," I said.

"With pleasure," Azureus replied. Mickelmas stepped on a rune, and the creature vanished like snuffing out a candle flame. Magnus rested his hand on my shoulder.

"What's the next step?" he asked Mickelmas.

"We've three representatives, if Maria counts as a witch. However, our knowledge does no good without an army. You said there were rumors of a coven nearby. Find them, and bring them into the fold. In the meantime, I'll summon the magicians," Mickelmas said.

"How?" Magnus frowned.

"I've Alice on my side. If she doesn't mind flying halfway around the country, I can tell her where to go and who to look for." He walked down the hill, whistling as he went.

"You need to sit down," Magnus whispered, ushering me in the direction of the tents. "You're pale."

"I'm fine." I touched my cheek and discovered that I had been crying. Well, perhaps I was less fine than I thought.

Inside the captain's tent, other soldiers waited for Magnus. He sat me by the fire and quickly dispatched his orders. I barely heard what was said; my mind wandered as I gazed into the flame. When the men had gone, Magnus gave me a mug of tea and sat down. The tea warmed me, though at my core I still felt frozen.

"I can't imagine what's in your mind," he said.

"What I think doesn't matter." I forced myself back under control. "Only what I have to do."

"You're not alone, though. Remember that."

I looked into his eyes. He gave a playful wink, but there was nothing boastful about him. Not anymore.

"I've learned to enjoy poetry," I blurted out. Magnus looked puzzled. "When we first met, I said I didn't think it was useful."

"I remember. That was our first breakfast together, wasn't it?" He chuckled and stretched his hands to warm by the fire. "Seems like a lifetime ago."

"Yes." I didn't know what possessed me, but I kept going. "The war's shown me how wrong I was. About poetry, I mean. I see now how necessary it can be. Art is strange, really. It envelops you in lies, but it also confronts you with such vivid reality."

"See? I knew you'd realize how right I was." Magnus laughed. I recalled, with a smile, how he'd brought me *Henry V* when I was feeling low. We'd spent an afternoon going through the play together.

"'Fair Katharine and most fair, will you vouchsafe to teach a soldier terms such as will enter at a lady's ear and plead his love-suit to her gentle heart?'" I quoted that particular scene. To my surprise, Magnus appeared blankly amused.

"I didn't know you'd read Shakespeare's histories. What about his dramas? That's the true meat of his work."

"Don't you remember giving me that play?" He continued to look as though I'd lost my mind. "We sat together in Agrippa's parlor for a solid hour. You made fun of my terrible French accent."

"Well, sounds like something I'd do. Pity, I'm sure it's a memory I would have relished—"

His smile vanished. I remembered when we had been under the ground in Mab's Faerie kingdom. Magnus had paid the toll for access to the Faerie roads: one memory. One memory of what he most loved.

I could not think of what to say.

Magnus stood.

"I'm sure it was good fun," he murmured, and left without another word.

23

TIME WAS SLIPPING FURTHER AWAY, AND EVERY DAY that passed made me more and more worried for Rook and Blackwood, for the magicians and the witches we'd yet to find. I would start awake several hours before dawn and lie in the quiet of my bunk, listening to the wind as it moaned over the snowy fields. I would half wonder, half pray that the surge of shadow in a corner was Rook. But the throbbing pain in my shoulder never abated; it was not he.

When the sun rose, we had to be all business. We agreed that we would have to find some of these highland witch covens, which meant a journey deeper into the wilderness.

Maria, Magnus, and I formed this particular hunting party. I'd been surprised to find Magnus leading his horse up alongside us, tightening his saddlebags and checking provisions. It had seemed ridiculous that he, the captain of the whole bloody enterprise, should accompany us. But he wouldn't be deterred.

"I've left my best lieutenant in charge. Besides, can't allow you ladies to have all the glory," he'd said, giving me a casual wink. Our moment in the tent was forgotten, it seemed. Which was good, because I needed to devote all my energy to staying on my horse.

I had never ridden before, in any capacity. Though Rook had loved horses, neither he nor I had the first clue about riding them. At first, I'd no idea how to mount the poor creature. It had taken a helpful young man to instruct me, and now I perched in the saddle, feeling entirely too high off the ground. Even though I'd flown to tremendous heights before, this felt somehow more frightening. I clutched the horse's mane, praying the wild beast did not buck me off and rampage down the road, snorting embers and kicking up sparks with its steely hooves.

"They gave you Gumdrop," Magnus said fondly. "He's the sweetest gelding we have."

Gumdrop nuzzled Magnus for a sugar cube, like the terrifying monster he was.

"Good horsey," I whimpered as we plodded into the forest. I clung for dear life. Maria, who'd dressed in trousers for our expedition, sat her horse with the air of an expert. She raised a single eyebrow as she passed by. "You mustn't judge me," I hissed.

"Aye, but I must," she replied.

Always, as we passed deeper into the highlands, I waited to sense Rook's presence, fearing and hoping that he would appear.

Maria took the lead. She could read the details of the earth with almost preternatural ease. We would often pause so she could interpret how snow dusted a particular tree trunk, or the direction in which a broken branch had fallen. Even Magnus was impressed.

"If it'd been up to me, we'd have circled round the same tree five times, made camp, and then listened to my heroic war stories for two hours."

"Now, now. I'm sure you'd have gone on for more than two," I said.

"I do love how you support me, Howel."

Then, two days after leaving the camp, Maria held up a hand. "Listen," she said. We all came to a standstill. "Do you hear it?" she whispered. I strained my ears but detected nothing. There was no sound, not even the soft plop of snow as it sloughed off branches and onto the ground. Dismounting from her horse, Maria took an ax from its place by her side. It was not her old ax, the loss of which she still mourned, but it was something. As she crept forward, Magnus and I exchanged worried glances.

"What should we do?" Magnus murmured.

"Hush up!" she whispered.

Ahead of us, a flash of gray cut across the sunlit snow. Gumdrop stamped his hooves, which meant I gripped fistfuls of his mane to avoid being flung to the ground.

The trees began whispering, as if they moved of their own volition. Voices soared on the wind, snatches of words here and then gone again. Forms came and went, visible only from the corner of my eye. I tried to catch sight of the figures while I reined in Gumdrop. Maria and Magnus turned in circles, until something moved from behind the trees.

At least a dozen forms appeared, all of them swathed in gray. They were faceless and nondescript. Maria and Magnus drew closer—Magnus even took Gumdrop's bridle, which I appreciated.

Some of these gray figures held daggers, while others went empty-handed. They did not raise their weapons to fight us—that was one good thing. But the power of something ancient flowed through the trees and around us.

"Who are you?" Magnus pointed his stave at one of the figures. It removed its cowl and pulled the gray cloth mask from its face.

The figure was a young woman, about my age. She'd wild, curling black hair and blue eyes. She was nearly as tall as Magnus, and she held herself with a kind of ease that indicated she'd never worn a corset. She looked from one of us to the other, her face unreadable—that is, until her gaze latched on to Maria. Both girls gasped and took a step back.

"Fiona?" Maria whispered. She clapped her hands over her mouth.

"Maria!" the black-haired beauty cried. They raced into each other's arms. Fiona was half a head taller than Maria. Both crying, they hugged tightly.

Then they kissed one another, a kiss explosive in its passion. Ah. Clearly their closeness was more than friendship. Maria was not so alone in this world as she'd feared.

"Apparently they're, er, allies." Magnus raised a hand in greeting to the figures around us. "Well, hello."

"Keep your hands at your sides," one of the gray figures barked. It was a woman's voice that spoke, and she lifted up a crossbow, a feathered shaft already aimed at Magnus's heart. The black-haired girl, Fiona, released Maria.

"Stop! Gemma, stop it!" she cried, holding out her arms. But the overall fear from the figures around us remained palpable.

"Perhaps *allies* is too strong a word," Magnus amended.

Gumdrop blustered and stomped his hooves, while I prepared to unleash a small show of my firepower. All right. Nothing too drastic, simply a display of strength; the witches might listen then. Of course, I'd have to get off Gumdrop first, then—

Oh no. I pictured being away from the horse on the other side of the trees, and then that certain frisson went through my body, which meant my porter runes were—

Gumdrop screamed as we transported. The horse bucked beneath me, and I felt myself lose control. We reappeared in the middle of the witches, who jumped out of the way. Gumdrop kicked, and I went flying out of the saddle.

My head collided with the tree first. That was all I knew.

"Wake slowly, now," a female voice said. Groaning, I opened my eyes and found a blurry image hovering above me. My vision shook violently for a moment, but then she came into focus. Fiona again. "Lie still," she said. "The worst should be past."

I felt something cool touch my head. Water trickled down my temples. Closing my eyes, I grunted as Fiona made me sit up. "Shouldn't sleep yet. We must make certain that head wound isn't more serious."

"Where are the others?" Rubbing my eyes, I leaned forward and put my head to my knees. Something felt wrong—my waist felt too light. With horror, I realized that Porridge was not at my side. Panic flared over my skin as I clutched the space at my hip where the stave ought to have been.

"Calm now. Nothing's happened to your stave." Fiona knelt before me and squeezed my hands. "They want to make certain you won't hurt anyone. That's all."

My stave wasn't all that was missing. I realized why the cloth of my gown sat heavier on my legs. "You took my petticoat," I muttered. Fiona stirred a wooden cup and nodded. She wouldn't look at me.

"Aye. Elspeth wanted you all to stay right where you are."

It seemed that porter runes were more widely recognized than Mickelmas thought. Then again, my spectacular job of teleporting about on horseback had to have raised a few witches' eyebrows. Fiona handed over the cup. "Drink."

"What's in it?" I sniffed, but it smelled pleasing enough.

"Willow bark for the headache, cherry for sweetness. You'll like it," she promised.

All I could picture was Eliza drinking what Maria—rather, Willoughby—gave to her. I put the cup back down, while Fiona sighed. "I won't poison you, girl. I'd never harm a friend of Maria's."

That I could believe; their kiss had not been faked. "Can you take me to her?"

"Drink, and I'll take you." Fiona spoke with a mother's tone. At least, that was what I imagined a mother to sound like, someone nurturing yet stern. Taking a breath, I did as she said. Wonderful heat flooded me from head to toe, and the nauseous dizziness evaporated. Even my shoulder felt better. I handed the cup back with a sigh.

"You have no idea how good that feels."

"Aye, I do. That's why I made it." She shook her head. "You English are funny."

Not sorcerers. English. "May I see my friends now? And when will they return my stave?" Fiona settled a cloak around my shoulders. It was warmer and heavier than my own.

"I'll take you to the others, but I can't promise when they'll return your stave." She shivered as we stepped out of the tent and into the icy wind. "Our coven doesn't take kindly to rebels."

"I've lived with the sorcerers for almost a year; the last thing I would ever call them is rebellious."

"Beg pardon, that's the witch's name for your kind. I

know it's history, but the older women have strong feelings about it."

I'd no idea what she meant, but as we walked into the coven's camp I rather forgot what we were talking about. The place was incredible.

The witches had settled in a large glen, surrounded on all sides by dense forest. It was as secure a location as one could find these days. Within the glen, twenty or so tents had been pitched in a large circle. Each tent was round and squat, covered with gray tarpaulin and tanned animal skins. In the center of the circle stood a tent much larger than the others. White smoke billowed out of the top. Fiona clucked her tongue.

"Elspeth's probably called a meeting of her council. They'll be deciding what to do with the three of you." She didn't sound cheered by the thought.

Despite the cold, the glen was filled with activity. To the right of us, a man in a gray cloak was studying a horse's hooves. The beast blustered and nosed at the man for something to eat. He stroked the animal's nose.

"I didn't know you had men in your covens."

"Aye, and how should we create new witches? Plant a rag doll in the ground under the light of a full moon and whisper spells over it?" Fiona pulled up her hood. "Our men have magical ability, but never as strong as the womenfolk. It's hard to keep a young man in the coven—they don't want to be forever taking orders. Many of our boys have gone off to fight in the war."

"On England's side?" I asked. Apparently, that was a foolish question.

"Of course. What kind of monsters do you think we are?"

Perhaps I should craft a spell to remove my own mouth. That might help matters.

"Forgive me. I thought the witches might hate the Crown, after what . . . happened." That was a polite way of saying "when most of you were burned alive."

"This land's our home, same as yours. We witches are people of the land." Fiona paused. "At least, that's what I think."

There were more cloaked men and women working in the yard. I heard the cries of pigs and chickens, and glimpsed young gray-outfitted children carrying eggs or bundles of wood. One man worked at stretching out a fresh deer hide. In a smaller tent, I glimpsed a pair of women with bushels of herbs all about them. They were grinding something with a sharp bit of stone.

"Here we are." Fiona pushed me inside another empty tent. A fire crackled in the center of the room, warming us at once. I might have started my own fire on our walk across the camp but wanted to keep that power concealed for now. Who knew exactly what these women wanted from us?

"Where are the others?" I warmed my hands while Fiona stood guard by the tent flap. Honestly, I wasn't going to run.

"We'll wait here, until Elspeth says they may enter."

"Who exactly is Elspeth?" That name sounded strangely familiar.

"Queen of our coven." Fiona's strong voice grew lower. It sounded as though she was afraid. "It was a fool thing to bring her granddaughter within shouting distance. You could not have planned it worse if you'd tried."

"Her granddaughter?"

Fiona looked as if I were simple. "Maria, of course."

Then I remembered Maria mentioning a wicked grandmother who had blamed her for her mother's death and tossed her out of the coven. Of course we'd run into such a woman in the middle of the highlands.

"Is Maria all right?" My pulse quickened to think of her back in her grandmother's clutches.

"Aye. Though likely not for much longer." Fiona worried her hands. She was trying to remain calm, but I read the signs of fear.

I was about to ask how long she had known Maria when the tent flap opened and my friends were shoved inside. Magnus entered with ease, a smile on his face and his hands bound in front. Maria was right behind him, also bound. She was not smiling—that is, until she saw Fiona. Magnus came to sit beside me.

"Never thought I'd say this, but three women searched me and I did not enjoy it." He held his bound hands to the fire. "Have you any explosive demonstrations planned to get us out of here?"

"I'd like to keep a few surprises handy, just in case." I

averted my eyes as Fiona and Maria wandered to a corner of the tent, speaking softly to each other. They should have a little privacy. "Are the horses all right?"

"Last I saw, they were eating apples and enjoying a rub-down. Some little girls even decorated Gumdrop's mane with holly berries."

Horses were the worst kind of traitors.

"What did Elspeth say?" I asked the girls when they joined us by the fire. Maria shrugged.

"She wouldn't see me." I could not tell if she was hurt or relieved.

"Well, I'm finding the whole thing enormously educational," Magnus said. "Who knew all the uses a person could get from one deer?"

"Never stop talking, do you?" Fiona regarded Magnus with amusement.

"Good lord, please don't encourage him," I moaned.

Voices drew nearer to our tent. We all got to our feet as three older women entered the room. They wore their hair long, and every one of them had eyes sharp and cold as a hawk's.

"Let me see her." The one in the center moved toward us. She was taller than any woman I'd yet seen—she might have reached six feet. Despite the massive difference in height, I saw a clear resemblance to Maria at once—this woman had the same pointed chin, the same broad forehead. There were shocks of steel gray in her once-red hair, and deep lines bracketed the corners of her mouth. Her eyes, a frosty blue, scrutinized Maria.

"So. It's you," the woman said at last.

"Gran," Maria replied curtly.

Elspeth looked about as unfriendly as I'd pictured her.

"This just got a great deal more interesting," Magnus said easily. Elspeth regarded him with the same warmth she might show a fascinating insect.

"What are these sorcerers doing here?" Elspeth said *sorcerers* as if she meant *vermin*.

"There's a war going on, if you hadn't noticed," Magnus replied with a smile. I believed he would only stop smiling when he was dead; given our situation, that might be soon.

"Please excuse the captain, he's taken a few blows to the head." I kicked Magnus's ankle.

"I'm not the one who smashed into that tree," he pointed out. Oh, I was going to smash *someone* into a tree before too long.

"Enough." Elspeth's gaze never thawed. "I pay no heed to the war. *Some* young people in this coven believe I am mistaken in that." Fiona lowered her head. "There is no need to notice what does not concern me." The women behind her murmured in agreement.

"R'hlem has a new plan that concerns us all," I said. Elspeth didn't even look at me.

"You've brought your stick-wielding friends to die, girl."

She sneered at Maria. "With that inferior blood in your veins, it should be no surprise you'd take shelter with the worst scum in the world."

Apparently, sorcerers weren't the only ones obsessed with blood purity. Maria's cheeks flamed.

"You've no right to speak of my friends that way."

"Friends?" Elspeth cast an unimpressed eye over Magnus and me. "I see children with stunted, inferior minds. Senovarus's rebellion created a race of tyrannical imbeciles." There was that word, *rebellion,* again. I hated not knowing key bits of information. "In the morning, I might kill you all. Or I might send you back to your futile war. It will depend upon my mood." With that, Elspeth made to leave.

But Maria spoke. "I call for the right of coven making."

Every witch in the tent gasped, save Elspeth. She did not turn around.

"There is no right for a sorcerer's bastard here."

"There is *every* right for a witch's daughter, and that I am."

Elspeth turned. God, she towered above Maria. "You know the victor may kill their challenger, if they so wish."

"Then you might finally get what you've wanted most." Maria did not flinch.

Damn everything to hell, we hadn't brought our chosen one to die in a stupid magical pissing match. "Madame, if I may," I began, but Fiona shushed me.

"Don't make it worse," she hissed.

Elspeth considered Maria. "Keep these degenerates under

guard until after the ceremony. If my granddaughter falls," she said, putting a bitter twist on *granddaughter*, "her friends will share in her fate." Then she left, her silent friends trudging after her. Maria looked at the fire; she apparently had nothing to say to us.

"So. When we say *share* . . . ," Magnus began, until I nudged him.

"You know what you're doing, of course," I said. Maria pursed her lips.

"I've an idea," she replied.

An idea was not comforting. Not at all.

24

I SPENT THE NIGHT IN FIONA'S TENT, UNDER HER watchful eye. I didn't know where they'd put Magnus and Maria, just as I didn't know what sort of challenge "coven making" was. When I asked Fiona, she replied, "There are some things a witch cannot give an outsider." After that, I learned to stop asking questions.

Come morning, we were awakened by what sounded like a clanging pot in the yard. We dressed fast and then emerged to head for the large tent in the center—Elspeth's tent. There were, to my eye, about forty witches, men and women. We all fit comfortably into the tent, which was set up rather like Magnus's had been. Furs stretched over the floor, a fire flickered in the center. But there were no tables here, and no papers. Dried bunches of lavender and dandelion dangled from the ceiling. A deerskin had been spread on the ground, with wooden bowls, mortars, and pestles strewn upon it. Fiona led me to sit beside Magnus. We'd been given the best seats for this particular show. Witches lined up on all sides of the tent; some even lifted children onto their shoulders.

I shivered. Magnus held up his hands, still bound at the wrist.

"If I could, I'd put an arm around you to keep you warm." Clearing his throat, he added, "As a fellow soldier, naturally."

"Naturally. They probably bound you because they feared your brute strength." I rubbed my free hands together. "Little do they know *I'm* the one not to be trusted."

"Howel, I do love it when you speak diabolically." Magnus made a noise of surprise as I slid my arm beneath his cloak and hooked it around his waist. I nestled against his body. It was a soldierly thing to do, naturally, and I felt a bit warmer. "You know, you could make a fire if you wanted."

"Waiting for the right moment." I eyed the growing circle of witches as Fiona sat down beside us. "Maria will win. I know it."

"She's always been a survivor." Fiona shivered as someone placed a few sprigs of black berries and two drinking cups on the deerskin.

"Are they going to have a tea party to the death?" Magnus asked.

Fiona pointed to the cups. "Inside each of those is pure nightshade essence. They must each take the berries and herbs provided and mix a potion that renders the poison harmless. Then they drink."

"Suppose they both die." I had seen death by nightshade essence. Remembering Eliza's agonizing final moments made this duel even more terrifying.

"Then someone else shall step forward and command." Fiona's brow furrowed as Maria entered the tent, a pair of male witches at her back. "Maria's never been great at potions. Always had a better head for fighting."

That was a revelation. "I thought she was marvelous at potion making."

Fiona cast me a tender look. "Indeed, to an outsider a third-rate potion maker seems a genius. Maria's got a healer's heart, but not the head. She's too rash." The girl's eyes softened as she watched Maria examining the items on display. "When we were girls, trying to get her to sit still and learn was a lesson in itself."

"I thought she wasn't part of your coven."

"It's not as simple as that," she began, but the beat of drums started and she gave up talking. My stomach dropped. It was time for the match.

Elspeth entered the tent, flanked by her two witches. Elspeth sat opposite Maria on the deerskin. The drums stopped.

A young witch with yellow hair stood, her hands raised. "Now may the mother judge who is worthy. Now may the healer turn death into life."

The match began. At first, Maria and Elspeth glared at one another across the bowls and herbs.

"You ought never to have come back." Elspeth's voice cracked. "I sent you away for your own good, child."

"You sent me away because you couldn't bear to think how

my mother died." Maria picked up a bowl and tossed some berries inside. Taking up a pestle, she began to grind. "Enough talk, Grandmother."

Elspeth smirked. "So soon to die. Poor little bastard."

"Rather a tough old bird, isn't she?" Magnus scowled, and I tightened my grip on him. Patience was a virtue, one I'd never truly possessed. But my fire waited for the right moment. I'd know it when it arrived.

Maria and Elspeth ground and stirred powders, and measured their progress with furrowed brows. It was in some ways the most boring match I'd ever observed, but the cups were life and death itself. One miscalculation would result in agony.

Sweat stood out on Maria's brow as she worked. I prayed Willoughby didn't overtake her now. How did she feel, working with the same poison that had murdered Eliza? Would it distract her, or spur her on to a better performance?

After several more minutes of measuring and stirring, they each raised their cups. "To the coven." Elspeth gave a rotten smile.

"The coven," Maria replied, and drank. Magnus turned his eyes away and winced. I was certain he, too, was thinking of Eliza.

A minute passed, then two. Elspeth looked puzzled, Maria quite comfortable. Fiona clutched my hand, not bothering to hide her relief. "She's made it through!"

Elspeth looked at the cups, stunned.

"I'd a good teacher," Maria said by way of explanation. Indeed, whatever else you could say about Willoughby, she knew magic. "So, Grandmother. What's next?"

"Next?" Elspeth put a gnarled, spotted hand to her mouth. I could see that it was trembling. "Well, my girl. This is your next challenge."

Elspeth squeezed her hand into a fist. Maria's smile fled; she began to cough violently, her face purpling as Elspeth stood. The old woman pumped her fist rhythmically, as though squeezing a rubber ball.

Or a heart.

"No!" Fiona screamed, though she didn't move. Every witch in the room bowed their head. Maria fell to her hands and knees, gasping for air. I had to do something, and fast.

"Blood magic," Maria gasped. She turned horrified eyes to her grandmother. "How could you?"

What had Maria told me of blood magic? A witch could access it, but it was an evil proposition.

Elspeth had ruled her coven by blood magic and fear. Now I understood why no one rose up to help. Now I understood why Fiona, though she cried to watch this, remained seated.

"After Sarah died, I knew there could be no peace with other magic folk." Elspeth's voice shook. Pain appeared on the woman's face, cracks forming in stone. "Better not to be slaves, no matter the cost."

Maria was going to die unless I did something. But I knew, deep inside, that any attempt to enter the fight would undo something powerful. Maria caught my eyes, and I couldn't help her. What could I do? All I had was . . .

Fire.

Praying that she understood, I willed a few sparks to fly from my hands. Before the cold air snatched them away, Maria summoned those sparks to her. With a thought, she whipped them up into a massive ball of fire, throwing it at Elspeth.

The woman's tunic ignited; flame rippled over her sleeve. As she beat the fire out, Maria stood. The witch's hold on her had broken, and she wasted no time.

She stretched her hand toward the tent's opening. The wind ushered in a gust of snow, which Maria transformed into a dagger of ice. With perfect aim, Maria flung the dagger, slicing her opponent's shoulder. Fresh blood spattered over the ground.

Maria went to stand over her grandmother. I gave a few more sparks, which she collected into a burning ball. Elspeth shielded her face as Maria lowered the flame to burn her.

"Have I taken the right of coven?" the girl asked. Silence. Until, finally, Elspeth groaned.

"It is yours," the witch hissed.

We all caught the words, so thin they were nearly lost. Something seemed to happen then, as though an invisible violin string had been plucked. The vibration went through my body.

Maria held her hand to her grandmother, but the old woman would not take it. Hurt glimmered in the girl's eyes. "I would forgive you," she said.

Elspeth never lost her sneer. "Anger is all I've left, girl." The old woman got off the ground without any help. "Take these fools, then. Lead them to their deaths in the name of those murderers. I want no part in it."

"You are a witch of this coven," Maria said.

"I break from the coven. I shall never take shelter in another; I shall live and die off the land alone." The words had the quality of rehearsal about them. Around us, the witches chanted in low voices. It was ceremonial; one of them was leaving the group.

"You won't survive on your own," Maria said. She held out her hand, but Elspeth struck it away.

"Then that will be the mother's wish. I accept it." Elspeth took up her cloak and stalked out of the tent. This time, her two women attendants did not follow her; they fixed their attention on their new queen.

Maria remained in the center of the circle. Slowly, she discarded her sadness and looked upon every member of her new coven. For it was hers, now, every bit of it.

"You know me," she said at last. Her voice sounded hoarse with nerves. "When I was a small child, Sarah Templeton left you to raise me with a lowland coven. Years after her death, I returned to claim my place with you. Elspeth Templeton said I'd no right to this coven, being a half-blood beggar." I expected this to turn into an accusatory rage, but that had never been Maria's way. Rather, her tone gentled. "Despite that, you never turned your backs on me fully. When I tracked you because I was too cold, you gave me kindling for fire, or dried meat, or an ax." Fiona offered a shy smile at the word *ax*. I now understood why Maria had been so attached to the thing. "I have not come back to hide. The Skinless Man wants to burn this country to the ground. His success means the end of all of us, witch, sorcerer, and magician alike." She pointed to Magnus and me. "My friends are sorcerers, yes. But they want what I want: to save our home. Will you take me as your leader and follow me into battle? To help the queen, yes . . . and the sorcerers?"

The crowd went stone silent. Who here had forgotten the agonized screams of loved ones burning on a pyre? Who had forgotten the smoke-ravaged skies, or the smell of cooking flesh?

"I'll say one last thing." Maria's voice wavered with emotion. "I've a powerful reason to hate the sorcerers. But I found a way past it." She looked at me. "With the help of a friend."

If Magnus had taught me anything, it was the importance of good dramatic timing. Sensing the opportunity, I erupted into flames, fully, from head to toe. Witches cried out in awe. Magnus, through the veil of fire, looked on me with pride.

When I extinguished I curtsied, very properly.

"Lines are being redrawn," I said. "If we survive, the new world won't be the same as the old."

"I won't ask anyone to march to death if they don't want it," Maria said. "But will you come with me?"

Silence reigned. Then, slowly, a low moaning began through the crowd. The hair on my neck prickled; it was the sound of mourning. And I could somehow picture the pyres as they had been, the ash of all those ruined lives. And then, the cries of grief began to change, and the images and colors changed with them. The cries became chants of war. Oaths of fealty.

The chants swelled. The witches stomped their boots and raised their hands above Maria. Blessing her.

She was their queen now. Their leader.

Finally, she had come home.

NOW THAT WE WERE GUESTS RATHER than prisoners, they brought both Magnus and me a change of clothes. I removed my knickers, stockings, and gown, dressing in the soft trousers and the tunic of the witches. They bade me take off my corset as well, which at first felt like freedom but quickly became painful. I'd rarely felt so sore.

"Probably fastened into a corset before you were three." Fiona managed to fashion me something like a corset, only softer and more pliable. I could bend quite easily at the waist, and it felt miraculous.

"Any chance I could have my petticoat back?" I wanted those porter runes, though it looked a bit hilarious with the tunic and the trousers. Deciding I'd wait until I'd a dress again, I took the petticoat from Fiona and put it in my pack.

None of the witches wore their hair up, so I brought mine out of its chignon, instead loosely tying it in a tail behind my head. When I emerged into Magnus's tent—he'd not taken off his uniform—he looked me up and down with an approving glance.

"Scandalous. A woman with legs!" he said, handing me a bowl of stew.

"Yes, I finally have a pair of my very own." We laughed as we ate. Liquid dribbled down my chin, and I wiped it on my sleeve without thinking. Truly, I was becoming a child of the wilderness.

We emerged from the tent later to find Maria already giving orders for what was to be taken. Tents were being pulled up, animals harnessed to carts and wagons. Women were cooking over fires, ladling concoctions into skeins. The men didn't seem to have much to do with potion making.

"That was how sorcerers were said to begin," Magnus told me when I pointed out the men's lack of participation. "Back in Constantine's day, one male witch, Senovarus, grew tired of being powerless. So he found a way to channel magic through an object—a stave. This was something that worked almost exclusively for men, setting them free."

Rebels, indeed. "Where'd you hear that?"

"My *grand-mère* was a perpetual outsider in sorcerer society. She adored digging up the unsavory bits of Order history." He winked. "Of course, who can ever know the whole truth?"

Nettie.

That was Rook's voice in my ear. I could feel him at the back of my mind, tugging me away from Magnus. I scanned the surrounding area for him.

"What is it?" Magnus asked. Making my excuses, I stole away from the group and wandered into the woods. I did not have to go far before the darkness encroached all around us. Rook appeared before me, halting me in my tracks.

His shadowy garb, and the oddly inhuman appearance of his face, stood out more starkly here in the natural world. He resembled a wicked faerie from a child's story. Yet I didn't care; being in the woods with him was like coming home.

"I never thought we'd be like this again," I admitted. He regarded me with gentle confusion. "Together, I mean. Free."

"Even when I was farthest from you, I could feel you as close as my own skin." Rook looked at the darkening sky. "It's funny, really, because that's what the Ancients are: always near to this world, yet eternally far." He spoke as if in a trance. I took his hand, much as I had the day we'd sat on the rock in the heather near Brimthorn. The day our lives changed forever.

"I missed you." I didn't mean for my words to catch in my throat. He kissed me on the forehead.

"You tethered me to this new life, same way you tethered me to the old. It was because of you I didn't succumb to darkness all those years at Brimthorn." He was silent awhile. "Will you save me from the darkness now?"

"Of course." I took his face in my hands. "I'd do anything."

He petted my cheek and said, "Then kill me."

25

THE WORLD DROPPED OUT FROM UNDER ME. NOT this again. "Be serious."

"I have never been more serious." His black eyes shimmered with hurt. "You swore you'd save me."

"Yes. I will *save* you. Not kill you."

"But this isn't about *me* any longer, Nettie." Rook sighed, ran a hand through his flaxen hair. "Try to understand. After Korozoth died, I inherited his abilities."

"Yes, and you became . . ." I stopped, because whatever I said would sound wrong. "Something more," I finished.

"Exactly. The danger is great, but so is the power." He drew nearer. "You could have that power, Nettie."

Oh, this was absurd. "So you want to turn me into . . . what you've become," I said at last, clumsily. Rook gritted his teeth. God, he was so obviously trying to be *patient*.

"I'm too far gone, Nettie. R'hlem is my master now; every day that I fight him, he hurts me. In here." Rook jabbed a finger at his forehead. "I could be turned into a beast again and force you to live as my slave. If that happens, we're all doomed. Don't you understand?" He spoke with gentle reason. "If you become the receptacle of my powers, there will be a period where you're still yourself. I was still Rook, the old Rook, at first, wasn't I? You've a strength I've never possessed; you could battle the influence while still wielding the power. With it, you could finish the war. Can't you see? This is best for both of us."

"For you to be dead?" I cried, finding my voice once more. No. Never.

"You're being foolish." Rook followed at my heels as I turned and ran deeper into the forest. "I never thought I'd say that of you, Nettie." The sounds of Yorkshire were returning to his voice, along with his old way of speaking. It made him sound too much like Rook, my Rook. It made everything worse.

"Get away!" I could feel the hum of that power between us. He could force me to my knees, if he wanted. Make me his servant. But I felt the invisible grip relax.

"You know there'll be nothing strong enough to kill me save your fire," he said. Then, "Please. I don't want to live like this."

"No!" The word ripped out of my soul. I fled again, fast in the opposite direction, back to camp. Tears froze on my cheeks, and my lungs ached as I ran harder than I ever had before. When a branch tripped me, I sprawled face first into the snow. Lying there, the sting of the ice on my face, I screamed for sheer frustration. Why? Why, after everything, did he ask for this? I could save him! I could find a way. There was always a way to what you wanted. In faerie stories from my childhood, there was always a woman with a wand, always a magic apple, always a kiss that released the sleeper from death. Be good and true, and you shall see everything right.

But this was not a faerie story. My breath frosted in the air as I sat up. I bit my fist until it bled to stop my sobbing, but the footfall behind me indicated I hadn't hidden myself as well as I'd have liked.

"Henrietta." Maria crouched beside me, brushed snow from my tunic. "What on the mother's blessed earth happened?"

"Rook." It all tumbled out of me. "He says he wants me to kill him."

Her eyes widened. "What?"

Then I told her all, and her expression morphed from horror to sorrow to pity. I didn't want anything that vile. I wanted to win. I wanted to have what *I* wanted. Because I deserved it! The same way Rook deserved to live free from this curse that he'd done nothing to earn. There was a way . . . there had to be . . . there . . .

I heaved like I'd be sick. Maria embraced and rocked me like a bloody child. And I wanted to be a child again, so that it all could be a nightmare. I wanted to wake in my bed and find that this was not true. I'd be happy to wake back at Brimthorn, even.

I did not want this responsibility.

"You don't understand." I shoved her away. "You don't know what it is to feel so bound to someone."

"When I fight off Willoughby like an invisible beast clawing at me? Is that not the same?" she said, not unkindly. "I won't

- 275 -

tell you what to do, but you've seen how others are frightened of him."

"They can go hang," I grunted.

"You're wiser than this, Henrietta. What if he possesses you? What if he succumbs to R'hlem?"

"So could I, if I take his power."

"The end of the war is near, one way or the other. You might survive without turning monstrous. But it's too late for Rook. He's so tired, and in so much pain." She rubbed her eyes. "It's not the same, but . . . once, when I was a child, I came upon a baby deer that had lost its mother. Such a bonny wee creature. I tried to feed it, but it withered before my eyes. One day, it fell and wouldn't rise again. I had to kill it. It was kindness."

"Rook is no deer!" I cried. Sorrow filled her brown eyes.

"Sometimes we must be harder than life itself."

I wanted to run from her until my lungs burst and my knees ached. But no matter how far or fast I went, this thing would dog my heels. Because there was a voice whispering in my head that I wanted to shut out—it was the voice of reason, which I had always prized.

"I'm not strong enough," I moaned. Maria nestled me against her shoulder.

"There is no force greater than you when you've your mind made up. You cannot master this." She kissed my forehead, as Rook had done. "But you are strong enough to see it through."

Those words reverberated in my head as we returned to the camp, and stayed with me as we rode out. Always, I could feel

Rook's presence on the periphery. He stayed by us that night, while I lay awake in my tent and made impossible plans. If I could get every witch to work at making a healing potion . . . if I could trap Rook in a cage . . . if I could find and kill R'hlem tomorrow, single-handed. If, and if, and if again tormented me throughout the night.

Come the morning, I was bone-weary and out of ideas. Maria forced some breakfast on me, while I felt Rook waiting deeper in the forest. I caught sight of him, his shadowy cloak thinning in the wind like smoke.

"You should speak with him." Maria tore a hunk of bread. "We'll wait."

Slowly, I walked away from Maria and into the forest, Rook at my side. We walked until we arrived in a glen. Sunlight broke through the dark, thatched forest ceiling. There was a fallen log, lightly dusted with snow. Brushing it off, we sat opposite each other.

I placed the tips of my fingers along his cheek. Besides the black eyes, the fangs, the sharper contours of his face, I could still see Rook beneath there. My Rook.

But he wasn't mine. He wasn't, thanks to my father, even fully his own any longer. My vision fractured as the tears came.

"It's all right," he soothed.

"It's not fair!" I tried not to sound like a child, but the words came out as a howl. Rook took me into his arms. "This wasn't how it was supposed to be." Why had I made him come to London? Why?

"It's better this way." He stroked my hair. "What would life at Brimthorn have been without you? When Korozoth died, I might have well become as I am anyway." He kissed my temple. "Even if it was only for a moment, I felt well and had you in my arms. I've no regrets in this life." He held me apart from him. "You won't succumb to the power, Nettie." He placed my hands on his face. I knew what he meant by it, and shoved him off. I couldn't. "Please." He sounded mournful.

"We found Fenswick again. He can help you," I said. Rook's patience evaporated.

"Would you have me suffer so that you can keep me?" he asked. Like a dog. Those had been his accusations the night he'd transformed. Now I wondered if he hadn't been awfully correct.

I wondered if we hadn't clung to each other because that was all we knew. All that was good in this war-torn world. Our love had been the love of childhood, of sweetness and security and home.

But all children must grow up.

"I want you to be free," I said at last.

We were silent as he looked around at the frozen glen. The trees were pillars of snow, the branches gleaming with ice. Like a fable of a winter world, where two children lived in eternal innocence. This was all a story now; I could not bear it otherwise.

"I was playing by the river the day Korozoth attacked,"

Rook said. "My brothers came to fetch me. I'd not remembered them in so long."

"Stephen," I said, trying to smile. "Stephen Poole is a nice name."

"It is," he agreed. He traced one long, pale finger through the snow. "I sometimes think that it was a curse that left me alive. The only bright spot in my life after them was you, Nettie."

I choked on my next words. "If I'd not brought you to London, do you think you'd have been all right?"

"Perhaps," he said. Rook would never lie to me. Another path might have led us to a happier outcome. But this was where we'd been brought, for better or worse. Gently, I put my hands to his face.

"Are you afraid?" I whispered.

"With you holding me? Never."

Trembling, I lit my hands on fire. The flames licked at his face, and

we run down the hill

The image was there and gone, like a puff of smoke. Back in London, the Shadow and Fog had stored illusions and memories, the memories of any who passed through it. I had seen a piece of Rook's remembrance, or perhaps mine.

"It's all right," Rook said. "Those are good things to see."

I pressed my lips to his forehead. He kissed me softly as well. One last time, his arms tightened around me. Burying my face in his shoulder, I whispered, "I love you, Stephen. My Rook."

"And I love you, Henrietta. My Nettie."

The flames swirled around us.

We run down the hill toward the pond. Rook is already tugging off his shoes.

"I'll catch you!" I yell, trying to pull off my own boots. But they are laced so much tighter than his, and I fall over. Wretched skirts.

"Nettie!" Rook is ahead of me, standing directly in the sun and waving. I leap up, even with one boot off, and charge after him. But he is too far ahead of me. The sun catches his pale hair. He jumps from the rock, to roll down the hill and into the pond. For an instant I think he might take off into the sky like a bird.

Lord, he is fast. I can't catch up, and watch as he flies along the path away from me until he is lost to my sight.

The memories vanished. My arms were empty. I was seated in the glen, alone. My hands were black as pitch and smelled of smoke. Glinting pieces of white ash hung in the air like snow. The seat before me was charred. I looked around the glen and knew I would not find Rook there. I would never find him again.

It felt like a cage door had opened in my chest and a rare and precious bird had flown out. I watched the shadows lengthen around me. I could not think of moving, no matter how cold I became. I had fire, after all. I had fire.

I sat there until Magnus arrived. He approached slowly.

"Maria told me."

He didn't try to make me stand, which was good. I couldn't leave this place.

I began to shake. Magnus took me into his arms, where I could feel the fast beat of his heart. Finally, the pressure broke. Finally, I found my voice.

"Please. It's the last place I saw him."

Magnus pulled his cloak around both of us for warmth. He understood.

We stayed there until the shadows grew around us, and I knew for certain that Rook was not among them.

26

THE JOURNEY BACK TO THE SORCERER CAMP TOOK two more days. For me, the time meant nothing. I felt no cold, and barely any hunger. Maria had to force food upon me, which I didn't want but still took. I didn't want to make extra trouble for her. After all, I knew I wasn't the only one who grieved for Rook.

Maria and I had both tried to save him, and we had both failed.

On the third day, I caught sight of the sorcerer lookout through the trees. Once Magnus and I revealed ourselves, he waved us on with enthusiasm.

Below us, the tent city was much as we'd left it. Magnus rode in to meet with several of his men and get their report. I went to visit the queen.

Her Majesty had been placed in a central, and protected, tent. She was not there, to my surprise. Rather, she'd made her way over to Magnus's tent, where I discovered her in deep conversation with several of his men and one of the engineers. That man was making a demonstration of a toy-sized model.

"It's something like a catapult," he said, springing the little birch and stone contraption into action. It launched a pebble across the room, nearly striking me. When they saw me, the men stood at attention. Queen Victoria looked pleased. There was color in her round face. She no longer appeared the pale, sickly young woman I'd first glimpsed at the commendation ball.

"They tell me you've brought a coven of witches," the queen said. "Strange to think of fighting alongside them."

"Some have ridden off already, to send for reinforcements." As queen of her coven, Maria had a right to summon other coven leaders to parley. Before we'd left our camp in the highlands, she'd spent half a day negotiating with the clan elders, discussing who should be sent where. Hopefully, the witches would arrive shortly. Even more hopefully, they would stay and fight with us.

"Speaking of reinforcements, Howel, there appears to be a congregation of magicians going on by the forest's edge," one of the sorcerers—Jackaby—said to me. He sounded wary.

Murmuring goodbyes, I went to meet our new recruits. Magnus soon appeared alongside me. "Don't you have a meeting?"

"I received the necessary information. If you think I'm about to miss a crowd of magicians, you're off your head." He hurried me along.

The lot of them had gathered by the forest's edge. I could see Mickelmas and Alice. The rest were strangers.

Magicians were, as I had discovered, the most ridiculous

people on the planet. I saw coats of bright pink and dyed purple, gloves that resembled snakes, women with shaven heads, men with hair that hung to their waists. I counted as many as thirty-two from where I stood.

"Alice did well," I muttered to Mickelmas as I came up alongside him.

"Every sage old man needs a young, energetic woman to do all his work for him." Waving a handkerchief in the air, Mickelmas attracted the magicians' attention. "Henrietta, I present to you our most noble and attractive saviors."

The magicians didn't look like saviors. Rather, they resembled a collection of hungry beggars, watching the world with eyes that had seen too much.

"Well." Everyone was staring at me. "I imagine you'll all want stew?"

A chorus of huzzahs erupted.

"I'll chat them up, Howel. We'll be friends in no time." Magnus began greeting magicians as if they had known one another for years. He'd a talent for this sort of thing.

While we fixed our newcomers with lodgings and food, a strange sort of peace descended over me. It wasn't until I was walking back to my tent that I realized my wounds no longer hurt. This morning, I'd woken up feeling healthy.

Rook's transformation had begun with the pain of his wounds vanishing.

Already, a tiny voice whispered in my mind. *Release me.*

Shuddering, I quashed that thought as I went inside to light a fire. Maria entered with a steaming mug of something that smelled foul, like old cabbage and burnt wood.

"Didn't add the honeyed belladonna this time," she said. Of course. She'd concocted the same potions she'd made for Rook. Recalling Eliza's death, I paused. Not because of Maria's skill, but Willoughby . . . "It's all right," she said. "Fenswick made the thing."

The taste was bitter, but the voice went away.

For now.

THAT NIGHT, A GROUP OF US gathered around a great fire in the center of camp. I felt bone-weary, having spent the day organizing and reorganizing groups of people until my head spun. My idea was to assemble ourselves into a decent army and then head for Sorrow-Fell, picking up whatever stragglers we could along the way. More witches had arrived—about two dozen or so. Not a great army, but every person helped. Provided, of course, that they agreed to stay.

That was a concern for tomorrow. Now I sat beside Maria, staring into the fire with a bowl of stew in my lap. The others were going around and telling jokes and stories.

First, Alice turned into whatever animal people could name. We had to stop the game when she started turning into people and insulted one of the magicians over the length of his nose.

Next, Lilly got up and sang "Red Is the Rose," an Irish ballad that had Dee gazing up at her like she'd invented music itself. "That was my favorite when I was little," he said when she'd done. He thumped the log on which he sat in applause.

"I know. That's why I practiced." Lilly kissed him lightly, which caused Dee's blush to turn crimson. People whistled and made suggestive comments.

Eventually, we got round to personal stories.

"So there I was, stark naked in front of a tea shop," one of the magicians, a man named Wilfred, said. He'd a long beard, which he'd woven into a single thick braid. "And this woman comes out, takes one look at me, and asks just what I think I'm doing. 'Ma'am,' I says, 'whatever do you mean? I am wearing the finest suit of clothes in all the land. My vest is purple, my stockings white cotton, and my shoes have silver buckles. Don't you see?' With a flick of my wrist and a few muttered words, well, she *does* see. She thinks I'm the best-dressed fellow she ever beheld. 'For three pound, I'll sew you a gown as fine as my own attire. What do you say?' So she gave me three pound, took off all her clothes, and tried to enter the Court of St. James's!" Wilfred kicked his feet, laughing hysterically.

"What happened then?" someone asked.

"I married her. Best three weeks of me life."

"What'd you do with her clothes?" Alice asked. A red-gold hawk perched on her shoulder, and she fed it bacon.

"Eh, turned 'em into jam."

"Not sure I'd want to spread someone's pants on my toast," Magnus said thoughtfully.

"Go on then, let's hear a sorcerer's tale." Wilfred slugged Magnus in the shoulder.

"Well, there is an ancient tale." Magnus took a swig of water. "One that I made up myself, of course." Clearing his throat, he began. "There once was a young prince. He was strong, and bold, and quite handsome. No, no, more than quite. Ridiculously handsome. The handsomest. And the best rider. And the best fighter. With the best smile, and always a witty rejoinder."

"Right, so this story's about you," I said to roars of laughter.

"Anyway, this prince lived in a fantasy land. He wore the finest clothes, drank the finest wines, and altogether lived the finest life. Companionship came swiftly and easily to him. But one day, he was out hunting in the glen when he met a faerie.

"The faerie girl was aloof. She appeared indifferent to him, which made the prince certain he must have her for his own, even if he was already engaged to a princess from a foreign land."

I stopped smiling. Magnus took out his stave and tapped the wooden stars embossed upon its length.

"Every day, the prince returned with honeyed words. He brought gifts, hired musicians. Every day, the faerie was gracious and kind, but composed. Still, he wore down her defenses with his charm. And the prince was sincere in his courtship— he somehow forgot how rakish his intentions were. He was a man who lived for the present moment.

"And one day, the faerie girl allowed him to kiss her. You

see, this prince had expected to enjoy the conquest. He had not anticipated being conquered in turn. He asked the faerie to come with him and live as his wife in all but name, thinking only of his own pleasure. He considered himself a good man, this prince, but how many princes are truly good?" Magnus did not look at me. "The faerie cast him out of her glen. When he emerged from the paradise of her company, he found that it was winter, and very cold."

"They're tricksy like that, faeries," one magician said sagely.

"The prince wandered back to his castle. But now the food in his mouth tasted of ash, and the wine of vinegar. The world's colors had muted. He thought a curse had been placed upon him. He went to a wise man to discover what had been done to him.

"The wise man replied, 'It is guilt you feel. If you desire wellness, return to the glen and beg forgiveness. Be all sincerity, and good fortune may yet find you.' So the prince returned to the glen," Magnus said, his mouth tightening. "But . . ."

He fell silent.

"But what? Did she turn him into a toad?" Alice cried.

"Into stone?" someone else asked.

"Into a wild boar, then had his own father's men hunt him down?" Maria asked, though she watched me carefully. There was a lump in my stomach. Magnus's mouth quirked in a smile.

"Ah, Maria guessed it. Well done." There were some groans of sadness, a smattering of applause, and one of the magicians offered an opinion as to how the story was rather derivative. Magnus walked away with only the hastiest bow. After a minute, I followed him. I tracked his footprints in the snow, until I discovered him standing in a patch of moonlight.

He remained still at my approach, as if I were some forest creature that might shy away.

"How did the story really end?" I asked.

"She welcomed him back, but she had placed an enchantment about herself—he could never touch her again."

"You make it sound rather her fault," I said sharply.

Magnus lowered his eyes. "It wasn't her fault. That was when the prince realized his greatest mistake. He had believed her to be a prize to attain. He had not known *her*: the strength and the honor of her. He had not known how the sight of her was sickness itself, and also the cure. To be near her was to suffer and grow stronger." He looked to the stars.

"Could we at least stop calling him 'the prince'?"

"I believe there was an oath never to speak of these things again," he said. I stepped in front of him, forcing him to look at me.

"I'm relieving you of that vow," I whispered. Magnus watched me with wide eyes. I kept my hands to my side, unsure of what to do.

He set his mouth in a firm line. "I don't want to hurt you, and I don't want to be hurt."

"How would I hurt you?" I said. "Because of Rook?"

Even saying his name was a wound, but Magnus shook

his head. "No." He glanced at my hands. "You still wear Black-wood's ring."

Indeed, I wore that blasted silver band with the pearl. Part of me wanted to rip it off and chuck it into the ice, but that wouldn't be right. I simply slid it off my left hand and onto my right. "I need to return this to its rightful owner." If Blackwood was still alive. My stomach cramped, even now, at the idea he was not. "But I can't marry him, after what he would have done to Maria. Even after I told him the truth, he was ready to kill her."

Magnus drew nearer. He was tall enough that I could raise my chin slightly, look up at him with caution . . . and hope.

"I've spent every night since we went to see that damned play wishing I could take it all back." His hand faltered, but he traced a lock of hair away from my cheek. "Well, not all of it. The kiss in particular, I'd like to keep." My laughter sounded weak. "Howel, you have to know that was the night I truly saw myself. I hated what I'd done and who I was. I never expected I'd regain your favor, but I at least wanted to be the sort of man who could earn it."

My entire body vibrated, my blood bubbling in my veins like sparkling wine. When I leaned up to him on tiptoe, he put a gentle hand on my arm.

"Are you certain?" he whispered. That was the glorious thing. I felt utterly, unabashedly certain. There were no questions to ask as I brought my mouth close to his. His eyes fluttered closed. His breath hitched as his hand slipped around my waist.

"Yes," I whispered. With a low moan, he kissed me.

Our first kiss, all those months ago, had been when we were tipsy. It had been full of fire and passion. There was the same explosive heat in this second kiss. He pressed his lips to mine, lining me up against the hard strength of his body. His hands roamed down my back, traced the curve of my waist. He claimed me, his kiss growing fiercer.

But there was also tenderness. He pulled away to plant a smaller kiss at the corner of my mouth. I placed a hand on his cheek, and he nuzzled my palm.

Running my fingers through his hair, I felt again how over-whelming it was merely to touch him. Magnus took my hands in his, kissed each finger in turn.

My face flushed as I remembered what I'd already given to Blackwood. "You don't mind, do you?" I looked down at our joined hands. "That I'm . . . well, that Blackwood . . ." I couldn't finish the words, but he understood.

"I don't need to be the first man who loved you. Only let me be the last," he said, and kissed me. Our embrace was no longer the burning, uncontrollable fire. He was the sun, all warmth and giving.

It was like waking from a dream to the morning light. Rook had been the one steady thing in my past, the rock to which I clung. Blackwood and I shared a destiny as deeply planted as anything the Speakers had ever prophesied. Magnus was different.

He teased me, and he listened to me. He was as comfortable being led as he was leading.

We were not hewn from the same rock or chosen by fate. We simply fit together because *we* chose it.

I had never known anything as easy, or as exciting.

"You're not at all the person you used to be," I whispered. He smiled.

"Neither are you. Yet I like you better with each day that passes. Isn't that wondrous?"

Sighing, he placed his chin atop my head. I felt the steady beat of his heart against my cheek.

And then it began to snow.

"Quick, before we catch our death." Laughing, we joined hands and ran. We arrived at the front of my tent and craned our necks about to search for onlookers. None to be found.

"Good night, my darling," Magnus whispered, and kissed me again. The snow had frozen on his eyelashes and in his hair. It dusted his shoulders, clung to the front of his coat. He looked as though he were made of starlight as he dashed back down the hill.

Giddy, I entered the tent to find Maria and Fiona nestled before my fire. Fiona had laid her head in Maria's lap, and Maria was stroking the girl's raven tresses. She hummed "Black Is the Color of My True Love's Hair."

No wonder she'd liked that song so much.

Fiona sat up when I entered. Maria didn't appear put out by my presence, but Fiona began to speak rather loudly.

"Well! There's nothing like a good talk to, er, set you to rights." Fiona blushed as Maria threw her arms around her neck. Smiling, I turned my back to give them some privacy, until Fiona blustered back out into the night.

"Don't you have your own tent?" I grinned. Maria cocked an eyebrow.

"Aye, but it has people in it," she answered. "The covens have been wanting to meet with me all afternoon."

I began to heat some water for a wash, while she examined me closely. Her nose wrinkled in glee. "See I'm not the only one as had a pleasant evening."

"I don't know what you mean," I said. She grinned, and whistled as she left.

"It's all right," she said over her shoulder. "I always liked him."

27

AS WE ENTERED YORKSHIRE THREE DAYS LATER, THE scout informed us that another army was riding up the hill. "Thirty men at most, but they are sorcerers," he said.

It could only be Blackwood. Relief and fear washed over me, and I tightened my hold on Gumdrop's reins.

We did not have time for arguments. The equinox was mere days away, and we needed to be friends as quickly as possible.

"Let me speak to him," I said to Magnus. He frowned, probably considering how such a meeting would go.

"I believe Her Majesty would like a word with Blacky as well." He clicked his tongue and urged his horse forward while I followed with a lump in my throat. So much had happened since I had last seen Blackwood. There was so much to discuss, and none of it would be easy.

I rode with Magnus and the queen to the front of the ranks. Queen Victoria sat very straight in her saddle and glared with the full fury of a monarch in command. Blackwood met us at the head of his men.

He looked terrible. He had lost weight; his cheekbones

were too prominent. His already slender physique looked all sharp angles now. Dark circles smudged his catlike green eyes, and his black hair was tangled. His triangular jaw was dusted with stubble; his clothes looked like he'd pulled them on in the dark. He seemed hollow.

But when he saw me, life sparked in his eyes. His mouth softened in apparent relief. Still, he did not rush to my side. There was business to attend first.

"Bring your sorcerers forward," he told Magnus. "Have them swear fealty to their Imperator, and there will be no violence today."

"Blackwood, how do you propose violence when you can't sit a horse properly?" Magnus returned.

Blackwood's eyes scanned me. I could not read his expression.

"I see you've found my bride," he said.

I lifted my chin. "Actually, I found *him*." Magnus snorted in laughter. "More than that, I've brought the queen an army."

Blackwood scanned the ranks behind us with a wary eye. The men behind him looked as haggard and tired as he—I didn't think they'd be difficult to bring to our side, with the promise of fire and food. I combed the ranks for Wolff and Lambe, and could have melted in joy when I found them. Lambe rode the same horse as Wolff; he'd been set in front, so that Wolff could keep him from falling out of the saddle. Lambe gazed blearily ahead, not appearing to notice anything.

Something glowed at Blackwood's side: he'd tied the

optiaethis to his horse's saddle. God, I hated that damned thing. I needed to warn him. But I also found that I could not tear my eyes away from it. It seemed as though I could hear a thin voice calling out to me. *Come,* it said. *Come to me.*

Azureus had told us that the *optiaethis* beckoned all Ancients within a thousand miles. Chilled, I forced myself to look away.

"We'll discuss everything in my tent," Blackwood said.

To my shock, the queen rode into his path. "I have not given you permission to pass, *Imperator.*"

"You cannot stop us," Blackwood said. The men behind him all put hands to their staves; they appeared to have got over Charles Blackwood's treachery.

If I didn't want this developing into a fight, I'd need to do something surprising.

"We must unite or we will die," I said.

Blackwood's eyes glinted with rage. "You must keep silent. Secrets can slip when one's blood is up." My father was his last remaining weapon. I would have to detonate that weapon myself.

I'd told enough lies and kept enough secrets for one lifetime.

"If you mean that I am R'hlem's daughter," I said casually, "that should be obvious."

There was nothing now but to hope.

The queen regarded me as though I'd turned another color. Magnus winked; I got the feeling he was pleased. The crowd behind me broke out in bewildered murmuring, and Blackwood's sorcerers appeared white with shock.

Blackwood gaped at me. I turned Gumdrop around to face the sea of people. "R'hlem's true name is William Howel."

"How the bloody hell do you know that?" Wilfred shouted. Around me, I could feel the crowd turning from shocked to frightened; outraged was usually the next step. I needed to work fast.

But more than that, I was sick to death of hiding what I really was, of feeling my pulse elevate every time anyone approached the truth.

"I know because he told me himself. My father was a magician who dabbled in the darker arts, but not for evil purposes. He wanted to prove to the king and to the Order that magicians are not England's enemy. Nor are witches." I caught Mickelmas's eye in the crowd. He was paying close attention. "We are all branches sprouting from a similar tree."

"How long have you known?" Wolff asked. He did not sound accusatory, merely baffled.

"Not long. I should have told the truth as soon as I knew it." The queen regarded me with a wary expression. She did not trust me. "Now you may all punish me because of who my father is, a situation over which I had no control." I turned Gumdrop around in order to face Blackwood's sorcerers. "Or you can lay down your weapons and parley with me. There is only one way to defeat my father, and I have it."

"What would that be?" the queen asked.

This was the part where everything could go pear-shaped. When we learned whether England would live or die.

I recalled Mickelmas's words to me all those months ago. *William had a vision of witch, sorcerer, and magician. All united. All equal.*

"We must form a consortium," I said. "Witch, sorcerer, and magician shall all work together, united in a common goal. Equal."

No one spoke. Then Mickelmas began to laugh. It started as a giggle and flourished into a maniacal cackle. Truly not the most encouraging thing he could have done.

"A consortium?" Blackwood said the word as if it were poison. "It goes against thousands of years of tradition!"

"We cannot face R'hlem's army without a united front. If we don't do this, thousands of years of tradition will be wiped clean off the face of the earth," I said. The men behind Blackwood started murmuring, and not in an encouraging way. In fact, the witches and sorcerers didn't sound all that keen, either.

"We shall discuss this further," the queen said, raising her voice as only a monarch could.

I was afraid that the different factions would begin breaking off, but the covens all agreed to stay, with Maria's encouragement. Mickelmas, too, was able to corral the magicians. As we headed downhill to make camp, Mickelmas walked beside my horse. He drew out a spotted handkerchief to wipe tears from his cheeks, still giggling.

"What's so amusing?" I asked, irritated.

"Forgive me. You see, it's as if William Howel himself were speaking through you."

GETTING MASSES OF PEOPLE TO AGREE on one simple thing was harder than I'd imagined. My initial proposal was to appoint one head of each magical "race." That leader would answer directly to Queen Victoria.

But every magical group had its own issues with this proposal. There were six covens, none of which would declare one leader. The magicians argued among themselves for the fun of it. As for the sorcerers, some backed Blackwood, and others supported Magnus and me. The meeting ground rang with a cacophony of voices. At the head of the assembly sat the queen, looking like a new schoolmistress contending with a pack of unruly children. Finally, she shouted, "Enough!" The talking died quickly. "Proceed, Howel," she said.

All eyes fixed on me, and I knew that many of the sorcerers regarded my attire—trousers, gray tunic—as belonging exclusively to witchery. I did not resemble one of "them" any longer, and that would make things more difficult.

"Great injustices have been carried out in the Order's name," I began, which apparently was the wrong first move. Everyone had an opinion, and everyone shouted it.

"The monsters killed my Bernard!" a magician woman cried.

"You think you've suffered? We lost our entire coven to their flames!" a witch shouted back.

"We must put these things behind us today," I said, trying for order.

"You can say that as you're one of 'em now!" a woman cried. It was Peg Bottleshanks, a magician I'd met in London.

"It's your fault!" a sorcerer cried, pointing at the witch who'd spoken. "Everyone knows the history. We sorcerers formed because the witches exercised a tyranny over the men in their coven!"

"And you responded by driving us into the hinterland and burning us alive?"

Weapons were drawn. Violence seemed on the verge of breaking out. I had to act.

Maria and I found each other, our look kindling a flash of understanding. We stepped into the center of the circle. With a wave of her arms, the ground beneath us rattled and rumbled. That shut up the lot of them. I summoned fire, and together we wove a net of flame, vivid blue and crackling orange. Agrippa had once taught me pyromancy, divining through fire. I plucked an image of R'hlem out of my mind and projected it onto the flaming disc. It was a bit dramatic, but it worked. The sight of our true enemy hushed the room entirely.

"We didn't pull this whole bloody army together for another scrap." Maria dropped the fire and turned to the assembly. "I've witch and sorcerer parentage. Henrietta's a magician's child. Don't you see it? The three of us're not far removed."

"Majesty, you've seen what Maria and I can do together. The three magical races are strongest when united." The queen looked pensive. "The Order has ruled by ourselves, for ourselves, for entirely too long. In the process, sorcerers have destroyed countless magical lives." I did not forget what my aunt had told me of my mother. "So I propose that our three societies govern themselves equally, and jointly, with the monarch."

"Are you daft?" Peg Bottleshanks shook her fist. "All you'll do is put us under another person's command. The Crown has no love for magicians or witches."

Queen Victoria stood, hushing all talk.

"I have seen enough to know that sorcerers serve themselves first," she said levelly. Blackwood, seated in the first row of sorcerers, paled with anger. "We face a great enemy who would tear our way of life apart. I can promise that should you join us, and should we take the day, there shall be a change in how we value magical life."

The meeting quieted. Maria returned to her coven. They spoke together, nodded, and she approached the queen. Taking a knife from her belt, she cut a lock of her own curly hair and cast it onto the ground. "The Templeton coven seals itself in a bargain."

A pause. Then another witch came forward, cut her own hair, and added it to the pile. Slowly, one by one and after discussion, coven leaders came forward. Six of them in all added their hair.

The witches had agreed to the consortium.

Mickelmas dragged me to the magicians' side for counsel.

"Don't trust it," Peg huffed.

"This could be our chance, though." Alice's eyes brightened. "Besides, if we all die by R'hlem's hand, what's the point of keepin' things as they are?"

Someone had placed a stool to the side of the group. It rocked back and forth.

"Alfred makes a good point." Peg patted the stool. "We can't trust a sorcerer, or a sorcerer's girl."

"That's not what Alfred said," I said flatly.

"Oh, now she speaks chair, does she?"

Bugger this.

Mickelmas cleared his throat. "What my dear burning rose is trying to say is . . . don't be daft." Not the most stirring words.

Of course. The burning rose: my sorcerer sigil and Mickelmas's name for his magician *army*.

"I saw several of you at a meeting for the army of the burning rose." I looked pointedly at Peg and patted the stool. Yes, I remembered Alfred. "We all want a way out of this darkness. Will you join me?"

Silence. "I went to that meetin' 'cause there was free ale," one of the magicians muttered.

"Well, I'll join you." Alice shook my hand and glared at the others. "If they've any sense, they'll do the same."

Apparently, Alice's was the voice they'd been waiting for. Soon after, we were able to deliver the magicians.

Witches and magicians had united . . . but what of the sorcerers? Blackwood crossed his arms in defiance.

"The Order is run by the votes of its seal bearers." Bloody hell. Seal bearers were the heads of sorcerer families. I was still one, as I was unmarried, but I knew which way Blackwood would vote. Scanning the group, I realized that the majority of seal bearers were on his side. The younger men were with me, but they weren't family heads.

Blackwood could destroy this consortium before it even started.

I wanted to give him a strong piece of my mind, but Mickelmas touched my arm. "Don't lose your temper. These fellows seek any reason to vote no," he whispered. He was right.

"Then I call that we hold the vote in one hour's time," I replied.

Blackwood narrowed his eyes. He understood that I wanted time to see if I couldn't persuade more men to give up centuries of tradition and join a harebrained scheme doomed to almost certain failure.

I needed to stop listening to my own thoughts.

Dee and Wolff were with me at once—Lambe, bless him, was asleep in a corner. Together with Magnus, we spoke with every seal bearer at the meeting. I did my best, but I wasn't certain it would be enough. Swearing inwardly, I had some of the older men meet with Maria or the magicians. I wanted to show how reasonable they were.

Magnus pulled me aside. "I'll be back in a minute," he said.

"You're leaving?" I needed him here! I needed every man I could get.

"Do you trust me?" he whispered.

"Yes." The word came out as naturally as a breath. I was shocked how easy it felt to speak. "But the vote's about to start."

"Stall if you must. You're good at distractions." He kissed my cheek and was off.

I grinned, until I discovered Blackwood watching me. He looked as if someone had struck him in the face. I wanted to speak with him, but the hour was up.

Time to vote.

I went forward first and voted for the consortium.

Blackwood went next. In a rigid voice that suggested he was barely keeping his anger in check, he voted to remain in the Order.

To my surprise, we had a few more seal bearers join our side. The older men had listened to me, thankfully, but a cursory glance told me that a few would not be enough. Dee, who had lost his father in the Battle of London, voted to leave. God, we were close, but it was going to come down to . . .

No. I realized, with a sinking heart, that we would be evenly split. If that happened, the Imperator got to cast a double vote, one as a seal bearer and one as Imperator himself. If he did that . . . the whole thing would be finished.

And so it was, a perfect tie. Blackwood smiled. "With an even split, I cast a vote as Imperator." I locked eyes with him, silently begging him to relent. I had always believed he would do what was best for this country. But in his eyes, I found only anger. "I vote that—"

"There's one more vote to be cast." Magnus broke through the crowd, a small velvet pouch in his hand. "The Magnus vote has not been counted."

Maria punched my shoulder, crowing with glee. I was so shocked I hardly felt the blow.

"The Magnus vote?" Blackwood sounded as if Maria had punched him as well.

"My cousin, Percival, has died. He left no children, making me his heir."

"You." Blackwood's voice cracked; he got it back under control. "You have no proof." He did not sound confident, though. With a flourish, Magnus opened the pouch and removed a piece of paper, along with a small metal disc.

The metal disc displayed a hawk winging its way above an ash tree. That was the Magnus crest, only gifted to the seal bearer of the house.

"My cousin perished during the march north," Magnus said. "I received word two weeks ago, just after we marched into Scotland. It took months to track me down, but here it is: death certificate and the seal." He handed the paper to Blackwood, who looked like he wanted to tear it to pieces.

"If I'd known . . ." Blackwood stopped there, but I could guess what he meant to say: if he'd known Magnus was now a seal bearer, he'd have known my side could win. He might have suggested an alternative plan.

Magnus had waited until it was too late for Blackwood to change his mind. Excellent strategy.

"As I've said, there is one more vote to cast." Magnus placed his seal back in its satchel. "The Magnus line votes to dissolve the Order."

I'd thought there'd be an eruption, but no one spoke. We had destroyed a six-hundred-year-old institution in the span of an afternoon. The sorcerer Order was done, and so was Blackwood's power. He looked ill.

The queen said, "As the head of the newly formed consortium, I choose to appoint the leaders of each branch until such time as we form a better system. For the witches, this . . . what was your name?" she asked Maria.

"Maria Templeton," she said.

"Yes. Miss Templeton shall lead. For the magicians." Her eyes scanned to Mickelmas, and her lips seemed to struggle to form the words. "Howard Mickelmas."

He bowed deeply in reply.

Finally, the queen looked at me. "Henrietta Howel shall have the sorcerers."

Head of the sorcerers and answerable only to the queen? I stammered my thanks. Blackwood put a hand over his chest, as though an invisible shaft had been plunged into his heart. He began pushing toward the exit, but on the queen's command was blocked.

"Lord Blackwood, you have violated your position most grievously," the queen said. "For that, punishment must be meted out."

Blackwood did not beg for mercy. I couldn't let this happen.

"Your Majesty, I beg you to spare him," I said. "We will need every possible soldier in the war to come."

"As the head of the sorcerer branch, you recommend this?" she asked warily.

"I do."

"Then it shall be done, though he must have eyes upon him at all times," the queen ordered. Blackwood looked like a ghost of a man as he fled the gathering.

I would have to speak with him, and right away.

But once I'd exited the tent, I found Mickelmas waiting. The magician was looking up to the oncoming night. Stars had scattered themselves across the deep blue of the sky.

"What is it?" I asked.

"Should we survive this final battle, in the centuries to come, some will speak your name with loathing. Some will speak it with praise." He gave me a strange grin. "But they will all speak your name, Henrietta Howel. The girl who changed the face of English magic. They will speak your name as long as there are tongues to utter it and ears to hear."

28

I HAD NEVER YEARNED FOR NOR DREADED ANY meeting this much. I trailed Blackwood as he made his way to the edge of camp. What I had to do was right, but I had not expected it to hurt so badly. When I called out to him, Blackwood regarded me with a bitter smile.

"You couldn't bear to be the second most powerful." He paced like a caged beast. "You had to wrench the crown from my head."

"I never wanted this." How different he seemed to me as I joined him on equal ground. He looked bruised and half wild. This near to him, I could feel tenderness creeping in. I couldn't allow that, not now. My feelings for him, real though they were, were also a product of some irresistible destiny. I would not be ruled by it. "Our goal was to save England. That's what we both wanted."

"What I wanted," he growled, turning his face away, "was to be the one to save it."

Yes, that was the dream to which he'd clung—a country's adoration to make up for a lifetime of warmth denied him. His mother had forsaken him because he was of his father's blood. His father had ignored him. Blackwood had done what so many other neglected children did. He had sought love from the world, and when he did not find it, he'd hated that world. I'd seen enough children like that at Brimthorn. Perhaps, if I were honest, I had been one of them.

But I had had Rook, at least. Blackwood had had no one. Even Eliza, much as he loved her, had been shut out from his secrets. And now I was taking away from him one more piece of love. If only I . . .

No. I could not give in. Sliding off my glove, I removed his engagement ring and held it out. He froze.

"Put that back on."

"Please don't make this hard," I murmured.

"One mistake." Pain tightened his features. "I made one hideous mistake. I should never have said those words to you in the library." He came closer. "I wasn't in my right mind."

"I know," I whispered. He pressed the ring into my palm.

"You could forgive Magnus for what he did. Forgive me, then, and marry me."

He saw my confusion.

"Our souls were wedded long before we were born. The ivy on our staves; the way that I feel when I'm near you." He put a hand to my waist, and despite everything my body burned with that touch. "Let the world collapse around us, let the Order fall and a new monument be raised in its place. I want you."

My last remnants of anger fell away. A horrible, aching sadness remained. "I do forgive you. Truly. But I can see now that we wouldn't work. We're too similar."

He didn't seem to grasp what I was saying. Boots crunched behind me as Magnus appeared by my side.

"Is everything all right?" he asked. I could see Blackwood remember what had passed between us in the tent. Black fury flashed over his face. He managed to tuck it away behind a stoic mask, but I had seen.

Blackwood gritted his teeth. "Haven't you snatched enough of my women?"

"Eliza and I weren't *yours*," I said, but he wasn't listening.

"Don't speak of your sister that way," Magnus said. They were going to come to blows if I didn't stop this. Already, Blackwood was backing up, and Magnus looked as if he'd rather welcome the challenge.

"Blackwood, these men want your head. Don't give them an excuse to think you unstable!" I cried.

He calmed, tugging at his coat to neaten it, buttoning and unbuttoning it as though to give himself something to do. Then he extended a hand to me. Despite Magnus's grunt of disapproval, I held out the ring once more. Blackwood snatched my wrist instead and pulled me near.

"Does he make you feel this way?" Blackwood's lips moved against my cheek. "Do you know this with him?"

No. You could never love two people in precisely the same

way. Even now, part of me still yearned to give in to him. But I knew my answer before I spoke.

"We were marked for one another in darkness." Gently, I put the ring into his hand. "I want a different life."

I wanted air, and light, and peace. Whatever thrill power gave to him did not prove as intoxicating for me. He stared at the ring.

Then Blackwood glowered at Magnus. "You should know she's spoiled for anyone but me."

It didn't feel as much of a slap as it had in the library. Before, he'd wanted me to feel worthless in his rage. Now he only wanted to cordon me off from Magnus or any other man. Shoving out of his arms, I looked him in the eye.

"I am not for anyone but myself," I replied.

Magnus strode forward, looking ready to do battle again. Blackwood dropped the ring in the snow. He wanted this, too.

Magnus stopped when I grabbed his arm, though I felt the strain in his body.

"I know what happened," he snapped. "It doesn't matter."

I thought Blackwood would attack, but instead he kept his hands by his side. Snow glistened in his hair, and his eyes were raw. Without another word, he walked off toward the trees. The ring lay glinting on the ground, and I picked it up.

"It's yours," he called over his shoulder before I could offer. "It will always be yours."

The way he said it, and the fact that it still felt as if my soul were being pulled after him, made it impossible to stay still. I turned and strode off in the opposite direction, my lungs burning with the freezing winter air. Magnus came up alongside and walked with me until I slowed and then stopped. No one could see us as he held me. He didn't try to kiss me or to coax assurances of what I felt for him. He only let me weep, the ring cold in my hand.

WE RETURNED TO CAMP, AND I found that Lambe was awake by the campfire, gazing into the crackling flames. Beside him, Wolff plucked at the strings of a cello. He coaxed "Greensleeves" out of it, and did rather well.

"How the devil did you manage to keep an instrument with you from London?" I sat opposite him.

"I didn't. A man sold it to me for two bags of potatoes." He began a piece by Mozart and got lost in the music. A smile stretched over his face.

"You didn't think the food had greater value?" I asked.

"What's the point of fighting without something beautiful to live for?"

"You want to ask a question," Lambe said to me. "Ask it." Of course he knew my mind without me saying a word.

"I was curious," I said as I watched everyone preparing for the night ahead. "Do you have any thoughts? Er, about prophecy, that is."

"You mean the prophecy tapestry that marked Maria as our chosen one?" He nodded. "There is a feeling you have, a fear that Maria is the one to destroy the Blackwood family. Indeed, I've wondered that myself. Sorrow-Fell is in the hands of the bloody king. Our chosen ones tend not to be so successful."

"Well, that's rather it," I said, my gut cramping. "Do you believe that destiny is unavoidable? Or can we make our own path?"

"You were our false chosen one, and you still destroyed Korozoth. Maria is our true chosen one, and she burned down Sorrow-Fell. The Speakers' tapestry hinted at both outcomes. Yet why did we seek a chosen one to begin with? Because the tapestry told us she existed. Without that prophecy, Master Agrippa would not have looked for you in Yorkshire. He would not have brought you to London. You, in turn, would not have found Maria. We hunted for our destiny because we were told it *was* our destiny."

"And it all came true," I said, puzzled.

"Because we told ourselves it would." He looked to the stars above. "Fate is inevitable, but there are many different ways to approach it. After all, the prophecy said poison would drown beneath dark waters of the cliffs." He blinked at me. "Were there any cliffs when you battled Nemneris?"

"I'm not even certain she drowned," I said.

Lambe coughed thickly, and Wolff stopped his playing.

"Clarence is sick. Let's not overexcite him," he whispered to me.

"Lady Blackwood may do as she likes," Lambe murmured.

I scoffed. "I am not, and never will be, Lady Blackwood."

"Oh" was his only reply. He slumped over as he fell asleep. While Wolff tucked a blanket around his shoulders, I felt a prickling on the back of my neck.

"Everyone. Be very still," I breathed. Taking Porridge, I walked away from the fire. I could feel the shadows beyond us. They seemed to be . . . watching me.

I felt the invisible tug that a mother might feel for her children, one that guides her to them no matter how far they are from her. Putting out a hand, I waited.

And the shadow Familiars of Korozoth came slipping over the snow to touch my outstretched fingers.

29

ONE OF THE CREATURES ROSE UP, THE BONY TIPS OF its fingers meeting mine. It felt like the touch of death, and yet I welcomed it.

"Hello." The voice was not mine, but it came from me. The black shadows skirted around, nudging at my ankles. They wanted to play. They wanted me to love them.

And now they were in danger.

"Don't move," I called to the men who were tramping forward to crush the threat. I focused on my strange shadow children. The Familiar in front of me bobbed. Its pathetic robes were a thin trail of smoke over the ground. Whimpering like a dog, it pressed its clay-cold palm to mine. A spark of recognition fanned into love. I wanted to keep this terrifying thing safe.

"Mistress," the creature hissed.

I'd got the feeling that the less I lost my temper, the more control I'd maintain.

"All of you come here. Assemble," I said, pointing a finger at the area around me. They fled in from across the snowy glen, out of the shadows of trees, and stationed themselves about me. They turned their faces up, rolling their smoke hoods away.

Their faces were gaunt and pale, lips chapped and ice blue from the cold.

One of them I recognized, a young woman with ragged white hair and eyes sewn shut with a needle and thread. Gwendolyn Agrippa, no longer threatening me or attacking. Now she rubbed her forehead against my knee like a devoted pet.

"Save us, mistress." She rubbed her arms as though she were freezing.

"The queen wants to talk strategy," Magnus said as he approached. He kept his voice careful. "Is all well?" He drew out his stave when my monsters hissed.

"It's all right. They're mine now." One of the beasts snuffled at my hand, as if I'd a treat to share. The perverse urge to cradle it returned.

No. I must be firm with these and keep them loyal, but I could not afford to love them. With a click of my tongue, I led them up farther into the camp. They trotted after me, some of them on all fours. Magnus and Wolff walked alongside, making certain that people did not attack. Despite their wariness, I believed they understood. And though many of the sorcerers in particular had horrified words to say about this, they did not argue.

So I was left with my little army of monsters. I opened my tent, and they surged inside. With a whistle, I directed them to lie low in the shadows of the room, and they obliged at once. They fit so neatly into the corners that it would be terribly easy not to notice them.

"Go to sleep," I said, puzzled for anything else to say. As I basked in the quiet of all my monsters, I felt a warm flutter of power. I smiled; I could imagine curling on the floor among my lovely shadows and drifting to sleep while they nestled close. Then in the morning, I would rise and don them like a garment and stride out into the world to burn down whosoever stood in my path.

I flinched, extricating myself from that idea as quickly as possible. I walked away to free myself from that nightmarish image. I would not become like Rook, or Korozoth.

But accepting these creatures as my responsibility had perhaps sped me down that path.

The next morning, we were a few days away from the spring equinox, and time was in short supply. Now that we had assembled our armies, all of our time that was not spent sleeping or marching was used in practice. Indeed, the sight of a whole yard filled with magicians, witches, and sorcerers, every one of them trying to out-magic the other, was indescribably bizarre.

"Sure, you can mix up a potion that makes time go backward. But can you do this?" Wilfred asked a blond witch as I passed by. Reaching inside his mouth, the magician turned himself inside out. His lungs, liver, spleen, and beating heart were all on proud display. The witch made a gagging noise; I felt like joining her.

The witches had gathered to show off more of their abilities to a group of sorcerers. As it turned out, potion making was not their only gift. They dug their hands into the snow, and we all watched as the great roots of a tree ripped up out of the earth and waved about. When a sorcerer laughed and called it a simple carnival trick, one of the roots knocked him down. Thankfully, the other sorcerers stepped in before their friend lost his temper.

I left all of them behind and made my way to the queen's tent. I'd left my little shadows back in my own room, where they would not cause any further trouble, I hoped. Today was when we put together a final plan. The time had come to discuss how we were to get ourselves into Sorrow-Fell and who was to undertake the ultimate mission to the stone circle.

The queen, Mickelmas, Maria, and I were the officials at the meeting. We'd each selected a few of our allies to join us and offer advice. Fiona was there at Maria's request, and Magnus at mine. Mickelmas surprised us all by bringing Blackwood, and Blackwood surprised me by attending.

"Are you certain?" Her Majesty asked Mickelmas pointedly.

Blackwood merely bowed. "It is my estate, Majesty. Mickelmas believes I can assist in the planning."

I wished I'd thought of it. "That's an excellent idea."

"I'm glad it meets with your approval," Blackwood muttered. He placed a hand on the map, which displayed a charcoal-and-pencil approximation of Sorrow-Fell. It was a simple blueprint, though. Blackwood knew the estate's secrets in his bones. "R'hlem will expect an assault through the southern woods." He pointed to the path that we had taken coming to Sorrow-Fell several months earlier. "That's the only way to launch a broad attack."

"We've been looking for another way through," Magnus said.

"Don't. We should give R'hlem what he wants: a frontal assault from the sorcerers."

"He'll have several of his Ancients patrolling those woods. It's suicide." Mickelmas looked as if he regretted inviting Blackwood. But I knew what Blackwood was getting at.

"You're thinking of my shadows." I placed a hand on that road, alongside Blackwood's. "I've about thirty or forty shadow Familiars that will follow me now . . ." I swallowed the words I'd been about to speak: *now that Rook was dead.* "We can use them to hide a large portion of the army."

"Not the whole of it?" Maria squinted at the map.

"R'hlem knows we will attack. If we try to hide entirely, he'll know we mean to trick him. If we drive at him with ten squadrons, though, he won't expect twenty more." I smiled at Mickelmas. "He's not one for details."

"Most of the sorcerers will drive in from the south." Blackwood took one of Magnus's wooden pieces and moved it to the eastern woods. "There's a narrower entry, though, which allows us to unleash another attack from this direction. The trees are ancient, so I'd recommend—"

"The witches." Maria twirled a curl of hair around her finger absently—always a sure sign she was thinking. "The trees'll help us. They'll listen."

An odd sentence, to be sure, but one I believed. "That leaves magicians," I said.

"Well, if you've the south and the east, I imagine we can take the west." Mickelmas snapped his fingers, and a wooden figure of his own appeared. This figurine was the shape of a hippopotamus and sported green polka dots. He laid it down, but it wandered away and started munching on a corner of the map. "Apologies. It was too adorable not to bring to life."

Blackwood sighed and rubbed his temples. He muttered what sounded like "Magicians."

"We'll be in Sorrow-Fell the day after tomorrow," Mickelmas said. "The day of the equinox, making our timing quite dramatic."

"Have your scouts located the Ancients?" the queen asked Mickelmas. He used his little hippopotamus to show where he'd sent Alice and her brother, Gordon—the red hawk to whom she'd been feeding bacon. They'd passed yesterday as ravens and had winged their way over the trees to Sorrow-Fell. They'd learned that Callax and Zem had been stationed along the southern road—a challenge for our sorcerer squadrons. Nemneris had been spotted near the west, Molochoron to the east, and On-Tez spent her time wheeling along the estate's perimeter.

In addition to our spies, we'd used scrying mirrors to look upon the stone circle. R'hlem had put his fanatics to work cleaning the stones. He was making them as perfect as he could.

"Of course, we can't win this battle through strength of

arms; R'hlem has the advantage there," Magnus said. "The point of this exercise is to set the place to chaos and draw R'hlem's attention. Once he's come to his monsters' aid, Howel, Mickelmas, and Maria will use Howel's petticoat to transport into the circle itself."

"And once there, we open the circle, draw the Ancients in, trap them, and send them home." I finished sounding far more confident than I felt. Opening the circle, attracting the Ancients, and shoving them through some portal in the sky was easy to say; far more difficult to make it happen. I'd the bone whistle from Azureus to help, and we would bring the *optiaethis* just in case . . . though I didn't want to use it.

"So," the queen said, "Maria and Mickelmas join you—"

"I shall join them," Blackwood interrupted.

Magnus gave him a sidelong glance. "That wasn't part of the plan."

"You need a defense," Blackwood said. He looked at me. "And in case we should need to beckon the creatures, I have the *optiaethis.*"

He might as well have slapped me. "Don't be bloody ridiculous. I've told you what that thing can do. It will kill you."

"I am not ridiculous." He put both hands on the table; all eyes were fixed on him. "If this is the only way to complete the mission, then it stands to reason someone must volunteer."

"Blackwood, I know you love envisioning yourself a martyr, but this is a bit much," Magnus snapped. Blackwood's smile was cold.

"Don't fight over this, you lot. I don't want to have you thumb-wrestling over who gets to give up their soul." Mickelmas punctuated his remark by slamming his fist on the map, knocking over all the wooden figures. The hippo kicked its legs helplessly. "Blackwood, you'll come along and assist. I like the idea of having someone to carry my bag, and adding a layer of defense is wise. If it comes down to the *optiaethis*"—he nodded solemnly—"I'll take care of it."

"Sir, that is gallant." The queen sounded impressed.

"It is. Perhaps we might discuss the incredible reward I should receive in advance, to compensate my gallantry."

The queen regarded him with half-lidded eyes. He didn't ask again.

"So. My forces will lead the charge." Magnus righted the wooden hippo. "You four ride with me as part of the frontal assault—we'll need Howel's shadows, like she said. The witches come from the east with everything they have: potions, arrows, the trees themselves, everything. Finally, the magicians ride in from the other side. Once we've drawn their attention, you lot can finish the job."

"It's all deceptively simple," Blackwood said, his arms folded.

"Perhaps. But with the forces at our disposal, it's the best we have."

"Well, I'm for it." Maria squeezed my hand.

"Good," I said. "So am I."

"If everything's settled, I imagine we should move on." The queen dismissed us with a nod. "We've ground to cover before the day's out."

We bowed and curtsied, then made our way out of the tent. Mickelmas whispered over the wooden hippo, and it vanished in a puff of smoke. He seemed regretful. "It was quite adorable, but no one should bring anything lovable into battle," he said.

Oddly wise words. Blackwood tromped ahead of us, his head down. I called after him, but Magnus took my arm.

"Let him go. Sometimes a fellow needs to sort his thoughts in private," he murmured. Perhaps that was true, too, but watching Blackwood walk away hurt. Of course he'd been the one to volunteer as a sacrifice.

Even surrounded by hundreds of people, he believed he was entirely alone.

Maria followed me back to my tent. I'd told her what—or rather, who—awaited us. Her shock had quickly given way to curiosity: she'd wanted to meet her sister. We entered to find my shadows seated on the floor, patient as dogs.

"Gwen? Where are you?" She stepped forward from the crowd and removed her smoke hood.

"Mistress?"

"I want you to meet someone," I said. Maria held her breath and approached. Extending a tentative hand, she watched as Gwen behaved like a spooked animal; she hopped backward, growling. Then her nostrils flared. Licking her lips with a long black tongue, she crawled forward and sniffed at Maria's fingers. She was taking the scent.

"So this is my sister," Maria said. She put a hand to Gwen's cheek, and the shadow girl clutched at her wrist. There was no danger, though. Rather, Gwen seemed to purr with contentment.

"Yes. They thought she was the chosen one at first."

Maria sniffed. "Makes more sense how she could give in to R'hlem. If Agrippa treated her as he did women like my mother, I'm sure she'd do anything to escape."

"Agrippa." Gwen whispered the word, then made a low, keening noise.

Maria had also gone to see her father out of a morbid sense of curiosity. He now spent his days in the medical tent, flat on his back and muttering nonsense. The doctors had examined him and confirmed that there was nothing to be done. He had survived the abuse and torture of R'hlem's camp only to succumb to a brain fever. He was alive, but not awake. He would never wake again. She'd watched him for thirty seconds before turning on her heel and storming out. She'd done her duty, she said when I followed. That had been enough of her father to last her a lifetime. How would Master Agrippa have felt if he could see this reunion between his two children?

Perhaps it was a mercy that he was unconscious.

Gwen came to cuddle against Maria; I suppose it was because she could smell the blood they shared. Maria sat with her elder sister for an hour, then abruptly got up and left the tent. Gwen whimpered, but on my order she went to sit with her fellows.

Outside, Maria's left hand was a tight fist. I approached cautiously.

"I'm all right." Her eyes shone with unspent tears. "Why did any of this have to happen?" she said at last. That question was far too big for a simple answer.

Horns sounded, signaling to start packing. We were on the move. Maria gave me a fast hug and kissed my cheek.

"Take care of her." With that, she was gone.

It seemed that the sun became brighter as we rose the next morning. The spring equinox was tomorrow, and though true spring was still weeks off, vitality was fast returning to the country.

Provided R'hlem didn't destroy the whole damn thing.

My Familiars dogged Gumdrop's heels, much to the poor animal's chagrin. Magnus always rode at my right-hand side as my most trusted commander. Blackwood came behind, never speaking with me.

When we camped that night, we knew that the morning would bring us within sight of Sorrow-Fell. We were to arrive before dawn, so as to allow our magician and witch troops time to find their way around the perimeter. If they failed, there might not be enough time or distraction for our small band to complete its mission.

I couldn't think of what I had to do. Rather, I busied myself by working with Lilly to peel some carrots for the last bit of stew. I wasn't nearly as skillful as she. Lilly chatted easily as she peeled and cut and prepared, while I found myself all thumbs. Maria finally joined in, just to pick up some of my slack. But the stew smelled heavenly when we got it bubbling. For some of us, this would be our final meal.

Then again, if we didn't stop R'hlem tomorrow this would be everyone's last supper. As I did every night now, I beckoned my shadows and sent them out to stand around the edges of our camp. As one, they secured us from prying eyes. How bizarre to be protected by Familiars.

"Miss . . . Henrietta." Lilly corrected herself. "Was wondering if you'd do me a favor?"

"What's that?" We were seated by the fire. Lilly toyed with her spoon.

"I'm marrying Mr. Dee . . . that is, I'm marrying Arthur tonight." She flushed. "Was hoping you'd be a witness."

Lilly probably didn't expect me to cheer so loudly; indeed, Maria spit out her food in surprise. But there was nothing I wanted more in these last few hours than to see a marriage. Whatever hell awaited us tomorrow, it could not have tonight.

"WAS A BIT NERVOUS AT FIRST, him being such a great gentleman and all." Lilly adjusted her flower crown as Maria and I helped prepare her for the ceremony. We'd borrowed a clean pink gown from one of the magicians—Wilfred had a surprisingly large collection of women's clothing. I had done up Lilly's hair, and Maria had begged a few dried flowers and evergreen branches from one of the witches. The roses, dry though they were, brought out the high color in Lilly's cheeks. The beautiful gleam in her eyes, however, was all her own. "When he told me he'd noticed me in Master Agrippa's home, I didn't know what to say. But after his injury . . ." She paused. It wasn't my place, but I hoped she wasn't about to say that she thought of him as a fragile bird to protect. "I never saw such strength in a man," she continued. "Not even Rook."

I had never asked, when we'd all moved to Blackwood's house together, if she'd still yearned for Rook. She told me now, without being asked.

"I thought Rook so beautiful, really, and so admirable. And he was." She turned her eyes to the ground. "But he wasn't mine."

"He wasn't anyone's," I said. "That's how it should have always been."

"I just saw Mickelmas. He gave me this." Maria came back into the tent, holding something that sparkled. Lilly was white with shock as Maria clasped a diamond pendant about her neck. "A wedding present, he says."

As Lilly went on about how kind the magician was, I pulled Maria aside. "It's not stolen, is it?"

"I'm almost certain it's not." She paused. "Almost."

Maria and I served as the bridal party, carrying candles to light Lilly's way up the hill and into Magnus's tent. Dee was waiting, along with Magnus and a minister. When Dee saw Lilly enter in her bridal gown, the flowers in her hair and the diamond at her throat, he looked as if he might collapse.

Magnus seemed worried about that, too. "Remember, if you die, I have to do my duty as best man and marry her." Magnus clapped his friend on the shoulder. "And I am not much of a substitute."

"Oh, I don't know. You might do for someone, somewhere." I went to stand beside him.

"You wound me, Howel." He grinned. "I like it."

Together, we watched Dee and Lilly join hands in marriage. The candlelight bathed them in a warm glow, and when a light wind gusted into the tent it carried snowflakes that glittered in the air for a brief instant before melting. Maria sniffled beside me when the minister pronounced them man and wife. "Don't look at me." She dabbed at her eyes. "I love weddings."

I could imagine Rook watching alongside us, grinning at Lilly's good fortune. And after the new couple shared a kiss and exited the tent to find an impromptu wedding dance in their honor, with Lambe and Wolff on the violin and cello, I pictured Rook clapping his hands in time to the music.

For the first time since the day he'd died, it did not hurt to think of him. At least, it did not hurt as much.

I clapped with the onlookers for the first two numbers. When the boys began to play a waltz, Blackwood approached me from out the crowd.

"May I have this dance?" He offered his hand. I hesitated, but the way he spoke made me think this was not about our canceled engagement. He escorted me to the floor. Lilly and Dee were dancing—I noticed he did not step on her feet, thank heavens. His dancing had improved since our days at Agrippa's. Maria had dragged Fiona along, and it was obvious they were each trying to lead.

"Is everything all right?" I did not like the haunted look in Blackwood's eyes.

"Have you even considered what happens if we win?" He turned us toward the edge of the dance; less of a chance to be overheard there. "What happens when the rules of our world are turned on their head?"

He wasn't wrong to be concerned. After all, monarchs might come after our queen with precious little regard for the power they wielded. Fitting the reins of English magic into one hand could lead to terrible things.

But the choice had been to unite or die.

"When we win, you and I can rewrite the rules together." I wanted it to sound friendly, but Blackwood flinched.

"Please don't speak as if you and I were going to be mere acquaintances. I can't bear it."

"What can I do to help?" He didn't respond. We both knew what he wanted, and what I couldn't give.

"Let me have this last dance."

So I did. We danced as we had the night we beat back Callax

in London, the night he had spoken of triumph. We danced in silence, as if to commemorate all that had passed between us. What we had loved and hated, longed for and lost in each other.

When the boys finished playing, Blackwood bowed to me. He kissed my hand one last time and left without another word. I watched him go, until Magnus arrived.

"How is he?" There was no jealousy in his voice. Rather, he sounded sympathetic. "Never thought I'd pity the Earl of Sorrow-Fell."

"I wish he didn't have to hurt like this," I said. Magnus held me close while Wolff and Lambe started in on another tune.

He sighed. "I haven't danced with you since the night of the commendation ball." He kissed the side of my head. "But I don't think this is the time to ask."

No. Much as I wanted to dance with him, it wouldn't have been kind. "Will you walk with me?"

"Anywhere."

We moved across the starlit field. I could sense my shadows standing guard in the forest beyond. We were safe.

"Look at them." Magnus gestured at several couples stealing into the trees. "Everyone wants a little privacy tonight. End of the world, and all that."

"Come along," I said lightly, glad he couldn't see me blush. We stepped off the path and into the forest. We stopped behind a tree, and Magnus kissed me.

"I've dreamed of this for so long," he whispered.

I reveled in the strength of him. We scarce drew breath for

several minutes; when one of us broke the kiss, the other began again. The kiss was a dance all its own.

This was possibly our last night to be together. We watched each other, neither sure what the other would do.

"Would you like to hear something truly idiotic?" He kissed my hand. "I've always spoiled everything good in my life by rushing. I want to take the time to do this one thing right."

I was giddy with relief. "So do I. Though we're both fools," I said.

"Horrible fools. You know what this means, of course."

"What?"

He smiled, and kissed me once again. "We've got to win now."

30

THE BLEARY PREDAWN LIGHT RENDERED THE world gray. As the battalions organized, we sorcerers formed several scrying mirrors. From every angle, Sorrow-Fell appeared unaware of our approach. Maria and Fenswick ladled a hot potion down all our throats for strength, but I was too tense to hold on to it. I ended up vomiting behind a tree.

At a quarter past six, the witches and magicians each rode off in separate directions. I rode at the front of the sorcerers alongside Magnus, Blackwood, Maria, and Mickelmas.

The last few miles to Sorrow-Fell passed quickly.

The magical folk did not face this battle alone. Many of the common men, and even some women, had come armed with kitchen knives and clubs, a gun here, a saber there, keepsakes from a grandfather's war. With the normal human men and women, our final army came to something like twenty-five hundred souls.

Two thousand magic users. All that was left of a once-great nation. Some of the older sorcerers must have bitterly regretted destroying so many witches and magicians.

Of the weapons we'd found in Ralph Strangewayes's house:

the bone whistle hung about my neck, Magnus had one of the corkscrew swords and a dagger, and Blackwood's *optiaethis* swung by his side. He'd slipped it into a black bag to hide its light.

My stomach still roiled, but I remained calm. We were as prepared as we knew how to be. I had my weapons and was wearing my aunt's rune petticoat, now hidden beneath a gray dress the witches had made for me.

Mickelmas rode up alongside me.

"You won't remember your mother. I don't know if R'hlem ever told you about her." His voice was tight; it sounded like nerves.

"My father mentioned her a few times."

"I've said before how similar you are to your father." He mopped his brow with a handkerchief. "But you've a cooler head than he has, a trait I believe you get from Helena. So remember, you are not only R'hlem's daughter. You're Helena Murray's as well."

Then, so briefly I almost doubted it had happened, he reached out and squeezed my shoulder.

We rode through the black woods, and the barrier to Sorrow-Fell drew closer. My shadows rode alongside us, sheltering a large portion of the sorcerer army. The hidden sorcerers had orders to cut around whatever attacked us and get them from behind. Magnus had asked if I wanted to ride under cover, but I'd said no.

R'hlem must see me coming.

Secretly, I worried about this meeting. If R'hlem's power was stronger than mine, he could regain control of my Familiars. I prayed our plan would hold.

"Awfully quiet," Magnus said, which was true. No Familiars or Ancients yet, and that concerned me.

With a signal, our army pulled to a halt and waited for Magnus's order to charge. He and I looked at one another, all that we could do in this moment. Surely we could not kiss in the middle of war. Dignity, after all, and propriety—

"Bloody hell," he whispered, and leaned over in his saddle. Our lips met once, but that was enough.

Magnus lifted up his stave. As he did, I saw something coming down the path toward us. Zem, the green-scaled serpent, crawled into view. The ridge on his back was shining purple, his lizard-like gullet bright orange. He regarded us with slitted gold eyes, and steam issued from between his crocodilian teeth. Behind Zem, I heard the rumble of many feet approaching. The enemy had spotted us.

The final battle had begun.

Magnus unleashed a stream of fire into the air as the signal.

Zem belched acid-blue flame. The front line sorcerers threw up wards in front of themselves and their horses; the flames licked around us harmlessly, though the heat made my eyes water.

Ravens dove from out of the sky, slashing and screeching as they went. I sent some of my Familiars up to meet them. A surprise for those ravens, to fight their own brethren.

Somewhere above us, On-Tez screamed in anger. She plummeted down, holding her wings close to her body. Crash-landing into a squadron, she crushed half of them beneath her bulk.

"Keep together!" Blackwood shouted to me, Maria, and Mickelmas. Already, the air was coppery with the smell of blood.

I blasted fire upward, using my magic to shape it into a grand, blooming rose—my signal, as the sorcerer squadrons moved into place behind the monsters. I raised my hand, calling off my shadows. My Familiars receded, leaving the concealed sorcerers to charge as one.

The surprise attack was a success, though now we were bottlenecked on the road, caught in a melee of death.

"Notice me, Father," I muttered as we crashed harder into the lines.

The clash of bodies was growing more feverish, and the screams of the dying rang around us. R'hlem had to find me and move out into the field. I put the bone whistle to my lips and sent up flame to scorch On-Tez. Cawing, she released her victims and soared higher into the sky.

As I played the whistle, On-Tez and Zem stilled to listen. Even when the sorcerers began to assault them with blades and torrents of wind and fire, they did not budge. But I couldn't keep playing forever. And we'd have to jump to the circle eventually. For now, at least, I kept them stupefied, letting the others get in some blows.

"You should go soon," Magnus called. He was ahead of me, still on his horse, fighting his way through the mob. My eyes moved with him as he went.

One of R'hlem's skinless Familiars rose up out of the crowd, slicing with a dagger. Magnus fell off his horse in a spray of blood.

I screamed. Gumdrop reared as I leaped off him, shoving my way to Magnus. Please, please, let him be alive.

"Henrietta!" Mickelmas shouted, falling off his own horse as Zem and On-Tez returned to their senses.

I found Magnus not ten feet in front of me, crouched on the ground and plunging his blade up into the skinless Familiar's throat. Black ichor sprayed over him; he turned from it and caught my eye.

"Go." Magnus stood, one hand to his face, which was a mask of blood. He'd his stave in one hand. "End this. Go, Howel!"

Hands grabbed me. Mickelmas shouted in my ear, "We can't delay."

Magnus spun around and parried another Familiar. He got it through the chest with his blade.

"Go!" he shouted, and disappeared into the carnage. Maria and Blackwood's hands found me. There was no other choice. Closing my eyes, I pictured the circle: the way the grass waved in the breeze, the bright blue of the sky, the slant of sunlight on the weathered stones. In a heartbeat, the chaos around us evaporated.

When I opened my eyes again, we were in the center of that eternal summer.

Thankfully, we were alone. R'hlem had taken the bait and abandoned this place to aid his armies.

The air buzzed with magic, the sound like a drowsy swarm of bees. Power coated the back of my throat. I felt drunk with it. Mickelmas wheeled about the circle, studying the runes. Maria's left hand was opening and closing fitfully; Willoughby could not be far away. I had to keep an eye on her.

"Quickly," I said, and we began to prepare.

Blackwood and Mickelmas unloaded wooden stakes and ropes from their packs, hammering the stakes into the ground at the edges of the circle, then hastily tying ropes to them. The ropes were to hold us in place. Mickelmas had not forgotten nearly being devoured by the portal all those years ago. If we couldn't control it, we wanted to avoid being sucked inside.

Mickelmas directed us to our respective spots. Within minutes, Maria, Mickelmas, and I were positioned at different points in the circle. Blackwood remained just outside, watching for danger. My eyes were drawn to the black bag at Blackwood's side; the *optiaethis*'s call to me had grown stronger as the days had passed.

Minutes ticked past as we waited for the sun's zenith. Sweat crawled down my face, but R'hlem did not appear.

"Prepare yourselves." Mickelmas took a silver knife, readying to cut his finger. "When it's noon, I'll throw blood on the stones. Then hold tight."

"Shouldn't we open it sooner?" I asked.

Mickelmas clucked his tongue. "If we did, it might not

take." He paused. "Or the whole thing could rupture and drag us screaming into hell with it. I might be the nearest thing we have to an expert on these stones, but only in the same way the world's smartest earthworm is an expert on Copernican heliocentrism."

"So we wait," I said after a pause.

He nodded. "So we wait."

The minutes dragged on. Maria's hand stopped clenching. She bent her head to her chest, mercifully peaceful. Every second, I feared R'hlem would show and spoil everything. But he did not arrive. Thankfully.

At last, the sun rose so high that the shadows disappeared. It was time.

Mickelmas flung his bleeding hand at a stone. As the blood struck, the runes hissed in response. Immediately the air above us warped like a whirlpool. I tasted my heart as the sky began to open.

Magic pulsed over my skin. I could feel it funneling into me, and it was almost too much to bear. Mickelmas threw out his hands, welcoming the power. I felt some of it siphon away from me and into him. Maria did likewise. I could sense the three of us, bound to one another, helping each other bear the burden.

The circle grew, and spread . . . and then stopped.

The tear in the sky was contained within the circle. Relief weakened my knees, and I exhaled deeply. We'd stabilized it, thank God. I lowered my arms—I hadn't realized that I'd raised them. It was like a current of energy passing through all three of our bodies. So long as we remained here, we had control.

"Blackwood. Take out the *optiaethis*. Don't open it unless I say," Mickelmas called.

"We've done it." I grinned at Maria. She picked up Mickelmas's blade, which he'd tossed aside.

"Indeed we have." That voice. That cold, joyless smile that she gave me. Oh my God.

"Look out!" My cry came too late. Willoughby lunged at Mickelmas, slicing him down the arm. He fell outside of the circle, yelling in pain. Willoughby leaped after him, laughing wildly as she kicked him again and again in his side. All of the energy funneled back into me, too much to hold. Too much for anyone to hold. My body shook violently, and I bit my tongue so hard that blood flooded my mouth.

Fight. The word painted itself in my thoughts over and over, in vivid red letters. I had to hold on. I clenched every muscle in my arms and legs, locked my knees. Squeezing my eyes shut, I tried to imagine myself as a bottomless pit into which all this torrential magic could drain. I could hold all of it. I could keep the portal stable. I . . .

I couldn't do this. I fell backward out of the circle, out of the flow of power.

The vortex overhead roared, and with a massive *crack* it

ripped once more. The portal was fast growing out of control. Cursing, I dug my fingers into the earth and dragged myself out of danger. I could feel it, trying to suck something living up into it.

"Blackwood, stop her!" I launched flame from my hands to scare Willoughby away. She dodged easily, then threw her knife at me as I prepared another spell. She missed, burying the knife in the ground. When I threw a blast of warded force, desperate to knock her out, she rolled across the grass. Coming up next to me, Willoughby caught at my skirt. When I pulled away, there was a ripping sound.

My blood went cold as I realized one of Agnes's runes lay in her hand.

I wouldn't be able to transport us out of here now.

All that kept me from murdering her on the spot was remembering that she shared Maria's body.

"You fool! Why—?" I screamed . . . and then shut up as every muscle in my body tensed. My jaw had locked. The same had happened to Mickelmas, who now lay next to me. Across the circle, I could see that Blackwood had also fallen.

R'hlem had arrived. Looking over his handiwork, he came to stand over me.

He had dressed especially nicely for the end of the world, regal in a crimson jacket.

Willoughby went to him, beaming with pride. With a wave of his hand, my father freed my jaw, though he held the rest of me prisoner.

"You tried so valiantly, my girl. I'll never say you didn't try." He was so indulgent; it was sickening.

There was one chance left, and only one. In the shadows just beyond the stones, I could feel my Familiars bristle with indignation. R'hlem was hurting their mistress, after all. They bubbled behind him, a sea of black.

My jaw was locked, but I was able to whisper through my gritted teeth. It took a few tries, but I managed my order: "Seize him."

My shadows surged forward. They went for R'hlem with daggers and teeth. My father took a few surprised steps back, with Willoughby beside him.

Then he held out his hands and unleashed the greatest wave of flame I had ever seen.

They fell at once.

Seconds later, they all lay smoldering in the grass. A wail of grief lodged in my throat. Tears blurred my vision, tracked down my cheeks. My children, all gone.

R'hlem snapped his fingers in my direction, and I felt my lips force themselves together. Now I couldn't even whisper; I could only moan.

I saw Gwen among the fallen, her sightless eyes closed forever. First R'hlem had broken her mind, and then the bastard had killed her. And he didn't seem to feel a thing about it.

The war was over.

R'hlem turned back to Mickelmas and me. Blackwood he simply ignored.

"I was going to kill you, my old friend." He knelt beside Mickelmas and slapped the man's face. "But I want you to watch. I want you to witness the smile."

I keened at the back of my throat, trying to beg him not to do this.

"Don't worry," he said softly, as though guessing my thoughts. "I won't let the Emperor harm you."

The tear in the universe continued to spread. Lying on my back, I glimpsed a barren black sky, devoid of starlight. R'hlem strode to the edge of the circle, Willoughby still flanking him. She stood on tiptoe to look at the void, curious as a child.

Taking the knife from her, R'hlem cut his hand. He flung droplets of blood into the air, and the circle sucked them up. R'hlem held out his arms, as if to embrace the tear above.

"Our Emperor will follow the scent of my blood. He will be so pleased with the bounteous world that I offer."

Blood was the hinge in the door of reality. I could feel the space around me . . . expanding.

"Come, Emperor!" R'hlem shouted. "Come and claim this world."

The wind picked up. Thanks to R'hlem's preoccupation with the Emperor's arrival, his control over my muscles diminished. I slowly stood and took one, two, four steps before I felt myself being inexorably sucked into the vortex. Crying out, I threw myself to the ground and dug my fingers into the earth.

Blackwood shouted something I couldn't understand. I got

to my feet again and moved carefully. Blood was the hinge of the door. If I could bleed on the runes, perhaps I could close the circle.

If that wasn't a large enough sacrifice, well, then I didn't know what to do.

R'hlem was paying me no mind. He delighted in watching the fabric of the world unravel. I kept a grip on the rope tied about my waist. At least I had that ready, should I need it.

I prepared to cut my hand, but the current of wind in the circle expanded outward and knocked me off my feet. Between one heartbeat and the next I was sucked up into the air, dangling in the wind, the rope around me digging painfully into my waist. I gasped, trying to get my bearings as I was tossed about. But I was all right. I was fine . . .

Until I felt the knot at my waist give way, unable to take the terrible strain.

I was untethered.

Gasping, I grabbed at the rope as it slid through my hand, burning me. By some miracle I managed to cling to the end of it at the last possible second. I hung there, my grip weakening. I couldn't let go of the stave. If it went through the vortex—that would mean suicide of my soul. But I was losing my grip on the rope.

R'hlem shouted my name in shock, but he could not enter the circle without being drawn into that void as well. Willoughby would do nothing. Mickelmas was too injured to help.

Blackwood—who had shaken off R'hlem's spell, rounded the circle, and found his way to my rope—was my last chance. He alone could pull me in.

He held his stave. I could see the warded edge of it glowing dimly.

"Blackwood, the portal! You can't!" Mickelmas shouted. And then I realized how it was. History had come full circle. Years ago, Mickelmas, Lord Blackwood, and William Howel had all played with the most dangerous object known to man. It had ended with Lord Blackwood cutting the rope that held my father, sending him into a hellish exile. Now here I was, dangling at the end of a rope at the edge of that same hell world, and Blackwood regarded me with a blade in his hand. He could cut it so easily, and no one could stop him. I looked in his eyes and saw fathomless rage there. Rage at me for disappointing him, rage at his family for burdening him, rage at the world for snatching away the things that he loved one at a time.

I was the perfect vessel for his revenge.

"Please," I gasped.

He locked eyes with me and grabbed the rope . . . and then put his stave away.

"Hold on." Blackwood tugged. I gripped so tight that my hand cramped. If I could only sheathe Porridge, I could climb down the rope myself. Instead I had to pray his strength would hold. I was nearly there. . . .

Blackwood's foot slipped on the grass. He fell forward and

released the rope. I flew back out and almost let go. I could feel my fingers slipping.

I closed my eyes, recalling the memory Mickelmas had shown me. When my father went into the portal, it had shrunk back to a manageable size.

If this portal stayed open much longer, the Emperor would come. At least I could spare the world that fate.

I breathed . . . and let go.

Opening my eyes, I found Blackwood's face frozen in horror. The world around me was blue and sunlit and brilliant. I'd take that with me into the darkness, to whatever horrors lay ahead. I allowed myself to fall upward.

Someone caught me by the wrist, suspending me in midair. He dragged me forward, out of the vortex's pull. I was back on the ground, Blackwood on his knees beside me. But he hadn't been the one to rescue me.

R'hlem was untying a rope around his waist.

"Are you all right?" His one eye was huge with fear.

I bolted from him on instinct, colliding with Blackwood, who moved in front of me, his stave ready.

"Don't touch her," he snarled.

R'hlem watched as I pressed close to Blackwood. He shook his head in disbelief, staring at the young earl. "You look so like *him*," he said to Blackwood.

Gently, Mickelmas sat down alongside us. "Charles is dead, William." Mickelmas looked more somber—and more pitying—than I had ever known him. "Please. George is not his father."

Blackwood kept an arm out to protect me. I pressed my cheek close to his, holding out my stave as well. I was ready for an attack. We were united.

"You went to save her." R'hlem sounded weary. I knew then that he had seen what I had—the same scenario that had once condemned him, only this time with a vastly different outcome. R'hlem looked at the vortex. He ran a hand over his face.

"Father." I tested that word once more. He didn't look at me. "How do we close it?"

"It's too late," he said as the pull of the vortex eased. At first I thought it a good thing, but I realized the suction had ceased because something large was coming through.

Something very large.

We would all witness the Kindly Emperor's smile.

31

WITNESS HIS SMILE. THOSE WERE THE WARNINGS I had read, written in blood or carved into walls.

But as the Kindly Emperor emerged into our world, I saw that there was no smile, only a gash in the universe. I felt inconsequential in its presence, as small as if I were gazing up at the black and infinite night sky.

I imagined the whole of humanity stretched out like a carpet of crumbs before this beast.

Its face resembled a Carnevale mask, with jagged teeth and blue triangles beneath the eyes. The emerging body appeared gelatinous, like a slug's. But the form did not matter: there was only that smile, that tear in the fabric of reality. Within that mouth, I glimpsed endless night, the rot of everything good and human. I had never faced anything like this. The Ancients were monstrosities, but merely that. Physical horrors.

The Kindly Emperor's smile ripped away the comfortable reality that had always enveloped me. In that mouth, I saw the truth. There was a universe beyond ours, and it was chaos. There was no reason, or light: only blood, and dead stars dwindling like dying embers in the endless void. The Kindly

Emperor's smile was not from hell; it was hell itself, come to swallow this world.

The earth went mad at the Emperor's presence. The grass rotted. The sky boiled and turned the color of a candy apple. Mickelmas dug his fingers into his eyes.

"The smile! The smile!" he wailed. I quickly turned away; I could feel my sanity unraveling the longer I stared.

R'hlem stood frozen, a hand over his mouth. Then, as if making a decision, he threw his arm down and ran toward the thing.

"Stop!" He planted his feet firmly in the ground. "Go back!"

The Emperor's eyes narrowed in fury. Spines bristled along the collar of its jelly neck.

Before I could even take a breath to scream, one of the quills shot out and speared my father through the center of his body, pinning him to the earth like a beetle. He coughed a bubble of blood, trying and failing to pull himself off the long spine.

I stared as his body went limp, as he slid down the spine.

The Kindly Emperor gave a scream of triumph. It was the sound of a thousand madmen being burned alive.

Nothing could stop this demon beyond time. Nothing except . . .

The world turned bright at the edges of my vision. Fire beaded on my hands, the shadows overwhelming the flame. I was a burning tongue of shadow now. And I ran my tongue along my sharpening teeth, and felt the cry of my five other brothers and sisters out there, fighting the sorcerers, the magicians, the witches . . .

And then I understood. Trying to hold on to myself, I turned to Blackwood. "We have to summon the Ancients."

"It's blocking the portal home!" Mickelmas shouted.

"Yes. I know." I fingered the bone whistle at my throat. "The *optiaethis* calls us home."

No, not *us*.

I fought against the impulse to tip down into that well of endless power, endless darkness. Korozoth's ability whispered through my bones, but I would not succumb. Not yet.

Blackwood did as I asked and took the lantern from its black satchel. The white light pulsed, calling me with the sweetest, smallest voice. *Come home to me,* it called. *Hear me and come.*

Mickelmas looked green but held out his hand to Blackwood. "All right, son. Let me have it."

Blackwood extended the *optiaethis* but paused. "Get Maria. She's fainted."

He was right. Maria was sprawled on the other side of the circle, unconscious. Was she free of Willoughby? I couldn't tell.

The human part of me wished to run and get her; the part that was increasingly Ancient wanted only my brothers and sisters.

"I can't go. Please, you get her," I said to Mickelmas, straining to remain in control.

He huffed. "Wait here." As he hurried over to her, Blackwood turned away from the circle. The *optiaethis* shone bright in his hand.

"This was always meant for me." Blackwood looked into my eyes, and I saw what he intended to do.

The sight of that lantern tugged at the beast inside me. Gritting my teeth, I forced back that monstrous voice. "No. Mickelmas will be right back," I gasped. Stop him. I should stop him. But he held up his hand to me.

"No, Howel. I wanted to be the one to save this country." His mouth twisted in an ironic smile. "Let me have that."

In my bones, I knew that our time was nearly spent. Fighting back the urge to scream, I realized that he was right. Clutching Blackwood's hand, I let him see the gratitude in my eyes, and the tears. I let him see that I understood what he was attempting—what he was willing to sacrifice. Here, at the end, all his bitterness and hatred had burned away. This was his great purpose. I could not take it from him.

He squeezed my fingers in return, and I felt the beast within me surge forward in hunger. "Do it," I growled, giving myself over to my need.

Without another word, he unhooked the latch and opened the cage door. A great burst of hot white light streamed out. Blackwood clutched the thing to his chest. He collapsed to his knees, his face taut with pain. Light shot across the valley, out into the winter and the snow.

The call reverberated in my blood: *Come here. Come home to me.*

Blackwood howled as the light grew hotter and brighter, so bright I was certain I'd go blind. A spasm racked his body, and he collapsed to the ground. The *optiaethis* tumbled from his hands, its light extinguishing.

No. I knelt beside Blackwood, forgetting Mickelmas and Maria, forgetting my father and the Emperor. Blackwood would not open his eyes, no matter how I shook him. The light from the lantern was dead—whatever creature was inside it had expired. I panicked, until I felt the presence of five other creatures.

With the ground trembling underfoot, the Ancients arrived in answer to the lantern's call.

Callax, the Child Eater, pushed his way into the circle first, his shoulders speckled and pocked with mossy disease. He squinted at me, opening his great jaw in a roar.

Nemneris, the Water Spider, crawled up beside him, towering over us on her long, long legs. A hot, steaming rope of venom dripped from her pincers.

On-Tez, the Vulture Woman, swooped in to perch upon one of the stones. The old woman's face glared down at me, the black vulture wings spread.

Zem, the Great Serpent, arrived, his gullet bursting with flame. His lizard eyes darted about, to me, to Blackwood, to Mickelmas, finally settling upon his master, R'hlem. His spines flared upon his back, and steam issued from his nostrils. As if he'd received a wordless order, he turned his attention to the Emperor. The enemy.

Finally, with the smell of bones and decay, Molochoron, the Pale Destroyer, rolled up beside Nemneris. The ball of mold swelled at the threat ahead of us.

Trembling, I put the whistle to my lips and began to blow.

And as I played, the darkness in the recesses of my soul spread.

My tongue traced the edges of ever-sharpening teeth. I closed my eyes, the monster inside me responding to the whistle's call.

I looked at my brothers, my Ancients. They did not need a whistle. They would follow *me*.

I pointed to the Emperor.

Send it home. I rose, my fire and my shadow rising with me.

Every one of my Ancients, save R'hlem, took up a gap in the circle.

It was as it had been in my dream, all those months ago in London. Only this time, Korozoth did not stand here. I took its place.

There remained a single thread of my humanity, and my soul swung upon it.

Desperately, I thought of Rook and myself on the moors, when we had played at King Arthur as children; I thought of Magnus's lips on mine under the winter moon; of Blackwood lying on the ground, having ripped out his soul for his country. I thought of giggling with Maria in the window on the night of Eliza's ball; of Eliza herself, opening the barrier, and the love between Wolff and Lambe, between Lilly and Dee. I thought of Mickelmas and Aunt Agnes. They were the people I loved; the people I protected.

They were the circle of invisible arms that kept me from pitching headfirst into the void.

So I remained myself. But the sharp teeth of Korozoth, and his black power, were at my beck and call.

"Attack!" I roared.

Callax plunged forward and struck the Emperor in its face. Nemneris sank her poisonous fangs into the beast's gelatinous hide. The Emperor gave a cry that could make the stars bleed. On-Tez sliced at the Emperor with her talons. Zem seared the Emperor's flesh with fire. Molochoron surged forward, knocking the Emperor back.

It was not easy.

The Emperor ripped one of Nemneris's titanic legs apart with its teeth. Black ichor gushed from the Spider's wound. Callax, as if defending his "sister," put a fist into one of the Emperor's hideous eyes. But the monster bit into Callax's arm, crushing bones.

My friends; my Ancients. Images flashed through my mind, tinged with emotions of bloodlust, of fear, hunger, rage, and joy. I saw England through their eyes; I saw the land as alien— too cold, too wet, too hostile. They yearned for home, which lay on the other side of the portal.

They needed my help.

I went to stand beside my father. He was not dead—not yet. He looked at me with understanding and lit one hand on fire. I followed suit. Together, we pounded the Emperor with flame. My fire came out black as pitch. I gave myself utterly to the magic.

My magician birthright, my sorcerer training, my monstrous blood, all combined to fight this emperor.

Our attack blindsided it.

Together, we drove the Kindly Emperor back up into the hole in the universe.

I imagined that barren hellscape I had glimpsed several times in different visions. I knew it to be the Ancients' home world, and it had always frightened me. This time, I experienced a surge of longing.

I sensed my Ancient brethren quiver with joy as they picked up on my emotion. The images of that world flooded my vision, and I spread that dream to each of my brothers and sisters. The longing for freedom was strong in them.

They knew exactly what to do.

Callax climbed up into the portal with a joyous cry, On-Tez flying right behind him. One by one, the Ancients crawled after the Emperor to a world beyond time and space.

Home. It was home that they craved. I could feel it, like cresting the hill after a long journey to find the lights in your house lit with a welcoming glow.

But as soon as the monsters fled into the void, the suction began again. Terrified and at the end of my strength, I stood beside R'hlem and set up a ward around us for protection. I watched in panic as the ragged maw grew wider.

"A sacrifice." R'hlem grunted in agony as he held on to the

pole that protruded from his chest. "It's grown too big. One of us must be the sacrifice." Yes, I recalled Mickelmas's memory. All those years ago, they had not been able to close the circle until it had devoured my father. He closed his eye. "I'm done for, Henrietta. Finish me."

I put a blade to Porridge, shivering as I contemplated what must come next.

At the corner of the circle, I glimpsed movement. Mickelmas was struggling with Willoughby. No. She'd already made this a catastrophe. What else could she possibly do?

Maria surfaced back into her own body. With a cry, she pulled out her ax and tossed it to Mickelmas. She threw herself to the ground. He shook his head; he didn't want to do it.

Not Maria.

"No!" I yelled as Mickelmas grudgingly took up the ax. She thrust both her arms forward, and with one deft swing, he severed Maria's left hand at the wrist.

The girl screamed in agony, and the scream was matched by another, deeper cry. Light flashed, and the hole above us shrank back to within the boundaries of the circle. Mickelmas smeared his bleeding hand on the nearest stone and shouted, "Close, damn you! Never open again!"

The vortex swallowed itself whole. In seconds, the sky returned to an August blue. It was as though there had never been an army of monsters, as though the country had not balanced on the precipice of an endless fall.

Maria cradled a gushing stump to her chest. Mickelmas

was working quickly to make a tourniquet to stanch the bleeding. I ran to Maria's side.

"It'll be well," she gasped, Mickelmas doing an admirable job of tightening the tourniquet. "Provided my heart remembers to pump." I buried my face in her hair, giving up prayers to whoever would listen to let her stay.

"Maria," a voice whispered. The faint outline of a woman wavered in the circle's gap. She was short and a bit stout. Her face was not beautiful, but it had a kind of hard knowledge about it. A coil of long dark hair hung to her waist. The ghostly shape of Mary Willoughby looked upon us all.

She had been our sacrifice.

"This child has suffered enough," Mickelmas said. Standing, he dusted his hands. "Mary. It's time to go."

"You left me to die," Willoughby said, focusing upon Mickelmas. Her voice and form was already growing fainter. "I'd have waited for you, you know. To warn you."

"You were the better of the two of us," he said gently.

The wind shifted, and the last traces of her snuffed out like candle smoke. Maria slumped against me. I felt the pulse in her neck, which fluttered entirely too fast for my liking.

"I've got her," Mickelmas said, taking Maria into his arms. "The others need your help."

Blackwood was facedown on the ground, unmoving, and my father was in an even worse state.

R'hlem was pitched at an awkward angle. The Emperor's

spine kept him upright, though gravity was doing its best to push him down. Blood dribbled out the corners of his mouth.

"Let me help you," I said, trying to think of a way to get him comfortable and off this blasted pole.

"It's nearly done," he rasped, "and I can hardly feel it any longer." I couldn't stand to see him like this and forced the earth to spit out the spine. He groaned as the pole left him.

"Please, let me look at you," he said as I knelt beside him. His hand grazed my cheek.

What did I feel for this man? I had never known him as William Howel. Until these last few moments, I had known him as a man who would sunder worlds for revenge. And for love, as well. Love of my mother and hatred for what had been done to her.

Shaking, I took his hand in my own. R'hlem—my father—struggled to keep his one eye open.

"I wish there were time," he said. His grip slackened, and he was gone. Between one heartbeat and the next, he had slipped away. There had been no moving final words, no declarations of love or forgiveness. There had been no explanations, or apologies. No real redemption. Nothing fair or just about it. There was only silence. And not enough time.

Everything within me gave out, and I collapsed beside my father's body.

32

I AWOKE WITH A START. IT DID NOT TAKE ME LONG to realize where I was—in Magnus's tent, back at camp. Outside there was cheering, and guns going off in celebration. The war was over. Truly over.

Before me, Magnus sat on a stool. He'd his head in his hands, looking rather wretched for the end of such a conflict. But he was alive, and here with me.

"Magnus." He looked up, a bloodied bandage covering half his face. The great wound he'd received in battle had slashed him from chin to temple. But the graveness in his eyes and the painful twist of his lip were the most striking difference. He looked as if he'd aged ten years in two hours.

He came to sit beside me. We were alive and together. He stroked my hair.

"This is all I wanted," he whispered. I kissed him. He kissed back, though more gently than I'd expected. "There's something you should know," he said. "Blackwood is alive."

"Oh, thank God." I could have cried in relief, but Magnus didn't smile.

"The doctors have seen him." He closed his eyes. "There's not much time left."

Time. It was always running out, always stingy. First my father on the battlefield, and now Blackwood. "May I see him?" I whispered. I wanted to curl into a ball and weep, but as Magnus had said, there was no time for it now. There would be time later.

Plenty of time to grieve.

"You'd better, I think. The doctors also examined you." He spoke stiffly, as if reading lines in a play, and badly.

" 'Examined me'? Magnus, what are you talking about, for God's sake?"

"You're with child."

My whole body froze. How? That is, of course I knew *how*. But . . . why? Touching my stomach, I felt as if some strange presence had placed its hand alongside mine in reply. After everything we had been through, this was not how Magnus and I should feel. And Blackwood . . . my God.

"I need to see him." Magnus helped me up.

"The doctors are with him. I've sent for the vicar as well."

Yes. Of course. We would need to be married, Blackwood and I. That is, if he still even wanted to. After everything . . .

I felt numb as Magnus walked me toward the queen's tent. The exclamations of joy all faded away as though swallowed by a rising tide. All I could hear was my own blood's movement. Magnus stared straight ahead. He would not break, and I could not break, either.

As we approached the tent, he stopped us. "Not so long ago, I might have asked you to marry me and pass it off as mine."

"Not so long ago, I might have agreed." I could not do that now. I'd known the pain of being deceived about one's family history. I knew the damage lies could do. I would not visit those same mistakes upon an innocent child, and neither would Magnus.

We had both grown into people who could properly love one another, but those people—those responsible, mature people—now had to part.

Numbly, I entered the tent. The men moved aside for me. I noticed how the doctor watched me when he believed I wasn't looking. I could only guess at what he thought.

All my anger fled when I saw Blackwood. They'd stretched him out on a cot. His right hand lay over his breast. His skin, always pale, had now gone nearly white. The most shocking change of all was his hair. No longer a rich black, it was pure silver, as though the color had been leached away. His green eyes were paler as well, and the blue of his veins stood out on his alabaster skin.

"You're alive," he whispered. I fell to his side, kissed his hand.

"I have something to tell you," I murmured.

"First, I want to ask you. Something." He could not draw enough breath for a full sentence. "Marry me." He swallowed. "I know. I'm dying. But as my widow . . ." He coughed, unable to finish. I knew what he meant. As a widow with no heirs, I would have a pension, and a house on the estate. I would be secure.

"I need to tell you something." I whispered the news into his ear. He closed his eyes. A tear tracked down his cheek.

"Then I suggest we hurry," he rasped. He craned his neck to find Magnus standing over the bed. The other men had left the room, and it was only the three of us. Swallowing, Blackwood said, "I know this isn't what you wanted, Magnus. But please, would you stand by us today?"

He wanted Magnus to be our witness. Magnus knelt by the bed—I couldn't bear to look at him. I needed to stay strong.

"Of course." He clasped hands with Blackwood.

"I'm sorry." Blackwood coughed. Patiently, Magnus gave him some water.

"Nothing to forgive," he murmured. The three of us sat there, all the blame washed away. Magnus and I looked at each other. I put all of my heart into that one glance, and he told me with his eyes all that he felt in return. "Did you ever think we'd shake hands and part friends, Blackwood?"

"Truly, the most"—Blackwood took a breath—"surprising development."

Finally, the vicar entered. Blustering, he began the ceremony at once.

I still had Blackwood's ring, I realized. Sliding it off my right ring finger, I let him put it on my left. Magnus stood to the side, watching all of it unfold. He was there when Blackwood and I murmured our vows, when we kissed lightly to seal it. Magnus did not flinch when we were pronounced man and wife, and even applauded.

"A handsome couple." He winked at me, then left with the vicar to give us privacy.

Now we were married. I'd his ring on my finger. I was Lady Blackwood, just as Lambe had said I would be.

Blackwood placed an ice-cold hand on my cheek. His thumb traced my bottom lip. "I still love you," he murmured.

Even though my heart was breaking, I spoke the truth. "And I you."

It was possible to love in different ways, to love Rook, and Blackwood, and Magnus, even as they were all taken away from me one by one. I lay down on the cot to give him warmth. Blackwood ran his fingers through my hair. Already, the strength in his body was depleting. Soon what little scrap of his soul remained would flee.

"Promise you'll raise the child to be better than I was." He kissed the top of my head.

"Any child would be proud to take after you."

"This world isn't mine any longer. I was forged by one thing, Henrietta. The Order. I don't have your flexibility. I don't know how to live in a different world, even if it's a better one. Raise someone who's the opposite of me."

"I don't want the opposite of you." The tears came hot and fast now. "I'm sorry I couldn't give you what you wanted."

"You did." He sounded amazed. "The war is over. The kingdom is saved. Sorrow-Fell will rise again, overseen by my wife and child. Even if this joy is an hour long, it is perfect. Don't pity me, my love." He kissed my lips. "Pity those who never know such happiness."

I traced my fingers across the beautiful planes of his face, his jaw, his lips. I laid my head on his chest. I told him how he had taken my breath away at Eliza's commendation ball. He'd seemed a prince from a fantasy. I believe that made him happy to hear. We spoke of all the things we had done and seen together.

"I think," he said, his voice faint, "that I know why the *optiaethis* could not take my entire soul. A part of it has its safekeeping with you, always."

After a while, Blackwood could not speak. He listened as I spoke. I told him of meeting him that first time in Agrippa's study, of feeling the stirrings of love when we waltzed together at his house. Finally, three hours after our marriage, Blackwood exhaled one long, soft breath. There were no more after that.

It felt as though I had always had an invisible cord tied to my waist, one that steadied me as much as the one in the stone circle. I had not known the significance of that cord until it was cut, sending me spinning into the abyss.

I gave a muffled cry against his chest, and my hands fluttered uselessly over him. His hair, his cheek, his chest, his hands. Trying to trap the memory of them forever. He was lost to another world now, hopefully a kinder one.

I couldn't let him go. Even when the men entered the tent, even when I felt Maria's soothing hand on me, and even when

Magnus lifted me into his arms to take me away, I wouldn't let go. I reached over Magnus's shoulder for Blackwood. He had been my enemy, then my greatest friend, my lover, my husband. He had been the worst and the best of sorcerers, and now he was gone.

"I'm sorry," Magnus said over and over as I wept. It took a while for me to realize that he, too, was crying.

33

I HAD NOT EXPECTED TO SIT IN BUCKINGHAM PALace ever again. But after the battle of Sorrow-Fell, and after Blackwood had been laid to rest on his family lands, we had journeyed back to the capital. London was still a tomb, a broken world filled with ashen air. But the palace remained. And the day after we had arrived, the queen summoned her three magical heads.

Mickelmas sent the Chen siblings, Alice and Gordon, in his place. "The future requires younger blood," he had told the queen. In truth, he did not want the responsibility of governing.

Maria also turned over the position, for similar reasons. Of our initial triumvirate, I alone answered the queen's summons. I now stood before her throne, raised upon a velvet dais. Lord Melbourne, the prime minister, had survived, and stood alongside the monarch. Certain members of Her Majesty's government had also made it through and were happy to slink out of hiding now the war was done. I didn't much trust politicians, I realized.

But I held Her Majesty in the highest esteem. Her warm smile indicated she felt the same about me.

"Lady Blackwood," she said. How odd it felt to hear myself called that. Henrietta Howel was truly gone. "For your sacrifice on behalf of our country and our people, We thank you. We honor you." So she'd begun to use the royal *We,* speaking for both herself and her nation. It suited her, as she had never seemed more like a queen than she did right now.

She turned a disapproving eye to her courtiers, who half bowed. Lovely.

"What may I do for Your Majesty?" I asked.

"I wish to truly set up my new consortium," the queen replied. "To that end, I will require only the noblest and best of my three races to lead." For a moment, I believed Her Majesty needed my help choosing one of the older men, perhaps a Hawthorne. Instead, she continued. "I wish you to take the place at my right side, head of all the sorcerers in my kingdom."

My jaw dropped; it had been one thing to assume the mantle in time of war, quite another to be gifted it now.

"I don't know what to say," I murmured.

"Indeed. This will involve, of course, remaining in London."

As one of the queen's most trusted advisors, I would need to stay close by her side, and I would have access usually granted only to the prime minister and other important heads of state. The power would be exceptional. "You've overwhelmed me, Majesty. I can never thank you enough."

"Well?" Her Majesty asked.

For me, there could be only one answer.

"I thank Your Majesty, but I regret I must decline." I gave

a deep curtsy. Some of the men snorted in derision. Well, they could all rot.

"I . . . We don't understand." Queen Victoria frowned.

"Your Majesty has given me everything I could ever want," I answered. "But Sorrow-Fell must be rebuilt."

"There are those in your late husband's family who can oversee that." But she had not given her word to Blackwood on his deathbed. She had not promised to raise our child in Sorrow-Fell. Beyond that, the queen did not know how homesick I had been for Yorkshire.

There was work to be done up there, taking care of the estate and, more importantly, the people.

"London is too political for me. I want to rebuild the ties between the magical races in the north." Indeed, being the regent of Sorrow-Fell would require a political hand all its own. "Also, I want to oversee the portal. That stone circle is still active and must be protected. But above all"—here I paused to keep my voice from breaking—"I would like to go home."

My voice was quiet, and so was the room. For a moment, the only noise was the patter of the rain outside.

Finally, the queen said, "Of course. You've earned your rest, How—Lady Blackwood." She extended her hand. I went and kissed it, much as I had when I was first commended.

"If Your Majesty would take my advice, Arthur Dee would make an excellent nominee."

Someone snorted. "Isn't he a bastard?" That was one of the queen's human councilors.

Forcing my anger to remain at bay, I said, "He understands the people in a way few others will."

I locked eyes with the man and let off a quick gust of flame. He wisely fell silent. I curtsied once more to the queen and walked to the door. Before I left, Her Majesty spoke again.

"What We owe you can never be repaid."

I looked back at her, the young queen with a ruined kingdom to reunite. I prayed she could do it. I believed that she could.

"There is no debt, Majesty. I only did my duty."

Alone, I walked the halls of Buckingham Palace and exited into the courtyard, where the spring air was beginning to warm through winter's chill.

"AMERICA. LAND OF OPPORTUNITY, PURVEYOR OF only the best in whale oil and rude political cartoons." Mickelmas led all of us along the dock. His children, the gaggle of orphans he'd taken in long ago, dragged his magical trunk and gaped up at the ship.

"I believe you've a limited idea of the country," Maria drawled. Fiona was beside her, the pair of them outfitted in gray cloaks. Maria's left wrist was wrapped in bandages. Fiona held her by the arm, treating her as though she were delicate china. Being Maria, she didn't love it, though since it was Fiona, I could tell that she didn't mind so much. After the war, they'd said that they didn't want to remain in England or Scotland any longer. "Too much pain and too many memories" was how Maria had put it.

"Will you be all right in America?" I asked Mickelmas as his children loaded the trunks. "They've still got those monstrous laws."

"I shan't be going south. New York, I think, or Boston. Besides, the young, upstart nation's views on slavery might make for a worthy challenge." He pulled his beard. "My most shameful secret, my hedgehog, is that I need conflict to thrive. It's how I stay looking so marvelously young."

"You really don't want to be at the queen's right hand, lauded as the greatest magician of the age?"

"What I want is to wake in a place that doesn't remind me of everything I've lost," he said. He narrowed his eyes at me. "If you weren't tied to that bloody estate, I'd suggest you come with me. A change will do you good."

"I'm afraid I'm not as adventurous as you," I said. Some required the constant hustle from one day to the next. I wanted to be useful and active, but at home. I was not the voyager that Mickelmas was, and I did not mind that. Mickelmas kissed my hand.

"You were my favorite apprentice," he said.

"Wasn't I your only apprentice?"

"Shut up."

Grinning, I kissed his cheek. Maria came up to me, her pack slung over her shoulder. Her red hair billowed in the wind as we clasped hands tightly. Already, I could feel this goodbye taking a piece of me.

"Are you certain you won't stay?" I whispered. Maria lowered her eyes.

"I . . . I don't know that I can do it. Too many memories."

She pressed the bandaged stump of her left hand against her stomach. After her rather ingenious move to rid herself of Willoughby and close the portal with the same blow, we'd inspected the prophecy tapestry once more. It displayed a white hand reaching toward the sky; the meaning of that hand was no longer lost on us. *She is two, the girl and the woman, and one must destroy the other,* the prophecy had read. Maria, the girl, had vanquished that woman, it was true. But the girl Maria had been was now gone as well. We were all of us struggling to find our feet in this new world. Maria smiled wanly. "I'll write. Spelling won't be much, but I'll do it all the same."

"Well, then. Farewell, Templeton."

Maria grinned; she'd always liked how we sorcerers used one another's surnames. "Farewell, Howel," she replied.

I hugged her, resting my chin atop her head. She was so bloody short, it made me laugh even as I cried. Fiona embraced me as well.

"Take care of that one, if you can," I said in her ear.

"That's an impossible task, but I mean to try." She winked. They turned and boarded the ship. I hurried back to Magnus, who was waiting with the carriage. The bandages had come off his face by now, and a line of stitches went from the edge of his jaw to his hairline. He claimed the scar would make him look even more dashing.

He said nothing, but the way he carefully helped me back inside the carriage showed he understood how much this hurt. As we drove away from the dock, I forced myself not to look back. The only way to survive in life was to move forward. That was what I told myself, at any rate.

"Did I tell you Her Majesty gave me a position?" Magnus asked.

"Lord, she's not made you head of the sorcerers, has she?"

"Thankfully that's fallen to Dee. Poor fellow was speechless." He took off his hat, studying the brim. "The queen wants me in her royal magical guard, spreading the news of our consortium. I'm to make a Grand Tour of the Continent, from Spain to Poland, probably with a semipermanent post in Brussels."

"That's . . . wonderful." I'd nearly said "far."

"A very grand post, you know." He said it as though he were convincing himself. There was nothing else either of us could do. My mourning garb would remain in place for at least a year. I'd hoped, perhaps, that he would stay in England and wait, but duty called.

I understood.

Though it still hurt.

"The coach will be awaiting us at Agrippa's," he said. "I'll escort you down to Devon, if you like?"

I would have liked that more than anything. But I knew

it would only delay the pain of parting for both of us. I didn't want that. Besides, I wasn't certain I would be able to say good-bye if he came with me.

"I believe I need to make the next stage of the journey alone," I said. That was not a lie. What I wanted to do should be done privately. Magnus did not argue. I allowed myself to memorize him as we drove, the way he sat, the way one stray lock of hair always fell in his eyes. He'd begun to grow his hair out of its military cut, and it hurt to think I would not be there to see it in full curl again. Once we arrived at Agrippa's, he kissed my gloved hand in farewell. What could I say to him? What would he say in return?

Tell him to come with you to Devon. The thought was there and gone. I was too afraid of my own feelings. Magnus sighed as he released my fingers.

"I'll write, Howel." He put his hat back on his head. "I know, I know. Lady Blackwood. But I can't help it. You'll always be Howel to me." With that, he got back in the coach and drove away without another word. I watched until he'd passed out of sight.

The new carriage bound for Devon was waiting, along with the wagon and its peculiar cargo. I'd chosen to start the journey at Agrippa's, because of one last call to pay.

Agrippa's staff had been reduced considerably. There was now only a butler, who answered the door with a weary expression. He bowed to me and seemed grateful for the basket of food I presented. His master was resting today. No, he could not have visitors. I was not surprised.

Agrippa had survived the final battle and been returned to his old home. But he was an empty shell, an invalid. As I walked down the path to the gate, I stopped to look at the house's front windows. I imagined I caught a glimpse of a wizened form seated there, watching the world without really seeing it.

This house would become a mausoleum to a vanished world, the world of sorcerer supremacy. Children might eventually run past the iron gates in mock fear of the ghostly man who lived inside.

I raised my hand once to my old Master and left him gazing onto a city that belonged to him only in dreams.

WHEN R'HLEM DIED, HIS BODY HAD not been given to me. The nation had paraded it down the highways of the country on our way to London. Some had spoken of hanging him by the neck from London Bridge, as in the old days of warning off barbarians. We had stopped in the fields where they were burning piles of Familiar corpses; after the Ancients had departed this world, their minions had fallen to the ground, lifeless. The men and women would cheer us and jeer R'hlem's casket. They hurled rotten produce at it. They made vulgar gestures. They had earned the right.

The queen, who had hated R'hlem as much as any of her countrymen, allowed the abuse of his corpse as we traveled to

London. She allowed the festivities, the burning him in effigy, and set up a place in town for a statue that would always celebrate how he had been vanquished. Indeed, I believe she even made a special order to have the pigeons relieve themselves on it doubly often.

But after the celebrations began to die down and the statue had been commissioned, Her Majesty had the body placed back in my care. It had been my sole request.

We took the long road to Devon. My morning sickness was making travel rather difficult, but I lay against the bumping carriage wall and closed my eyes. I wasn't even certain if my aunt's cottage would still be there. Perhaps, like much of the country, it had been burned to the ground. When we emerged onto the downs, however, I saw it again.

I'd forgotten how sweet it looked, a snug little whitewashed building with a thatched roof and red-painted shutters. Flower-beds of yellow and blue nestled against the walls of the house. I'd been born in this little cottage. It had belonged to Aunt Agnes, willed to her by her late husband. My mother had left this place to do what she could for my father in London. She'd been tortured and killed by Charles Blackwood, by all the Order, really. At least with a consortium, that could not happen again. I'd avenged her in that.

My gut twisted to think of the cottage standing empty. After Aunt Agnes had helped me escape, I knew that R'hlem had killed her. I could only pray it had been quick.

The carriage halted when we came to the plot of land behind the cottage. My uncle was buried beside the chestnut tree. Aunt Agnes had buried my mother here as well, and as a child I'd sometimes played there. I'd laid wildflowers on the stone, and kissed it.

HELENA HOWEL
BELOVED WIFE AND MOTHER

I had them dig a plot right beside my mother's, and the men took the casket off the wagon and lowered it into the earth. Only the vicar seemed to have an inkling of what was going on. Wisely, he said nothing.

Soon there would be another headstone beside my mother's. It would tell of William Howel, solicitor, beloved husband and father. Perhaps it was more, far more, than R'hlem deserved. But in the end, he had saved our kingdom, and he had loved my mother. For her sake, as well as his, I wanted them together.

I was surprised to hear footsteps coming up the path, and shocked when I discovered my aunt standing behind me, dressed in black mourning garb. Her long veil streamed in the breeze.

"How?" I squeaked. Impossible. She'd died. I'd seen her dragged away by the Familiars, and R'hlem would never forgive such betrayal a second time.

She put a hand to my cheek: a hand that was no longer bandaged.

"He wanted to kill me." Her eyes told of sadness and love. "But he could not."

We both turned to the grave. R'hlem, my father, was gone. The men patted the grave flat with their shovels and walked back to the carriage.

"How are you, Nettie?" she asked. I had several responses. *I'm well, I'm ill, I've a child on the way, I'm married, I'm widowed, I'm the regent of Sorrow-Fell and the north, I haven't eaten since this morning.*

But all that came out of my mouth were the words "I'm alone."

And then the facade shattered, and I wept. My aunt took me in her arms and shushed me as she rocked me back and forth, much like I was a child again.

34

AUNT AGNES RETURNED WITH ME TO SORROW-FELL to help. The place was as bleak as I'd feared it would be. Much of the main house remained a smoldering wreck, now dampened by the snowfall. Only a handful of the surviving servants returned when I asked them. We resided in the Faerie part of the house, which seemed to breathe and whisper in the night when we were asleep. I lay on a cot, a thin blanket stretched over me, and listened to the drips from the leaking roof.

Sometimes it seemed I hadn't come so far from Brimthorn after all.

Still, we made progress. Aunt Agnes, as it turns out, was a superlative manager of household economies. She got the servants into shape and sent out for men to come and estimate how to rebuild the house. But the land was barren. The forests had lost the sheen of magic. Perhaps the power might never return, and the pine and rich earth and willow leaves would be all that remained of a once-great power.

That would not be much of a legacy for me, or my child.

One day, not too long after we'd returned to Sorrow-Fell, my aunt called me to come and look at something. We found a new spring lamb, bleating and covered in cottony fluff, as it bounded up the path to our door. Someone had tied a ribbon about its neck, with a note attached. I took it up and read while my aunt fussed about what to do with the creature.

My dear Lady Blackwood,

This is to say that we are fine and well. After the battle of Sorrow-Fell, we went to the queen and resigned from the consortium. Clarence is too ill to continue serving, and I must remain by his side.

Our only desire is to find some quiet corner of the earth where we might live without magic.

I confess I wanted to move on without even telling you, though it would have pained me, but Clarence insisted. I find I must give in to his wishes. I cannot say no to love.

Please accept this gift as a token of our esteem and friendship. I doubt the pair of us will ever forget you. It is rare to meet a true lady in this life, much less a true sorcerer. We shall always remember.

With great love,
Isaac Wolff

I folded up the note and asked when the lamb had come. The butler, Cranford, replied that it had only just arrived. I walked around the corner of the house and drew up a scrying mirror, focusing upon the southern road that led out of Sorrow-

Fell. Soon I glimpsed a carriage. Through the window, I caught sight of pale hair and a delicate face.

Wolff and Lambe could not see me, but I raised my hand in farewell nonetheless. I watched the carriage until it rounded a bend. Then I dissolved the mirror and went back inside.

THE SPRING GREW, BUT THE MAGIC did not. I would sometimes go to the stone circle and sit there, feeling the balmy air of summer on my face and listening for the quiet hum of the circle's power. So far, I had heard nothing.

What would that mean, for all of us?

Still, the snow-sorrows were withering with the coming spring. I had to believe that melting sorrows were a promise of good things to come.

One day, a few weeks after our arrival, I was out walking in the woods when I heard the steady clop of hooves coming down the path. It was true spring; the grass had begun peeking through the frozen soil. The whole world smelled of new earth and budding promises. Ahead of me, two ladies in gray cloaks led a horse and wagon. Their skirts were well muddied, and they chatted amiably.

"Hello," I called as they approached. The one nearer me lifted back her hood. It was Maria.

"I thought you were gone!" I gasped.

"We could not be away from the land," Maria said. Her eyes crinkled at the corners as she laughed.

"This one's such a liar. We could not stomach the sea."

Fiona stroked the horse's nose. "Though a witch's spirit is indeed tethered to the earth. The things that live in Yorkshire bind us."

Maria grinned cheekily. "Besides, I missed you."

I hugged her about the neck. I hadn't realized how badly I'd needed a friend. We walked together back to Sorrow-Fell, while I insisted the two of them stay awhile. Stay forever, if they could.

And then we stopped, because on the path ahead stood a white stag. The animal's snowy fur glistened in the sunlight, and its shimmering black eyes watched us with caution. One soft ear flapped. Finally, it galloped back into the forest. Maria hummed to herself.

"That's a lucky sign."

"Aye." Fiona looked after the stag. "It's a call to the forest itself."

As we continued to clear and plant, to clean and build, the world around us sprang into new life. It was more than just a place, Sorrow-Fell. It was the pin in the whole of English magic's garment, the force that kept everything from falling apart.

More than my work as an upholder and enforcer of magical law, I was the guardian of English magic itself. Its blood was my blood, and its heart my heart. My fire was brighter than ever, without a whisper of shadow.

But I could not help the feeling that I was forgetting something important.

One morning, as dawn lit the sky, I walked out with my hair long and unbound, a shawl about me. I breathed in the dew, and felt the earth beneath my slippers quivering into new life. Sorrow-Fell was urging me on to *something*. But I had done what I could. I'd visited the stone circle. I'd carted away the rubble and made plans for the house. What else could I do?

I thought of that white stag. And I thought again of Queen Titania, standing before me in her regal robes of snow white. She had traced a letter—a rune—into the air, embedding it in my mind.

I knew what to do.

I knelt, Porridge in hand, and drew the rune that Titania had gifted me into the dirt. I wasn't certain this was how it worked, if it would even work at all. But as I finished carving it—those wavy lines at the bottom of the *M*, the three dashes through the center—I felt the very air around me crackle to life. Glimmers of Fae magic appeared in the corners of my eye, gone before I could turn my head. Piping song from the reed flutes of forest nymphs floated to my ears on snatches of the spring wind.

In the distant woods, I knew that toadstools would sprout from the earth, and that fairy rings would form. Beyond, in the old druid lands, the circle would hum back to life with awful and wonderful power.

The ivy on my stave bound me to more than Blackwood: it bound me to Sorrow-Fell itself.

Magic returned to the world, and I knew that I had done my job. I was truly and finally home.

Maria walked over to me as the land revived. "Well." She whistled. "What now?"

I turned to my friend.

"Now," I said, "we begin again."

ONE YEAR LATER

EPILOGUE

ON THE FIRST DAY OF SUMMER, I FINALLY REMOVED my mourning clothes. It had been well over a year—nearly fifteen months, to be exact. I'd found safety in the black satin and crepe that I dressed in every day. Those clothes had been my armor against the world, an unspoken excuse to keep to myself. Still, my maid Dawkins had insisted that I finally remove the "drab items," as she called them. Since children were coming over for a picnic, it would not do to look like a frightful old woman. Besides, summer was too hot to be always in black.

"You are far too young, m'lady, to be shuttered away," the maid clucked before laying out a new periwinkle gown. She'd taken particular care to choose the color. I'd insisted on finding a maid with a quick tongue and a solid head, and Dawkins suited me fine in that regard.

She helped me step into my gown and began the work of pinning and buttoning me into the yards of taffeta silk. Already, the girl I faced in the mirror looked years younger than she had before. Dawkins sniffed and gave a discreet tug of my bodice to get it into place. "Much better, if I may say so."

"You may," I said with a grin. Sitting at my vanity, I let

Dawkins attend to my hair as my secretary entered. People had questioned why a lady should need a secretary, conveniently forgetting that I'd matters to attend to besides parties and salons. Laurence was the younger son of an old, if minor, sorcerer family, and he was a quick study. With a short bow, he began to read off a list.

"I'm afraid we've only two hours for the picnic." He sounded like he regretted this whole affair. Indeed, he'd tried to convince me that I had too many items on my itinerary to attend to children. However, I'd insisted. "Afterward, the minister of York wants to speak with you regarding the magician situation. Apparently there are protestors against the consortium."

"I'll be glad to remind the minister that the people are allowed to criticize." I clasped a bracelet around my wrist. Dawkins gave a meaningful sniff. She didn't approve of people "rising up," as she called it, but any healthy society needed to hear multiple voices.

"Indeed." Laurence sighed and returned to the schedule. "Followed by tea with the head of the Order . . . beg pardon, the sorcery branch." His lips pursed. He was one of the people who missed the old ways.

At least Dee and Lilly would be here today. That brightened everything.

"Anything else?" I asked as Dawkins hooked my necklace in place.

"The queen intends to make her way north for an inspection with her new husband. She wants a show of support for him." Wise choice. Many did not approve of a foreign consort, though I'd heard Prince Albert was a good man. "She asks to be received at Sorrow-Fell. Also, you've invitations to the Duke of Roxburgh's ball on Thursday next. His eldest son will be in attendance. The duke, er, made certain to mention that."

Ah. That. Since the period of my mourning had passed, I'd received several letters from eligible gentlemen professing themselves enamored of me. Enamored of my status and estate, rather. I frowned; this was not what I wanted to hear. Laurence quickly changed the subject.

"You've a letter from Genoa." He laid it on my table. "And Master Stephen is rather fussy."

Genoa. I forced myself not to grab for it.

"Thank you." I took up a letter opener. "Let me know when the guests arrive."

Laurence bowed, and I dismissed Dawkins as well. When I slit open the letter, my hands shook so badly I nearly cut myself. I'd recognized the large, jagged handwriting at once. Tearing the letter open, I read.

> *Lady Blackwood,*
> *Still feels odd to call you that, Howel. Would Blackwood-Howel be an appropriate name? Feels very modern.*
> *Got your letter in Brussels forwarded to me here. That was a miracle, as I've been on the move since April. Did Stephen enjoy the toy soldier I sent from*

Hamburg? I'd planned on sending him one from here, but the Genoese don't seem to have a great selection. Perhaps he'd like a fine cheese? Plenty of that about.

You must also tell me if Templeton figured out the riddle I sent in my last letter. She probably knew it within instants of reading. She's rather clever like that. Just between us, do tell me what the answer is, because I still can't make it out.

Most importantly of all, how are you, my dear Blackwood-Howel? I ponder this question by the fountains of Rome or on the boulevards of Paris. I find I've taken you with me across the great expanse of the Continent, and my picture of you is forever lovely, and always troubled. Please set my mind at ease. Tell me if you smile, and how often, and for what reason. Nothing would make me happier.

However, you may need to wait on the reply. I'm afraid you won't be able to write me here. I'm leaving on something of an important journey. Perhaps my most significant mission yet. You'll know of it in due course, I assure you.

Your obedient friend,
Julian Magnus

As I put the paper down, my heart sank. So. He'd had nothing to say about my last letter.

After he'd gone to Europe, Magnus and I had corresponded

frequently. I'd receive postcards from Paris, Venice, Berlin, all of them inquiring after the estate. How was I? Did I realize that Bavaria produced the finest pastries in Europe? I received sugared ginger and peppermint tea to ease my pregnancy, and chocolate and candied fruit afterward as a treat.

In the darkest months after Blackwood's death, Magnus had made me laugh again. Soon I found myself eagerly awaiting his next letter. I'd needed something to look forward to.

When I'd entered my confinement, Magnus had offered to come back to Yorkshire to see me. He'd asked his superior officer for a leave but had been rejected. Maria and Aunt Agnes had stayed by my side during Stephen's delivery.

I had never told Magnus exactly how agonizing the birth had been. The pain was nearly beyond endurance, and Maria said there was a time she feared I wouldn't survive it. Of course, the moment I held Stephen in my arms I'd have been glad to endure the pain again twice, or a hundred times. He'd been small and perfect, with a rosebud mouth; more than that, he had been mine absolutely.

Still, without Maria I'd probably have died, and I'd told Magnus that much. He'd begun sending everything he could lay hands on, comfits and cushions and herbs and spices. He provided everything he could for my comfort, and Maria's, and little Stephen's.

But he had never come himself.

As the months wore on, and as his superiors kept him on the Continent, I began to worry that my friendship was a burden to him. Perhaps I was holding on to the memories of those few days we'd spent together at the war's end.

In truth, I'd let doubt creep back into my heart. A person could only change so much. Perhaps the near proximity of certain death had brought out the romantic in Magnus. Perhaps, once he was free to see the world, he had realized that he didn't want to settle with me.

So I had written a letter. It was a letter I couldn't bear to think of now, and I had sent it with my heart.

And he had returned that heart in a simple white envelope.

Perhaps I was reading too much into his letters.

Perhaps I ought to accept the duke's invitation.

I wouldn't allow myself to sulk. I left my room and walked down the hall to the nursery. Aunt Agnes was there, standing over his cradle.

"He's quieter now." She smiled warmly, though she always appeared distinctly puzzled to see me in here. Surely, as a countess, I should have been content to see my child for an hour at teatime. "He's been fussy all morning."

In the cradle, I found Stephen Blackwood, tenth Earl of Sorrow-Fell, gurgling up at me.

"Have you been a nuisance?" I lifted him into my arms. Stephen was bright-eyed and effusive and squealed with glee as he tugged at my coral necklace. Perhaps he'd just wanted my attention.

Stephen had his father's black hair, and I could already see the shape of Blackwood's nose and jaw, and his long fingers.

But Stephen had my own olive coloring, like his grandfather before him. His eyes—the pupils a pure and shining black—were indicative of another gift. I settled my son back into his crib. Then the curtain by the window fluttered, and a flush of shadow spread over the carpet.

"Stephen. No." I looked at the child with disapproval. He grinned gummily and kicked his legs. The shadows dispersed.

Whatever bit of Korozoth's power I had carried had spread to my son. He was in no danger of turning monstrous, Maria had assured me. The shadow abilities were merely an added quirk, as she called them. That would be a challenge in itself as he grew up. Sighing, I leaned over and kissed him. One day, I'd have to explain to him the many challenges of his powers and position. I was determined to do as Blackwood had asked and keep Stephen from becoming too comfortable. The master of Sorrow-Fell would learn that his good fortune came with a lifetime of duty.

Duty. That had been the name of Blackwood's stave. It now resided in a glass case underneath his portrait in the hall. The picture showed him standing upon a hill with the dawn rising behind him. He looked strong and splendid in a green waistcoat, which brought out the color in his eyes. I'd had the painting commissioned soon after Blackwood's death so that his son could see him every day, and so that I could remember.

I had one last thing to see to before the party. I kissed Stephen and left him with Aunt Agnes.

THE FAMILY GRAVEYARD WAS NOT AS impressive as one would have expected, at least on first inspection. Most great families had crypts, but this graveyard displayed only standard stone head-pieces. The sorcerer way was to be swathed in black silk and buried in the rich earth, so as to be absorbed back into nature all the sooner.

Blackwood's headstone rested beside Eliza's. I went to hers first, to kiss it as I did every morning. Perhaps that was why today had thrown me into such a tizzy: there'd been no time to make my visit. Then I kissed Blackwood's and leaned my cheek against it. It had felt natural to come here when I was dressed in mourning garb. Now, in my periwinkle dress, I felt like an interloper.

I didn't want that.

"I didn't tell you about Stephen today," I whispered to the headstone. "I believe he understands what I say to him. He's the cleverest child."

The words on the gravestone, GEORGE ROBERT BLACKWOOD, 1822–1840, were the only response I received. Still, I made the full report of Stephen's laughter, of his trouble with shadows. When I'd given Blackwood all the details I could, I traced his engraved name with my fingertips. I hated to think of that name wearing away over the years. Finally, I got up and wandered to a small corner of the graveyard. Here, I'd placed three commemorative stones.

Rook's body was gone, but I had given him a memorial. Stephen Poole's name was carved into one of the black stones.

I had made him my son's namesake. I could think of no better way to have him with me every day, or to thank him.

The dead did not speak to me here. They had passed on, but their memories haunted me. Indeed, I sometimes felt as though these graves anchored me in the violent waters of memory. Shuddering, I left the graveyard and walked toward the sounds of the party. It was wrong of me to neglect my guests.

THE GIRLS FELL OUT OF THE carriages as I came across the lawn to meet them. One little girl in a pink frock raced toward me with her arms open in joy.

"Miss Howel!" Even two years later, Sarah still looked like the smiling little girl I'd left behind at Brimthorn. Though I was pleased to note that she appeared better fed, and her clothes were new. I gathered her in my arms. "They said you wouldn't come back, but I knew," the child said proudly.

"It's Lady Blackwood now," tsked the new headmaster, though he patted Sarah's head rather than struck her with a cane. Mr. Portman had been my personal selection to replace Colegrind at Brimthorn. I'd chosen him for his dedication to education, his reputation as a kind man, and the fact that he was a married father of two. His children seemed to love playing with the Brimthorn students.

"Come along," I said to all of the children. We'd set up a rather splendid array of tables and blankets, along with as many good sandwiches and cakes as the kitchen could provide. Since becoming the benefactor of Brimthorn, I'd made it a priority to see the girls cared for.

The girls crowded around the nurse when she brought out Stephen. He was quite the beautiful boy, and he loved being the center of their attention. Giggling, he'd grasp at every ribbon and lock of hair that dangled in his face. How unlike his father he was in that regard.

Stephen had Blackwood's hair, his grandfather's coloring, and Rook's black eyes. What of me was there? Perhaps time would reveal it.

"Look!" one of the girls cried through a mouthful of cake. She pointed down the road. "Oh, it's such a beautiful horse!"

I turned to see a young man on horseback cantering toward us, dressed in a dark blue riding coat and cream-colored breeches. He took off his hat to the girls, revealing a shining mass of auburn hair. My breath caught in my throat.

Magnus.

But what the devil was he doing here? The surge of excitement turned to nerves.

"Well." Maria came up beside me with a little girl climbing on her back. "Strange to see him here. Did he tell you he was coming?" She did not look displeased. I swore Dawkins had laced my stays too tight. As Magnus dismounted and passed off the horse's reins to a groom, I found it harder to breathe.

"No. Did he tell you?"

"Haven't heard from him in a month." She glanced sidelong at me. "Perhaps he missed you."

Lord, Maria was not helping my nerves. It had been one thing to pour out my heart to a blank sheet of paper. But with him here in the flesh and blood, my embarrassment threatened to undo me.

"I'll be back shortly," I murmured to Maria, and dashed away before she could stop me. I hurried to the edge of the forest. The needle-strewn path carpeted my footfall. Closing my eyes, I wished myself away. Perhaps he'd come to tell me face to face that I was placing too many foolish hopes upon him. Perhaps . . .

I had to stop behaving like a child. Soon Dee and Lilly would arrive, and I would have to behave normally. I would . . .

Magnus appeared before me on the path, with the sun at his back.

"There you are," he said. My heart pummeled my chest; really, Dawkins had laced me too tight. That was the problem. "Why did you not come and see me?"

He was unchanged. True, his smile was a touch crooked now because of the gleaming scar that raked up the left side of his face, but it seemed to complete him. I could no longer imagine him without it.

"Why did I not come say hello?" I echoed. Magnus approached, but I shied away. "I . . . I thought you were in Italy."

"Yes. Well. I'm not." He frowned.

"You've, er, come at an odd time. We're having a picnic," I said lamely. Why was I behaving this way to him? Because I was afraid he'd tell me he'd come here to announce his engagement to a foreign duchess or princess. Or that he'd had time to consider it in a distant land, and realized we simply weren't well suited. Too much time had gone by. We had not seen each other in almost a year and a half.

A love that had bloomed for a few days could not weather such a long absence. That was a fanciful idea. Surely.

"How is the Continent?" I tried to smile.

"Well, it was splendid, but I shan't be returning for some time," he said. "I've come home."

"To see to your estate?" It was in Shropshire, on the border of Wales. Beautiful country, and a good place to settle. Magnus regarded me rather closely.

"Actually, the work is here. They've made me a colonel and stationed me about three miles east of Sorrow-Fell. The northern regiments are filling up, you know."

I felt strangely hot. Embers bloomed in my hands, and I quashed them. He'd come home, to England. He was so close now, to Sorrow-Fell . . . to me.

My mouth was cotton dry. "You gave up the Continent?"

Magnus went positively rigid. "You're . . . you're not pleased with this?"

"What? No!" I cried, feeling more and more lost. "I mean, I am."

"Good." He drew near to me in one breath, his hands taking mine. His eyes pinned me in place. "Because you are the reason I've done it."

I felt suspended in some kind of dream.

"I thought your feelings for me were done," he said. "That you wanted only friendship. Your letters never mentioned anything too personal. When we parted in London, the day you said I shouldn't come with you to Devon, well, I assumed you meant to say goodbye."

That was a mistake I'd cursed a thousand times.

Magnus continued, "I didn't want to interfere with your life, especially when you'd have suitors far richer and nobler than I could ever be."

"And I thought you'd done with me," I said at last, trembling. How could any of this be happening?

"Howel, you must know by now that no power on earth could force my heart from you," he murmured. "But I thought you wanted only my friendship. Until your last letter." His eyes searched my face. "One passage in particular leaped out at me." He began to recite: *"You must know how I rely upon hearing from you. Sometimes, I wake and imagine we are still in Agrippa's house. I think I will go down to breakfast and find you seated at the table. Sometimes I yearn for those days. They were simple, weren't they? We were simpler.*

"I confess that when you wrote to me of Camilla, the young lady you found so intriguing in Naples, I felt a surge of something. Shall I call it envy? Magnus, I would give most anything to go back to that night when you told your faerie story. But I'm afraid, my dear, that we may have missed our last chance. At least, I have missed mine. I

should have let you take me to Devon. My mind is never free of you. If I could exchange the whole of Sorrow-Fell for one more opportunity to speak my heart, I might do it."

I closed my eyes. "You memorized it?"

"I read it over and over again; I have never hoped for anything in my life as violently as I hoped that you meant what you wrote." He came one step nearer. "I want to say this, Howel. So that there are no misunderstandings." He took my hand and placed it over his heart. "My feelings will never alter. The war made me a man, but . . ." He looked into my eyes. "You made me *want* to be a man. I'd no way of knowing, when I went on a bet after Master Agrippa's carriage that day, that you would become the center of my life. They say you should know the minute you fall in love, but it came on so gradually. All I know is that one day I realized it, and that realization can never die.

"If today you tell me no, I shall never speak like this again." He dropped to his knee, both of my hands in his. The world grew hazy—Magnus alone stood out in sharp focus. "I won't live and die a coward. Henrietta Howel—because that is who you are to me, now and always—will you be my wife?"

I knew that I loved him. I had spent over a year hoping for another moment like this, where I could give voice to the words burning inside me. I touched his cheek.

Yes, I was still afraid. Behind me waited the ghosts of all those I had lost . . . how could I move forward and leave them behind?

I could feel them, suddenly. Blackwood, Rook, and even

Eliza seemed to whisper in my mind. Not that they were truly here, but I sensed their hands pushing me forward, toward Magnus. It was one thing to take off the black dresses and the veils; it was another to choose to live without them.

As that idea came to me, it seemed the darkness evaporated around us. The sun broke through the canopy of branches, dappling the forest with light. I could feel the magic in the world around me.

A world I wanted to face with him.

"Yes," I said.

A look of wonder came over him. "You will?"

"I will." My whole life, I had concealed my real thoughts and feelings to protect myself, but that wouldn't do any longer. I had written a letter from the safety of my desk; now I had to voice my feelings aloud, to him. Without fear. "I've loved you for such a long time, Julian." It sounded odd—yet wonderful— to speak his first name. "And I never want to be without you again, from this day to my last."

I did not feel shy or self-conscious. Rather, I was utterly free. *This* was what the truth felt like.

Magnus rose, his expression suffused with pure light. He took me in his arms, and there was nothing left but to kiss him.

The instant our lips touched, I forgot the world. I had heard those old tales of princesses awakened from an enchanted slumber by a true love's kiss, but I had been awake for so long. Now I needed something of which to dream.

"I love you," he whispered.

"I love you." I tasted the sweetness of those words.

"So." Magnus raised an eyebrow. "You're sure you wouldn't rather have a prince or a duke for young Stephen's stepfather?"

"Oh, you mean I'd the choice? Well, in *that* case . . ." I laughed as he kissed me.

"Hush. Or I'll ride off again."

"I'd have to hunt you down, as you're still on my land."

"Mmm, that sounds rather delicious."

Arm in arm, we strode back up the path until we found ourselves at the edge of the party. The girls tumbled over the grass with squeals of glee. Lilly and Dee had arrived and were seated upon a blanket with a plate of strawberries. They spoke with Fenswick, who had worn his best violet coat for the party. Aunt Agnes bounced Stephen on her knee and dangled a toy before him. He clutched at the puppet with forceful concentration. Maria and Fiona hung by the tables, speaking softly to one another. When Maria discovered Magnus and me standing side by side, she gave a sly wink.

They were all waiting for us.

"Shall we?" Magnus gave me his arm again. I felt a quick flare of fire under my skin, and the blue flame appeared and disappeared as quickly as breathing. My joy had been light and heat incarnate. Swiping ash from his sleeve, Magnus chuckled. "Suppose I'll have to watch out for that from now on."

Our hands clasped. With the summer day blazing overhead, and the party waiting for us, we moved forward. Together.

"Yes," I said. "It will be quite an adventure."

Acknowledgments

To finish a book is one thing; to finish a series, another. It feels less like the end of a project and more like the completion of a chapter. Henrietta and her friends have been a large part of my life for half a decade, and now I'm leaving them behind. They changed the entire course of my life, as did the people who helped bring them to publication. Thankfully, I'm not saying goodbye to the people, but I would like to say thank you.

Thank you to Chelsea Eberly, for fighting so hard for this series. From the first phone call, I knew you were the creative partner I needed to grow these characters and this world. The series wouldn't be what it is without your guidance, and I'm forever grateful to you, as a colleague and a friend.

Thank you to Brooks Sherman, for your savvy, your humor, your know-how, and your won't-back-down-ness, which is not a word but should be. Henrietta and I landed in the safest of hands when you offered to be my agent.

Thank you to the Random House team for welcoming and believing in me, and in this series. Special thanks to Barbara Marcus, Mallory Loehr, Michelle Nagler, Barbara Bakowski,

Allison Judd, Hannah Black, Jenna Lisanti, Mallory Matney, and Ray Shappell. It's been a perfect pleasure. I hope we can do it again.

Thank you to my closest friends, Gretchen Schreiber and Josh Ropiequet and Brandie Coonis and Jack Sullivan and Alyssa Wong. You make every day a delight. The Rosenblums and the Forbes-Karols, thank you. Thank you to Alexa Donne and Alyssa Colman, for nights of Cobbler Club and more than a few drinks. Thank you to Adriana Mather, for coffee dates and brainstorm sessions. Thank you to Alwyn Hamilton, Stephanie Garber, Roshani Chokshi, S. Jae-Jones, Gwen Katz, Margaret Rogerson, Elly Blake, Erika Lewis, Kerry Kletter, Audrey Coulthurst, Arwen Elys Dayton, Kiersten White, Amie Kaufman, and Jay Kristoff. Being welcomed into a community of excellent writers is good. Being welcomed into a community of friends is even better.

Thank you to Traci Chee, Tara Sim, and Emily Skrutskie. More than anyone, you three have been there for me for every wild DM session, every frantic question and nebulous fear. Traci, your generosity and genius know no bounds. Tara, you are a strong and fabulous writer and friend. Hello, Yuri. Emily, why *Kung Fu Panda 2*? What is wrong with you?

Thank you to my family, for cheering for me and loving me.

Thank you to all the teachers who have helped to shape and inspire me.

Thank you to all the readers and teachers and librarians

and bloggers who have supported this series. You are the reason to write.

Wherever I go from here, this will always be the first step on the journey. As such, it'll always be the most special. Thank you for coming along.

About the Author

JESSICA CLUESS is a writer, a graduate of Northwestern University, and an unapologetic nerd. After college, she moved to Los Angeles, where she served coffee to the rich and famous while working on her first novel, *A Shadow Bright and Burning*. When she's not writing books, she's an instructor at Writopia Lab, helping kids and teens tell their own stories. Visit her at jessicacluess.com and follow her on Twitter at @JessCluess.